PRAISE FOR AVA MILES

NORA ROBERTS LAND
Selected as one of the Best Books of 2013 alongside Nora Roberts' DARK WITCH and Julia Quinn's SUM OF ALL KISSES.
--USA Today Contributor, Becky Lower, Happily Ever After

"It {NORA ROBERTS LAND} captures the best of what I love in a Nora Roberts novel..."
--BlogCritics

"...finding love like in the pages of a Nora Roberts story."
--Publishers Weekly WW Ladies Book Club

FRENCH ROAST
"An entertaining ride...{and) a full-bodied romance."
--Readers' Favorite

"Her engaging story and characters kept me turning the pages."
--Bookfan

THE GRAND OPENING
"Ava Miles is fast becoming one of my favorite light contemporary romance writers."
--Tome Tender

"The latest book in the Dare Valley series is a continuation of love, family, and romance."
--Mary J. Gramlich

THE HOLIDAY SERENADE
"This story is all romance, steam, and humor with a touch of the holiday spirit..."
--The Book Nympho

THE TOWN SQUARE
"Ms. Miles' words melted into each page until the world receded around me..."
--Tome Tender

COUNTRY HEAVEN
"If ever there was a contemporary romance that rated a 10 on a scale of 1 to 5 for me, this one is it!"
--The Romance Reviews

FRENCH Roast

AVA MILES

ISBN:1492110159
ISBN-13:9781492110156

To my grandmother, Lanone Miles Bosn, who taught me how to tell stories by recounting amusing tales about the family farm, which ushered me into a peaceful sleep when I was a child. She also taught me how to cook, so everything food-related in this book has its roots in the summers I spent with her although she later said I always took cooking up a notch. I miss you, but know you are always with me.

And continued thanks to my divine entourage, whose support and love make life the beautiful and magical thing it is.

ACKNOWLEDGMENTS

There are always so many people who support us in giving birth to our dreams. Here are mine:

The earth angels of Team Ava, including my publicity helpers, Joan Schulhafer, Debby Tobias, and Alissa Di Giacomo of Joan Shulhafer Publishing and Media Consulting; Elizabeth Bemis and Sienna Condy of Bemis Promotions for my website; my wonderful editor, Angela Polidoro; the Killion Group for the cover art; my copy editor, Helen Hester-Ossa; Gregory Stewart for my publicity photos, the awesome Dare Valley map, and always being willing to pinch hit when something comes up; and Janet Geary for being my research consultant on all things law enforcement.

My former agent, Jennifer Schober, and her early comments on this manuscript.

Christi Barth and her heaven-sent support in my writing journey and for embracing this book and providing wonderful feedback to make it shine even more.

My old chef and all my other colleagues in the back of the house who taught me egg whites could be frozen, how to make a traditional tiramisu, and a million other things.

My family, whose love, laughter, and support mean the world.

My T.F. For infinite reasons.

All of you reading this book. You are priceless jewels in my life.

Lastly, just a note to say that I've played with time regarding the city council aspects in this story to make everything come together. Don't you love fiction? Have fun reading.

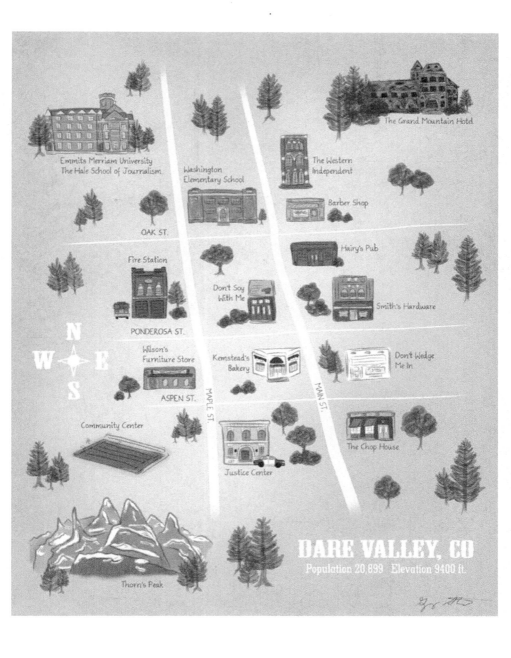

Emmits Merriam University
The Hale School of Journalism

Washington
Elementary School

The Grand Mountain Hotel

The Western
Independent

Barber Shop

OAK ST.

Fire Station

Hairy's Pub

Don't Say
With Me

Smith's Hardware

PONDEROSA ST.

Wilson's
Furniture Store

Kenstead's
Bakery

Don't Wedge
Me In

ASPEN ST.

Community Center

Justice Center

The Chop House

N
W E
S

MAPLE ST.

MAIN ST.

Thorn's Peak

DARE VALLEY, CO
Population 20,899   Elevation 9400 ft.

PROLOGUE

Jill Hale surveyed the cookie sheets dotted with her mother's famous mocha chocolate chunk cookie dough. The clumps would already be spreading in the oven by now if her mother had written down the baking temperature on the recipe. Jill hoped her mom would get home soon from shopping for Jill's high school graduation party. They had about six hours before family and friends descended upon the house.

Too bad a party was the last thing on Jill's mind. The song, *It's my party,* seemed appropriate, since all she wanted to do was cry. She gave into temptation and plucked one of the dough clumps off the cookie sheet.

The garage door to the kitchen opened. Finally! "Mom, what the heck do I cook these at? The temperature isn't on the recipe."

"Three hundred and seventy five," a young man's voice answered—one she'd desperately hoped never to hear again.

Her childhood friend and the love of her life, Brian McConnell, stood at the edge of the kitchen, shoulders hunched. His navy shirt brought out the blue of his eyes. He shoved a hand into his cargo shorts, jingling his keys. Of course, *he* would know the temperature; *he* was taking off in a few days to train as a chef at the Culinary Institute of America in New York, blast him.

"You don't have the right to just walk in here anymore," she answered, dropping the rest of the cookie ball in the sink and wiping her fingers on a yellow gingham towel. Praying she wouldn't tear up, she turned around to face him.

"Jill, I've been walking into this house since the day I could turn a doorknob. Don't lay down new rules because we had a fight. We need to talk."

She threw the dish towel aside and strode across the kitchen. "A fight? That's tame. What we're dealing with here is pure betrayal. The kind that ruins friendships."

His brow furrowed "Don't say that. Look, I'm sorry I didn't tell you I was going to the Culinary Institute instead of Cook Street in Denver. I didn't know how."

What a bald-faced lie. Her hands gripped the kitchen island's granite countertop. "You've always been able to tell me everything. That's why we were best friends. I decided to go to the University of Denver so we could be together. I thought..." The first tear rolled down her face. She scrubbed it with her palm.

"Shit, don't cry. Look, I know it's hard, but I need to do this." He walked forward and reached for her.

She shoved him back. "No. You don't get to touch me. You made it clear you didn't want that either." Her cheeks heated into horrible red splotches. She would never overcome the humiliation of his rejection.

He pinched the bridge of his nose. "Jill, I know you're upset because I wouldn't be with you, but—"

Unbelievable that he'd even try to defend his actions. "But what, Romeo? Did you want someone more experienced? Is that why you turned me down and hooked up with Kelly Kimple?" The roar inside her head was reaching epic levels, so she dug her teeth into her lip.

His throat moved when he swallowed. "Dammit, I knew I was leaving. Jill—"

"But I didn't." She slammed her hand on the tan granite counter, her palm smarting from the contact. "*Why* did you ask me out anyway? It's what I've wanted for years, but you always held back. You kissed me senseless, and then you turned me down when I said I wanted to be with you. You're a tease."

His lip curled. "I didn't ask you out before because I didn't want to ruin our friendship if things didn't work out between us, and I didn't want to lose your family, who's meant more to me than my own ever could. Dammit, you know that."

She stared at the baby blue wall over his shoulder, not wanting the trickle of compassion she felt to weaken her resolve.

"But when I knew I was leaving Dare, I couldn't fight what I felt for you anymore. I didn't want to leave without going out with you for real. It was a mistake. I was selfish, and I'm sorry. I didn't know you'd want me to be your first after one date. Jesus! It freaked me out, okay? I could almost hear your dad telling me he'd kick my ass. Jill, you always jump in the deep end head first. I know I hurt you. Please tell me how to make it better."

Her hands fisted at her sides as the shock waves of his rejection coursed through her again. "You can't!"

"Kelly was nothing. It didn't mean an-y-thing." He pronounced each syllable as if that might change things.

She put her hands over her ears. "I don't want to hear it." Kelly was a perky, blond, petite cheerleader, whereas Jill was red-haired, tall, and *so* not petite with her size eleven shoes. He'd chosen the prettier girl. And she'd live with that stab to her self-esteem for the rest of her life.

Brian grabbed her hands and yanked them against his chest. "You *will* listen. Dammit, I am not leaving Dare like this. We're going to get through this together."

His strength had outpaced hers when they were sophomores. She couldn't dislodge her hands, so she kicked him in the shin.

"Oww," he cried, falling back and jumping on his good leg. "Jesus! Cut it out."

Swiping at her tears, she dashed over to the door to the garage and threw it open. It smacked into the wall so hard it left a mark on the white paint. "Maybe if you'd only done one thing wrong we could make it, but the Culinary Institute omission was too much. Bri, you've told me everything since we learned how to talk. You didn't mention this. Not once. And it affects me too."

His hand massaged his shin. He straightened and looked her dead in the eye. "I haven't told you everything, dammit."

Her breath sucked in. Right. The other girls...the ones who weren't just friends. They'd never discussed *that*.

"I didn't know if I'd get into the Culinary Institute, but I had to try," he continued. "It's my dream come true. When I found out, I didn't know how to tell you. I knew you had the whole Denver scenario worked out in that stubborn brain of yours."

"Stubborn? Get out!"

He strode over to her. "You *are* stubborn. When you're like this, there's no talking to you. I'm sorry I hurt you. This whole thing is tearing me to pieces. I'm leaving everything I know, all my friends...and you. I don't want to lose you, Jill. I don't know how to go a day without talking to you."

Her lip quivered. Seeing his anguish hurt her, but she couldn't relent. Wouldn't. "You're going to have to figure it out. I can't trust you anymore, and that's worse than anything."

He grabbed her to him and hugged her, his taller frame making her feel less like a giant than she had before his growth spurt. "Don't say that. We can work this out before I leave. I won't lose you, Jill."

His scent—a mixture of cedar aftershave and salt—tickled her nose. She muffled her cries against his chest as his hands rubbed her back.

"Don't cry, Jillie, please don't cry. We'll get our balance back."

His earnest, aching voice broke her heart into tiny, unfixable pieces. She pushed away and met his eyes. "You don't get it, Brian. It's over. Go to the Culinary Institute. Have a good life. But this ends here."

His eyes narrowed into his telltale determined look. "No, it doesn't. I'll call you."

"I won't answer," she replied with an edge. How was she supposed to go on being his friend after everything, particularly when she'd thought their date would lead to what she'd always wanted—them falling in *love*, getting married, raising their kids in Dare. He could pretend not to know how serious she was about him, but he did. She'd never been able to hide anything from him.

His face fell. "Jill, we've always made up before."

She rubbed away the tears and straightened to her full height, reaching deep for the inner strength to do what must be done. "I don't want you at my party. I mean it, Brian. We're done."

His mouth gaped. "But our friends. Your parents. It's the last time the Four Musketeers will be together for months, maybe years. What will Jemma and Pete say?"

"They already know how I feel." Their best friends were high school sweethearts, just like she'd always wanted to be with Brian, but he had never pulled the trigger. Any compassion evaporated. "It's better this way."

His head lowered. He kicked at the linoleum, silent for a long moment. "Okay, Red, I'll honor your wishes now, but I'm going to call you when I get to my new place. I'll give you some time to cool down."

An Alaskan winter wouldn't change her mind.

He dug into his pocket. "I just bought it at Old Man Jenkins' jewelry store, so it's not wrapped, but here's your present."

She stared at the little black box. Numbly reached for it.

He strode toward her and kissed her forehead before she could duck. "Don't stay mad." And with that parting command, he shut the door behind him.

Jill opened the box. A heart-shaped necklace winked at her. Her finger flipped the shape over, searching for answers. The engraving made her knees give out. *J&B, BFFs.* She sank to the floor, clutching it to her chest.

CHAPTER 1

Eight years later

Jill Hale's heart fluttered when Brian McConnell's silver SUV turned onto Route 44 ahead of the vehicle she was riding in—Dare Valley's newest red fire truck. The fire chief, Ernie, had given her and her sister, Meredith, rides growing up, and he'd suggested one today to cheer her up. Her inner child had jumped at the chance.

Her eyes tracked to Brian's rear-view mirror, hoping for a glimpse of his face. She only got a partial view of his strong chin and easy smile. She gave a breathy sigh.

Jill had loved Brian since she was a toddler, but before his return to town the previous summer, she hadn't spoken to him for eight years. Their falling out had left wounds that had scabbed over without fully healing. She had forgiven him now. Mostly. The death of their childhood friend, Jemma, had pulled them together, sparking a tenuous reconciliation.

They'd been hanging out a lot—going to the movies or the pizza parlor, skiing up in the valley. It was all very enjoyable...and very platonic. She was trying to play it cool, but the waiting was driving her crazy. Brian *had* to make a move after everything that had happened between them.

"Earth to Jill," her sister called over the roaring engine. Meredith Hale's wedding ring flashed when she waved a hand in Jill's face. "Man, you have it bad. You go into the Zombie Zone every time you see him. Even his car."

Gripping the brass fire pole as the truck accelerated through a traffic light, Jill said, "I can't help it! Brian's been back for months, and I've finally decided to make him mine. Mua-ha-ha."

"Don't do the scary laugh," Meredith pleaded jokingly, her red hair swinging as she shook her head.

Jill didn't know where Brian was going, but she hoped he was driving to her coffee shop to see her. When he turned onto the road leading to downtown Dare, she smiled to herself—it was in the direction of Don't Soy with Me. "Hey, Ernie, can you head south on Dare Avenue?"

The old fire chief, who was dressed in a uniform resembling a yellow jacket wasp, glanced over his shoulder and smiled at her. "Sure thing, honey. After all, this ride is supposed to cheer up my favorite girl."

Her heart contracted. The whole town had been trying to help her cope with Jemma's sudden death. Most of the time it warmed her heart, but sometimes it just reminded her of all she'd lost—their day-long banter while working at the coffee shop together, girls' nights out at Hairy's Irish Bar, a shoulder to lean on whenever she needed one.

Brian cruised down the street, the fire truck in hot pursuit. Maybe this wasn't what Ernie had intended when he'd offered her a ride, but this whole car chase *was* raising her spirits. She hadn't seen Brian in a week, and she was feeling a bit starved for his company.

They continued to follow the silver SUV. She leaned with every turn in the road, her cork-screw red curls brushing her flushed cheeks. Ernie spun the massive wheel to follow Brian onto Main Street without being asked. Yeah, he knew. Heck, everyone in town knew about them.

"Can I hit the siren when we pass the newspaper?" Jill asked, dancing in her winter boots. The fire truck sparkled in the Cut and Curl's front window like Dorothy's ruby red slippers as they passed.

Meredith raised an eyebrow. "We're on Main Street with no fire in sight. It's against the rules."

"I *like* breaking rules." She gave a pout. Her older sister could be such a party-pooper. Why not have a little fun?

Ernie chortled. "Okay, but only because your grandpa bluffed me out of fifty bucks last night at poker."

Jill put her hand near the button as they closed in on the headquarters of the family newspaper.

Putting her hands over her ears, her sister said, "As a current employee of *The Western Independent,* I should note you're going to have at least four reporters—my husband and our grandpa included—scurrying out of the front door like ants to see what all the commotion is about."

Jill pressed the button, and the siren's circular, ear-piercing wheeze rolled out. "I know. Isn't it great?"

Her sister stuck her tongue out. She reciprocated and hit the horn, punching the air with a *cronk*.

Brian parked his car on Main Street in front of a row of brightly painted shops. Her heart rate escalated. He *was* coming to see her!

"Ernie, can you swing around the back? I need to do something at Don't Soy with Me."

"Sure thing, kiddo."

She ducked down as they passed Brian's car, curling her tall frame into a ball.

Her sister crouched next to her. "I'm only hiding with you because I love you. Everyone—and I mean *everyone*—is going to know we rode the fire engine today since you blasted *The Independent.*"

A black fireman's mask banged into her head when she wobbled. "Shit. You're right. I don't always think things through."

"You can say that again. It's like your spontaneity card gets jammed, overriding all logic."

What was so great about logic anyway? "I didn't *have* to bring you along on my ride."

"Girls, girls," Ernie shouted, making her smile. How many times had he said that to them while they were growing up?

The brakes whooshed when he pulled to a stop. He spun in his seat. "Guess I should be grateful Brian wasn't heading to Denver. I don't have enough gas to make the two hour trip."

Jill leaned forward and kissed his bearded cheek. "You old buzzard. You know you would have done it for me."

He held up a hand. "You've had me wrapped around your finger since you were a kid, wearing those red pigtails like Pippi Longstocking." He pointed to Meredith. "You too, missy. Now git on out of my fire truck." The radio crackled. "Calls are starting to come in about the siren. Can't wait to talk to your grandpa. Hope he's aggravated enough to take Maalox."

The sisters hopped down from the truck, narrowly missing a puddle of snow melt. "Thanks, Ernie!" they chimed.

The thick burn scar around his mouth shifted when he smiled. "Oh, go on with you."

Meredith grabbed Jill's hand and—in unspoken agreement—they ran to the back of the shop together. "You know you've lost your mind, right?"

"I wasn't in my right mind anyway."

They hurried through the back door and down the hallway past Jill's office, skidding to a halt when they reached the main part of the shop. Don't Soy with Me had exceeded everyone's expectations—hers, her family's, and the town's. Though the Hales were a big name in the newspaper world, it had been a while since a Hale had found success in something other than paper and ink. And the shop showcased Jill's unique style to a tee. The bold color scheme of fire engine red—so appropriate after today—and sunshine yellow was eye opening, and the walls were lined with local artists' paintings, most of them modern, with splashes of bold, primal color.

Her patrons ran the gamut: students from the local university studied here, while their professors graded papers; locals talked about the weather; and the California transplants ordered soy lattes and tofu-stuffed croissants.

She'd found a way to draw everyone in, making Don't Soy with Me more than just a coffee shop. It was *the* local meeting place. She'd expanded her menu to sandwiches, pizza, and light plates, and now they served food and drinks from 6:00 a.m. until midnight. Not too shabby for a business that had started as a class project.

"Compose yourself and stop wheezing," she told her sister, smoothing down her hair.

"Wheezing? I swim four miles—"

"Blah-di-blah-blah," she interrupted. "Margie, our favorites, please," she called out to the barista—one of the perks of being the boss—and they darted over to a table that had opened up near the front window. Jill scanned the street with laser focus, immediately catching sight of Brian's green Spyder jacket. He was heading away from them. *Darn it!* She'd interrupted a ride in a fire truck so she could sit like a wallflower in her own coffee shop.

"You're right. I'm pathetic."

Her traitorous eyes couldn't stop following his progress toward the drug store. Even though he was wearing a coat, her mind conjured up those rigid back muscles. Those broad shoulders. The way he filled out a T-shirt at the gym, all sweaty and ripped. He'd been handsome in high school, but eight years in New York City had only honed his appearance. He had the whole casual sophistication thing going for him now, and he was all man.

"Do you even have a clue where this is leading?" Meredith asked, a hint of older sis in her voice as Margie set their drinks down.

Brian turned to greet an old lady in the street, his bow-shaped lips tilting into a smile as he laughed at something she said. His easy gait hinted he wasn't in a hurry. No, he was never in a hurry, not with her or anyone.

"Hey!" Meredith punched her lightly. "Did you hear me?"

"Yes! Well, I know where I want it to go, anyway. Us together. Finally!" She'd decided he was The One in second grade after he socked Timmy Caren for calling her carrot top and pulling her ponytail. She'd drawn pictures in colored pencils of the two of them holding hands, and all her notebooks had been scrawled with "Jill McConnell" in hesitant cursive.

She'd waited for him to make a move. And waited.

In the history of courtship, two turtles could have come together faster.

Then he'd changed the rules, and everything had gone to hell. Before leaving for the Culinary Institute of America, he'd promised to keep calling until she relented, but after six months, he had finally given up. Until his return to town, that was.

Meredith neatly placed her napkin in her lap. "You think he plans on staying? New York can be hard to get out of your system. Dare's not exactly a hot restaurant scene."

She bit her lip. "I know. That's why I've been trying to persuade him that we should open a restaurant together. He'll cook the food. I'll handle the biz. I need a new project now that Don't Soy with Me is a huge success, and this will be a great way to reconnect with him. Plus, it fits in with my plan to be a big-time businesswoman someday."

"Give it time." Meredith hugged her. "I know you want this to work out, but have you thought about setting the whole restaurant idea aside? If things don't work—"

"It'll screw everything up." She tugged on a red curl.

"Jill, seriously, why don't you give your relationship some time to develop before pushing ahead with this?"

Rolling her eyes seemed appropriate. "Meredith, seriously," she mimicked, "why don't you stop raining on my parade?"

"You darn well know what I mean. It just doesn't seem smart to me."

"Well, it does to me," she said, lifting her chin, telling herself it would be fine.

"Promise me you're going to be reasonable."

"When have I ever been reasonable? Drop it, Mere."

Her sister held up her hands in surrender. "Okay, okay, but take it slow."

Big sisters. "I've only been trying to talk Brian into it. It's not like I've drawn up plans yet or taken out a loan. Jeez."

"I'm only trying to gently say you've been through a lot with Jemma dying. Heck, we all have."

"Easy for you to say. All your 'stuff' ended up turning out great."

Meredith and Tanner had just gotten married on New Year's Eve after a whirlwind courtship and were living in their own Nora Roberts Land—just like in the sisters' favorite novels.

"Don't worry, Jill. Yours will too."

"I miss Jemma, Mere."

"I know. That was so sweet of Ernie, trying to cheer you up like that." She scooted her chair closer and leaned in toward her. "Are you still visiting her grave?"

Jill straightened. "I know you don't like it, but I need to talk to her. She was my best friend!"

"The family's worried," her sister said with a sigh.

"I'll stop going when the time is right." If only she could shut the grief off like it was a porch light. "It helps that Brian and I are hanging out so much." It was true, even if it wasn't as hot and steamy as she'd like it to be.

"I still don't understand why he came back to Dare Valley." Meredith licked the foam off her chocolate mocha.

"Me either," Jill replied. Brian didn't say much about his time in New York or why he'd returned to town. In some ways, it was mysterious and a bit sexy, but in others, it made her realize they were no longer the best friends who could finish each other's sentences.

He came out of the drug store with a small bag in his hand. Had he bought shaving cream to slowly scrape off the day's growth of beard darkening his face? She hoped not.

As if sensing her speculation, he looked straight through the window, then lifted a hand and waved. Great. She'd become a stalker. First the fire truck and now this. The movie could run on *Lifetime*. She waved back as if to say ta-ta, not watching you like some lovesick chick. He entered another store. Her frown just about cracked her lip, so she reached for the bubblegum lip gloss in her tiger-print purse.

The punch on her arm interrupted her speculation.

"Hey!"

"You're in Lust Land, lil' sis."

"Spoken like a happily married woman."

"Yep, but I remember feeling all itchy before Tanner and I got together. The same thing's going on with you, except you've known Brian forever."

"I know. Makes it...weird sometimes."

"You'll get there. Your whole getting-to-know-you phase has been short-circuited since you grew up together. You just need to catch up on all the years he was gone."

"Sometimes he seems so familiar," Jill said. "And then others... Well, it's like there are these new layers of caution, quiet, and...confusion." Like he didn't always know what to say or how to act around her.

Of course, the freaking lust shooting through them both might have something to do with that. She knew he was attracted to her, and he darn well knew how she felt. And yet they hadn't touched each other recently. Okay, except for a couple of weeks ago when she'd slipped on the ice as they were walking to the movies. And that *so* didn't count.

The new-customer bell chimed. Her head swiveled. Brian strolled into the coffee shop—all tousled and rugged like he'd just rolled out of bed. His maple-syrup hair curled at the nap of his neck, and his blue eyes never failed to pack a punch.

"Hey!" He stuffed his hands in his jeans, drawing her gaze.

"Hey, back," she answered, trying not to sigh at his bulge like some groupie. She was a Bulge Watcher. Her mother would be so proud.

"Hey, Brian." Meredith stood and gave him a quick hug.

"You hear where the fire was?"

Jill bit her lip. "Nope."

"They have a lot of false alarms," Meredith said. "Cats in trees. Morons who—"

"I'm sure he's not interested in fire statistics, Mere."

His mouth curved, unfurling a ribbon of lust in her abdomen.

"Jill and I were just talking about you, Brian. You've never told us why you left New York. The city's a hot food scene. You must miss it."

The muscles around his mouth tightened. Even though Jill wanted to know—was dying to know, really—it was mean of her sister to ambush him.

"Give him a break, Mere. Guys don't blab their life stories."

Or they only do to the women in their lives. Brian definitely had a story. Like *I met someone in New York, but it didn't work out or I saw a dead homeless man in an alley during winter, and it changed me.*

Meredith glared at her. "Reporter's prerogative. Okay, I've gotta get back to work. See about that fire." She gave Jill a kiss and sailed out.

Without Meredith there to take off the heat, Jill felt her bones dissolve into tissue paper. Sliding out of her chair would be ridiculous, but she suddenly understood the reason for those Victorian reclining couches.

"*So,*" Brian drawled. He turned those blue eyes away for a moment, allowing her to take a deep breath. "Business is good."

When he turned back, the hummingbird pace of her heart increased again. "Yes. Ah, do you want me to make you your favorite?"

Jill realized she'd do pretty much anything for this man. Hike the Continental Divide in the snow. Darn holes in socks. Cripes, she needed to get a clue. Or a life.

"No...I thought I'd drop by and see if you wanted to come to dinner tonight. I'll cook."

Her head darted back. They'd been spending time together over the past few months, but cooking...from scratch. This was new.

"Like a real date?" she asked. Dammit, maybe the whole fire truck ride had infused her with life-and-death energy, but she wanted to be clear.

"Ah, sure. If you want to call it that." He jiggled change in his pocket, ducking his head, hitching his shoulder up like he did when he was nervous. "I want to cook for you."

He did? Her heart warmed like she was holding a puppy. "That'd be awesome! I'd love that. I mean..." Overdone, she realized. "Great, simply great." Shut up, Jill.

"Why don't you pop by at seven?"

"Can I bring something?"

"Just yourself."

And the way he said it made her knees quiver, actually quiver.

"Great!" she breathed out and ground her teeth. Maybe she should study the dictionary so she could learn to form cohesive sentences.

"Okay." He edged back. Then, he rushed forward to kiss her cheek. "See ya then." He turned, bumped into the table, and cruised out, not looking back.

Jill righted the paper cup he'd knocked over, fighting the urge to touch her cheek. The patrons' muffled chuckles only made her lovesick grin grow wider.

She wasn't the only one off her rocker. Brian was making a real move.

It was about damn time.

CHAPTER 2

Brian zoomed toward his car. Man, what had happened to his mojo? Jill was putting him on edge. He felt like a high school teenager around her again. The boy had wanted her. The man craved her.

But knowing her, it would be the deep end or nothing.

Brian needed to find himself again. He didn't want to rush into things with Jill before he knew if they could find a balance between their friendship and the hot-as-a-kitchen-blow-torch attraction they felt for each other. He was terrified of screwing things up with her. Losing her eight years ago had been like losing a part of himself. It would be unconscionable for it to happen again.

He yanked on the wool scarf around his neck. Managed to smile at the people he passed on the sidewalk. Inside, his mind was a mess, like one of those splatter paintings in Jill's coffee shop. How much longer could he keep this up? How much longer could he spend time with Jill without telling her his reasons for returning to town? If she could learn to fully trust him, maybe she'd understand. But how could she when even he didn't?

Cooking for her had seemed like a nice gesture to kick their relationship to the next level. Hell, he was a chef and the only person he'd cooked for since returning to town was his buddy Pete, also Jemma's ex, and the current subject of Jill's hatred.

He changed course and headed to the Food Pantry for ingredients. When he entered the produce aisle, there were seven women selecting everything from bananas to onions. The gossipy old guard hadn't changed their ways. Their conversations swirled around him.

"Did you see Kerry Jenkins sitting next to Mitch Miller at the basketball game the other night? People are starting to talk. Something's brewing there."

Another trio talked about the mystery car in their neighbor's driveway that morning. "You know what that means," a woman wearing a severe ponytail whispered, her voice projecting loudly.

His gut tightened. Some things about Dare made him happy—the close-knit community, the outdoors, the familiarity. Then there was this.

New York had its pros and cons, too, but there he'd had the ability to do what he wanted, when he wanted. The problem was he had taken things too far.

There were always consequences, no matter where you lived.

The small organic produce shelf called to him. It was a positive addition, probably added to cater to the Californians who'd moved into town. He picked up an avocado and looked at the mottled emerald color.

"My goodness, Brian McConnell."

His hand automatically clenched at the sound of the shrill voice.

Vivian Thomilson still wore all black and had a chin hair that was about two inches long. "It almost made me do a double take, seeing you selecting produce."

He picked up on the censure in her comment. God, he'd hoped the old talk about him cooking had gone away.

Brian made his lips form a smile. "Well, I don't have a nice woman like you to buy what I need for me, Mrs. Thomilson."

She laughed in a high, staccato tone, her cameo clasp earrings dancing dangerously on her sagging lobes. "Well, I used to tell your mother she was so lucky you turned out to be a chef. We were worried you were gay when you started baking those quiches in high school."

The dig stung. Being a teenage boy in Dare who liked to bake and plate dishes in artistic ways, he'd been subjected to name calling and then some. Apron Boy. Nancy. He hadn't forgotten.

His parents had been ashamed of his interest in French food, especially given the way it had set off the town rumor mill. His mother had tried to prevent him from cooking by taking them out to eat all the time and not buying groceries. His father, who thought *real* men had no place in the kitchen, had grounded him for showing an interest. When that had failed, his father's campaign had escalated. He'd berated Brian for not being a man, calling him horrible names, even threatening to beat it out of him.

Jill's mom had saved his dream from dying by letting him cook at the Hales' house. Growing up, he had spent more time there than at his own home. They were the family he had always wanted. And when his parents divorced after twenty-five years of marriage when he was sixteen, he'd poured all his anger, heartache, and confusion into his food.

Meredith had asked him why he was back. Well, that was one reason. He still had something to prove in Dare.

"Uh-huh," he muttered, his jaw tight. He wished she'd go away before he gave into the temptation to bean her with an eggplant.

"The Chop House is a good place for you. Nothing like a good steak."

He'd gambled that the Chop House would allow him some creative freedom after he'd proven himself. It was a slow process, but he'd persuaded the owner to consider a beurre blanc sauce for the ribeye, to rave reviews. Of course, they had called it a white wine butter sauce, not wanting to use the French.

He just nodded. You didn't converse with Mrs. Thomilson. You listened...or pretended to.

"Tom Kenders tells us you're doing well."

Brian's brow rose. He wasn't pleased that his boss was talking about him, but he wasn't exactly surprised either.

"He said you got some ideas in New York, but you understand Dare isn't the Big Apple and doesn't want to be."

"Dare's always been its own place."

"Exactly," she harrumphed, her grin more a grimace. "Well, good to see you. Tell your mother I said hello. We miss her."

He'd tell her when hell froze over. They didn't talk. Three months after his parents' divorce, she'd moved to Phoenix to marry a tight-assed podiatrist whom she'd met online, leaving her son with a father who was ashamed of him and didn't care to understand him. Thank God neither of them lived here anymore. "Sure thing."

When she left, he rolled his tense shoulders and let the avocado drop. It wasn't ripe enough for tonight. He needed something else. He caught sight of the watercress and grabbed a shiny Clementine. He could toast pecans with honey and bourbon. The combo would make a killer salad. He bagged everything and strolled down the aisles.

Going into business with Jill would silence anyone who'd ever suggested he was gay or a little loony for adding saffron to the church potato salad. *Up yours, Mrs. Thomilson.* He pushed his cart to the meat aisle.

Meredith wasn't the only one who wanted to know why he was back. Everyone wondered. What none of them knew was that he didn't have anywhere else to go. He'd bombed through a device of his own making in New York, and now he needed to rehabilitate his career and figure things out.

Then he would leave again. Move back to a Michelin-star restaurant. Please, God!

At least, that had been the plan before Jill came back into the picture. Of course, part of him had come back *because* of Jill, but he hadn't known how deeply she'd affect him. He hadn't known that her zest for life would leap out and grab him by the throat.

He'd had a hard time leaving the girl behind—untouched.

He didn't think he could take the woman and be the same.

His phone rang, and his heart stopped when he saw the number. Why in the hell was Simca calling him again after all this time? This was the third day in a row. He hadn't picked up, although part of him wanted to know why his former lover was trying to get in touch with him.

She and her husband owned the restaurant where Brian had worked in New York. She'd told Brian the marriage was over, and they'd started an affair while her husband was abroad, opening another restaurant. As soon as he'd returned, he'd fired Brian in front of the whole kitchen. To top it off, he'd accused him of stealing secret family recipes. The end of the relationship had left Brian with a bunch of what-ifs and whys, about as filling as a side salad after a day-long hike.

Wasn't this another reason he didn't want to jump into an intense relationship with Jill? He snorted to himself. Right. What about them wasn't intense?

Brian hit the ignore button and tucked his phone away, pushing the cart forcefully. No, he had nothing more to say to Simca. He was here. And the past needed to stay in the past.

His future depended upon it.

The meat aisle called like a siren, whispering *pan-seared, roasted, stewed*. The tantalizing voice loosened the knots in his gut. So many possibilities. He stood there, letting inspiration rise while the carts around him slowed down to watch.

He heard other whispers from the past—both from Dare and New York—but he tuned them out.

CHAPTER 3

Dare's Trio of Truth, as the citizens jokingly called them, walked into her coffee shop. Two generations of journalists ran the Hale family newspaper, *The Western Independent*, one of the leading national independent presses in the country. Jill's grandpa had started it back when coffee had cost five cents. Since then, he'd shared that timeless beverage with countless presidents and world leaders. Now her sister had taken over for their newly retired dad, and their grandpa couldn't be happier. Add Meredith's new husband into the mix—a former international correspondent—and Arthur Hale had as much of a spring in his step as was possible for a guy in his seventies.

Meredith held hands with Tanner like always, and he paused to hold the door for Grandpa Hale. If you didn't know the old geezer well, you'd think his scowl sprung from a dislike of Jill's establishment. But while he might bitch about her frou-frou coffee and the prices, it was all an act. Of course, she egged him on to keep his heart ticking.

"You in the mood for a raspberry mocha, Grandpa? Just in time for Valentine's Day."

His bushy eyebrow lifted. "Are you addled? Give me a damn normal coffee. Don't understand why people want fruit in their coffee. In my day—"

"People put fruit with Jello, marshmallows, and whipped cream and called it a salad," Jill interrupted, tapping her hot pink fingernails on the counter. "In my day, a real salad had lettuce and—"

"Hi, Jill," Tanner interrupted, his dark hair and eyes a dead ringer for her mocha espressos. "I'll have a café Americano. And my beautiful wife would like..." He studied the board and then turned to study Meredith. The jolt between them was like one of Zeus' lightning bolts. Jill sighed with envy. Would she and Brian ever be like that?

"Oh, for cripes sake," her grandfather muttered. "They're like this all the time. Order that fruit coffee. Anything to stop the goo-goo eyes."

Tanner's shoulders shook with laughter. "Goo-goo eyes? Wow, that's a blast from the past."

"Well I'm as old as dirt, too. I can't believe I walked all the way over here in the cold for this coffee and this conversation. My hip." He patted it for effect.

Jill rolled her eyes. His health couldn't be better. "Mere?"

"The raspberry one sounds scrumptious."

Tanner fiddled with his wallet. "We're discussing a new editorial, and we needed some neutral space. These two were going at it pretty hard."

"And you're what?" Meredith frowned. "Jimmy Carter at the peace talks? I happen to remember ..."

Jill grabbed his twenty and headed off to make their coffees, waving off her barista, Margie. When they turned all journalistic, there was no talking to them.

She made sure her grandpa's mug didn't have a single water mark on it, or he'd give her a hard time. Some families patted you on the back to show love and support. Other families teased. The Hale family could have won an Emmy for best comedy.

The new raspberry coffee featured for Valentine's Day made her think of Brian. Of course. Would they do anything for Valentine's Day after having their first date tonight? It was only a week away.

"Here you go," she called.

They automatically reached for their coffees as they continued their discussion of health care. They made their way to a table, greeting other patrons as they went. The group was so intent on each other that it was hard not to feel left out.

It didn't usually bother her that she wasn't part of the Hale journalism club, but with The Trio of Truth in *her* place, her old feelings of being a black sheep nagged at her.

Don't Soy With Me was an inarguable success, but she wanted more. Some people still thought her place "too cute for words." Man, stuffing a croissant in their mouths was tempting. She wanted to show Dare and her family she could make it big, as big as the family newspaper.

Mostly, she wanted to prove it to herself. And opening a restaurant with Brian seemed to be just the ticket. And it would have the added benefit of keeping him here.

Margie bumped her hip. "Lost in thought?"

"Not enough coffee this morning."

"Let me make you something special." Her eyebrow ring winked in the light.

"Thanks."

She turned away. Jemma had always done that for her. Her best friend had helped her create Don't Soy With Me. She glanced up at the plaque she'd mounted on the back wall after Jemma's death. Her picture was on one side, with the inscription *Our Coffee Angel. You'll Always Be In Our Hearts.* on the other.

The phone rang, interrupting her reverie.

Margie hooked it by her neck. "Sure thing." She put the phone down. "Hey, it's that guy with the sinfully gorgeous voice that keeps calling you and won't leave a message. I'm almost sad you're here because I've started looking forward to his calls."

The mystery made her do a little jiggle. "Well, I'll just have to find out what he wants."

"Just wait. His voice...it's like French silk pie."

"Seriously?"

Margie mimed a faint. Jill headed back to her office. This call had better be as interesting as billed. If it was some sicko calling to ask what she was wearing, she'd tell Peggy later and let her friend go all deputy sheriff, talking animatedly about how the law needed to handle weirdoes better before they became a threat. The strangest things improved Peggy's mood.

Her recently painted purple desk made her smile. She'd updated it to match her coffee table at home. With the red and yellow walls, green chair, and blue lagoon painting on the wall, her office pretty much screamed rainbows and unicorns. She loved it.

"Hello. This is Jill Hale."

"Ms. Hale, you're a difficult woman to reach. My name is Mac Maven."

His voice *did* prompt a delicious shiver. French silk pie fit the bill. "Mr. Maven, how can I help you?"

"I'm interested in meeting with you about a business proposition. We have a common friend, Jack Higgins."

What on earth could this be about? Jack was a regular who'd been coming in more than usual recently. Just last week, he had taken lots of photos of her shop, telling her he was trying to convince some friends in Silicon Valley how civilized Dare was so they'd visit. Was this guy one of them? Jack had made millions out there before moving to their small town with his wife and two kids to enjoy a less-frantically paced life, consulting on the side. What she really liked about him was how down to earth he was in spite of all his money and success.

"Jack's a great guy. I'd be happy to meet with you." As a favor to Jack, if nothing else. "What do you have in mind?"

"Well, it's a bit complicated." He paused. "I know it's rather unorthodox, but my business interests require a confidentiality agreement. Jack can vouch for me if you're concerned."

She spun her lucky Flying Purple People Eater pen in a circle, beyond intrigued. "A confidentiality agreement, huh?" Now that did sound Silicon Valley-like.

His laughter erupted—a rich, easy sound. "No, nothing like that. It's a formality. I'd really love to waive it, but my lawyers would be unhappy, and they'd use it as an excuse to raise my fees."

This time she laughed. She kept Stanley Kepok on retainer, but he was the paper's attorney and didn't charge her a dime. "I've heard tales."

"Why don't you take my number and call Jack for a reference? Then you can call me back."

She wrote his mobile number down when he recited it. "Okay, but I should warn you. I'm thinking about another business venture right now." Brian's gorgeous face popped into her mind.

"You strike me as someone who'd be intrigued by the type of business proposal that would come with a confidentiality agreement."

"You're right, but my partner and I go way back."

"Ah," he murmured, making her wish Margie was the one on the phone. Jill had no interest in anyone but Brian, but this man's voice did make her tingle.

"How far back?"

"To my first business. A lemonade stand."

"How'd you do?"

"We raked it in. I convinced my grandpa to let me do an ad in our family newspaper. Then I got my mother to buy all the fresh lemons in Dare and help us bake cookies. My partner thought oatmeal raisin would go better than chocolate chip. Not as sweet." She paused for a second, warmed by the memory. "He was right."

"So you're destined to turn lemons into lemonade again?"

"Something like that."

"Just do one thing for me. Call Jack."

"Okay, but I can't promise anything."

"It's *intriguing*."

"Stop. You're worse than the Pied Piper."

"Okay. And Jill, I just have one more thing to say, scout's honor. After everything I've heard about you and your coffee shop, I can't wait to meet you in person. Enjoy your day."

"Thanks," she breathed out. "You too."

When the phone went dead, she stared at it. The intrigue *was* getting to her, so she emailed Jack for more information. Then she opened her laptop. Mac's name popped up in the search bar before she'd even keyed in three letters.

His picture almost made her call in Margie. Oh my God. His green eyes seemed to follow you—kinda like people said about the great portraits. He was all high cheekbones and mischievous smile, with straight hair so brown it was almost black, and a dimple in his chin. He looked about Tanner's age—mid to late thirties. Wow, he could have been on a soap opera.

She hunkered down when she found his bio. Mac Maven was a major player in the world of poker, and he ran a business called Four Aces, Inc. It specialized in boutique poker hotels—not the huge casino types with flashy slot machines. He was so not from Silicon Valley. She laughed.

"Maybe he wants to franchise my coffee shop for his hotels." He had famous chefs at fancy restaurants, but no coffee joints. It was a possibility. Jill did a little dance in her chair.

He was big time. And he wanted her. The big question was: for what?

As usual, she was getting carried away. *But this could be so much bigger than any restaurant,* she heard her Inner Businesswoman whisper into her ear.

She was a terrible person. She did believe bigger was better.

Well, she and Brian were only *talking* about opening a place together. *He hasn't agreed yet,* the little voice added. She'd have to see what Jack said and how things went with Brian.

She clicked her laptop off so she could focus on the present moment.

She had a date to prepare for. One she'd waited for all her life.

CHAPTER 4

Deputy Sheriff Peggy McBride cruised down *her* streets, as she now thought of them, heading home. She and her seven-year-old son had only been in Dare for a month since moving from Kansas to be closer to her brother, Tanner, and to take a new job, but it already felt like she belonged here.

The mountains had smothered the sun again in their daily contest, cloaking the town in an eerie twilight. She still hadn't gotten used to nature's majesty, so different from Kansas' rolling prairie, where you could see storms coming miles away.

She was cruising down Adler Street when she saw Jill heading to her car, dressed like a woman who wanted to see some action. Peggy would bet her ass she was going to see Brian. She angled her car over and rolled her window down.

"You planning on doing anything illegal tonight, Ms. Hale?"

Jill's eyes sparkled, a mischievous smile breaking out across her mouth. "I'm not sure I should tell an officer of the law."

"I have to relieve the babysitter, but do you have time to come over for a minute and tell me all about it?"

Making friends wasn't easy for Peggy. She understood the penis-carrying gender best. Peggy knew how to shoot pool—and a gun; she didn't get offended when men belched or adjusted themselves; and she could play bad cop so well her buddies joked that she made their balls shrink. But she was trying to click with Jill, especially since Jill was her sister-in-law's sister, a part of her new extended family.

Plus, no one entertained her like Jill, who always acted like she was on speed—but in a good way, not a get-your-ass-busted way.

Jill walked closer and lifted her sleeve. Even in the muted light, the electric purple watch dotted with fake crystals couldn't be missed. "I was going to buy a new lip gloss, but I'm being neurotic. Pink passion is fine. I'd rather use the extra time for a girl chat. Thanks."

A *girl* chat. What did people drink for that? Tea? "Okay. See you in a sec."

Dare's quiet streets drew her in as she drove off. Parents were coming home from work, greeting kids at their garage doors. Lights popped on in simple A-frame houses.

Jill was waiting by her front door when Peggy pulled up.

"How in the world did you beat me here?" Peggy asked, getting out of the car.

Her friend strolled over to her. "You must drive like an old lady. I thought one of the perks about being a deputy was never getting a speeding ticket."

"Officers are expected to model *and* enforce the law," Peggy said primly.

"Sounds like a bad deal. I love to speed."

Peggy laughed and headed toward the house. "Let me pay my sitter. Then I'll get your tea."

"I hate tea."

"Thank God. I was worried we might be reenacting *Little Women*."

"I like *Little Women*."

Peggy let herself inside. The immediate sound of pounding feet made her day—every day.

"Mom!" Keith raced around the corner decked out in a superman sweatshirt and blue sweatpants. His cheek was creased from his habit of watching TV with one hand under his chin. As she leaned down to hug him, he wrapped his arms around her waist.

"Jeez, I thought you'd never get here. Can we have pizza tonight?"

"No, we had it Sunday. Say hi to Jill."

Jill stepped through the door after stomping her boots, crouched down, and held her arms out. "How's my favorite guy?"

"Jillie," Keith yelled like an incoming war party. He zoomed into her arms. It was a mutual love fest. Most people took easily to Keith. She didn't know where he got the approachable spirit from—certainly not her or her ex, another cop.

"Mom, now we've *got* to have pizza. Jill, don't you want some?"

"Can't. I've got to head over to Brian's soon. I'm just here for a girl chat. I like the digs," she added, looking around. "You guys are settling in well."

"Yeah, mom's got everything up. I told her if the pictures were straight."

Uprooting her son from Kansas had been an easy decision. No one wanted to be closer to Uncle Tanner than Keith. Okay, she was a close second. She loved her brother dearly. Hell, he'd practically raised her when their dad had left. And her ex was so out of the picture he barely remembered to call or send child support.

"The house looks great, but it could use more color," Jill commented.

Peggy shuddered. "No way. I *like* white and gray." She glanced at the landscape prints on the wall, thought of the train set she'd assembled after midnight. So, it wasn't Jill's style. Peggy craved order and clean lines—a safe haven for her and Keith. She couldn't give him a father and a normal family life. Her ex's cheating ways had blown that possibility to bits. She tried to make it up to Keith as best she could. She didn't want him to think he was missing anything.

"Keith, don't you want a pink room?" Jill asked.

His gagging sounds were a little too good.

"I'll go make some coffee," Peggy said. The irony hit her. She was making coffee for a coffee shop owner. And she didn't have anything but the super-saver brand the grocery store sold, nothing exotic from another country like Jill's shop headlined. Maybe her friend wouldn't notice if she added enough milk and sugar.

She paid the sitter, who had been waiting patiently in the kitchen, and doctored the coffee while Keith and Jill played tug-of-war with her scarf. After she set it on the kitchen table, with a paper napkin instead of the usual paper towel, she sent Keith off so she and Jill could talk. He zoned out again in front of the TV, watching *Toy Story* for probably the seven-thousandth time.

Jill sipped the coffee she'd concocted. Peggy caught her wince.

"Is it that bad?" she asked.

"It's fine."

"Please, I interrogate people for a living. Let me get you something else."

"Is this instant?"

"No, but I have that if you'd prefer." She laughed at the look of horror on Jill's face. "I have good memories of drinking instant coffee when I was a rookie."

"That makes me want to save cops everywhere."

"When you've been on shift forever, you quit tasting it."

"Stop. You're making me tear up." Jill pretended to wipe her eyes. "So, since I'm going on a *real* date tonight, what do you think of my outfit?" She jumped up and swung around.

Peggy's mouth dropped open. Girls twirled for each other? Thank God she didn't have a baton in the house. *This* is why she wasn't comfortable with having female friends.

"I'm not exactly the fashion police."

"Ha ha, but you can tell me if this works, right?"

Could she? She categorized what she saw as she would if she were giving a suspect's description. "The green sweater matches your eyes. The jeans are pretty tight, if you're going for that. And it's got the whole..." She gestured toward the low V-neck. No way she was talking about boobs with her kid in the next room. "It looks...nice."

Jill rolled her eyes. "That's encouraging. Could I seduce a lawman into doing something illegal?"

She lifted a shoulder. "Cripes, what have you been watching?"

"Okay, next time I'll drive up and ask Mere, but she and Tanner are still in honeymoon paradise, so I don't like showing up unannounced."

"Please, he's my brother." She so didn't want to think about him like that.

"Point taken."

"You and Brian must be getting serious if he's cooking for you."

Jill wacked her hand on the table. "Yes. Finally. We've been hanging out, but this is our first *real* date. I asked."

"I don't remember those. I'm a single mom. I watch cartoons, listen to kiddie music, and assemble toys late into the night."

"You need to get out more. We'll have to do a girls' night at Hairy's Bar. You can sit on the leprechaun's lap."

Peggy cracked her knuckles. "In your dreams. So tell me about you and Brian."

Instead of answering, Jill stirred her coffee with a spoon. After a moment, she said, "When someone doesn't want to talk about their past, it usually means something bad happened, right?" It was clearly something she'd been thinking about for a while. "Brian won't give me a straight answer about why he came home."

Peggy looked at the clock and realized she could serve Keith some macaroni and cheese in twenty minutes if she multi-tasked. She rose and pulled out the blue box.

"Why don't you just ask him? I'm sure it's nothing criminal. Maybe he's still figuring out how much to share with you. You did give him a hard time when he first came back to town."

Jill picked up a pan from the stove and filled it with water.

Peggy stopped in her tracks. "Thanks."

"For what?"

"Helping." Peggy turned around, the sense of awkwardness returning. She wasn't used to help. She sure as hell wasn't used to someone doing it without being asked. Well, except Tanner.

"I tend to be an all-or-nothing person," Jill clarified. "I don't know if I can be with him without wanting more...and that scares me."

Peggy ripped the box open. "What does?"

"Getting hurt again. Brian was always an open book growing up. Then he broke my heart and left for a cooking school I didn't even know he'd applied to."

The macaroni dribbled into the pan, the impact turning the water cloudy. "You don't trust him?"

"Not fully." She bit her lip. "Plus, there's this other thing I haven't told anyone. I was with Brian on the night of the Halloween party when Jemma..."

The blush that broke out across her face made Peggy drop the spoon she'd been using to stir the macaroni. "You were *together?* she asked in a lowered voice.

Yanking on a curl, Jill said, "We were out on the porch. He grabbed me and kissed me, and it ...got heated. I don't know what would have happened if..." Tears popped into her eyes. "We heard people screaming Jemma's name and ran inside. Part of me wonders if I would have been able to save her if I hadn't been with Brian. I think it's why we've kept things platonic even if we felt otherwise."

Survivor's guilt was the prime bitch, but Peggy knew how to deal with it. She walked closer to Jill and looked her directly in the eyes. "There was nothing you could have done. I know it's hard, but don't fall into the trap of thinking you could have saved her. When someone has an undetected heart murmur that acts up, there's not much anyone can do. Not without an AED, anyway. It's tragic, but it's not your fault."

Jill's sniff had made Peggy's knees lock. She hated seeing people cry. She reached for the napkin and handed it to her friend.

Jill's sigh came out shaky. "Part of me knows that. The other part can't accept it yet."

"You will. And listen to the professional here. This tragedy is something else that you and Brian share. On top of everything else between you, it's a hell of a lot."

"You're right."

"And you want to start a new business, together" Peggy said, shaking her head. "You're taking on a bunch."

Jill's shoulder lifted, and her blush faded. "I always do. I *need* to move forward. Work fulfills me, and it will help to have something new to focus on."

"Then do it—with or without Brian. Have a great date, but listen to your gut and try to take it slow. Deep down, if you don't trust him, there might be a good reason."

"Thanks, Peg." Jill squeezed her shoulder. "I need to run. Keith, come kiss me goodbye."

Peggy's son rushed in, grinning like crazy as Jill planted a kiss on his cheek. Jill didn't hug her at the door. Peggy was glad. That *would* have been too girly.

"Be careful," she said as Jill waved on her way out.

"I'm planning on it."

When the door shut, Peggy studied her mud-brown hair and eyes in the entryway mirror and had to wonder—not for the first time—other than having girl parts and a kid, what really made her a girl?

CHAPTER 5

Brian's unhurried perusal of Jill's outfit left her with no illusions about how charged this night would be. Sexual tension sizzled along with whatever was crackling and popping on the stove.

His navy V-neck sweater showcased his strong shoulders while his faded jeans snugly fit his muscular butt and legs. Her mouth watered from more than the smell of food.

"Hi there, he drew out, pulling her flush against his hard, warm frame.

Whoa! The slow kiss caught her by surprise, but yearning and lust sparked through her. She wrapped her arms around his neck and dove into the kiss. His tongue slid between her lips without preamble and explored her mouth with the same leisureliness of his heated gaze. She moaned deep in her throat. After years of fantasies, she was putty in his arms.

He broke the kiss and buried those warm lips against her neck. What in the world had gotten into him? She took a moment to quiet her panting. Jeez. She needed to go to kissing boot camp to get into shape for all this action. When he pulled back, she raised an eyebrow.

"Aren't you supposed to kiss me *after* dinner?" she asked although she hadn't dared to expect that.

"I couldn't help it." His wink was playful. "Cooking for you kept you on my mind all day. What you might like. What textures might delight you. How you'll respond when my food hits your tongue."

If she didn't have a good grip on him, she probably would have slid to the floor. *Oh. My.*

"I see," she managed to say with a dry throat, trying to banish Peggy's cautionary words—and her own—from her mind so she could enjoy the moment.

"It's also a *I'm glad you're not in jail for the stunt on the fire truck today* kiss."

She cleared her throat, praying he wouldn't say anything more—like he knew she was a stalker and needed serious medication. "Me too."

He helped her out of her coat, brushing errant curls down her back. Then he took her hand and led her into his loft-style apartment. It had high industrial ceilings, and the main floor boasted a family room and kitchen area separated by an island surrounded by bar stools.

She reached down to say hello to his bulldog, Mutt, who lay drooling on the rug, as they passed the leather sofa. Like everything in his trendy loft, the walls were black, white, and gray. Brian clearly didn't mess with color. Even his artwork had a monochromatic feel. She felt the urge to add a bop of red paint to the wall-size landscape of a foggy Paris bridge.

The kitchen was serious business with stainless steel appliances, black granite countertops, and a mega-industrial stove. He had canisters meticulously printed with the names of herbs and baking ingredients. Man, he had four kinds of flour—pastry, white, wheat, and rye.

He tugged her over to the stove. "I made chicken fricassee, potatoes with a beurre blanc sauce mixed with fresh parsley, and a watercress salad with orange segments and honey bourbon pecans."

She'd thought she was putty in his arms? Try a puddle at his feet. "Wow! You're going to spoil me."

"Come taste."

The smell of onions, wine, and herbs blended with roasted chicken wafted up at her, making her mouth water. He held the wooden spoon to her lips and placed a gentle hand on her waist. She opened her mouth, acutely aware of his touch, feeling a little off balance. He was feeding her like they were characters in a silent film about the Roman Empire, sans the succulent grapes.

The creamy sauce just about exploded her taste buds. "Yumalicious."

"Is that a Jill-ism?"

"Maybe."

The sauce's seductive flavor only inflamed her desire for him—a lifetime of repressed feelings. She linked her arms around his neck again and brushed her lips across his, wanting more, needing it. She ran her fingers across the base of his skull, and he tilted his head to make the kiss deeper. A wooden spoon clattered to the counter. The stove's heat only added to the rising burn in her body. She yanked her mouth free.

"God! I *love* kissing you." The connection, the texture, the heat was even better than she'd remembered.

"Yeah," he murmured against her neck, sending chilly bumps down her legs.

"And I'm going to absolutely *love* being able to do it any time I want." Dating and kissing. Learning about each other. Peggy was right. Let things take some time. Evolve. She almost snorted. God, she sucked at that.

Those warm lips nipped her chin. "That's not all I want to do."

Her nerves came back, full force. She wasn't ready to make love with him. There were things she needed to know first. His past. How he felt about her. Where he wanted this to go. Her mind wandered away from the kiss.

Brian must have sensed the change in her mood because he ran his hands up and down her spine and stepped back. "I know you don't care much for wine, so let me grab you a beer. Then I'll finish everything up." He'd set the bar for two. Even stuck flowers in a clear blue vase. The cloth napkins surprised her.

"Can I help?" she asked when he placed a frothy beer mug in front of her after pouring an ale into it.

He turned, brow furrowed. "Ah..."

She made a slicing motion, shaking off her heavier emotions. "I...can...cut...bread," she mimed like an ignoramus.

He snickered. "Sorry, I'm not used to...normal people helping."

"So I'm a normal person now?"

He lurched forward and kissed her smack on the lips. Then he darted back to the stove. "No, you're the least normal person I know. Which is exactly why I like you." And he sent her another wicked wink over his shoulder.

The "like you" comment dropped her firmly in reality. Right, they were still getting to know each other again.

"How was your day?" He plated the food with flair. His right hand swept out like a painter with a paintbrush as he squirted sauce onto the dishes from a clear bottle.

Mac Maven's call came to mind, but she didn't want to go there, not when she was after Bryan to start a restaurant with her.

"Meredith, Tanner, and Grandpa came in the shop today, arguing about an editorial," she said instead.

"Ah, the Trio of Truth strikes again. They've been sparking some lively debates lately. I've heard Tanner had them attend the evening journalist class he's teaching at Emmis Merriam. The students loved it."

"Grandpa gave me a hard time when I offered him a raspberry mocha. He said couldn't believe someone would drink fruity coffee."

Brian cleaned up the plates' edges with a towel. "I love his descriptions. He's eaten at some of the best restaurants in the world. I wonder what he'd say about them."

"He's probably on his best behavior at *those* places."

"You know he was only kidding."

She fiddled with her napkin. "Yeah, but it's like a burr under my saddle sometimes. I've always wanted his approval."

He set the towel aside. "Trust me, he doesn't care that you're not a journalist. He knows you're happy running the shop. He's proud of you, Jill. We all are."

"Does it bother you, ever? Cooking in town, where people used to make fun of you for wanting to be a chef?" His family had been brutal about it. She still couldn't believe all the horrible names his asshole father had yelled at him, especially after Brian's mom had skipped town.

"Funny you should mention that." His eyes narrowed. "I ran into Mrs. Thomilson today in the grocery store."

That nosy old biddy, she thought, clenching her fists. "Whoever came up with the term battle axe had her in mind. Ignore her. She wouldn't spend the money to eat at a nice place." Jill dashed over and wrapped her arms around him. His back resembled iron. "Trust me, you're the most smoking hot, manly man I know. All those people who used to call you terrible names can eat Spam."

His laugh snorted out. "What a punishment. Thanks. Now go back to your chair and let me dazzle you."

She stayed where she was and kissed the place between his shoulder blades. Let her fingers drag away slowly. Smiled at the hiss of his breath.

"You're playing with fire."

"Uh-huh." But she did as he asked, watching the play of his back muscles as he finished adding the pecans to the salad.

He presented a finished plate to her. *"Voilá."*

"Incredible! Five stars all the way." As she draped the white napkin in her lap, Mutt started audibly snoring. "Does he sleep all the time?"

"Pretty much. He's my dog couch potato," he replied, bringing over his white wine.

"You always wanted a dog."

"Yep." He gestured to the food. *"Bon appétit."*

She responded with her best Julia Child imitation.

His hand slapped his forehead. "Please, don't *ever* do that again. It's like taking the Lord's name in vain."

"Like that bothers you."

"Eat, Jill. I want to see what my food does to you."

That comment stopped all conversation and almost made it difficult for her to swallow the first bite of mouth-watering gastronomic magic. The cream sauce clinging to the juicy chicken held hints of garlic and thyme. The potatoes couldn't have held less than a stick of butter. And together, they gave her a foodie power-packed punch. Her eyes closed in sheer delight.

"God," she cried out, awash in a food stupor.

Even without looking, she felt his body tense beside her. Her lashes fluttered open. As she watched, his fingers flexed on his leg like he was itching to grab her. She cleared her throat in an attempt to get a grip. "Did you get Mutt in New York?"

His fork paused before it reached his mouth. Then he took a bite and chewed. "No. My work schedule was too crazy for a dog. The Chop House doesn't stay open late, so I decided to go for it when I moved back. Plus, I can run home on my break to let him out. He's pretty easy going, and he's good company." Brian speared a potato. "For a while, the only people I thought would ever talk to me in this town were Mutt, Jemma, and Pete."

As she fiddled with the watercress, some of the magic of the night faded. Their past was a minefield, and if they were going to move forward, she needed to stop being afraid it would explode. "Bri, I need to ask you something," she whispered. "Did you go to New York and not Denver because of me?"

His eyes narrowed as if he didn't understand the question. Then he sighed. "How long have you thought that?"

"Since you left."

"Are you sure you want to know the answer?"

Her heart fluttered like butterfly wings, fragile and slow. "Uh-huh."

Maybe. Not really.

He swiveled on his barstool and took her hand. "You thought that it would be perfect if we both went to school in Denver, but I knew that if I did, we would have gotten serious. I was afraid I wouldn't be able to give you what you needed. I knew how demanding culinary training was going to be."

"So that would be a yes." Jeez, the sharp pain in her heart made her blink.

"We were so young, Jill. My parents married right out of high school and look how that turned out."

They were nothing like his parents. A spurt of anger rose up in her. "We might have been young, but I knew what I wanted." You.

He let go of her hand. "You didn't know what you wanted to do for the rest of your life. Heck, you didn't even really want to go to college. You figured things out just like I did."

"And what did you figure out?" she asked, hoping that he would give her a straight answer.

The way those Bengal-tiger blue eyes studied her made her want to turn away. "I figured out I want to be a chef more than anything."

The fiery determination made his eyes look like blue flames. "Why did you come back if New York was your oyster?"

Brian speared the chicken. "Because I missed my friends." He cleared his throat and looked away. "I wanted *us* to be friends again. I couldn't stop thinking about you, even after so much time apart. We were friends for eighteen years. It was hard to lose a relationship like that. I'd...never had what we had...with anyone else."

God, she'd waited forever to hear him say that. "I missed you, too. I blamed myself for you leaving."

He spun her around and pulled her against his chest before she could blink. "I'm sorry," he whispered. "Jill, I needed to prove to everybody—and maybe even to myself after everything my fucking dad used to say—that there was nothing wrong about a guy wanting to cook French food. Hell, if they could feel the heat off the grill, feel the sweat dripping off them in gallons, hear the cursing, and heft the pots as heavy as dumbbells, they'd realize how much of a man's world a restaurant kitchen is."

His pine and musk aftershave tickled her nose. "You didn't work with any women?"

His fingers tensed on her back. "Ah...some. Like I said, the kitchen's mostly a man's world."

She let the sexist perspective go and drew back. "So you weren't driven away by some mystery woman or anything?"

His head darted back. "Why would you think that?"

"Because you never talk about it."

He lifted a shoulder. "There's not much to tell. I went to school. Then I worked like a dog from the time I got up until the wee hours of the morning at a five-star French restaurant."

Had his determination led to isolation? "Didn't you have friends?"

"You make friends with people in the business, casual ones you drink with after a shift." He ran his fork over a potato, making a train track.

"So you didn't have a long-term girlfriend?"

He broke eye contact immediately and scooped up more watercress. The silence made her bounce in her seat.

"No, I didn't have a girlfriend." Another pause. "But I wasn't a monk, Jill," he finally said after taking a bite.

She looked down in her lap and fiddled with her napkin. She knew it wasn't rational, but she didn't like to think about him with other women. In fact, she hated it.

"What about you? Jemma never talked about your personal life."

Her insides turned raw. "She wouldn't." Because there wasn't much to tell.

He ran a hand down her back. "I know, but that doesn't answer my question. Was there anyone serious?"

"No," she replied, feeling her face grow warm.

"Okay, then."

He leaned in to kiss her, his lips brushing hers like she was a crème brûlée-coated spoon. Chances were good Brian wouldn't disappoint her in bed like her only other lover, who'd brought new meaning to the saying zero-to-sixty...as in he hadn't lasted more than sixty seconds. Still, he didn't know her experience quotient was worse than a farm team's batting average. Would he freak if she told him? She didn't want him to turn away from her again.

He swiveled on his barstool. "Are you sure you want to explore going into the restaurant business with me, Jill? I want this, Jill, and I need you to be sure. The Chop House is a...temporary plan for me. My plan has always been to have my own place someday."

She thought back to Mac Maven's call again, but pushed it to the back of her mind. Infusing her voice with more certainty than she felt, she said, "Yes, I think we should explore it."

"Is being with me the only reason you want to open a business together?"

He'd always been able to read her. "Well, I won't lie. I want you to stay." Hadn't he just said his current job was temporary? "But I also think Dare is ripe for a new restaurant that's geared toward the Californians and the student/professor crowd. I need a talented chef to make it shine."

"Then I'm your man."

The vision she had of the restaurant rose to mind. The food would cater to their small town with its farm-to-table simplicity while serving a streamlined menu of *avant garde* cuisine for the more adventurous. Brian would give the job everything he had. Together, they could create something truly spectacular, and working together would give them the opportunity to combine their love for their work with their friendship and interest in each other.

"Let's do it."

He took her hand. "Deal." His palm stroked hers. Their warm skin ignited fires in her body again. He pulled her closer and caged her against his body, taking her mouth in a wild kiss. He pressed her against the counter. It dug into her back, so she pushed forward. Off balance, he grabbed her and sidestepped them to the couch. He lowered her while caressing her all over with his hands and lips. Her neck, shoulders, waist, hips.

When he tugged her sweater off, she tensed for a moment at the newness of his touch, but then his hands covered her breasts, and the sensation made her writhe and moan. God, it felt good. Before she knew it, he had her bra open, his mouth tugging one nipple and then the other. Her chest rose, seeking deeper contact. The tug and the pressure sent electric shocks down her toes and up her spine. Jill gave another anguished moan.

He pulled his sweater over his head and threw it aside. Her mouth dropped at the sight of his six-pack abs, and when he brought their bare chests together, the heat and sensuous slide of their skin made her clench with pleasure. He thrust his hand in her hair, pulling her mouth to his and stroking her with his tongue, nibbling her lips with his teeth.

Her body turned to water. Thundering, forceful, rushing, always rushing, like a mountain-fed stream. A new longing had her running her hands down his back to his butt, fitting her hips close to the hard bulge of his groin. God, the feelings inside her. He let out a throaty groan and undulated his pelvis in a way that made her fight for breath and call out his name. She pressed against him, seeing starbursts behind her eyes. The current inside her could go anywhere, do anything. It was so much...

"I want you, Jill," he whispered as he sucked on the skin where neck met shoulder.

The hot breath and the incessant rhythm of his hips had her wanting more. But when he dipped a hand into her jeans, she pushed him away. Took a few shaky breaths to clear her head even while her body thundered.

She wasn't emotionally ready for this.

His blazing eyes scorched her. Years of understanding passed between them. After a moment, his face fell. Her heart clamored in her chest, making it hard to breathe. Tears burned her eyes. He looked away. Took a few deep breaths. Then met her gaze, the pulse pounding in his neck.

"It's okay, sweetheart." He stroked her cheek with a finger. "That was pretty fast."

She disengaged from him with a lump in her throat and stood there blushing. Her body pounded with unmet desire. She covered her breasts and watched the muscles in Brian's stomach clench with each ragged breath.

He stood, his mouth pinched. "I need a moment. After all these years...Jill, I can't look at you right now without touching you."

Her pulse pounded in her neck. She eyed her sweater and bra on the sofa. "I'll get dressed and take off. I can't eat anything else now."

"Me either," he agreed, his voice strained.

Her hands fumbled with the bra strap, but after three attempts it finally hooked. She tugged on her sweater and stumbled to the door.

"Thanks for dinner," she rasped, jolts of electricity still igniting in her thighs.

"You're welcome. I'll call you." He didn't move from where he stood, his bare chest all hard grooves of sinew and bone.

Her last glimpse of him stole her breath. She opened the door and ran down the hall. So much for being on the path to liberation.

CHAPTER 6

$\mathfrak{I}$t was pathetic to wear a jacket with a pocket in it just so you could carry your phone around waiting for some stupid guy to call. After her evening with Brian had ended so abruptly a week ago, pathetic pretty much summed it up. Brian had texted her, but he hadn't called. Hadn't popped by, either. Without anything else to distract her, she had dived into the plans for the restaurant, wanting to have something more concrete to share with him. She'd convinced Morty Wilson to allow her some time alone in the furniture store he was selling so she could assess it as a possible location.

In a low blow, when she'd asked Brian to get together to discuss some of her new ideas for the restaurant, he'd begged off, saying he had too much work. She'd started to doubt herself, them, everything.

But today was Valentine's Day! And she'd had so many dreams about spending it with him growing up. This was her chance, or so she'd thought. She'd hoped he would send her a card or something, even if it was super early in their relationship. Maybe they didn't have a relationship. God, she was becoming neurotic. No, she *was* neurotic.

"You sulking?" Meredith wrapped her arms around her from behind as she finished making a latte.

"What makes you think that?"

"Your face is as long as your hair. It's Valentine's Day. Why aren't you happy?"

"Because I don't have plans."

"I'm sorry. Maybe something will turn up. Tanner's taking me to a lovely cabin up in the mountains. Roaring fire. Nice bottle of wine and—"

"Someone needs to put a lid on it. There are single mothers around here who might break down and cry," Peggy announced, stepping up to the counter and shrugging out of her coat.

Jill and Meredith turned, greeting Peggy in unison.

"I need a jolt to get through this *love brings out the worst in people* day. I've already had to pick up one peeping Tom who blubbered all over me about how he couldn't live without his ex-girlfriend. After seeing all his surveillance equipment, I think the girl did the smart thing."

Jill handed Peggy her regular. "That makes me feel better. I forgot that it's a field day for stalkers. At least I don't have to worry about that."

"Like you'd be upset if Brian stalked you," Meredith quipped, grabbing a chocolate from the red and white cupid bowl.

Peggy assumed what Jill thought of as The Police Position, hands on hips, legs planted wide. Her forest-green button-down shirt with the Sheriff patch and Eagle County logo emblazoned on the shoulder screamed authority, while her tan slacks begged for help from *What Not to Wear*. The police belt holding her radio, gun, mace, and handcuffs looked like it weighed a ton of bricks. "You got problems with the guy?"

"No." Jill shoved away thoughts of the other night. "He's working."

Meredith rested her hand on her shoulder. "It's a big day for The Chop House. Heard it's booked solid up to 10:15."

Jill snagged a chocolate—the consolation prize for girls everywhere who had no V-day plans.

"Why don't you have lunch with us?" Meredith asked. "Peggy, you can take off, right?"

"I have an hour."

"Okay," Jill agreed. "I'll get my purse and coat. Margie—"

"We've got it, boss," her barista responded without missing a beat, filling the machine with more beans.

When Jill reemerged, Peggy was talking with Margie. "Where's Meredith?"

"She's warming the car up."

"What a wimp. It's gorgeous outside. If I didn't have to work, I'd head up to the canyon, maybe eat outside."

"You must be nuts. It's winter! The sun appears for a second, and you people wear shorts."

She handed a cookie to Peggy. "This is for Keith, since I really do want to marry him someday."

"Thanks. He's mastered the farting armpit sound this week. I'm so proud. Oh, he made you a card." The red paper had glue globs of glitter in star shapes. "You ready?"

"Sure."

Her hand mimed the royal wave, eliciting a laugh from Margie and the customers. She pulled her sunglasses on as she stepped onto the street. Her whole body froze when she saw Brian standing next to her sister—all decked out in winter gear.

"You ready for some cross-country skiing and a picnic, Red?"

Her hand thumped her heart. "You...you..."

"At a loss for words? That's a first." He produced a bouquet of red roses. "You thought I forgot? That'll teach ya."

Her eyes burned. Meredith and Peggy smiled. People stopped on Main Street to watch.

Brian's silver mirrored glasses reflected her face's shock as he sauntered forward. "Happy Valentine's Day, Jill."

She wrapped her arms around him, their parkas making a sound like cicadas. "I thought...I thought..."

He kissed her head. "Keep working at it. You'll get it out."

The loving sarcasm stopped her stuttering. "I thought you had to work."

"Tonight. No getting out of that. But we have the afternoon to ourselves. Okay?"

"Okay!"

He framed her face and kissed her gently on the lips. In front of the whole town.

"You're making quite the public declaration here."

"Like it's a newsflash that I want you."

Her stomach clenched as she thought about all the ways he wanted her. Her breathing hitched.

He leaned closer to her ear. "Get your mind out of the gutter, Red." And he kissed her smack on the lips again.

Meredith hefted a bag forward. "I brought your gear. Brian already has your skis stowed. Go inside and get changed. Margie's taking care of the shop."

"You were all involved?"

Peggy shook her head. "Yeah, Jill. Duh."

"Oh, my God!" She stumbled back into the coffee shop to change, realizing she might float off the mountain if her skis didn't keep her grounded.

***

Brian savored familiar motions: snapping cross-country skis into place; planting poles into the snow; feeling the sunshine beat down on him, warm and bright; sliding along the glaring white banquet Mother Earth had laid out in Mountain Laurel Canyon. And best of all, Jill was right there with him. The basin stretched out in front of them, flanked by mountain laurels, aspens, endless rows of pines swaying in the breeze, and rugged mountains dotted with white swirls, making him think of whipped cream.

He'd missed afternoons like this in New York, where everything was quick and cramped and the streets were all dirty concrete.

The drive hadn't dimmed Jill's happiness, but she'd recovered her powers of speech. Damn if he wasn't pleased with himself. Who said women were the more romantic sex? The *text-message-only* run-up had totally worked. After all the Valentine's Days they'd missed spending together, he wanted to make this a day to remember for both of them.

Brian cast her a glance. "Remember how we used to come up here and drink in high school?"

A roll of her eyes. "I seem to remember a few falls on the way back."

"Good times. Everybody was so happy back then. So alive."

When she looked away, he caught the tear running down her face. "You missing Jemma?" he asked softly.

Her sniff was audible. "Yeah."

He could see her now in his mind's eye—that emerald green snowsuit she'd always worn and her crazy, hand-knitted purple hat, complete with ear flaps. "Me too," he said, "come here."

Leaning over awkwardly, he pulled Jill into a hug. The sparkling snow, the sunshine, and the punch of the evergreen trees had his heart expanding. An eagle flew overhead, casting a majestic shadow.

"That gives me goosebumps," she whispered.

His arms squeezed her tightly as they watched the eagle.

She skied alongside him for a few miles on the flat stretch, a comfortable silence descending between them. The scissor movement only accentuated her legs' graceful length. She might have felt awkward about her height growing up, but he thought she was perfect. He couldn't wait to have those long legs wrapped around him.

Okay, McConnell. No need to get heated this early.

Their destination loomed ahead. The large boulder sported one of the best vistas in the canyon and was as high as they could ski cross-country. Plus, they could sit on the rock and not freeze their asses off. The stone wouldn't be much warmer than the white stuff, but it absorbed the sun's rays.

Her pace increased. "Up for a little race, McConnell?"

The grin just about split his chapped lips. "You got it, Red."

Firming her shoulders, Jill shot forward. He planted his poles deeper and used his strength to add length to his stride. But then she crossed into his path.

"Hey!" He veered to the right.

Her laughter echoed loud and clear across the valley. "You must be out of practice if that throws your panties in a twist."

The crazy woman continued to zigzag in front of him, making it impossible to pass her without causing a collision. "You always did play dirty."

"Please. It's like NASCAR. Once you take the lead, you keep the other guy behind you."

"Like you've ever watched NASCAR."

Her legs slid across the snow smoothly. He skied through her tracks and looked for an opening. Brian's heart was pumping like crazy, while she didn't even seem to be breathing hard. God, was she in better shape than him?

"Jemma and I used to watch it together. The men are so hot—especially in those tight suits. Kinda like you look now."

"Okay, that's it." He dug his poles in even deeper and shot forward. She smiled when she saw him coming and stuck out her tongue. He headed right at her. Why wasn't she veering?

"Dammit, Jill!" He had two more yards, and he'd be on her.

Her laugh trilled out again. She angled sharply toward him. His right pole stuck in ice-crusted snow, and he lost his balance, toppling like a bowling pin. His skis came off as he somersaulted—his pack digging into his back. He spit out snow, sat up, and wiped his face off.

Her shoulders shook. "You really *are* out of practice."

"And you hate to lose. You crushed our picnic."

Her ski pole waved like Gene Kelly doing a dance. "At least you didn't blame me winning on you carrying that *heavy* ol' backpack."

His snort carried across the distance. "As if. I also won't say you weigh less and move like a gazelle."

Her hand reached for his. "A gazelle? Really? That's probably the nicest thing you've ever said to me."

He tugged her forward.

"Hey!" Her long frame fell in an inelegant heap next to him.

"If you think that's the nicest thing I've ever said, I clearly need to work harder." He flipped her, looming over.

Her mouth opened in surprise as he kissed her. Long and deep and hot, his heart racing from their contest and from how much he wanted her. Her gloved hands clenched him. With their snow suits on, he couldn't touch the curves he dreamed about, so he concentrated on kissing her senseless. His body nestled between the V of her legs, his hips moving against hers, their suits scraping. He sucked her tongue into his mouth and heard her groan.

The angle of her jaw called to him when she turned her face. Pressing a kiss there, he went lower, running his tongue above the bare skin over her yellow scarf. Her mouth glistened in the sunlight, so he sucked on her lower lip. Elegant fingers played at the back of his neck, while her tongue danced against his. Her hand moved down his back and fell away. Then it slid back up, igniting a string of fire until he felt snow slide down his neck. He darted back.

"Shit, that's cold."

Her laughter gusted out as he tugged his glove off and dug out the snowball. When he turned back, his breath caught. She looked like a winter goddess lying there in the snow—her long, lithe frame, the red hair trailing out of her yellow hat, her lips swollen from their kisses.

"You're so beautiful."

The smile he loved seeing faded. "You've never said that."

Yeah, because growing up, he hadn't wanted to lose her. She'd been an anchor in his life. And he'd seen from his parents' ugly divorce how horribly wrong romantic relationships could go.

Razor-sharp guilt rose. He tugged his glove on and then hunched over her, pushing his sunglasses up. It was important for her to see his eyes. "I may not have said it, but I always thought it."

"I'm glad," she said in a small voice, which told him she didn't believe him, not really. "So, have we a squashed picnic?"

"I only made macaroni and cheese." He pushed off the snow so he could stand and help her up. "Let's eat."

They brushed snow off each other and skied to the spot he'd picked out for them. She unclipped her skis and planted her poles. He followed suit and trudged through the white, shrugging off the pack, trying to cool down.

While Jill took care of business behind a tree, he spread a white cloth on the boulder. They couldn't have candles and flowers, but he could still plate her food. He popped the champagne, poured, and buried the bottle in the snow. Ice crunched, signaling her return.

"You totally lied! Macaroni and cheese, my ass. Is that champagne?" She trudged through the snow and sank down beside him.

"Like I'd make you mac and cheese. Jesus, Jill, what do you take me for?"

She kissed him. "A genius. Oh, I adore tapas! Let's see. Marinated mushrooms, chorizo, and olives. Oh my God, is that ceviche?"

"It loves to be cold."

"Tell me that's Man-chengo," she said, popping a wedge in her mouth. "Yep."

"If you're referring to the cheese, it's Manchego."

"Not like Jemma and I...used to call it. We dubbed it the Man-chengo."

Ah, that wicked sense of humor. Hadn't he always loved it? "Why?"

"Because it's a funnier name—and really nutty." She kissed him again, deeper this time. "You did all this for me?"

"Sure."

She tore her sunglasses off. Her green eyes outdid the lush pines snaking up the mountain. His heart shifted, and it felt like it was falling clear out of his body. He didn't want to tear his eyes away from her. Realized he could gaze at her forever.

His insides shook. God, he so didn't want to screw things up between them. And after his parents, he wasn't sure he could ever have a *forever* with anyone. Even her. Time for a toast, he decided, grabbing a glass, cursing himself for thinking about his parents at a time like this.

"To us," he said because any romantic words had evaporated from his mind.

Their glasses clinked. "To us." She took a sip. "Yum. Thanks, Bri."

He popped an olive in his mouth, off balance. Their relationship made him feel a whole hell of a lot more than he was ready to feel. Hadn't he just gotten out of an insane relationship not too long ago? One that had consumed him, annihilated him. He loved being with Jill, but when she looked at him like that...She had always looked at him like that. Like he was everything, could do anything.

He couldn't be her hero.

He wasn't a hero.

Hadn't he proved that in New York?

She dug into the food, talking with her hands. Everything she said came from her whole heart. God, he didn't want to hurt her by not being able to give her everything she wanted.

A blue jay cackled from the nearby tree, and squirrels chased each other, jumping from branch to branch. Occasional moans danced across her lips as she ate and drank her champagne. He ate in silence. He'd gotten carried away. It was Valentine's Day for Christ's sake. He'd feel normal tomorrow.

He fed her more tapas. They ate. Sipped more champagne. Took a few pictures of each other and then one of them together. Then he put the picnic away. She seemed to naturally end up with her head leaning against his chest as they both looked out over the valley.

The quiet unnerved him. Being with Jill and not needing to talk was new. Part of him wanted to talk about anything and everything to take away the intensity.

When she turned her head and met his gaze, his breath caught. He could drown in those luminous green eyes. His hand cupped her cheek. *Drown* was too scary. He could wade in them.

The tightness in his chest didn't ease, but he fit his mouth to hers like it was the most natural thing in the world.

***

Jill kept her eyes open as he kissed her, tracing his dark brows, the slash of his high cheekbones. Was there anything more dear to her? Hadn't she missed this face?

He sipped at her lips and stroked her tongue in long sweeps, making her heart sing. Her blood boiled. She tugged on his lower lip as he turned her onto her back.

"Do you have any idea how much I want to kiss your breasts right now?"

She inhaled sharply. Everything inside tightened. "Well, it *is* pretty warm in the sun. So long as you cover me up from the rays, I can give you a little skin."

He tugged on her zipper. "Afraid of a sunburn?"

She helped him lift her shirt. "Jemma and I tried sunbathing topless once when we were teenagers. You have no idea how much that hurt."

Her nipple tightened. "You mean here?"

"Yes, there."

He met her gaze dead on. "What do you want? Tell me."

Voicing her desires was new and awkward and...kinda hot. "I want you...to kiss my breasts."

His mouth tipped up. "So do I," he murmured as he lowered his head and took her nipple between his beautiful lips.

Her back arched. The sun warmed her face, while his mouth incited a different kind of heat. He kissed his way across her chest until her nipples were wet and hard and aching. A cold breeze blew, making them tighten even more.

Her soft moans couldn't be contained. Cold then hot, hot then cold. She was being exposed to more than just the elements.

Her body strained under him. When he slid his hands down her sides and into her snow pants, she stilled. Waited for the touch she sensed was coming. His mouth gentled on her breast and his hand slowed, as if he were seeking a sign. She wrapped her arms around his neck and urged him on. His fingers parted her folds and traced the V of her thighs to her core, his touch delicate, a mere brush. When her hips jerked, he deepened the caress, slipping one finger inside.

She moaned at the sensation paired with the raw tug of his mouth on her breast. The bold touch of his hand. Her body struggled against him, wanting more, wanting to give *him* more.

He eased back from her breast. "Shh…it's okay. Let me show you." He leaned up and took her mouth in a long, hot kiss.

She dug her boots into the snow as his palm continued to press against her center. Another finger joined the first. They caressed, rotated, and swirled until she was throbbing with desire. Her pulse beat wildly, erratically. Her body broke out in pure heat. Their tongues danced. He sucked on her neck, her earlobe, her lower lip. Her hands reached for him.

"No." He pressed them over her head. Opened her legs wider. Stared at her with those Bengal-tiger blue eyes. "I want you to feel this, all of it."

She closed her eyes as his fingers picked up the pace, stroking and stroking until lightning bursts raced up from her toes. Still his mouth tugged on her breast as his fingers swept deep and hard into her, his palm pressed against her. She convulsed with a loud moan, coming apart, anchored by him. Then sensations drummed all over her body until she relaxed against him in one long liquid line. He kissed her lightly and released the pressure between her legs. Rearranged her clothing. Pulled her head onto his chest.

Wow, was all she could think. Simply wow. It didn't equal anything she'd experienced on her own, and wouldn't it be even better when they had sex?

Her cap must have come loose because his fingers threaded through her hair. Even her scalp sizzled. She inhaled long and deep and turned in his arms. His mouth looked pinched, but he tried to smile.

"What about you?" she asked in a voice she didn't recognize.

He pushed a curl behind her ear. "This was for you. I want you to know how it's going to be between us."

Her mouth turned dry. In that moment, she made the decision. Soon, very soon, she would make love with him. There was nothing she wanted more. Hadn't he shown how much he cared by giving pleasure to her so unselfishly?

"I'm sorry about the other night. I wasn't ready. I—"

"It's okay. I won't rush you."

She thought about mentioning this was her first orgasm with a guy, but she didn't want him to think she'd been waiting for him, even if it was partially true. She hugged him tight.

"Did you bring me out here because you knew it couldn't go too far?"

He squeezed her and then moved away, sitting in the snow. She had a moment of guilt as she realized he was trying to cool off.

"Partly. Rolling around like two sunburned jackasses wasn't my idea of our first time together."

"Then there are the satellites," she added, making him laugh.

"I brought you up here because we always came here when we needed to get away from school or our parents."

She tugged her cap on. "This was our wishing spot."

"Our wishing spot?"

The sky seemed endless when she raised her hands to it. "We always talked about what we'd be when we grew up, remember? You talked about becoming a famous chef."

"I did, didn't I?"

"Yep, and you made it." She sang a few bars of *New York, New York* by Frank Sinatra.

He turned away quickly. Something about the new lines around his mouth made her cut off the song early. What *had* happened in New York? After what he'd done for her, she didn't want to ruin their mood by asking again, even though she knew he hadn't shared the full story. Patience wasn't her virtue, but she'd try with him.

She rose, her legs still unsteady. "So, I've been thinking about our place. Mortimer Wilson is going to be putting his property on Main Street up for sale in a few weeks. I went by his furniture shop. Took some rough measurements."

"You did all that while I was MIA?" he quipped, throwing the pack on his back.

"I told you I had some new ideas to discuss, but you wouldn't meet with me. I thought you were backing out after what happened last week."

"Sorry. I was trying to build the surprise."

"Well, you did." She grabbed a ski pole. "I've done some sketches. Thought about the layout." She drew the general space in the snow and then segmented it with lines for walls. "I thought we'd put the kitchen here. Office across the hallway by the walk-in cooler. We can split the front section into two. An informal one to cater to families—something funky, maybe with an Impressionistic feel. Monet blue on the wall with clouds and bright yellow flowers in chunky Provencal vases."

She sketched the second section more slowly when he rubbed his hand against his temple, the lines around his mouth as pinched as her Aunt Gladys before her morning prunes.

"Ah, it's just a brainstorm."

No smile.

"The second section would be more elegant, with a real French café feel. Dark wood tables with feminine-shaped chairs. Butter-yellow walls. Maybe a mural of somewhere in France."

"Like the Eiffel Tower?" His voice might be silky soft, but she heard the edge. And she had no idea what had put it there.

"God, no! Umm...A field of wildflowers. Wait. They have sunflowers, right? Like Van Gogh."

His silence was as vast as the valley.

"Or we could do something else."

He looked up. Gave her a fake smile. Touched his wrist in the telltale gesture of time ticking away. "We need to get going if I'm going to make it to work."

She grabbed her other pole and snapped into her skis. "They were just ideas, Brian. Why don't you tell me what you have in mind? This is never going to work if you're not honest with me."

"Let's talk about it another time."

He took off. She had to dig her poles in deeper to keep up with him. "Was there anything you liked about what I said?"

"Jill..."

"You don't need to spare my feelings. If we're going to be partners, you need to tell me what you think."

"Fine." Snow flew as he swished to a stop. "It's not in line with what I've been thinking. I don't like theme restaurants."

"But you like French food. Plus, the locals love pretending to leave town. It's the best of both worlds." Her heart pounded hard under her suit, drumming up a dangerous tune about their potential partnership.

He cleared his throat. "And the whole thing about two sections. I didn't imagine this as a place for families."

Her mouth dropped open. "But Bri, that's the fastest growing market in Dare. So many people are sticking around after college and starting families, not to mention the young professionals from California who are moving here to raise their kids in a small town. These people have good taste and the money to spend. Plus, they like introducing their kids to new things." Her throat tightened. Jill blinked back the tide of welling tears. So she'd lied about being impervious to his opinion. "Did you like anything?"

His sigh carried across the space. "I like to see you this excited."

She shot ahead of him, not wanting him to see her devastated expression. "That's not much."

"Hey!" he called, but couldn't catch her.

All the way down the mountain she struggled with herself. Brian's reaction made her think they could never work together after all. Her traitorous mind spun scenarios of Mac Maven's mysterious offer. Jack had emailed her back mid-week with a glowing review and then followed up with a call, but he'd been just as darn cryptic as his friend both times. She couldn't turn off her curiosity button. What did Mac want from her anyway?

Brian was breathing harder than she was when they reached his truck. She unclipped her boots and felt his hands on her waist, turning her toward him. "Look, we'll work it out. Everything's going to be fine." His voice was about as soothing as a dentist who was about to start drilling for cavities. "I don't like color. That's no surprise. I'm a guy. I'm looking for something understated. I don't want the décor to outdo the food. Let's set up a meeting for sometime this week and go through all of the details."

She almost rolled her eyes. Some boring place that didn't cater to families wouldn't last eight months in Dare.

"Hey." He tipped up her chin. "When we used to come here and make our wishes, what did you used to say? I can't remember." He put his arms around her. Her head fell to his chest without her conscious realization.

"I talked about making it big. Like my grandpa. Being a major town player." No change there.

"That's all?" he joked.

"I had other dreams." Jill didn't mention that the main wish she'd made on that boulder was to be Mrs. Brian McConnell someday. She pulled away, opened the car door, and reached for her boots. When the lace on her ski boot wouldn't untangle after a minute, she let out a low shriek.

"Let me help," he said from outside the vehicle. He'd been watching her struggle. "You need to be more patient."

But that never had been one of her virtues.

Brian sank to his knees and angled her boot onto his thigh. The sun illuminated his face as he frowned, working slowly with the knot. His puffy lips reminded her of what he'd given her today. That he'd wanted to give her pleasure without taking it for himself. Her concerns about the restaurant faded. He was back. He was here. And he wanted to be with her. What could be more important?

"You got pretty tangled up here," he muttered.

You've got that right.

He slid one boot off, a gentle hold on her ankle. As he pressed her stocking-clad foot into her hiking boot, Cinderella and the glass slipper popped into her mind. The handsome prince on his knees, his touch loving, his face indulgent—exactly how Brian looked in this moment.

She fell back against the seat as a major realization descended. The girl inside her had always loved Brian McConnell. Now she knew for sure that the woman inside her did, too.

Too bad Prince Charming hated every idea she had for their place together. He might be able to cook, but it was becoming abundantly clear that he had no head for business. She could run the castle, and she didn't want to have to smash her glass slipper on his sparkling kitchen floor to drill that home.

CHAPTER 7

Peggy didn't understand how Meredith and Jill had corralled her into joining them on a girl's shopping trip to Denver. Jill had announced she needed lingerie after the successful Valentine Day's picnic with Brian. D-Day was dawning, Jill said—the *Deed* Day.

Great, like Peggy needed to know her friend had picked out a day to get it on with Brian.

Still, the two sisters made her laugh, and she'd been wanting to see Denver. So far the tour sucked. They'd spent three hours in Cherry Creek Mall.

She detested shopping, especially this lingerie binge. The bright colors, lacy teddies, and padded cups had her stuffing her hands deeper into her well-worn jeans. Padded cups? Heck, she wished they had something to squash her "girls" down.

Didn't they understand *jiggling* was embarrassing? Busting into a crack lab and pursuing a fleeing suspect with your girly parts bouncing like basketballs suited a porn flick more than it did real life. Cops weren't supposed to have cleavage. She couldn't lean over a perp and squeeze out a confession with her décolletage sticking out.

Jeez. These people must think women sat around dreaming of situations where they could *push 'em up, push 'em up, way up.*

Exotic mannequins *with nipples* were propped up all around in various sex get-ups, some of them so obscene she wanted to shield her eyes. These weren't the androgynous figures she'd grown up with at JC Penney. She eyed one lone guy fingering a black lace mesh body suit. What in the hell was the purpose of putting on something that made you as buck naked as a jaybird? Plus, wouldn't it rip? Was that the point?

"You should try this on, Peg," Jill suggested. "It compliments your dark hair."

The purplish nightie's price boggled her mind. How could it cost that much when there was hardly any fabric? Plus, she lived in a winter state. She'd freeze her ass off wearing something like that.

"I've got a kid. Remember? I can't prance around the house in that."

"It's all about intention." Jill held up a neon-green padded bra. "If you buy it, you're telling the universe you're ready for some action."

"I'm a single mom. That's not high on my priority list."

"Tanner is going to love that, Mere," Jill told her sister, who was holding up a black lace teddy.

Peggy shuddered. "Please, that's my brother you're talking about."

"Like you don't know we have sex." Her sister-in-law dropped it in her pink shopping bag.

"I don't need any details." She shifted on her feet. Would it be impolite to suggest they meet up later?

"Oh, come on. There has to be something you like," Meredith said.

"Look, I sleep in a T-shirt and sweatpants."

The lone guy dug through the bra bin like he was digging for gold, making Peggy wonder if he was a cross dresser.

"Didn't you wear lingerie when you were married?"

The guy picked up a black bra studded with silver spikes. Dear God, it was straight out of an old Madonna video. He dangled it, eyes as bright as a drug user's. She looked over at the security guard and wondered what kind of crap he had to deal with in this joint. There couldn't be enough money in the world to entice her to work here.

"No, not really. Frank wasn't into that stuff."

Jill snorted. "Every man likes lingerie, trust me."

"Not Frank." She stilled. He'd cheated on her, hadn't he? Maybe he *had* been interested in all this crap. She walked over to the cosmetics aisle to give herself some room. The cloying fragrance made her eyes smart.

Who the hell cared if Frank liked this stuff, anyway? If he cheated on her because she didn't wear some scoop-your-boobs-up bra, then he was even more of a weasel than she thought. She shrugged it off. Her hands sought out her badge in her purse. She knew who she was.

"Hey, Peg, do you think Brian will like this?" Jill held up a tropical print nightie.

If you're going to a luau. "Jeez, I don't know. Stop asking me. Do I look like I'd have a clue?"

Jill shook it like a burlesque performer. "Come on, you work with guys. Would they find this hot?"

"Why don't I send a photo to the sheriff?"

"Haha. Seriously. I want my first time with Brian to be perfect."

Her head started to pound from all the questions and the perfume. God, gunpowder from the firing range smelled better than this nonsense.

"So long as you're putting out, men don't care. All this crap is for a woman's confidence."

Meredith slung an arm around her shoulder. "As someone who wore La Perla after her divorce for that very purpose, I can confirm that you're right. However, I will add that your brother loves this stuff almost as much as I do."

Peggy gave her a light shove. "Jeez, could you give it a rest?" Maybe if she changed the topic, Meredith would lay off. "Jill, I'm glad you've finally decided you can trust Brian enough to let him into your pants. After all these years you could wear a potato sack, and he'd still drag you to bed."

"Probably true, but I want to reward him. He's shown incredible patience."

"I'll bet," she drawled and realized how cynical she sounded. "You're blushing again."

"I need to go to the doctor. See if there's a pill."

"It's called embarrassment. Now, please have mercy. I *really* need to leave this store. If I have to watch that guy touch one more thong and wipe his mouth, I'm going to tell him to take a hike. Plus, it stinks like a whorehouse in here."

"You ever been in one?" Jill flicked another bra into her bag.

She rolled her eyes. "It was more of a crack house, not really the bordello type."

"Oh, the good ol' days. Satin and lace. Men with cigars."

"You have a pretty romantic view of prostitution."

Meredith stepped in. "Okay, let's try these things on. Peggy, I won't ask you to come with us."

Her fingers rubbed her brow as they disappeared behind a cream and pink wall. The weirdo wandered her way, holding three black thongs and snap crotch teddies. God, imagine being the person who invented that. What a proud moment in science—or fashion—or whatever.

The sisters' laughter carried out of the dressing room. Who knew some girly outing would become a comedy show? Still, it made her smile, hearing them. They were like an alien species sometimes, but they always drew her to them.

She texted Tanner to check on Keith, ending the message with, *Save me. I'm in shopping hell.*

His immediate response pinged. *Keith is fine. You decided to go. Save yourself. Is Meredith buying anything interesting?*

Her mouth twisted. *I am so not describing your wife's undies,* she texted back.

Sweet. Something to look forward to. Have fun. Snort.

God, he'd been acting so weird lately. The Hale alien species had converted him.

Crowding into a corner seemed like the smartest strategy. A brown velvet nightgown drew her gaze. It reminded her of a bear's hide. Her fingers itched to see if it was as soft as it looked. She checked over her shoulder to make sure Meredith and Jill weren't around and darted a finger toward it. The rich, smooth texture rippled. Finally a color she could approve of. Weren't most men color blind anyway? Bold colors were wasted on them.

Plus, this looked warm—well except for the missing sleeves. But the length was good. Then she realized she was thinking about taking it off, letting it fall in a puddle at her ankles. She needed to get a grip. Maybe it was that hideous smell, making her light-headed. The price tag boggled the mind. She could feed her and Keith for a month on that amount.

"See something you like?"

She spun around and shoved her hands in her pockets. Meredith raised an eyebrow. Jill gave a dopey grin.

"You two sounded like drunk sorority sisters."

"This brown one would suit you," Jill said. "It's not slutty."

"I appreciate the character reference." Peggy's gaze slid back to the gown. "It's not the worst thing in here."

"Hmm..." Meredith elbowed her sister.

"I'm going to check out." Jill said, grabbing Peggy's arm.

"I need to change a size." Meredith sauntered off with a skip.

Peggy waited by the counter as the clerk wrapped Jill's medley of carnal clothing like it was fine china. This store was so weird. Why waste money wrapping stuff that couldn't break in bright pink paper?

Jill produced a flashy credit card when the clerk recited her total.

"You know you aren't going to have those on long enough to justify the debt."

"I don't care. This is what you do when you date someone. Wear hot lingerie, have blistering sex. I've wanted to be with Brian for what seems like forever. Don't ruin it for me."

This is what people did? She never had. "Sorry."

The sight of liquid gel pad breast lifters made her nose scrunch up. She could just imagine wearing one on a raid and popping it when some guy threw a punch. She'd die of embarrassment. The guys would never stop giving her crap.

"Okay." Meredith appeared at her side, having checked out at one of the other cash registers. "I'm ready."

"Me too." Jill lifted her bags. "They should call this place Sex 'R Us."

Peggy led the way out of hell. She gave the lone guy her scary smile, making him drop the underwear. Brightened her day.

"Hey," Meredith said, catching up. "I bought something for you." She held out a bag.

Oh, please don't let it be something with animal print. She didn't want to look, but she didn't want to seem ungrateful. Peggy reached into the bag and her fingers brushed velvet. She stared at Meredith as she pulled the brown nightgown halfway out of the bag. Her mouth turned dry. "I...this is too much. Meredith, seriously, I'll never wear it." Still, her fingers curled around it.

Meredith slid her arm through Jill's. "Never is a long time. Please, it'll hurt my feelings if you don't take it. Think of it as an early birthday present."

"My birthday's in December," she protested, her fingers betraying her by playing with the texture once again. When she realized what she was doing, she dropped it back in the bag.

Jill nudged her hip. "Let's do lunch. This is the best shopping spree ever! And I'm having sex this week. I am woman. Hear me roar. Okay, Mere, your turn."

"I am reporter. Hear me scoop."

Jill swung their still-linked arms. "Good one. Now you, Peggy."

"I am cop. Hear me shoot."

They both laughed like loons and slapped her on the back. The sudden tightness in her chest almost hurt. She stuffed the pink bag into her purse, reminding herself that girly things weren't for her. She was a cop and a mother—first, last, and always.

She'd throw the bag in the back of her closet when she got home where Keith wouldn't look. Peggy McBride had no use for it—never had, never would.

Even as she told herself that, another part of her cried out, making the feeling in her chest so unbearable that she pulled out an antacid for relief.

CHAPTER 8

Was there anything more rip-your-clothes-off hot than envisioning making love for the first time to the man sitting across from you?

Well, there was the *actual sex,* but Jill would get to that.

Her thigh brushed Brian's muscular leg as he continued to talk through those seductive, bow-shaped lips. She imagined them trailing down her neck and going lower, nipping at her heated skin as her hands curved around his corded back, then trailed over his washboard abs.

He sucked in a breath. "Stop looking at me like *that.*"

"Like what?" she flirted back, reaching for his hand and stroking the palm with her newly manicured vixen-red thumb.

"Like you don't know. Seriously, you're killing me. Right here in your damn coffee shop. You should call it Don't Toy With Me instead of Don't Soy With Me. Jesus." He shifted in his seat, the hard line of his mouth pronounced.

This man was toast—and she was going to be the butter. She'd studied the Kama Sutra all week until she knew it as well as the Gettysburg Address. Whether or not her body could twist into the "Splitting-the-Cicada" position like a Cirque de Soleil performer was another matter.

"Sorry." Brian tucked one of her corkscrew red curls behind her ear, his brilliant Bengal-tiger blue eyes soft and slumberous. Everything in her core settled into peace and certainty.

"I love you, you know," she uttered in a low voice, following her heart. Saying it today, before they had sex, seemed important somehow.

His eyes narrowed a fraction, but he rallied by raising her hand to his lips. "That's a pretty important thing to say in a coffee shop," he tried to joke.

Her heart squeezed like it was a piece of meat on the grill clutched by his metal tongs. So, he wasn't ready to say it back. Well, he would in time. Hadn't he been showing her how much he cared over the past week?

"Let's get back to our plans." Brian held her hand while he resumed talking.

Her mind drifted to the emerald green negligee she'd selected for tonight. Aromatherapy candles would light their first steps into passion, give the room an exotic touch of musk.

"Are you even listening?" Brian angled his head closer to hers. The overhead lights illuminated his dark eyelashes.

"Of course," she lied, her heart beating like she'd sucked down too many espressos. "Don't I always?"

His snort had her skin cooling. Jill settled back, watching his fingers caress the rough plans they'd drawn up for the restaurant. They weren't discussing anything controversial today, just the layout. After what had happened on the Valentine picnic, they were dancing around their differences. Brian had gone to see Morty's place a few days ago while she was working, and he'd liked it. Thank God Morty wasn't planning on putting the space on the market for another month. Plenty of time for her and Brian to work out their creative differences, right?

Her mind drifted back to that afternoon. His touch on her core, the sun warm on her face, the deep convulsions in her body. My God, she was going to experience it all again—tonight. It was going to be so much better with him. Her thighs contracted.

His hands clapped in her face. "Earth to Jill. What is *wrong* with you today? You're more spacey than usual."

Because *Sex, Sex, Sex* was flashing through her mind like gaudy lights at a sleazy Vegas strip club. "Words to make any girl's heart pitter patter, Bri."

"You don't want me to talk normally to you anymore?"

"A little romance would be nice." She toyed with the crystal on her necklace. She'd dug into her top dresser for the black box holding the heart-shaped one he'd given her for graduation, but she hadn't been able to put it on. To her, it still symbolized the end of their friendship. She didn't want to jinx their happiness by wearing it yet.

He rolled his eyes. "Listen, if we're going to work together, I can't be Casanova and Wolfgang Puck at the same time."

Now she snorted. "No, you have much better hair."

"Okay, smart ass, as I was saying, I need more space in the kitchen."

"I'll make it worth your while." She ran a finger down his blue V-neck sweater. God, flirting with him and knowing where it was going to lead made her feel bold and sexy.

He swatted her hand aside, putting a damper on her enjoyment. "Jillie, you can't negotiate like that if we're seriously going to form a business partnership." He blew steam from his coffee before sipping it. "I mean it."

"You're *so* stern. Why can't you have fun with this?"

"Because sex and business don't mix well. Trust me I…"

Her butt scooted to the edge of her seat. "Do I hear the voice of experience talking?"

He didn't speak for a moment, adding a sugar cube to his macchiato with incredible concentration. "You're like a horny teenager. I need your mind on our ideas—and nothing else—when we're working. We can have fun after. This will only work if we can keep business and pleasure separate."

Perhaps they needed to have *fun* so she could stop being horny. "Fine." She grabbed the hand-drawn design. "What do you want?"

"Six more feet for the cooler."

Her heels dug in like an oak tree extending its roots. "I need space for the office. I am *not* working in a cracker jack box."

"You can use your office here."

"No, I want to be on site." With you.

"Doesn't make sense. You can shuttle back and forth."

It usually delighted her the way his brows framed his brilliant eyes. Right now, the line in between them made her want to shred her signature lime green and black napkins into tiny pieces and throw them in the air like confetti.

"I'll split the space with you, Bri. It's the best I can do."

"A measly three feet? That's impossible."

The disagreements were giving her an ulcer. Not much had changed since the picnic—even though they were both trying to compromise. The Brian Groupie in her wanted to give in—like she had about a monochromatic scheme, which she hated—but she just couldn't do it.

"Give it up, McConnell. That's the best you're getting."

"Fine, but when we don't have enough food to feed everyone, Red, I'm going to remind you of this moment."

Her fingers squeezed the bridge of her nose—hard. Brian was sipping his espresso, watching everyone but her. They had to find a shared vision. Deep inside she knew they'd fail if they couldn't find some common ground.

Her nerves increased. Suddenly, having sex with him didn't seem as daunting as opening a restaurant together. Her mind pinged back to Mac Maven's mysterious offer. He'd called again to check in with her, pouring on the charm, but not too hard. She'd told him she was pursuing a business with her childhood friend, but had Meredith been right from the beginning? Was opening a place together putting too much strain on her relationship with Brian?

The bell chimed, announcing a customer. She was a newcomer—and a stunning one. Her honey-blond hair seemed to bounce lovingly around her exotic face. A cliff diver could have committed suicide off her cheekbones, and her movie-star almond eyes shone in gold and cherry-wood tones. Her full-length black mink wasn't buttoned—a dangerous choice given all the Colorado environmentalists—exposing a red dress clinging to a frame that should only have been possible with accompanying air brush fairies. The matching four-inch red heels were totally impractical in winter and left snowmelt dots all across the walnut floor.

Jill's sigh bordered on a wheeze. Oh, to be so beautiful—even in your forties like that woman. She *had* to be a California transplant. In a roomful of casually dressed patrons, she looked like she belonged on Rodeo Drive.

Jill stood to introduce herself.

Brian grabbed her hand. "Where are you going?"

"New customer." She inclined her chin.

He jerked like he'd been electrocuted. His color went from normal to white to green in one second flat. She'd only seen this happen three times. When he'd broken his leg skiing. When he'd told her his parents were getting divorced. And when he'd stopped CPR on Jemma.

"Bri-yan," the woman singsonged out in a sultry French accent. She sashayed toward them like a glittery Christmas ornament.

Brian dropped Jill's hand like it was a hot potato and stood. Venus incarnate reached over and grabbed his face, kissing him ardently.

Jill felt her mouth fall open like a bad cartoon character's. When the woman's tongue swiped at Brian's lips, she straightened to her full five foot ten inches. She tapped the woman on the shoulder as Brian's hands *finally* pushed her back.

"Simca!" Brian stuttered, breathing hard.

"You know her?" Jill asked. It was a stupid question after that kiss, but it was the only thing she could think to say.

The woman's perfect red lips curved into a knowing smile. "We were involved. In New York. Brian, I told you I was coming."

He'd been in touch with this goddess? Her hand gripped the chair. "You were?" She looked at Brian for confirmation, but his eyes were fixed on the mystery woman.

"Yes. He did not tell you?"

"No, he told me he didn't have a girlfriend." And this omission felt like a betrayal.

He looked from Simca back to her, his pupils wide. "Well...that wasn't...what I called her. Jill...I'm sorry."

As an explanation, it sucked. Why did he think he could withhold vital information about an ex, particularly an ex who was coming for a visit? An apology improved nothing.

Simca linked her arm through his. "In my country, we don't use childish descriptions. We were lovers."

"Jill..." Brian broke off, rubbing his throat.

Seeing him with this gorgeous, blond woman—so much prettier than she was—made all the old insecurities rear their head, just like when he'd chosen perky blond Kelly Kimple over her.

After a few seconds of silence, the woman tsked. "Ah, Brian, you are overcome at seeing me again. Let me introduce myself to your friend. I'm Simone Moreau. My closest friends call me Simca."

How could he not have told her about this woman? And she was *older!* Jill's spinning mind conjured up images of the two of them together. So not what she needed.

"How did you meet?" she made herself ask. Part of her wanted to know. The other part...

Brian cleared his throat. "Simca was...ah...one of my restaurant bosses."

"Really? I seem to remember you saying a restaurateur's life was mostly for men." She turned to Simca. "I take it you're an owner, not a chef?"

"No, I am a chef, too." She settled comfortably against Brian's side like a French Barbie and her American Ken doll.

Becoming aware of all the stares focused on them, Jill broke out in a blush. In a small town like Dare, the news would travel as fast as a forest fire. Her questions would have to wait.

"If you'll excuse me," Jill muttered through tingling lips.

The woman's gold bracelets clicked together. "Brian, let's go somewhere and catch up. I've missed you so much."

Jill ran into an empty table before sailing out of her shop. She listened for the door chimes to ring again as her boots slapped the sidewalk. Surely, Brian was coming after her.

When nothing rang except the ding to Smith's Hardware, tears gathered in her eyes. Dammit. She would *not* cry over him again. She'd get mad instead. Let the pain sear through her like a hot poker, heating her freezing body. He'd *lied* about having someone special. Hell, he'd invited her here. And to top it all off, she was an *older*, beautiful French woman with a sultry accent.

She felt like a fool. The new life she'd spun for them might as well have been made of toothpicks.

CHAPTER 9

Brian watched Jill stride down the street like she was taking on the blustering north wind in the boxing ring. She wasn't even wearing a coat. Shit, he thought, tugging his hair. This was bad.

Simca's fingers, those delicate instruments that could filet a twenty-pound fish or make a man beg himself hoarse, caressed his collarbone. He pushed her hand aside.

"What are you *doing* here?" He felt as loopy as when he'd taken a baseball against his temple in junior year of high school.

Those pouty French lips didn't lose their small smile, but her sherry eyes narrowed a fraction. "Correcting the worst mistake of my life."

Her sultry accent alone had made a slave of him back in New York. It had made him understand why so many people chose to study abroad. A book dropped on the floor, making his head turn. Customers were literally leaning forward on the edge of their seats to get a better look.

"Let's take this backstage." He brushed his hand under her elbow, knowing she would dig her heels in if he manhandled her. Simca led. Men followed. It was a rule of the universe.

"Margie, I'm using Jill's office for a minute."

He escorted her back there, the itch to follow Jill climbing up his spine. This could ruin everything. The explosive colors in the office added to his headache. Red door. Yellow walls. A new modern art landscape, vibrant with blue and orange.

"What the *fuck* are you doing here?" he asked, sitting on the edge of Jill's purple desk.

"I called you. Didn't you listen to my voicemails?" She closed the door, leaning against it like a starlet. "My divorce is final. You were right. Andre didn't love me." The ghost of a smile flickered across that movie-star face. "But you do, *mon cher.*"

"What?" He almost fell off the desk. "You have a hell of a nerve to show up after all this time and say shit like this to me."

"Don't be mad at me. I wanted to contact you when Andre fired you, but my divorce lawyer told me it would hurt my settlement. The minute my divorce was final, I called. I want to be with you again. I want to work with you again—and make amends."

His mind buzzed from total shock. "You've got to be kidding me.

Jesus!" Brian paced. "Why didn't you help me when he accused me of stealing his recipes? You didn't say a word!"

"Yes, I did!" she said, raising her voice. "I told the police you couldn't have done it. That you were with me."

That revelation deflated some of his anger. It explained why they'd dismissed the charges so quickly. "He black-balled me, Sim. Said I was a thief. I couldn't find a goddamn good job anywhere."

"I know. That's why you had to come home. I'm here to change all that. Think of me as your Food Fairy Godmother."

When she pushed off the door, her eyes liquid with desire, he held up his hands. "Give me a damn minute here. This is a lot to take in." He took a shaky breath.

"But of course," she politely murmured.

It was weird, seeing her in Jill's space—it was like his two worlds were colliding, and he was caught among the debris. "I came home to rebuild my life, and I'm doing a damn fine job of it."

"I am so sorry for everything, *cherie*." Simca twirled her bracelets in a nervous gesture. "I want another chance. I want to open a place together. We were so good together, *mon cher*. In the kitchen and in bed."

He had to shut her down fast. "The girl you met. I'm with her now."

"I see. Is it serious?"

His rubbed his tight chest. "Yes, it's headed that way." He realized it was the truth even as the ever-present fear of what that meant stole his breath. "We're thinking of opening a place together."

"Where?"

"Here."

Her brow rose. She watched him gently. Hadn't she always listened? The ongoing disagreements with Jill about their conflicting visions flickered through his mind. "We're still working out the details."

"You don't sound convinced. This is a small market. What would you say if I told you I want to open the place we always talked about? I have the capital now from my divorce."

His heart skipped a beat. God, he could be part of a Michelin-star restaurant again. His dream. Even though he'd returned to Dare to rehab his rep, he hadn't been sure how long it would take to get back to that level. And now it was within reach. Now. Plus, he and Simca never disagreed when it came to work—that aspect of their relationship had always been pure harmony. "I don't know. Jesus, Sim. I was so mad at you. Still am."

"I don't blame you. I want to help. I'll do whatever it takes."

Her determination had always matched his. His fingers drummed the desk. "I was serious about what I said before. I'm with Jill now. What if I can only work with you in a professional capacity?"

She caressed her throat. "I would be very disappointed, but would still want to work with you. We French are practical about sex and business."

Yes, he'd seen that firsthand. God, could such a thing even be possible? His mind conjured up the restaurant they'd discussed. Trendy lighting, monochromatic décor with simple geometric patterns, an eclectic seasonal menu. Was he really thinking about returning to New York or another big city? And Jesus, what did it mean for him and Jill? Could they do the long distance thing?

"I need to talk to Jill." It would be like lighting dynamite. "And I need some time to decide what to do."

He could feel the walls closing in. If he took her up on her offer to set the record straight, everyone in Dare would know what he'd done. *Jill* would know. He sat down, exhaustion deflating him like an undercooked soufflé. "Look, no one here knows what happened."

"I won't say anything if you don't want me to."

The picture on the wall of Jill with her family made his stomach hitch. They'd been everything to him growing up, and it had hurt like hell to lose them. They wouldn't understand. No one would. "For all its trendiness, Dare is a small town. What we did was wrong. I've grown up."

"So I see. It only makes you more attractive."

She approached him with a natural shimmy, and the notes of her specially blended Parisian perfume of hyacinth and frankincense consumed him. Few women could carry off a perfume so exotic. She was the embodiment of a sensual goddess, and she knew it.

"Think about it. I'm staying at The Kenilworth Inn."

"Okay." He walked to the door.

Her hum lingered in the air like her fragrance. "Á bientôt, Brian."

Her *see you soon* haunted him as he left the coffee shop to find Jill, his mind awash with new possibilities—and what they might cost him.

CHAPTER 10

The snow-covered cemetery looked like a sheet of paper from death's typewriter, gravestone markers pounded into the ground by its destructive keys, dotting the land with painful stories of lives ended short, long, and somewhere in between.

Jill walked carefully down the slippery sidewalk, needing her best friend—even if she wasn't *here* anymore. The pine trees waved a forlorn greeting, whispering about nostalgia and grief. A fresh bouquet of yellow daisies and pink roses decorated Jemma's grave. She tucked her arms around herself to ward off the chill. In her haste to get the hell out of Don't Soy With Me, she'd forgotten her coat. Another smart move.

Jill knelt and traced the angel on the tombstone, summoning Jemma in her mind. Short blunt hair. Wickedly narrow eyes. Petite frame. Animated hands. A laugh as light and airy as cotton candy.

"Dammit, Jem. I need to talk to you like we always did." The wind blew her hair away from her neck, causing her to shudder. "Brian lied to me, and just when everything seemed to be coming together so well. He had a lover in New York. An *older* French woman. She's like something out of a Fellini movie—except she's French, not Italian. God, it hurts."

She gripped the stone, her skin burning from cold. "How could he lie about something like that? Did he think I'd freak out about him being involved with some older chick?" She sniffed. "Of course I am. She's even hotter than Kelly Kimple. I was going to sleep with him tonight, Jem. I've been waiting for this moment all my life."

She sniffled and wished she had a Kleenex. "Did the French chick dump him? Was he too devastated to tell me? Maybe she changed her mind. It sounds like they've been talking. Doesn't that mean he wants her back?"

She thought of the familiarity of that woman's heated kiss, and how Brian hadn't exactly sprung away. He might as well have diced her heart with his chef's knife. "What am I going to do?"

Being here made her feel a bit better. It was almost as if she could see her friend staring at her with bright eyes, pushing her bangs out of her face like she always did when she listened. Jill's knees protested the freezing cold, so she sat on nearby bench. Her body felt like peanut brittle ready to crack.

She heard a car pull up. Pete Collins—Jemma's betraying, scum-sucking ex—walked toward her. He held a bouquet of pink, orange, and yellow Gerbera daisies, the flowers he'd always given Jemma before he'd told her he wasn't ready for marriage, dumping her a few scant months before she died. Jill brushed away her tears, turning her back to him.

"I was just going to leave these," he said, rubbing the back of his neck.

"Why the hell are you here?" She pointed to the bundle, which was identical to the other bouquets she'd seen at the gravesite over the past few months. "If you think that wipes away your guilt, you're dead wrong."

He laid the flowers down and drilled her with an icy stare. "I'm not going to argue with you."

Her rage bloomed like a mushroom cloud. "You made her last months miserable."

"Stop this," he said, shoving blond hair out of his eyes when the wind gusted. "I'm grieving too. I know you don't want to believe that, but just because Jemma and I broke up doesn't mean I stopped caring for her. Jesus, Jill."

She trudged around the grave, her shoes sinking into the snow. "You broke her heart in two, and then you just had to show up with a new girl at the Halloween party to shove it in her face. That's the last memory Jemma had, Pete."

He thrust his gloved hand in the air. "Believe me when I say this: If I had known what would have happened that night, I never would have come. I can't talk about this anymore."

Even hearing the strain in his voice, she couldn't forgive him. He shouldn't have wanted anyone else.

"What the hell are you doing here without your coat?" He pulled off his North Face jacket and shoved her into it. "You're freezing."

"Just leave...me...alone." Her teeth chattered.

"You can give my jacket to Brian," he said as he took off down the path, not looking back. His Jeep fishtailed around the corner a few moments later.

"Oh, Jemma. Pete gave me his jacket." His kindness—a reminder of the friendship they no longer shared—snapped the ribbons of control. The sobs rushed up her chest and out of her throat with a roar. She clutched the tombstone and held on.

"Jill," she heard Brian say as he rounded the bench. His strong hands lifted her and pulled her into his warm body. "Don't cry."

The arms holding her were giving her the gentleness she'd craved. Yet she pushed back. "Leave me alone."

***

Brian took note of the daisies and Pete's jacket. So Jill and Pete had had a run-in, too. As if things weren't bad enough. Jill had a huge heart, but it was a two-sided coin. When her emotions were positive, they were as inviting as the Ferris wheel. When they went negative, they were like a class-5 hurricane.

He was about to get the ass-kicking he deserved.

He planted his feet and hunched his shoulders against the brisk wind coming down from the mountain. "We need to talk about—"

"Your French lover? You lied to me *again!*" She lifted her chin, a proud move at odds with the mascara streaking down her face. "How could you? I thought we were getting close."

"We are." He took a deep breath. Her obvious pain deepened his guilt. "I'm sorry, okay? I don't know what else to say. Let's go somewhere and talk. You're freezing." She stepped away when he reached for her, making his gut clench. "Jill, please don't turn away. We've come so far." His mind flashed to those dismal months after graduation when she wouldn't accept any of his calls. Panic descended.

"Have we? From where I'm standing, you wouldn't have lied to me if we'd *come so far*. How could you not have told me about her?"

"It wasn't relevant to us."

"I asked you point blank, and you don't think it's relevant to us?" She hit her forehead. "Gee, why didn't I think of that?"

"Because you take everything too seriously," he stormed, his frustration with himself and her blurring what was right and wrong. "I was with Simca in New York. It was...complicated." Her mouth formed a thin, straight line so he rushed on. "I told you I wasn't a monk. It ended before I came back here."

"I'm not mad you were with someone, but you lied about there being anyone *special*." Her green eyes cut into him like lasers. "It was serious enough for her to come here. Have you been in touch with her?"

It hadn't occurred to him that she'd think that. He took her shoulders and rubbed them briskly. "No! I didn't answer any of her calls or texts. I had no idea she was going to show up like this."

"And you didn't think to tell me your ex-whatever was trying to reach you? When did it start?"

Shit. He looked away. "A few weeks ago."

"So, when we were 'involved.' And you didn't think to mention it to me? Wasn't it bothering you?"

His shoulder lifted. "I ignored her. I thought she'd give up."

Her laugh was bitter. "Yeah, well that clearly worked. I saw how she kissed you. And it sure took you a long time to push her away." She wrapped her arms around her middle and rose to her feet.

"That's not true." He thrust his hand out to stop her from leaving. "I was in total shock. She was the last person I expected to see." Brian rocked back on his heels, squishing snow. "I told her I'm with you."

Jill snorted. "Great, problem solved." She pressed a hand to her chest, her wet eyes making his chest hammer. "If it were over, you would have told me about her when I asked. We're supposed to be friends—first, last, and always. The rest of it..." Her voice broke.

He ducked his head, not knowing how to respond. Telling her the full truth would be the stupidest thing he'd ever done. She would shut him out again, and he couldn't go through that again.

"So what does she want? 'Cause you don't come to Dare by accident."

His cough couldn't clear his throat. "She wants me back. I told her I'm not interested."

She wiped her nose with her sleeve. "I hear a 'but' coming from a mile away."

He took off his gloves, grabbed her hands, and put them on her.

"Oh, Bri." She rested her head on his chest and sniffed.

His arms wrapped around her and he kissed her hair, wanting to make the anguished sounds cease. His eyes burned when her tears plopped against his coat. "Jillie, please don't cry. I'm sorry."

"Tell me exactly what she wants."

He could at least tell her that. He tucked her close. "She wants to open a restaurant together."

She jolted and tried to pull away. "But..." she said. He kept his grip firm. "Oh God, she wants you to go back to New York."

Even now the shock gave him a headache. He tried to cup her cheek, but she jerked back. "Yes."

"You had talked about opening a place together?"

His insides jittered. "Yes."

Her face crumbled. "And New York is where all the action is. Not like boring ol' Dare."

"Don't say that! You know I love being here with you."

"But you're considering it."

"Well, I can't just discount it... It's my dream to run a big-name restaurant. Don't you remember what I had to overcome to get where I am? All the bad names my dad and lots of other assholes called me? This is important to me, Jill." He punched the air. "And, dammit, I'm pretty confused right now, too. I never expected this, never!"

She wiped at more tears. Seeing her wet, blotchy face and runny nose undid him. He took her hands. "I couldn't stand to lose you again." He kicked the snow so hard it flew like gunfire. "But the thought of forever still scares me, and the last thing I want to do is hurt you."

She finally threw her hands up in the air. The wind blew her red hair behind her like a flaming kite. "Well, you already have. You top the list of *People Who Have Hurt Jill Hale*. You need to decide what you want because I can't *not* be serious about you. I don't know if I can do this anymore. It's like high school graduation all over again."

The panic hit him like a haymaker punch. He hadn't even told her everything, and she was already pulling away, retreating to past hurts. He snagged her arm when she turned away. "Don't say that."

She sniffed, looking down at her feet. "You still look at her like there's something you haven't resolved. It's why you came home, isn't it?"

"Yes, partly." He opened his mouth to tell her the truth. Fear strangled him.

She tapped her foot, waiting.

He cleared his throat. Tried again. But he couldn't utter the words.

She would run away for sure if she discovered Simca had been married. He couldn't take that. She was the only stable thing left. The only piece of Brian McConnell he still understood.

"There were lots of reasons," he finally said in a shaky voice. Even to his ears, he realized how paper-thin that statement was. He grabbed her shoulders. "Jill, please give us a chance to work this out. I'll tell you everything...in time."

She raised her hands. "What? Like in installments? Do I look like a bank?"

"I need more time, Jill." God, he couldn't tell her now. Not when she was this close to walking away. "There are reasons, Jill, and they don't affect only me."

She put her hands on her hips. Pete's coat gave her the appearance of a light green grape.

"They affect her, right?"

"Not just her."

"You must have your reasons if you're being this stubborn. So let's cut to the chase, shall we?" Her green eyes met his, all drenched and entreating. "I told you earlier that I love you."

The wind carried the cold straight into his heart. He knew what was coming.

"Do you love me, Bri?"

His heart stopped pumping. His mother had said she loved him, but she hadn't hesitated to abandon him for some man. What the hell was love? He took in a ragged breath through a bone-dry mouth.

"Jill, I've known you...all my life. Of course...I love you." Even the blue jay in the pine tree seemed to laugh at him. It was pathetic.

Her spiky, black-caked eyelids flickered. "That's not very convincing. Let me know if you decide what you want to do. You just can't keep coasting through life not making a real decision about anything. In the meantime, I'll be looking into other options."

He squeezed her arm. "What the hell does that mean? You plan on hooking up with some guy to get back at me? Jesus, Red, that's not you."

She ripped off his gloves and thrust them out. "No, it means I'll be looking into other business options. All we do is fight about our plans anyway. My life is here. You've always wanted to be in New York. Maybe you should just go back there."

And in that minute, he knew he could never ask her if she was willing to do something long distance.

He could live without them working together, but it shattered his heart that she would tell him to go. "You want me to leave?"

She bit her lip. "No, but I want...you to be happy. You've chosen your career over me before. Why should this time be any different?"

He stood rooted in place, his whole frame shaking. "Dammit, that's not fair. Just give me some time to think things over. Then we can talk," he promised. Maybe she'd listen once she cooled down a bit.

Her hands pulled at her coat, her distress obvious. "I was going to sleep with you tonight. Did you know that? Funny how your whole chef thing has messed everything up. Again."

She ran off the path, punching holes in the hard snow. He watched her until she disappeared down a side street.

Why did he feel like she was disappearing from his life again? He rested his hand on their best friend's tombstone, suddenly worn to the bone. God, he'd hurt her.

"Oh, Jemma, what am I going to do?"

CHAPTER 11

Jill headed up Peggy's sidewalk. God, she needed to talk to someone who could talk back—the reality of Jemma's absence had been hammered home after the double whammy of Pete and Brian.

Peggy opened the door after one knock. "What happened? Are you okay?"

"No." Jill stomped her feet on the rug. "But no one's molested me, if that's what you mean."

"Clearly you've been crying. Let me grab you a washcloth. Is that Brian's coat?"

"No," she whispered, trying to reel the pain back in. She couldn't think about Pete—not when her talk with Brian was front and center in her mind.

"Do you need a hug, Jillie?" Keith said in a froggy voice, peering down from the staircase. He'd been suffering from a bad cold all week.

"You need to be in bed, young man," Peggy called up to him.

"Well, I *am* sad." Jill took a deep breath. No need to bawl in front of Peggy and Keith. After she cleaned up, she'd have Margie bring her stuff over from the shop and drop her home. "You feeling any better, Keith?"

His coughing answered for him. Peggy darted up the stairs. "Jill, there's a washcloth in the half bath. Keith, back to bed. Now."

"But mom," came the pathetic, congested response. "I want to hug Jill, and Uncle Tanner is coming over."

"Jill needs to talk to Mommy. I'll send your uncle up as soon as he gets here. Now, get in bed, or I'll handcuff you."

Peggy picked him up, and he curled around her. "You only cuff bad guys." He waved a limp hand at Jill as he was carried up and out of sight.

Throwing Pete's coat onto the crayola-colored rack, Jill headed to the bathroom to clean her face. The person in the mirror resembled someone she didn't want to be—a grief-stricken, broken woman. The warm water felt comforting as she washed. Restored, she retraced her steps to the main room. A knock at the door made her jump. She headed to the door.

"Hi, there," she said with forced gusto when she opened the door for her brother-in-law.

"Well, hey, didn't expect to see you here."

He gave her an easy hug, and she wrapped her arms around him. His big, strong body was a comfort. She hadn't had a brother growing up, but she appreciated having one now.

"What's the matter, honey? You look like you've been crying. Did you and Brian have a fight?"

"Brian's ex-something came back from New York today. She wants him back, and she asked him to open a restaurant with her in New York."

He lifted her chin, his brown gaze gentle. "So? He's with you now."

She rabitted away. "It's what he always wanted. Plus, he's conflicted. And it's no wonder. She's this gorgeous French chef, and here's the kicker. I'd say she's got at least ten years on him."

"An older woman? You don't say."

She punched his arm. "He left New York over her." She got all angry and hurt again just thinking about it. Whatever.

Tanner led her to the kitchen. "Did he confirm all this?"

"Mostly. He's still being pretty evasive." Still feeling shaky, she appreciated that he held out a chair for her. "And cut the reporter lingo. You sound just like Meredith and Grandpa."

"You're from a newspaper family. You should be used to it." He grabbed three sodas from the fridge and sat down across from her, sliding one of the drinks over. "What exactly did he say?"

Since he was still giving her that *trust me, you can tell me things* look, she pulled her hair and kept talking. "He wouldn't tell me everything."

"Who wouldn't?" Peggy asked, coming into the kitchen. She hugged Tanner. "Little man has been waiting for you all morning. He's watching a video upstairs. Oh, a beverage. Thanks. I've been getting zero sleep. He was up coughing all night, poor guy." She tugged on her wrinkled black T-shirt. "I look like shit, don't I?"

"Mommy shit, so it doesn't count," he answered.

Peggy kicked him under the table. "Funny. So, I take it we're talking about Brian?"

"Yes." Jill played with her soda's pull-top.

Tanner cleared his throat. "Seems Brian had a secret relationship with an older French woman he worked with back in New York. Now she's in Dare, she wants him back, and she's hoping to open a restaurant with him in New York. Jill thinks he's conflicted. How's that for journalistic efficiency?"

Jill crossed her arms. "I think it sucks."

"That explains the raccoon eyes. How much older?" Peggy asked.

"Hard to tell. She's got perfect skin."

"Bitch," Peggy said. "Okay, start from the beginning."

Her account covered everything except for the whole *sex tonight* plan. She brushed at her tears when she finished. "What? No advice?"

Peggy's leaky faucet was the loudest thing in the kitchen.

"Well, that explains the coat," Peggy murmured. "It sucks that you had to run into Pete on top of everything." Her friend knew she was having a hard time forgiving him for what he'd done to Jemma.

"Yeah...So, we're totally screwed, right? Brian won't admit he loves me, he's keeping secrets from me, and—"

"'Secrets' is a strong word," Tanner interrupted. "He didn't tell you the full truth now, but said he would. All of us have things in our past we're not proud of, things we don't want to share with our loved ones."

Really? She'd missed the boat on that one, since she didn't have much of a past. "Are you saying there are things you haven't told Meredith?"

"Let's return to the subject at hand," he said. "There might be good reasons for him to keep quiet, but you need to remember something. When he chose to leave New York, he didn't go to Chicago or Los Angeles. He came here. That's telling. As for the business offer, you'll just have to see what he decides." He stood up with his soda. "I'm going up to see Keith. Jill, you Hale women are made of strong stuff. Don't forget it."

Right, she felt like the Rock of Gibraltar right now. Jill leaned forward after he'd left. "I was going to have sex with him tonight," she whispered. "No way that's happening now. What do you think?"

Peggy rubbed her face. "I don't like secrets either. I lived through all that crap with my ex. Keith was a newborn when I found out Frank was having an affair. Plus, if Brian had told you he loved you—none of that *best friends forever* crap—it would have helped you feel better."

Jill knew what Peggy was leaving unsaid: Yes, it would have, but he didn't do it. Jill chugged her soda. "I don't know where we stand or what to think."

"You don't think he'll stay?"

Banging her head on the Toy Story placemat seemed like a good idea. Maybe it would help clear the fog. "I don't know. It's not New York, and I'm certainly not Chef Barbie. We both like the idea of working together, but we disagree on just about everything when we try talking business." She lifted her head and scratched at a fleck of food on Woody's sheriff outfit.

"Then maybe it's better to focus on the personal stuff." Peggy grabbed a napkin and spit on it, reaching across. "Last night's macaroni."

Jill lurched back. "Gack, did you just do the mommy thing?"

Her eyes narrowed like Jill was a murder suspect. "Don't make me hurt you." She threw the napkin aside. "I need to get back to work. Cuff some drunk and disorderly college students or something. God, I even miss the paperwork. I love my kid, but he's *no fun* sick. And now I'm afraid he's given it to me. I had a sore throat this morning. I can't get sick!"

"Well, don't get any closer. I can't get sick either."

"Like I was going to lay one on you. I may be a single mom, but I'm not that desperate."

A laugh huffed out, and it felt good. "If I were a guy, I'd totally marry you. Then I wouldn't need to worry about Brian. We could raise Keith together. Plus, you know how to use handcuffs."

The corners of Peggy's mouth tipped up. "I can get a resisting suspect cuffed in five seconds. Made the guys hang their heads in shame."

"Not that you're not competitive or anything..."

"Like you're not? Okay, wise ass, back to Brian. What are you going to do if he decides to open a restaurant with her?"

Brian leaving? God, the thought hurt. Jill leaned back in her chair. "Well, I have another option." Even without knowing the details, she didn't think Peg would approve of Mac Maven. "Not sure how viable it is though."

"What aren't you telling me?" Peggy asked, drumming her fingers on the table.

Was she that transparent? "Do you have ESP?"

Her friend leaned back in her chair like she had all day. "Comes with the job. Now spill."

Jill threw up her hands. "Fine, but I don't really know much. He won't discuss it without a confidentiality agreement. The one thing I do know is he's smoking hot."

Peggy's eyebrow arched. "Single?"

Jill made a trilling noise, this conversation a welcome distraction. "Have you decided it's time to join the land of the living and dance the horizontal mambo?" The thought sent a few bars of laughter bubbling through her, easing the tension in her diaphragm. "He's *so* not for you."

"Just because I look like Mommy slime doesn't mean I don't clean up well. What's his name?"

Jill cocked her head. This wasn't prurient interest. "You're planning on running him in your whatchamacallit police database, aren't you?"

"Guy wouldn't make you sign a confidentiality agreement if he's up for citizen of the year."

Jill grabbed her hand. "Peg, seriously, he's a good businessman. I'm sure there are excellent reasons for the confidentiality." Even if she didn't know them. "One of my regulars vouched for him." Jack had been using a soft-sell strategy on her each time he came to the coffee shop, telling her how incredible Mac was and how much he wanted to work with her. But his lips had remained zipped about the nature of the business, which frustrated Jill to no end. Didn't a girl at least deserve to know what she was being courted about?

"If that were true, you would have told Brian about it, and you wouldn't balk at giving me his name."

Dammit, she never should have said anything. "How did you know I didn't tell Brian?" Jill popped out of her chair. "I wasn't planning on pursuing it." Until now. "Please leave this alone."

Peggy stood. "I don't like you holding out, but back to Brian. What do you want to do?"

God, what *did* she want to do? Jill rubbed a hand under her tingly nose. "Honestly, Peg, I don't know, but I'm done waiting for him. I've done that most of my life."

What could it hurt to inquire about Maven's offer? If nothing else, it would keep her mind off Brian. If he left, at least she'd have something else to pour her broken heart into.

***

Peggy shut the door after Jill and headed upstairs. Poor girl. Men could really mess you up. She'd had her quota of that with Frank; as far as she was concerned, she was done for life.

Tanner was reading Keith another story, and her kid was curled against him like bread dough in a pan. Too bad her camera wasn't handy.

She ducked into the bathroom to clean up. Her eyes had a glassy shine like she'd been on an all-night stake-out. Were those dark circles? She really did look like Mommy shit. Thank God, she wasn't the type to go *mirror, mirror, on the wall...*

But her T-shirt smelled, and that was pretty bad even for her. When had she last done laundry?

She eyed her badge, propped on the vanity. Frank thought she was weird for keeping her badge in the bathroom when she was off-duty. For Peggy, it was a reminder of the kind of woman she was. Far more than just cold cream and hair products. She twirled the plastic slinky Keith had left on the side of the tub when he took his bath. She was a mommy too. Sometimes the two people inside her seemed incongruent. Staring at her reflection, she wondered where the woman had gone. The cop and the mom seemed to have taken up all the space inside her.

She reached for a new shirt and pants. At least she could wash her face. Brush her hair and teeth. For today, it would be enough.

When she came back out, Tanner was waiting.

"He's out cold. Poor kid didn't even make it through one chapter with me."

She walked downstairs with him. "This virus has zapped him." Her sore throat spiked her worry quotient. Sometimes being a single mom was as nerve inducing as bursting through the door to a perp's house.

Tanner put his arm around her. "Meredith and I can help."

She knew she was having a girl moment, but she wanted to lean on her big brother and let him take care of everything. "I think I'm coming down with it too."

"It's no wonder. You've pushed yourself to the max. You bought this place and set it up faster than anyone I've ever seen; you started a new job, where you've had to clean up after a dirty cop; and you got Keith settled into a new school."

"When you put it that way..." she said. "You coming over here every day means so much to Keith." She patted him on the arm. They weren't sentimental people, but she wanted him to understand. "It means a lot to me, too. I missed you when you were overseas."

The hug he gave her was oddly comforting. He'd never been into hugs before meeting Meredith. Then again, neither had she.

"I missed you, too. It's funny. With you guys and Meredith, I don't have the itchy feet I was so worried about."

"I'm glad. I didn't know if you could stay state-side."

His arms fell away so she stepped back.

"I need to head back to the university for my class."

"My brother, the journalism prof." When he reached the door, she called out his name. "Could you do me a favor?" she asked when he turned around, going with her infamous gut.

"Anything."

"Could you get me a list of people who've bought property in the area over the last six months?" Time to see if she could find a thread to pull. She didn't have much to go on from Jill.

He tugged on his navy coat and leather gloves. "Are you going to tell me why?"

His intense gaze didn't make her squirm like it would other people. "It's nothing to be concerned about."

"Is this about this French woman?"

She almost laughed. "Not at all."

Silence filled the hall for a full ten beats. "Okay, but if you want to let me know why you can't run this at work, you can trust me."

She nodded. She was too new at The Justice Center to use their resources for something personal. But she didn't want him to know about Jill being approached by a mysterious investor. He'd have to tell Meredith because of the marriage rule, and Meredith would likely do the sister thing of talking to Jill. Peggy had zero desire to start a telephone game.

"I'm sure it's nothing."

He kissed her cheek. "Okay. I'll bring a list over. Call if you need help. I mean it, Peg."

As she closed the door, she pressed a hand to her jumping stomach. She wasn't psychic, but she knew when something didn't feel right.

Dare was her home now, and she'd do what she could to protect it—and Jill.

Hopefully her gut was wrong. If this investor was bad news, she'd have to find a way to shut down whatever confidential thing he was planning.

Even if Jill didn't like it.

CHAPTER 12

Going back to Don't Soy with Me held about as much interest as bowling on the frozen river up the canyon. Jill wasn't up to the whispers, questions, or assessing glances.

Instead, she went home and dialed Maven's number. Time to explore new options.

"Mac Maven," the baritone voice answered with a hint of impatience.

"Mac, it's Jill Hale."

"Jill," he responded with a liberal dose of charm. "It's good to hear from you. I hope this means you've reconsidered."

She flipped a photo of her and Brian playing pool at Hairy's Pub face down on her purple coffee table. "That's correct." She refused to feel guilty, trying instead to focus on the excitement of this mystery business deal.

"Wonderful! Can you meet me at my office in Denver?"

"Sure." She wrote his address down.

"Is tomorrow possible? I can be flexible since you're driving down. How about I take you to lunch?"

Might as well get a good meal out of the trip. "Sure."

"I'm glad you reconsidered. I look forward to seeing you tomorrow."

The phone clicked.

She headed to her closet. Her taste in fashion didn't run to power suits, but hopefully she could pull together something appropriate. Tomorrow she'd finally discover why he'd contacted her. Part of her couldn't wait.

Then she'd talk to Brian. She understood how difficult relationships were for him and how badly his parents had messed him up. But if he wanted to preserve any kind of bond between them, he'd tell her the rest of his secrets. She needed to be able to trust the people in her life.

If he didn't come clean, she couldn't even be his friend anymore.

CHAPTER 13

Brian took another pull from the Jack Daniels bottle and threw a dart across the living room of his apartment. It hit the wall and bounced. Mutt didn't even flinch.

"I'm sucking pretty badly today, aren't I?" He scratched the dog's head. "I miss Jill." He drilled a dart into his Paris landscape instead of the dartboard.

He took a draw on the drink, reveling in the way it made his throat burn.

Someone pounded on the door. Mutt rolled his eyes up like *are you going to get that?*

"You're a terrible watchdog. Maybe it's Jill." Mutt barked. Brian rushed over and opened the door.

Pete held up a brown bag. "Brought some medicine."

His friend strode into the kitchen. After finding a highball glass, he poured himself a drink. He sat across from Brian, who had sprawled back on his black leather couch, rubbing Mutt's floppy folds.

"How could you not have told me about the French chick?"

Because he'd sworn to himself that he wouldn't tell anyone. Returning to Dare had been hard enough without adding more complications. "I don't want to talk about it."

"Well, no one in Dare can stop talking about it. That scene in Don't Soy with Me will keep the grist mill going for weeks."

"*Fuck.*"

"I take it you and Jill are on the outs." Mutt gave a *ruff*.

"Yes, we're talking about Jillie, boy. We went a few rounds at the cemetery after she talked to you."

Pete stood, fists at his side. "I wouldn't call it talking. God, every time I see her, it's one accusation after another, which only makes me feel worse. I know she needs someone to blame, but goddammit, I'm having a hard enough time as it is."

Brian heaved himself up. "You're not to blame for what happened to Jemma. No one is."

Pete threw back his drink. "Nothing's how it used to be, and I don't think I can take it much longer. You're finally back, but Jemma's dead, and Jill's declared me her mortal enemy. Now I understand how you felt when you left for New York, and she wouldn't talk to you anymore. When I broke up with Jemma, I knew I'd lose Jill's friendship, too. I just didn't know it would suck this much."

"Yeah, it sucks balls." And thinking about how he'd felt before only added to his current misery. The problem was that any explanation would make Jill crazy. And she had the right—he'd been a dick for not telling her, for not being able to give her a firm commitment, either on the restaurant or their relationship.

"So this Frenchwoman wants you back?"

He turned away from the Paris scene on the wall. "Yes, but I told her I was with Jill. She wants to open a restaurant together."

Pete whistled. "Are you thinking about taking her up on her offer and heading back to New York? I never did understand why you came back here."

Even though Pete was his friend, he felt like Jill should be the first one to hear the whole story.

"Why are you still here if you feel that way about this place?" he asked, hoping to change the subject.

Pete shrugged. "I've been thinking about moving on lately, and I've put out some feelers. I can finish my dissertation from anywhere. It might be good to have a fresh start."

He hated to think about his friend leaving just when they were getting their rhythm back, but he understood. "You'll figure it out."

"I'm headed to Hairy's tonight. Wanna come?"

"Nah." His stomach churned like an ice cream maker. He should have eaten with his drink. "Grab me that salami and cheese in the fridge, will you?"

Pete dumped the contents on his granite countertop. "You've become such a food snob. What happened to you?" he asked jokingly.

"I got taste. You didn't," he concluded in their form of male bonding. Brian cut a piece of sopressata salami and bit in. The cured pork was like a shaft of light, and the truffle cheese made anything seem possible. Food made life seem good again.

"Sure you don't want to go to Hairy's?"

"I don't need to hear people talking about me."

Pete slapped him on the back. "Understood. Catch you later McConnell."

The door slammed. Brian gripped the counter. Well, if he was going to stay in tonight, he needed a distraction.

And nothing calmed Brian like cooking.

***

To keep his mind off Jill, he decided to go with comfort food. A quiche? No, nothing French. Nothing he would have made with Simca. He'd go Italian and make homemade lasagna. He pulled some sausage out of the refrigerator. Making the noodles by hand would soothe him. He threw a pan on the stove and added the sausages, spacing them apart.

Some ingredients needed room to reach their true potential. He was one of them. Leaving Dare hadn't been easy, but it had been the right decision. It had helped him grow up. The question was what he needed now.

When a knock on the door sounded, he turned down the burner. Mutt's eyes fluttered open, and he gave a jaw-cracking yawn, drool trailing to the floor like melting wax.

Brian hoped it was Jill. He threw open the industrial door and stilled. Seeing Simca twice in one day made him feel off balance.

"Hello, Brian," Simca said quietly.

"How did you find out where I live?"

"I am resourceful, no? I had something special to give you and didn't want to wait."

"I wish you'd called," he said, but not wanting to be rude, he let her inside.

She leaned against the door and undid a few buttons on her black silk blouse, revealing the tips of an even darker lace bra.

"Sim, you need to stop that."

"What?" she asked with a slow smile.

"You know. I told you I'm with someone else, and you can't stay if you're not going to respect that."

Her smile dimmed, but she buttoned back up. Thank God.

"I like your loft, *chérie*. It's very European."

She'd get that. Her attention to detail had impressed him, from the kitchen orders to remembering how he folded his T-shirts.

"And you have a dog too. I remember you saying you wanted one." Mutt put his paws over his eyes. "Your gift." She crossed over to the kitchen in her ice-pick black boots, already dressed in a different outfit from the one she'd been wearing that afternoon—so Simca.

His taste buds leaped straight off the cliff. He knew that bag. To the naked eye, the leather satchel could be a purse. Inside it held coolant freezer packs to store specialty food items. Leave it to the French.

"I was just in Paris. I brought you back some Epoisses de Bourgogne."

The bag's zipper purred slowly. To a chef, the unveiling of this rare cheese was akin to a striptease at an upscale club.

"You take too many chances with Customs, Simca." Saliva pooled at the sight of that round orange wrapping shaped like a pin cushion. Nine ounces of sheer orgasmic delight. He suspected she remembered him equating the cheese to raunchy sex. She could have chosen any foodie gift, but a sexual reminder was so her style.

"Do I look dangerous?" She broke the vacuum pack and pulled back the ruched orange corners.

He edged closer, the earthy smell drawing him in like a siren. God, he was weak. He remembered the last time he'd sampled Epoisses. She'd returned from Paris and fed it to him in bed.

He didn't stop her from taking out a toast point and spreading the cheese on it with an engraved butter knife. He eyed the washed rind that had been coated with Marc de Bourgogne, a French alcohol, during the ripening process. How could nine ounces take you to heaven?

When he took the toast point, he inhaled deeply, the aroma punching him in the face. To the untrained nose, it smelled like hell. To Brian, the worse the smell, the better the cheese tasted.

He closed his eyes. Opened his mouth. The exquisite creaminess covered his tongue as flavors of fecundity, grass, and old milk danced around his mouth before elongating into the pleasant dip of sour lemons at the end. The mixture of flavors converged into a dazzling combination—like the harsh notes of a Chopin overture blending together in sheer harmony.

"Jesus, God." His eyes closed, a shaft of pleasure shooting straight to his toes.

He jumped when a hand caressed his arm. "I have missed you like this. Your eyes closed in delight as the passion of flavor travels down that long, hard body."

"I told you. It can't be like this anymore, Sim." He removed her hand.

She angled her head to the side. "Are you sure?"

Needing air, he cracked open the patio door. The winter wind whistled in, cooling his heated flesh and clearing his head. Mutt howled and lumbered out of the room.

"Yes, I'm with Jill now. I...won't betray her in that way."

She leaned against the couch. "I admire that, after Andre. Are you still mad? Andre and I may not have been legally separated, but in the important ways we were not together. There were other women for him. Why could I not find my own happiness? There was only you."

He wondered if she was telling the truth. "We're not going to solve this tonight. I need some time to think about your offer to open a place together."

She wrapped a honeyed curl around an emerald-ringed finger. "I understand. In the meantime, I hope to share some new ideas with you. Being in France again really inspired me. I think you'll like what I'm thinking. It's only an addition to what we've discussed before, of course."

Their visions of the restaurant they'd like to open had always been perfectly in sync. He had no doubt it would wow customers and garner a prized Michelin rating.

He could so easily imagine himself back in New York—the cars rushing by, the people striding down Broadway as they talked about business, food, and art. His reputation in the food world would be restored by their partnership. It would change everything for him professionally, and after all the hard work he'd invested in his career, longing flickered through him.

Her body sashayed as she walked toward him. "Let me help you, chérie."

"I know you can. I just need...to decide what's best for me." Was leaving Dare for his career the answer? But that would mean losing Jill again. It tore him apart, having to decide between the two things he wanted more than anything: his dream and the girl who had always meant home to him.

"We always worked well together. It won't be any different now." Her smile flashed like a sunburst. Turning on her heels, she walked to the kitchen for her satchel. "I will leave the cheese and bid you goodnight. I will draw up a menu while I wait." She shrugged into her coat. "*Bon nuit.*"

Brian laid the cheese down carefully in the refrigerator and slammed the door. He fingered a photo of him and Jill held by a Don't Soy With Me magnet.

What in the hell was he going to do? Jill would never go for a long distance relationship because she'd interpret it as him choosing his career over her. And given his fear of long-term commitment, he wasn't sure he could make that leap either. He wanted to be with her now, but what if something changed? Hadn't his parents suddenly up and decided they were done with each other? That decision had pretty much destroyed everything in its wake.

God, could she even trust him again when she found out the whole story about Simca? Hell, she didn't even know everything yet, and she seemed just as upset as she'd been after high school. He understood why she was hurt. She deserved to be with a man who knew what he wanted, one who was willing to making a real commitment to her.

He had to make a decision.

This was the real world. He couldn't have everything.

CHAPTER 14

Keeping watch outside someone's apartment made you slime, just like that Peeping Tom Peggy had arrested on Valentine's Day. With the temperature in her car hovering only a few degrees above the temperature outside, Jill was cold, hurting slime. She'd come over to have it out with Brian, but when his French ex had arrived, she'd decided to hide and wait her out.

The minutes ticked by. She slumped in her seat when Simca came sailing out of the building, a smug grin on her face.

Oh God, had this been a bootie call?

Jill wrapped her hands around the car keys. Should she leave? Her body was vibrating from head to toe. No, she needed answers—now more than ever. If he'd slept with her, then he'd made his decision.

As the Corvette purred away, she uncurled her stiff, cold frame and strode inside. She pounded on the door. When it swung open, Brian froze.

"Jill." His expression was a combination of horror and panic that seemed straight out of a slasher movie.

"She was here! What was she doing here?" The hurt exploded inside her like a bomb. Before she realized what she was doing, she slung her purse off, rushed inside, and smacked him.

"Hey! Stop it," Brian cried, fending off the attack while trying to slam the door behind her.

"No!" she huffed out. "Tell me the truth. Did you actually *invite* her over?" Her voice held a tinge of the venom that had done in Cleopatra, so not her.

"No! Christ almighty! Were you spying on me?"

"I wouldn't have to if I trusted you, but you've blown that to bits. Again."

"Jesus, she looked up my address. Will you calm down?"

"No, I won't calm down. She had this smug smile on her face." Her voice hitched. "Tell me you didn't have a quickie with her."

"Dammit, of course not. Is that what you think of me? Why even come over then?" He grabbed her purse and tossed it on the loveseat. Mutt trudged closer.

She started stroking the anxious dog without even thinking about it. "I was coming to *talk*. To make you tell me the truth, but after this..." Her stomach radiated with pain, so she curled her arm around it.

"Jill, you're jumping to conclusions. Nothing happened!"

All the evidence suggested otherwise. "How am I supposed to trust you when you won't tell me the truth?" She pressed her hands to her temple. "Do you have any idea how much it hurt to know she was in here? After ten o'clock? That's when people come over for bootie calls."

"It wasn't a fucking bootie call." He rocked on his heels, taking a few deep breaths. "I'm sorry it hurt you. She came over to give me something perishable. A French cheese I enjoy, okay? Do you want me to get it out of the fridge?"

His explanation made her want to bawl. God, they were in a bad place. Her deepest fear clawed at her throat, demanding release. "I'm afraid you're going to choose her over me—like you did with Kelly. I'm afraid you already have."

"Jesus." He strode over and gripped her shoulders. "Don't think like that."

How could anger and comfort exist in the same moment? "Nothing happened, I promise."

She edged back against the couch, shaking. The tense muscles around his mouth and eyes told her he was just as upset as she was. She'd seen that earnest look before. Mutt crawled to the edge of the rug with a high-pitched whine. "I want to believe you."

He sat down beside her and took her hand. His eyes held hers. "Then do."

How many times had he held her hand and stared straight into her eyes that way? Thousands. Yet she could only look away. "God, I can't do this. I thought I wanted to talk, but every time I get near you I feel like I'm a rocket coming back into the airspace with its tail on fire."

His mouth twitched. "Well, it *is* a nice tail."

"Humor won't work."

He leaned closer. "Then I have another idea. You know what they say about not being able to hide the truth in a kiss. Kiss me."

Her mouth salivated just at the prospect, even though it was ridiculous after what had happened. "You've *got* to be kidding."

"Look, I know you. Remember how I used to give you a cookie when you were upset. Words don't work, Red." He held out his hand again, eyes as calm as the sea. "Come here."

She sat in front of him. He cupped her face and slowly moved his head, watching her the whole time. His lips brushed hers like a feather. The gentleness undid her, and her eyes welled with tears.

"When I saw her, I thought..." Jill broke away as the truth bubbled up from her tight diaphragm. Her forehead rested against his. "I don't want to lose you."

"Oh, Jill," he whispered and fitted his mouth to hers again, taking the kiss deeper, infusing each stroke of his tongue and press of his lips with an emotion so pure her head throbbed. "Close your eyes and listen."

His mouth settled over hers without demand. He stroked. He

caressed. He wanted *her*.

Everything opened.

Her heart uttered a soul-anguished cry, the force echoing up her chest, clawing at her throat. Desperation. Wanting. Love. Confusion. Fear.

She could taste them all.

He was right. There was truth in a kiss. And the power of it was more than she could deny. This was what she'd always wanted. His lips. His heat. His body. Him.

She grabbed the back of his head and fed the starved part of her who'd always wanted him, was terrified of losing him, and didn't think she could love anyone but him.

It was like setting a match to gasoline. His mouth devoured her. He pressed her into the couch, the leather sighing with her, covering her with his long, powerful frame. She opened her legs to take his weight and groaned at his hardness. Her arousal spiked like a thermometer plunged into boiling water. She fisted her hands in his hair and thrust her tongue into his mouth. He responded with force, grinding against her pelvis with an urgent roll of his hips.

She gave a long moan as his hands pressed under her sweater and tugged at her bra, freeing her breasts. Her back arched when he twisted and pulled on her nipples.

Teeth scraped. Lips swelled. Tongues laved.

Jill clenched her legs around him, thinking, *Take me. All of me. Devour me.*

"God," she cried aloud when his mouth pressed against her neck and bit gently.

Passion took on superhero speed. She shoved him back blindly and tugged off her coat, her sweater, her dangling bra. His hands fisted around her ribcage as she pulled off her jeans.

"Wait...are you sure?" he rasped.

She yanked his mouth back to hers, not wanting to hear reason. The compulsion to be with him blew every thought out of her mind. She had to have him or die. Years of wanting burned her to ash. She wanted to rise like the Phoenix in his arms.

She ripped at his shirt, buttons flying, her hands digging into the tight skin of his corded abdomen.

"Jesus, God," he uttered in a voice she didn't recognize.

He helped her drag his shirt off. She struggled with his zipper, and then she had her hand on him in seconds, his heat and hardness pulsing in her palm.

He threw back his head, thrusting against her. "Okay, we need to slow down."

His texture was new and hot and incredible. Jill gave him a few feather strokes and then increased the pressure. "No," she hissed back and fitted her mouth to his again as he rolled her under him.

The deep thrusting of his tongue, the feel of his furnace-hot body against hers, and the perfect suction of his mouth had the sexual energy flying north, south, east, and west. Brian flipped her onto her back, his hand cupping the V of her thighs. She opened her legs wider, giving him access, and uttered an anguished moan when his fingers rubbed her core and thrust inside. Her pelvis shot up, seeking more contact. Jill became a mindless fiend of sexual desperation.

She had only one desire. To be filled. Entered. Penetrated. By him. Finally. Her mind nudged her about the need for a condom, but she didn't want to interrupt things. The odds of her getting pregnant their first time seemed miniscule. She fell back into the moment.

Freeing her mouth, she panted. "Now! Right now."

His neck arched. "God, let me get—"

"No, it's fine." She yanked him close.

He surged into her with a deep thrust, lifting her off the couch. Given her near-virgin status, the fit was tight, and her senses were flooded with a mixture of pleasure and pain. Her legs wrapped around him. He sank deeper and pumped, hands pulling her hips to him, sealing them together. She met his rapid thrusts. Mindless, she was nothing but sensation, rhythm, movement.

Their mouths fused, deepening the connection, breaking for a breath every few thrusts. The energy built until the crown of her head tingled along with her hands, fisted at his waist to anchor him to her. She felt the urge to bear down and tighten all her muscles around him. She arched as he drove straight to her heart.

Her body became a long sweep of electricity from loins to head, and then she exploded. She pulled her mouth back to breathe shallowly, crying out as she pulsed with pleasure.

"Jesus," Brian shouted.

He tunneled his head against her neck and surged into her with three deep thrusts, lifting her from the couch. He growled as he came, his whole frame shaking against her. She took him deeper into her body as the sensations built again, taking her higher.

"Brian," she murmured, somewhere between rapture and bliss.

Quiet moans sang from her throat with the shallow, rapid breaths. Ecstasy filled every pore as their chests rose against each other, their hearts beating in time. Deep inside, she knew this was where she belonged, a destination she'd been traveling toward all her life. A white light spread through her, uncurling a new ladder of love into her existence.

She drew it all inside her. His shallow breath. His earthy smell. His perfectly-made body.

Her Brian.

Her ankles went lax around his waist, and her hands fell open in total surrender. To him. To herself. To what they were together, whatever it meant. She leaned her head closer, wanting a deeper connection with him as her awareness returned. His shallow pants on her neck tickled, but she didn't care. Couldn't move. Didn't want to.

When he lifted his head, his hair was mussed, a sheen of sweat tinting his ruddy face. His eyes shone like bright stars, piercing light into the recesses of her soul. "Jesus, Jillie," he uttered with a trace of awe.

Then, slowly, like he was awakening from a dream, his face tensed, his eyes narrowed.

In that instant, she knew he was more afraid than she'd ever seen him. And all because of what they'd done, how right it had felt while they were doing it, and how wrong it felt now.

He lowered his forehead to hers. Mutt barked, drawing her attention. Drool pooled from the dog's mouth as he stared at them. Something inside her cracked. Oh God, this wasn't how it was supposed to happen.

She closed her eyes, shaken and exposed.

He wasn't ready, and they'd done it in front of his dog. Where were the candles? The quiet murmurs? The slowness? The soft professions of love?

This was madness.

Pleasure faded like raindrops down a windowpane after an intense storm, leaving regret in its wake. The words *I love you* surfaced, but she knew she couldn't say them now—not when he wouldn't be able to say them back. She'd allowed herself to be swept away. After all this time, they'd come together without a clear vision for a shared future. Right after his ex-whatever had visited.

Stark vulnerability cast a dark cloak over her. A tear slid out of the corner of her eye. She tried to wipe it away before it fell on his skin. When he lifted his head, she was more emotionally naked that she'd ever been with him.

After all this time, *this* was what was between them. As if they were two symbiotic organisms, she read his thoughts. Pleasure, yes—even ecstasy—but laced with the combustibles of fear and uncertainty. They'd traveled far beyond anywhere she'd known, like the far edges of the Dark Continent on maps of old.

How could he still not know this was love?

"Don't cry, Jillie," he whispered in a hoarse voice, rubbing her tears away. "Please, baby." He stared at her, his fear as plain as day.

He knew it. She could see it in the mistiness of his eyes. They had reached the farthest boundaries of their souls and nudged the door open to a whole new realm...but he wasn't ready to live there with her. He didn't think it could last because nothing else in his life had.

She turned her head away and closed her eyes. Why was she surprised? The hurt crawling through her wasn't rational. She had to get away. Shield herself. Grow some new armor.

"Would you please get off me?" She coughed to clear her throat.

His fingers traced her cheek without the sureness of his usual touch. "I know this isn't how we both imagined it, but don't ask me to leave you now, Jillie."

The howl inside her started to build. She pushed at him. "Please, Bri, let me up."

The slickness of their skin, the wetness between her thighs, and him pulling out only made her more aware of how monumental this mistake had been.

She picked up her clothes and struggled to the bathroom. When she slammed the door, she used a towel to clean herself up, her hands shaking. She scrubbed her eyes with cold water as sobs trickled out of her mouth. God, she had to get a grip. This emotional monsoon was a bunch of shit.

When she emerged, he was sitting on the floor by the bathroom, wearing only his jeans. His Adam's apple bobbed.

"I heard you crying. You aren't the only one affected by this, Jill."

She took a deep breath and strode away, aware of the tenderness rubbing against her jeans. "No, I'm not."

"We didn't use anything."

His words made her squirm, but she needed to face the truth. She pressed her hand to her forehead. "I know," she whispered.

She didn't think his face could have fallen more, but the grooves cut deeper around his mouth. "We'll deal with whatever comes."

She crossed her arms around herself. God, they'd made an enormous mistake. Now she understood *in the heat of the moment*. "I don't—"

"Would you please let me hold you?" he nearly shouted, pushing up off the floor. "Goddammit, Jill. We finally made love, and you're further away from me than you've ever been."

"I'm not the only one," she whispered, making him look away. "It was a mistake. You weren't ready."

He was in her face before she even blinked. "I don't know what you're talking about." His hands cupped her cheeks. "Jillie, it was intense and passionate, and the strength of what I feel for you tears me in fucking two."

Why couldn't he admit how afraid it made him? Did he think it would make him less of a man like his father used to say?

She tucked her hands behind her back so she wouldn't smooth down his hair, caress his skin.

"I came over to get you to talk, so talk."

He stepped away and firmed his shoulders, his posture rigid, drawing back into himself. "Jesus, you're shivering," he observed, helping her to the couch. He tucked a green fleece throw around her, tearing her heart a little more with his gentleness.

When she didn't respond, he dropped his hand and reached for his shirt.

"All right," he said with resignation. "I'll tell you what you want to know, but we have to talk about this, Jill."

The blanket took the edge off her chattering teeth, but her body seemed to have sucked in all the winter wind from outside. "Start talking."

He sat across from her at the coffee table, their knees bumping. He took a long breath and rested his elbows on his thighs. "We worked together and became involved. It went on for six months until..."

She stared at the top of his head when he lowered it. Silence stretched out taut between them.

"The other owner got jealous and fired me. Then his secret recipe box disappeared—or so he said—and he accused me of the theft. He couldn't prove anything, but it didn't matter. He's super powerful in the culinary world, and he trashed me to everyone." His sigh was long and deep. "People won't give a potential thief a job. I didn't want to work anywhere but a Michelin place, so I came home for a while to build up my professional credentials and let the talk die down."

God, that must have destroyed him after working so hard to achieve his dream.

His hand rested against her knee. "I also missed Dare and felt like there were some things I needed to resolve before I could move on. You topped the list."

The hurt spread. Hadn't she suspected this was only a stopover? Brian didn't believe in forevers, and being a chef here would never be the same as it was in a big city.

"So, you wanted to 'resolve' me?"

His breath rushed out like a leaking tire. "I didn't want to go through life with this rift between us, Jill. You're a part of all my good childhood memories. Playing in the sandbox. Swimming at the quarry. Hanging out after school. You were my family."

Instead of responding to that, Jill said, "Why didn't Simca stand up for you? If she was part-owner, she could have stopped you getting fired."

He toyed with the hem of the blanket for so long she wasn't sure he would answer. Finally, he said, "She didn't want to endanger her...partnership over us."

"So what's changed?"

His hand gripped the cloth, his knuckles white. "The partnership dissolved over it. She says she told the police I was with her when the recipes were stolen. It was probably why the charges were dropped."

There was something more. She could feel it. "What else?"

"There's nothing else."

When his eyes flicked away for a second, she was sure he was holding back. "I don't believe you."

He clenched her hand, hard. "Look, this is difficult for me. Talking about this after we've just made love for the first time. Jesus. It's like hammering another stake between us. Can't you understand that?"

Her stomach quivered, but she nodded.

"I don't know if I was in love with her. We had food in common...and other things. She was older, confident. It's what I wanted at the time. I didn't want to be with someone who wanted to get married."

"Of course you felt that way after your parents divorced the way they did." Their sudden split had even scared her for a while, but she had her parents' marriage as a role model, so that fear had eventually faded.

He cleared his throat and rubbed his hands over his face. "Do we have to keep talking about this? I want to talk about what happened between us."

She firmed her lip to keep from being swayed. "So how much older is she?"

He gave her *the look.*

They engaged in a no-blinking contest.

"She's forty-four," he hissed. "Satisfied?"

He'd turned twenty-seven last month. "Seventeen years. Aren't you the child prodigy?"

"Look, I didn't tell you because I didn't want any other shit standing between us. We had enough to sift through when I came home. I would have understood about...other guys. I don't have the right to be jealous."

She pushed off the couch. "Well, good for you, but it wasn't so easy for me when you left. I was in love with you, and I couldn't seem to move on. I tried to date other guys. I even found someone to sleep with—someone who I thought would make it good for me. It was horribly uncomfortable and short. Sex wasn't what I'd expected."

Still wasn't after tonight, she realized.

"Afterwards, I wished it had been you with all my heart."

He flinched.

"He dumped me the next day, saying he didn't want to get too serious. I hadn't told him I was a virgin. He freaked out." The shaking started again. "I went out with other guys after that, but never got serious with anyone. I couldn't. And I didn't sleep with anyone else because I didn't want to be disappointed again. It was always you, and I couldn't seem to make myself want anyone else."

He rose slowly and approached her with an outstretched hand, like he was worried she was about to bolt. Poised on the balls of her feet, she thought about running for the door.

"I'm sorry. More than you can know." He stepped closer, but didn't touch her.

His voice's rough sandpaper quality held her in place.

"You need to decide what you want."

"I know that. Christ."

She swallowed over the thickness in her throat. "I think we should give each other some space."

He pinched the bridge of his nose. "I know you were hurt when I didn't say *I love you* back. Jillie, love isn't clear and straightforward for me. My parents said they loved me, but then my own mother left me for someone she barely knew, with a father who despised what I'd become. I don't know what the fuck love is anymore, but I *do* love you. There's friendship, laughter, and passion all mixed in with hundreds of happy memories."

"That was then, this is now." She brought his hand to her heart. It thumped against her ribs as a vicious pressure manacled her chest. "Let me show you. Love is clear and straightforward. Can't you feel it when you touch me?"

His face fell when his hand did. "Jill..."

She stepped back. "I hear what you're saying. I do. I'm not sure it's enough. Her offer is...she can help you with your career, which I know is everything you've ever wanted—and on a bigger stage than Dare." It was one of the hardest things she'd ever said. "Even if you decide to stay, I'm not sure we should work together. Especially if you think you might want to move on in a few years."

"Where does that leave us?"

Good question. "I don't know."

He reached for her, but she edged away again. His fist punched the air. "We just made love for the first time, and you won't even soften enough to let me hold you. I'm afraid I've already lost you. How do I fight for you, Jill? And why am I sounding like *the* girl all the sudden?"

"You're not sounding like a girl, Bri. You're sounding like a *friend*." She reached for her coat and zipped it up. "I want more than that."

"Fuck that! I'm more than your friend, and if you'll stay here with me instead of running away, I'll take you to bed and banish any doubts you have."

But would he feel as swept away as she did? Or would he still be holding back, uncertain about her and what she meant to him?

"I don't think I could handle that." She walked to the door. "I need to think. You need to think. About us."

He pushed the door shut after she cracked it open. "And if by some chance you're pregnant?"

Her insides vibrated like an out-of-tune violin, creating disharmony with every note. "I wouldn't tie myself to you just because there's a baby in the picture. I'd never know if you stayed for me—or it." The words killed something inside her.

"Damn you, Jill." His hand fell from the door.

The quiet words made her lip quiver. "You have to choose me on your own, Bri."

Since there was nothing else to say, she left his apartment and raced down the hall.

CHAPTER 15

The windows of Mac Maven's Denver office sparkled—a rare sight in winter. The brass doors shone like Colombian gold, and even the elevators gleamed. Everywhere Jill turned, her reflection mocked her, from her puffy eyes to her chalk-white face. Getting out of bed this morning hadn't been easy, but she'd pushed herself through the pain.

She turned her phone off in the elevator and chucked it into her enormous gold leather bag, smoothing down her belted navy cashmere sweater and sand-colored pencil skirt. Her legs still felt like rubber bands, so she locked her knees. Her two-inch tan boots were throwing off her balance, but she hadn't wanted to wear flats. She hated getting slushy snow inside her shoes.

The elevator doors opened, revealing a plush room with burgundy walls and caramel leather furniture. The arresting woman seated at reception seemed like she belonged at a blackjack table rather than in an office. Her long blond hair hung in happy, snake-shaped curls.

"Ms. Hale, welcome. Mr. Maven's been expecting you. I just have something for you to sign first."

Jill took the fancy pen and scanned the confidentiality agreement. It was pretty straight-forward, so she scrawled her name. The woman took the clipboard and led Jill down a glass hallway. When they reached the walnut double doors, the woman knocked softly and gestured Jill inside.

Mac Maven stood as she entered, a smile transforming his GQ-handsome face. His thick, black hair, dark brows, and lashes hinted at mystery. His jade green eyes held wisdom and watchfulness. The dimple in his chin altered his dark presence when his smile reached full tilt. Charm mingled with confidence. She admired the package like she did a sleek sports car—stunning, but not something she'd buy off the lot. She could feel him drawing her in even as he took her hand in a warm clasp.

"Jill Hale. Welcome. It's good to finally meet you in person."

Her brow rose as she gazed up at him. She was a tall woman, but he was taller. She appreciated height in a man. He didn't make her feel like Jillie the Bean Stalk, as the kids used to call her at school.

"Do tell," she replied smoothly.

His well-defined lips curved. "You're young, hip, and smart. Serious about business, but not the kind who needs to wear Ann Taylor to prove it.

It's not your market anyway."

"You're right." She took the red leather chair he pointed her toward. Her cursory scan took in his office. Navy walls. Brass lamp fixtures. Gleaming wood. And a mixed bouquet in a crystal vase. His desk was organized, but had plenty of paper on it. There was no doubt he was a working CEO. "Dare isn't the Ann Taylor type. I'm not sure whether to be impressed or curious about your knowledge of women's fashion."

He laughed, sitting across from her and not in his tan leather office chair. "It's all part of the game. The details people show me—how they dress, what they smell like—well, they're as critical as their tells."

She'd seen her share of poker movies. She knew what a tell was. "So you can 'tell' lots about me from how I dress?"

He tilted his head to the side. "You're tall but you wear high heels. My instinct is you're comfortable with your height. Your face is too open and honest to be the kind who likes to lord it over men. The navy sweater and pencil skirt are conservative. The belt adds a hint of couture, telling me you keep up with trends."

He pointed to her feet. "Your boots are well worn at the heel. You feel comfortable in them and wear them frequently. You didn't buy new shoes for our meeting although some might have." His assessment continued up her body, but not in a creepy way. "Your jewelry is bold and a bit funky, conveying a larger than life personality."

She fingered Jemma's amethyst necklace, which she'd worn for luck. Damn he was good.

"You've decided to embrace your unique style by leaving your *very* curly red hair as it is and not straightening it. That signals an ease with who you are—not surprising in someone so successful for being so young."

"You make it sound like more than it is. I own a coffee shop in a small town." Amidst all this splendor, her accomplishments seemed meager.

He gave a throaty murmur. "And you're modest. You have one of the most successful places in an increasingly attractive small town nestled in the mountains. You cater to the college crowd, the long-time residents, and the Californians. Your eclectic menu and space appeal to everyone, including families."

He steepled his hands. "That's not easy to do. You've made it more than a coffee shop, and by keeping your doors open until midnight, you catch the student crowd before they collapse into bed. Few people can make a place that opens at six in the morning and closes at midnight such a success. And all from a college business plan."

Her palms started to sweat, so she placed them on her legs. This game was becoming too reflective. His skills were top-shelf, and she didn't like being read so well. "That's your homework talking. You didn't get that from studying my outfit."

"You're right. But I can also tell you didn't get much sleep last night. I'd like to think you were excited about this meeting, but there's an inner somberness that suggests a personal struggle. Whatever that may be, I'm sorry."

Her stomach twirled like a baton thrown by the marching band. "I think that's enough. Shall we get on to business?" She'd like to know what was behind all this secrecy for starters.

The silent regard he gave her made her want to squirm. He was like a wizard looking into a crystal ball. She drew in a deep breath, but didn't look away. "So, now that I've signed your papers, what do you want with me?" It had better be worth her while.

His smile beamed again. "You don't intimidate easily."

Funny how much bolder she felt in the business world. Brian's ex intimidated the crap out of her. "No."

Standing, he tagged his coat off an elegant pineapple coat rack. "Good. Let's go to lunch, and I'll tell you everything you want to know."

The devilish waggle of his eyebrows made her want to salsa as she followed him to the door. "I can't wait."

Suddenly the excitement of something new made life seem less bleak.

**

Her brother's impending arrival gave Peggy a momentary sense of connection to her sane, adult self. Keith was going on his third sick day. She was losing her mind.

And the tickle in her throat was starting to burn like hellfire, making her wonder if brimstone was around the corner.

She missed the antiseptic smell of the office. The mustiness of the old case files she read when she didn't have anything hot going on. She'd resorted to listening to the police scanner while Keith watched another Disney movie. How many ways could they animate something? Would they ever run out of singing animals? She was convinced she'd never see an R-rated movie again, something with curse words like "fuck" and "damn" and hot sex between two writhing, gorgeous bodies.

Today was not a good day in Mommydom. Perhaps if there had been a Daddy Prince to bring home takeout and give her a break, she'd be in better shape when Tanner arrived. As it was, the seconds were ticking by as slowly as Keith's toy turtle moved.

She leaped off the couch when the doorbell rang. Her sainted brother was finally here. She could leave the sickroom and slink off on her own, shedding her mommy-nurse skin like the proverbial snake for a few hours. Thank you, God!

Tanner pulled her in for a hug. "You going nuts yet?"

"I could do an ad for Planters. Mixed Mommy Nuts. How about it?"

He ruffled her unbrushed hair. "It'll probably end up on the cutting room floor. How's he doing?"

"About the same. This cold's dug in deep."

He pulled out a file. "Diversion for the deranged. A buyer's list of new properties in the last six months. Have fun." Tanner headed in the direction of the Disney song blaring on the TV, *Kill the Beast.*

She caressed the pages like they were a secret treasure map. Work! Something to engage her mind. Oh, the pleasure tickled her tired soul.

"You sound like you're coming down with it too," he called over his shoulder.

"No way. I'll make it eat lead. I can't get sick." True, but her throat flamed like a charbroil grill.

She bounced her way to her office like a kid who'd received a new kite, her legs losing their rubbery lethargy.

She unbound the file, and her finger traced its way down the list. The eighth property had a business name, Four Aces Incorporated. It was a conditional sale—odd for residential listings. The house stood at the foot of the mountains with several acres of land and a hefty square footage.

Her police gut quivered like a divining rod. She'd start there. A simple Internet search gave her what she was looking for. Four Aces owned and built high-end boutique hotels. Their additional attraction gave her a jolt. Poker? She scratched her head. That explained the business name. The president and owner was Macalister Maven. A company promoting gambling would definitely opt for a confidentiality agreement.

She switched to her specialized background software, which allowed her to run people at home. His profile appeared. Born in Atlantic City to Carol and Len Maven, who'd divorced five years after he was born. Single. Never married. A younger sister named Abigail. Attended Princeton for three years before dropping out. Joined the professional poker circuit at twenty-one. Won the World Series of Poker tournament at twenty-five and twenty-eight.

The list of other tournament championships was endless and eye-widening.

He'd started Four Aces at twenty-nine, building four boutique poker establishments in the southwest. Each of his small, exclusive hotels showcased an upscale night club and a swanky restaurant run by an acclaimed chef. There was poker—and only poker. No loud, garish slot machines. No craps or blackjack tables.

He didn't fight the big boys, one article noted. Maven created an exclusive venue for the poker enthusiasts, a group that was growing in leaps and bounds across the country. She had no idea the interest in poker had swelled like a balloon ready to burst. There was a seriousness here that went beyond the poker nights she'd experienced—the kind people played with red, white, and blue plastic chips for pennies, nickels, dimes, and oh, a quarter if you wanted to get real dangerous. Peggy chuckled at the thought.

Maven was as much the allure as the venues. He played frequently enough to draw fans and opponents. His estimated worth had her blinking a few times to make sure her vision hadn't been permanently damaged by too much Disney.

He had a few speeding tickets, clocking in at NASCAR limits. So he liked the fast lane when he wasn't at the table. She had the VIN numbers for the six cars he owned, a mix of expensive classics and top-of-the-line racers. Great, he loved cards and cars. Could he be any more stereotypical?

She clicked on his properties, marveling at the designs. Not what she'd expected. Classy. No flashing lights or fountains. And surprise,

surprise, lots of squeaky clean windows. Weren't gaming establishments supposed to blot out the light? Stop time?

The room prices were highway robbery. She clicked on the spa service list and sighed. She didn't understand the whole hot rock massage thing, but right now, her body moaned for some serious pampering. Clearly she was at the end of her rope if she had a flash of digging up rocks in her backyard, boiling them in her spaghetti pan, and asking Tanner if he'd put them on her body. Get a grip, McBride.

Her eyes narrowed at all the styles of poker offered at his hotels. She'd heard of five-card stud and Texas hold 'em, but Omaha and Razz were new. His places boasted poker packages for different player levels and poker types, mostly stud and Texas hold 'em. There were a few discreet mentions of Mac Maven playing in his hotel-sponsored tournaments with dates.

Not Macalister, but Mac.

Her famous intuition put the puzzle pieces together. She'd bet her bottom dollar Mac Maven wanted to open something in Dare.

He had a house in each of the four cities where his businesses were located, plus one in Denver, where he kept his office. That was a little too close for comfort. He'd bought land here, conditionally. Did that mean he had an inside track on something new? Or an ace up his hand-tailored sleeve? *Jill, what in the hell have you gotten into?*

She crumbled Tanner's file. She didn't want gambling in Dare. She was a deputy, so she knew the kind of crap it generated. Drunk and disorderly. Fraud. Violence. Prostitution. People spending their last paychecks gambling, going from poor to poorer. This was *so* not going to happen. She was raising her son here. This was her new home.

A memory surfaced of her dad drinking and playing cards while they struggled with rent and food. Sometimes he'd swing his arm out and catch her in the cheek if she asked if he'd won when he hadn't.

She shook off the past and clicked on a blue link with Mac's name on it. A picture popped up. Her mouth went dry as an unexpected punch of attraction socked her in the gut. His coal black hair was cut about an inch longer than his skull, curling over a strong forehead. The dark eyelashes were about as shocking as the stoplight green eyes, which made a woman think *yes, go* as opposed to *no, stop*. The nose seemed like a poetic afterthought between high, rugged cheekbones, and his ruby chiseled lips kept him from looking like a bruiser. The strong chin had a dent in the middle, transforming him into a charmer.

Having studied perps for years, she thought she was pretty good at reading people. She saw a lot of things in this man. Power. Control. Confidence. Will. And a smoldering sexuality he appreciated, but wouldn't exploit.

The deputy and mommy in her slid away from the shore of her consciousness with a tide of new awareness. The woman inside cried out, a faint echo after a lengthy silence. *Well, hello there, handsome.*

Her body grew warm as those eyes seemed to stare deep inside her. He would know what to do with a woman. He'd enter forcefully and drive deep. The thought almost made her moan.

The tide came back in. The deputy and mom returned, pushing the woman back out to sea like flotsam. Disgusted, Peggy forced herself to breathe out the jittery desire racing up her spine.

She would have to talk to Jill about this situation. Maybe she didn't know Maven's game. Damn, he was smart, she had to admit. Jill was an asset. She could bring the town along. Was that what he wanted from her?

Cop reason prevailed. She'd have to see what the local laws said about gambling and how she could use them against this man. Keith called her name from downstairs, his voice hoarse from coughing. She stood, praying she wasn't going to sound like that in a couple of days. Hadn't Keith had a sore throat before whooping all over the place?

"Coming, honey."

Her mommy persona snapped more firmly back into place. Time to take care of her most precious gift.

Maven was not bringing gambling into her town.

CHAPTER 16

The small talk irritated the heck out of Jill, especially since she was dying to know what Mac wanted from her, but he didn't seem to be in any hurry. They were lunching in a five-star restaurant illuminated by cozy gas lighting yet decorated with modern art—a compelling contrast to her artistic eye. He controlled the conversation, asking her about herself, her family, Dare. Jill suspected he already knew most of the answers, but his interest didn't waver, his charm didn't fade.

She poked at her roasted chicken, not wanting to rock the conversation boat. "I'm curious why you dropped out of Princeton when you had a full scholarship. That's when you hit the poker circuit, right? Were you bored with school? 'Cause you're talking to someone who totally understands."

He was silent for so long she wasn't sure he would reply. Then he set aside his silverware. "Since you have a strong sense of family, I'll tell you. My sister, Abbie, got pregnant in high school. There were some...medical issues. We didn't have insurance. My father was a small-time gambler in Atlantic City who had more ups than downs. I'd sworn never to become drawn into that world after he left us. The only problem was I'd shown an innate skill at cards. Some parents sing nursery rhymes to their kids. I played cards with mine. My mother was a dealer. She died when I was ten. Dad left when I was sixteen, telling me I was old enough to take care of things. Abbie was twelve then."

Jill felt a surge of gratitude for her loving parents and happy childhood, and just like that, Brian popped into her mind again. She wished she could wave a wand for people whose parents totally sucked. "That must have been tough."

He shifted when the sun came out from behind a cloud, streaming through the windows. "My nephew, Dustin, was premature. There were complications. The bills started mounting, and the two jobs I worked couldn't make a dent, so I did something I'd sworn I'd never do. I went to Atlantic City—our hometown—with the mad idea that I could grow the measly savings we had into the funds we needed to pay her medical bills."

Jill smoothed her hands in her lap, trying to imagine how much pressure he'd been under.

"I didn't get what we needed overnight, but I grew it over three months. My classes were in jeopardy, so I took a leave of absence." He smiled in an absent way—he must have thought of something private and amusing. "By then I couldn't deny the truth. I loved poker. I was like Moses in the Sinai finding his inner calling. It wasn't an easy transition, but my sister and nephew needed more care, so I could justify my choice. When everything...settled down, I'd developed a certain reputation and received invitations to other events." His gaze returned to her. "The rest, as they say, is history."

Wow, talk about will power. "That's quite a story. I'd be lying if I said I wasn't impressed."

"That's not why I told you the truth. You wouldn't want to work with someone you couldn't trust."

Brian came to mind. Wasn't that one of the reasons she was sitting here with Mac and not trying to iron out their different visions for the restaurant? She tapped her fingers on the table. "You're right. It's a bit scary how well you read people."

His chuckle was as inviting as wind chimes on a breezy spring day. "I usually don't share my observations, but I know I only have one shot with you."

"So what did you major in when you were at Princeton?"

"Engineering. I always wanted to build things."

"And now you do."

"Yes," he murmured, inclining his fork.

They continued to eat. Her stomach couldn't quite settle even though she'd opted for the blandest thing on the menu. No sleep. Too much caffeine. Personal stress. Not appetite material. He coaxed her into looking at the dessert menu. On any other day, she'd have jumped at the pumpkin soufflé.

"Your mind is working overtime," he finally said after the waiter set down his espresso.

Yes, it was. The coffee scent tickled her nose. The restaurant used a roasted blend of Kenyan and Guatemalan beans, she'd guess. Not too strong or smoky. An Italian would liken it to piss water, but it worked for Americans.

"What are you smiling at?" He cocked his head to the side in that intense way he had. Funny how it reminded her of Tanner.

"I was deciphering the beans in this espresso."

"And your guess?"

She told him. He signaled the waiter over and conveyed her assessment.

"Your guest is correct, Mr. Maven," the waiter responded when he returned. He set down a plate of small chocolate coins dotted with espresso beans. "The chef's compliment. For the lady's good nose."

Delight at being right prompted her to sample her prize. Perhaps the chocolate would calm her stomach. Unleash those chemicals it was so famous for. "Why did you ask?"

Mac drained his espresso and leaned back in his chair. "I can't help it.

It's like calling someone's hand."

"So the hand went to me." She rolled the coin with her tongue.

"It shows you know your business. May I share the chocolate?"

She extended the silver dish, ready to get down to business. "Do you finally want to tell me a little more about what you have in mind?"

"That's good chocolate." He threw his napkin on the table with an easy flick of the wrist. "I assume you know of The Grand Mountain Hotel."

Well, that was totally weird. Why was he interested in that run-down, haunted old place? "Of course. We call it Pincari's folly." Her brows drew together as she tried to recall the local history. "Robert Pincari had some cockamamie idea he could build a European mountain resort in Colorado in the 1920s. His family owned some gambling places when Denver was a big venue. He spent tons of money on it and drew in a motley clientele, from mobsters to East-coast businessmen. The resort combined skiing and vice."

"Exactly. I'm impressed."

Cheered by his praise, she decided to share the rest of what she remembered. "Don't be. It's my journalist family rubbing off on me. Pincari lost a chunk in the crash of 1929, but he couldn't sell the hotel, so he tried to keep it open. There was a ghastly murder in it a few years later. Some gangster. A local disappeared too—can't recall the family now. I think they moved away. Isn't that terrible?"

Since he gave no agreement, she continued, "Pincari closed the hotel shortly thereafter." She snorted. "Everyone in Dare thinks it's haunted."

"Interesting." His face didn't give anything away. No urbane charm now. "And why is that?"

His intensity had her wondering if he was into ghost hunting like the other tourists who pestered her with questions when they visited the coffee shop. She shrugged. "My grandpa talks about people sneaking up there to make out or scavenge around. People came back with tall tales. Moaning sounds. Shrieking laughter. That kind of nonsense. It's a wreck now." She leaned forward, beyond curious. "Why do you ask?"

"I've put in a conditional offer to buy it," he responded like he hadn't said the most asinine thing in the world.

Her mouth dropped open—totally unprofessional. "Are you kidding? It's a disaster! I know it's only a few miles out of town, but it's a dead loss, investment wise." Reigning in her babbling, she took a long breath. "Okay, you're a smart man. Why?"

"The gambling license comes with the hotel. It's grandfathered in. I informed the Colorado Gaming Commission that I'm going to rebuild it once I get Dare's city council to approve the restoration plans. Everything is contingent."

Holy. Shit. This was huge! Her hands grew damp just imagining the boost it would give Dare. Her town couldn't compete with Aspen or Breckenridge, but with a restored poker hotel in the mountains, it would be a unique tourist attraction. She could already hear cash registers in town ringing from the influx.

Mac made room on the table for his briefcase. "The hotel is *not* a dead-loss. Trust me, I've checked." His wink competed with the twinkle in his eyes. "It's made of brick, so it will be easy to strip it down to the frame. Gut everything. The main highway up the canyon makes the road to the hotel 1.3 miles now. I can pave that. Taking away some of the 150 rooms, I can convert some of the space into the club I want. The original plan had only one restaurant, which I'd expand."

He drew out sketches from his briefcase. Jill marveled at how far along his plans had come. She'd seen black-and-white photos of the hotel at *The Independent*. The face-lift Mac had designed was guaranteed to make the hotel a showstopper again.

"The restaurant will be in the left wing. The club will flank the right side, back against the open valley, so the noise won't echo. The poker floor will have a combination of open rooms and private spaces. And of course, we'll have a spa, health club, and swimming pool."

Freaking cool.

His smile flashed when he raised his head. Then he focused on the sketches again, his finger pointing to different parts. "Pincari laid five miles of ski lifts, which we'll re-secure. The trails will be cleared. In summer, people can go to the top of the mountain, do some hiking."

"What about parking? People have a hell of a lot more cars now than they did back then."

"Didn't I say you had first-class smarts? We'll add onto the back. Here, between the right side of the hotel and the start of the mountain. We'll also run a shuttle service from Denver airport and downtown Dare."

Sweat broke out on her palms. She rubbed them on her skirt. He was already including her in his vision. Her brain made the leap, imagining it all. She could see herself in front of the hotel. Thousands of questions swirled, but only one mattered. "Why do you want me involved and in what capacity?"

The way he sat perfectly still was unnerving. He could have taught yoga.

"I can't make it feel like a Dare institution or have the Dare stamp of approval without the help of a local."

She gave a slow nod. "So, you want my expertise in making this palatable to Dare citizens?"

"Not just that. I want you to be the creative manager, putting your special touch on the property, like how you've made Don't Soy with Me a local meeting place and not just a coffee shop. Things like what music the club should play, what menu and spa services will draw in locals. You'll have a sense of how it should look, feel, and taste."

It was even more incredible than she could have imagined. Her feet tapped on the floor.

He reached into his briefcase and pulled out an envelope. Inside were sepia photos from a different time. The hotel at its finest. Women in long velvet skirts and hats dotted with swirling feathers. Men in pin-striped suits and Fedoras. Antique automobiles with running boards as long as bridal trains flanked the drive. When she stared at the pictures, she could almost hear a crackling radio playing a jazz hit by Al Jolson.

"I'll also want you to greet guests, especially the locals. Make them feel at home. I had Jack do a little scouting for me in Dare because I didn't want to risk anyone recognizing me. Even poker players have followings, although the whole thing makes me uncomfortable. Anyway, the first thing he told me about you was that you know the name of every customer who walks into your shop, and if you don't, you immediately introduce yourself. You know what they order, who they're dating, what their story is. That's a special gift. I want it at The Grand Mountain Hotel."

Everything within her went still. This was the chance of a lifetime. She could stay in Dare and become a world-class businesswoman. It would allow her to achieve far more than she could alone...or with Brian.

Right. Brian. "It sounds incredible." She gripped her napkin with a fist. "What are your plans for the restaurant? Would you be open to having a local chef run the kitchen?"

"I usually bring in someone from the outside who has a strong culinary reputation." He steepled his hands. "Let's cut to the chase. You're asking if I would consider Brian McConnell for the position. Jack mentioned you were exploring the idea of opening a restaurant together."

Of course he had. He'd been the scout. "Yes."

"I checked into Brian's background before our meeting, sensing this might come up. His reputation among elite chefs isn't the hottest. There were some problems at his last restaurant. I don't want any complications like that. Plus, I usually hire someone with significant head chef experience. I wish it were different, Jill."

Well, their partnership seemed like it was over now anyway. At least she'd tried. Jill threw her napkin aside. "It sounds incredible, but I'd like to take some time to think about it." She'd already made one impulsive act. No need to do two in twenty four hours.

"Understood." He handed her some papers. "Here's the formal offer, which is negotiable. I really want you to be involved, Jill. Read it over. Then we can talk more. You'll find I'm willing to go to great lengths to have you involved."

It was awesome to be wanted.

Mac took care of the bill. "I hope you enjoyed your lunch."

She stood up, her palms damp again. "It was excellent."

"Why don't you spend the rest of the afternoon at the spa in the hotel next door? I have an account there. Relax. Think it over. If you don't want to drive back to Dare, spend the night. Just use my name to secure a room. We could meet again in the morning."

Not heading back to Dare sounded like a great plan. "I'll stay over, but I'll need more than a day to think things through."

Mac helped her with her coat. "Fine, but I need a decision quickly. I have some friends at the Gaming Commission who are going over our plans to make sure there won't be any state concerns. Once that's done, I'll submit them officially. Then I'll take them to Dare. This whole deal has three weeks to come together."

That was fast. She clutched her purse. "Only three weeks?"

He snapped his briefcase shut. "I don't like to waste time. My offer's contingent on everything falling into place. I don't want the city council to draw this out. They either like my plans, or they don't. And if I put a shorter time limit on the decision, there's less time for any opposition to mobilize."

This was the big leagues. What a learning opportunity. "So, the council either agrees or you walk." Her low whistle turned a few heads. "That will make folks jump."

"It's simple. They either want the millions of dollars in revenue and new jobs or they don't. Gambling can be a sticky issue, but from the research I've done, Dare will be receptive."

"I agree," she replied, running through community groups in her head. "There will be some resistance, but nothing significant. Likely something religious or environmental."

"I can't address any religious concerns, but the plans represent the highest environmental standards. Platinum LEED Building Standards, if you know the term."

She didn't, but it sounded impressive. "That's good. The economic infusion will be a big draw."

"It always is. I'm counting on that."

As they left the restaurant, her entire future looked different.

CHAPTER 17

Brian made his third pass by Jill's house since the crack of dawn. Her car was still gone, and Margie had told him she wasn't coming into the coffee shop today. He kept calling her phone, but it went straight to voicemail each time. Where could she be? He'd driven by all their usual places after tossing and turning the whole night and realizing she was right.

He was terrified of what he felt for her. Always had been. As an eighteen year-old kid, he'd had the excuse of youth and inexperience, but he was a man now. It was time to step up.

And even though his fear made him feel like a boulder was pressing down on his chest, he needed to find her so he could assure both of them they'd be okay. Losing Jill was not an option.

He hoped to Christ he could find her before he had to head to work.

He was pacing in his apartment when his cell rang. "Hello," he answered, not recognizing the number.

"Brian," the rough voice scratched out, "it's Arthur Hale."

Jill's grandfather *never* called him. For a split second, he imagined the worst. Hadn't he been looking for Jill for eight hours now? She'd been so distraught when she'd left... Just look at what had happened to Jemma. Life could change in a New York minute. Frozen in place, his heart rapped so hard against his ribs, he was sure it would burst through his chest.

"Is Jill all right?" he rasped out.

"Why would you think something's wrong?"

"Something's wrong. I can't find her *anywhere*. Her phone is off. And she's not at the coffee shop." She was always there.

"Don't panic, Brian. I'm sure everything is fine." The phone clicked, and the local radio station started streaming over the line. Arthur Hale had put him on hold. The broadcast droned on about a winter clearance sale at Rugged Trails Sporting Goods.

He resumed his pacing, wanting to throw the phone against the wall. He shouldn't have let her drive home last night. The roads were icy. She'd been emotionally distraught. God, should he call Peggy? Part of him knew he was overreacting, but she'd been so upset, and she loved to drive fast. She could have rolled down an incline. His gut gripped, thinking about her lying in a canyon. Dead.

In that one moment, he saw a life without Jill.

No corkscrew red curls bobbing around her face when she laughed with gusto. No soft, silky skin to caress in the middle of the night after they'd made love. No one to be his confidante. No one to have his back always, even when he was the one at fault. How could he keep going if she wasn't there to make him smile?

He put his hand to his temple as realization dawned. He loved her. *Really* loved her. Not just as a friend.

How could he not have seen it?

"Meredith said Jill texted her that she was going to Denver for the day," Arthur said when he came back on the line.

He had to sit down, the relief making his head spin. "I see."

"I take it you two fought about the French woman?"

Twelve rounds. He rubbed his temple. "Yes."

"Why don't you come over to the house? I have something I want to discuss with you."

That didn't sound good. In fact, it sounded downright foreboding. Arthur Hale asking him over on a work day? "Fine."

"See you soon."

Brian darted to the bathroom to change—no way was he meeting Arthur looking grungy. He nicked himself twice shaving.

He tried Jill's phone again and left a message. "Jill, will you please call me? Your grandpa said you're in Denver for the day. Why are you there? Please, call me. We need to talk. I have something to tell you."

He wiped the blood running down his chin. He wanted to say he loved her, but didn't want the first time to be over the phone. She deserved better than that. Starting today, he was going to treat her like she meant the world to him.

Once he was presentable, he headed over to Arthur Hale's home. When he arrived, Arthur gestured him inside with his ivory-topped cane. He hadn't been in this house since he was a teenager, but he had a lot of wonderful memories here. Arthur's deceased wife, bless her soul, had made it an inviting place, blending pieces from her husband's trips overseas with items from local handicraft stores.

Usually, he felt at home.

Today only a cold draft welcomed him.

"Thanks for coming," Arthur said. "Let's talk back here." He gestured down the hallway.

Palms sweating, Brian followed Arthur into his office and halted abruptly. Tanner and Meredith were sitting on the brown leather sofa below the wall of photos of Arthur shaking hands with presidents from this country and others. The feeling of being ambushed crawled up his neck.

"Meredith. Tanner," he managed to choke out. "I assume this must be about Jill."

"In part," Arthur confirmed. He tapped his cane on the floor like a judge would a gavel "I'm glad we don't have to dance around. Meredith and I both did some digging about what happened with you in New York.

We wanted to talk to you about the alleged theft of your boss' secret recipes. I have to admit we were all surprised to find out the police had questioned you."

Being called out by the Hale family burned like a blister. He hated to think of what Jill's parents thought of him now. They'd been his lifeline growing up. "I didn't do it if that's what you're asking." He locked his knees. "I'm pretty sure Andre, my former boss, staged the whole thing."

"Don't you mean Simca's husband?" Meredith snarled, her eyes full of fire.

"Mere," Tanner cautioned.

Meredith's arms resembled a straight jacket. "I won't leave Jill in the dark about something this serious."

Right. Sisters. "I've already told her about the recipe incident." But not about Simca being married. His worst fear had been realized. If they knew about the affair, then Jill knew too—or would soon. Shit. "Wait a minute. Is this why Jill's gone radio silent? Did you tell her all this?"

"No," Arthur answered, crossing his arms over his navy cardigan. "We wanted to talk to you first. We know you and Jill are thinking of opening a restaurant together."

Jesus, he hadn't expected this. He shifted on his feet. He wasn't much relieved by the fact that they hadn't said anything yet. If Jill didn't know, then *last night* had made her bolt. Not encouraging. "So you didn't want her partnering with a thief. Thank you very much." He'd taken a lot of insults in New York after the incident, but coming from them, it felt like a knife in the gut.

But it was time to come clean, starting now. "Jill doesn't know Simca was married. Yet." He cleared his throat. Man, that had been hard to say.

"I see." Meredith's words shot out like gunfire. "You'd better tell her, Brian. Or I will."

"I'm planning on it. I haven't yet because I was worried about how she'd react. I wanted—"

"Then you know my granddaughter well," Arthur interrupted, a frown on his face.

"How could you do this, Brian?" Meredith asked, her voice strained. "I've known you since you were born. You were raised better than this."

"Meredith," Tanner reproached. "It's not our business."

Her words made Brian clench his fists, but he understood why she was being so harsh. Her ex-husband had been unfaithful. "Look, I was stupid and reckless, and I paid for it. At first, I thought they were separated. When I found out that wasn't totally true, I didn't end it. Simca wasn't concerned, and it wasn't hurting anyone. I'm not proud of it."

"And what about now?" Arthur asked.

"I want to try to make things right with Jill." His mind spun, wondering if that was even a possibility now.

"Then why is that French woman hanging around here?" Meredith asked, her voice hard.

Standing before them defending himself made him realize this conversation would be even harder with Jill. "She wants us to open a restaurant together in New York."

"And you're considering it?" Meredith spit out.

Now that he knew he loved Jill, everything looked different. He needed to talk to her about this, not her sister. "Jill and I are talking about things." Or they would. Once she returned.

Meredith pointed at him. "From where I'm sitting, you need help rebuilding your rep after what happened in New York. That's why you came home, right?"

He nodded. "And to persuade Jill to be in my life again."

"Was Jill only the means to securing your own place?"

"Babe," Tanner cautioned again.

Brian ground his teeth like he was chewing one of Arthur's red hots. "I didn't come back thinking we'd open a restaurant together. I came here to get back on track and see if I could resurrect friendships that were important to who I am. Jemma. Pete. And, most of all, Jill. Opening the restaurant was her idea, remember? I was reconciled to putting in some time at the Chop House."

Meredith leaned forward. "I don't know if you being here is good for Jill."

His heart blistered like peppers over a gas flame. "That's for Jill to decide."

"I don't want her to get hurt." Meredith clenched Tanner's hand so hard her knuckles turned white.

"I don't want her to get hurt either, Meredith. I'm trying to fix it."

"Then tell her the truth," Arthur encouraged. "You have two days."

Great, an ultimatum. Like he needed more pressure. "I was trying to."

"Jill will be back," Tanner assured. "She probably just needs to lick her wounds a while."

Right. Her wounds. His mind flashed to the sound of her crying in the bathroom after they'd made love. His energy crashed. "Are we finished here?"

Meredith stood and put her hands on her hips. "If you're really planning on leaving Dare, you should let Jill go now. She never got over you leaving the last time."

He drilled Meredith with a stare. "I know that, dammit." His head buzzed. His hands were clammy. He needed to get out of here.

Arthur inclined his cane. "Brian, be good to my granddaughter, or else you'll answer to me."

"And me," Meredith intoned with an edge.

Brian gripped the chair's arms, not bothering to explain how terrible he would feel if he hurt her like that again, how it would tear out his own heart. "I will," he promised and walked out.

He checked his phone again. Nothing. When she got back from Denver, he'd tell her everything and see where that left them.

Loving Jill was a game changer.

CHAPTER 18

Jill held her head high as she strutted into Don't Soy With Me the next day. Mac had provided her with more details in their morning meeting.

She'd managed to maintain her cool while they discussed his hefty financial offer. And since she was the queen of building scenarios, she'd numbly bought a pregnancy test before leaving town in case her period was late. If she bought one in Dare, the rumors would travel far and wide.

Her night in Denver had given her a renewed sense of control over her life. She had options. Facing Brian wouldn't be easy, but she was confident she could do it.

"Hey, Margie," she called out to her barista.

"Well, hello there. How was your stay in Denver? More importantly, *where* did you stay?"

Rumors were probably already flying, given that Denver was normally a day trip for most Dare Valley citizens. "Wonderful. I decided to have a night away at a nice hotel." Something she'd never done.

"Mm-hmm," Margie muttered.

Jill just smiled enigmatically as she circled the counter. Let them think what they wanted.

The evening crowd was hunched over with fatigue. Late night studying and partying made this one of their busiest times. People needed a caffeine fix to keep going. The new cashier, Pat, was working out well, and he kept the line of customers moving along.

She jingled the bell on the counter, deciding to give herself her favorite pick-me-up. "Okay, everyone. Mamma's here, and she wants to make coffee."

Margie smirked, her eyebrow ring winging up like someone had pulled it with a string.

"You up for dueling espresso machines?" Jill pushed up her sleeves.

Margie flicked her wrist. "You are frisky. Bring it."

Jill danced a salsa step, loosening up her muscles. "Pat, get the timer. Take the line's order, and we'll split them down the middle. See who finishes first."

A few guys *woofed*, and people sidled up to the bar to watch. Jill hadn't done this for weeks, but it was always a real crowd pleaser. Pat switched the smooth jazz to boisterous Irish music. Flutes, fiddles, and drums wove a peppy melody, bringing to mind leprechauns racing against each other for a pot of gold.

"You ready, Margie?"

Jill placed the list on the counter and waited for Pat's signal. When he brought his hand down, she spun into action. Blocking out the raucous crowd, she memorized the first five drinks on her list. Double espresso. Hazelnut mocha. Carmel macchiato. Triple chocolate hot chocolate without the whipped cream. On it went. People bought second rounds just to keep it going. She brushed moist curls back from her face as she made the last order—a vanilla latte with extra foam.

"Go, go, go, go," the crowd chanted in the background.

She ran through the motions and topped off the foam. When she set it aside, Pat called, "Stop."

Jill put her hands on her waist, her heart knocking in her chest. Margie froze in the act of pouring milk into a chai tea latte.

"Winner," Pat shouted, lifting Jill's hand. She thrust the other in the air. Shaking her stuff in a victory dance, she felt her mood lift.

"Eight orders in a little over two minutes." Pat showed her the clock. "Not too shabby, boss."

"Pretty damn good."

Margie came over. "It's one of your best times. Maybe *I* need some time off. Wink. Wink."

"Feel free to ask," Jill smartly responded. Then she turned to their audience. "Who makes the best coffee in Dare?"

Like a crowd at a Justin Timberlake concert, people yelled, whistled, and cheered her name. The buzz swept her along in a tide of delight. She wiped the moisture from her face, grinning like a fool.

"Fairly impressive," a voice called in a husky French purr.

Jill's mind stuttered, the intruder instantly deleting the joy program from her system. She turned. The French Barbie stood at the counter in skinny jeans, knee-high stiletto boots, and a cashmere wrap. Her blond hair glowed against the black neckline. Jill considered her own outfit—a pink fleece, jeans, and Uggs. Great.

She was so removing French Roast from her coffee menu. She'd never liked its bittersweet taste and charcoal briquette tones, cemented by a thin body. Rather like the woman in front of her.

Pat stepped forward. "I've got this, Jill. What can I get you?"

Simone fingered her oversized designer silver purse. "I'll try your espresso. See how it compares with mine."

Jill bit her lip to keep her mouth shut. "Why don't you go to the office?" Margie asked, tugging at her arm. "I need your signature on some purchase orders."

"No, it's fine." She needed to find her spine. Today was a good day.

"I'd like to speak with you while I wait for my espresso," Simone added.

Jill met her gaze. "Fine. We can talk in my office."

The change in the crowd couldn't be more noticeable. The rowdy fun fizzled, and her customers' sudden silence made her cringe.

She led the way, the ice-pick taps of Simone's shoes echoing on the hardwood floor. When they were both inside, she shut the door and headed for her chair.

Simone stood, hands on her cover-model hips. "I wanted to tell you I only have Brian's best interests at heart. I am here to make amends for what happened in New York. He's an incredible chef. He should not waste his talents in this small town. I hope you will not try and keep him here."

Oh, yeah, this woman was not to be underestimated. "That's up to Brian."

"Yes, it is. If he returns to New York, I will do everything in my power to convince him that we are made for each other. Of course, you dislike me. That is no surprise. I feel the same way." The woman fingered the white tips of her manicure—French, of course. "But you need to understand. Brian *loves* cooking. If he is not able to do it the way he desires, his spirit will die. How would you feel if you were responsible for that?"

Guilt. Manipulation. This woman knew how to wield her weapons. "You're one to talk. If you had stood up for him in the first place and offset your partner's accusations, perhaps he wouldn't be where he is now."

Simone made a humming sound. "That is true. I am doing what I can to rectify that now."

Her Good Samaritan act pissed Jill off. "Why don't you date men your own age?" Sheer jealously got the better of her.

"You are so provincial. Brian is an amazing man. Why would I let something as meaningless as age stand in the way?" Then her eyes narrowed. "To answer your question though, it's rather Pygmalion. There's nothing better than helping a man grow into the person he wants to be—and the chef, of course. And then, of course, there is that youthful sexual stamina..."

She wanted to hurl her stapler between the woman's eyes. "I think you should leave now."

Simone stroked her purse's strap and made a tsking noise. "Surely, you see what a waste it would be for him to stay here. He needs to go back to New York and fight my ex-husband. Take back his rightful place at a Michelin restaurant. I can make that happen."

What? Jill's head roared like an espresso maker's steam valve was jammed in her ear. "Your *ex*-husband?"

"Oh, what a terrible slip of the tongue. Brian asked me not to say anything."

Her thoughts shifted in slow motion. Suddenly it all made sense. "Let me make sure I understand this. Brian had an affair with *you* at the restaurant you owned with your *husband*?"

"*Oui*," Simone responded in that breathy voice.

She stood up even though her knees wanted to give out. How could he? After all the damage Meredith's ex had done, she hated cheaters with a passion. Everything she knew of him was being shifted upside down like sand in an hourglass.

"See, there are things you still don't know about Brian."

No kidding, and it hurt beyond belief. Jill looked down at her desk, unable to reply. What could she say?

"If you care about him, you will encourage him to leave. That is what I came to tell you."

She stared at the woman for whom Brian had destroyed his life. "Let me be clear, as you said. You didn't come here today to 'persuade' me to free Brian. You came here to make sure I knew your relationship was an affair."

Her icy blond hair swished against her shoulders when she shook her head. "As I said, it was a slip of the tongue."

"I'll bet. Get the hell out of my office. It's Brian's decision. It always was."

"If you hold him here, he will come to hate you." Simone walked to the door.

Hadn't she already thought about that? "Just get out. Now." Jill gripped the edge of the desk with white knuckles.

"It's nothing personal, you understand. He has outgrown you and this place."

How come people always said *it's nothing personal* while they destroyed your world?

French Barbie finally left the room, and Jill curled back in her chair. The picture of them laughing together on their Valentine's Day picnic mocked her. They looked so happy, a thread of familiarity and longing visible in the way they embraced and gazed into each other's eyes. She remembered how unselfishly he'd pleasured her. Her lips trembled, and like ripples in a pond, the tremors spread to the rest of her body.

"Oh, God," she whispered.

Her renewed sense of control over her life melted like butter left out on a sunny counter.

CHAPTER 19

Jill turned onto her street and saw Brian's SUV parked in front of her house. How dare he come here after his shift and uncover her spare key?

She'd wanted more time to process Simone's revelations and bury her hurt and anger, but he was not going to force her away from her home. After leaving her car, she increased her stride, rage growing inside like a thunderstorm.

Aromatic smells assaulted her nose when she let herself in. Usually the intoxicating smell of garlic, onion, and tomato would reduce her to a drooling puddle. She firmed her shoulders. Did he think a homemade meal could erase what had happened? He must be insane.

Brian came out of the kitchen and made a beeline for her. His arms clamped around her, lifting her to her toes. "Thank God, you're back. Jesus, you scared me. Don't you ever do that again!"

Struggling in his embrace, she shoved at him. "Stop this!"

"Don't you *ever* disappear on me."

"I don't—"

"Jesus. Before I found out you were in Denver, I imagined you lying at the bottom of some canyon after hitting some black ice. Dead like Jemma."

She stopped struggling, sensing the raw emotions radiating from him. She was angry, but not cruel. "I didn't mean to worry you."

"Well, you did. Took twenty years off my life. Dammit, Jill. How could I not be worried after the way we left things?"

Stepping away was her only form of protection. This didn't change what he'd done. "You shouldn't have made yourself so at home."

His mouth tightened. He lowered his arms from her waist. "I'm sorry. I didn't know what else to do. You wouldn't return my calls, and I didn't want to sit in my car like some stalker. I... I needed to see you. I...Jill, you scared the shit out of me. It felt like when I left Dare after high school, and you wouldn't return any of my calls."

Her pain rose swiftly. Here he was, standing in faded jeans that hugged his gorgeous legs and a simple navy zip fleece over a white T-shirt. His beauty stole her breath away. The face she knew and had caressed with love—the thick brows, silky eyelashes, and square jaw—seemed the same. Yet, with the evening's revelation, he was a stranger.

"How could you?" she whispered.

His whole body paused like a movie frame. "Dammit! They said they wouldn't tell you."

She threw her purse down on her orange couch. "I have no idea what you're talking about."

His jaw clenched. "Your family. They did some sleuthing and called me over for a Hale smackdown."

It clicked. Her hands turned to ice as her internal temperature dropped. Her family? They knew about the affair? Of course they did—they were reporters, they looked into everything. She wrapped her arms around her middle, a new hurt spreading.

"Wait." He grabbed her. "If your family didn't tell you, who did?"

She met his gaze without flinching. "Your lover."

"Ah, fuck." He pulled her to his chest again before she could evade him. "I'm sorry. Is that why you disappeared? Jesus, I didn't want you to hear about it from anyone but me."

Self-deprecating laughter bubbled up. No, it hadn't been why she'd left, but that didn't matter now. She pushed back. "Don't you mean you didn't want me to hear it at all? Isn't that why you lied?"

He gripped her shoulders, holding her in place. "Dammit, can you blame me? I knew how you'd feel."

And that made it right? "I'm dying to hear this one."

"You're afraid you don't know who I am. That you can't trust me."

"Bingo," she snapped.

His hands squeezed. "I was going to tell you, but then we made love, and we fought. I was scared, okay? It was *so* not the time to tell you another horrible thing about me. When you disappeared, I finally realized how I feel about you. I knew I had to tell you everything when you came back."

When she yanked her arms away, his grip firmed, making her struggle all the more. "Oh, so you know how you feel, do you? Why don't you tell me since I still don't have a clue?"

He took a deep breath, eyes as blue as a stormy ocean. "I love you, Jillie. All the way."

He could say that *now*? His words shredded her heart. "How can I believe you after what you kept from me? I don't feel like I can believe anything you say anymore." She jerked away. When he wouldn't let go, she struggled. "Stop it!" Her arms strained. "I want you to leave."

He angled them over to the couch, pushing her down with his weight. "Dammit, I don't want to hurt you. Stop fighting me."

"Let go of me," she growled, kicking at his legs.

He pressed his forehead to hers. "Please don't ask me to do that. I *can't* do it again."

"Too bad." Jill tried to wiggle away. "I don't want you anymore," she lied, desperate to make him leave.

His sigh blew over her face. "Yes, you do. We both want each other so bad we can barely stand it."

She shifted her lower body away from his arousal. "Yes, I can feel that," she snapped and tried to shut out the terror that she could want him so badly—even after everything she'd learned.

He rubbed his forehead against hers, the gesture charged with longing. "That's not what I meant, but Christ, there's that, too." When he lifted his face inches away from hers, his expression utterly naked, her heart squeezed. "*I love you. That's why this hurts so much. I don't want to lose you over this, Jill. I want a second chance.*"

She'd already given one to him, and she couldn't bear the thought of another. "I was offered a job in Denver. I'm thinking about taking it."

He blinked, the spell of longing turning to confusion. Then he flinched. "What the fuck are you talking about? Denver? That's why you were gone?"

She took a few breaths, realizing she'd misspoken. No shock given the way her head was buzzing. "The interview was in Denver. The job would be here."

His bemusement gave her the chance to free herself from him and slide into a chair across from the purple coffee table.

He rubbed his hands over his face as if unbearably tired. "So, just like that, you don't want to talk about going into business together anymore? I told you I needed time. What about me loving you?"

"It's not like waving a magic wand and deleting the past. Simca's changed everything." Her fingers clutched a pillow in her lap. "I'm starting to think you were right from the start. It's not a good idea to mix business and pleasure. Anyway, we're not in a good place right now."

His face shuttered. He threw a navy pillow against the wall, hitting the African mask there. She trembled as he slowly rose to his feet.

"Let me take the food out. It's going to burn."

She followed him, shaking down to her toes. "I hate that I feel like I should say I'm sorry."

The pan crashed on the gas grates when he flung it down. Lasagna steamed violently, bubbles of cheese and sauce casting a spell like a magic cauldron. The oven door slamming sent a tremor through her. He threw the pot holders off like they were boxing gloves.

"Why, Jill? Tell me how you really feel. Let's get it all out in the open."

Fine. No reason to dance around it when the hurt was this great. "I don't trust you anymore," she cried, clutching her chest. "The Brian I knew wouldn't have an affair with a married woman, and he wouldn't keep it from me when his cougar ex contacted him. Don't you see how this looks?"

He planted his feet. "Fuck that. The Jill I know wouldn't go to a job interview without telling me and then do a one-eighty on wanting to explore opening a restaurant without discussing it with me first. At least I told you about Simca's offer."

"Don't try and compare the two. I only reconsidered his offer because your French Barbie came to town. I wanted to tell you the other night, but...we made love. I forgot." She nearly winced at that last sentence.

"So you held back too." His brows slammed together like two cars in a fender bender. "Wait. This wasn't the first time you talked to this guy?

Why didn't you tell me before?"

He thrust the salad he'd made into the refrigerator. *Slam.* The violence made her vibrate like a tuning fork.

Was kicking a chair a reasonable reaction? "Because I wanted to explore our idea first."

"Bullshit. You ran away instead of working things out between us."

She pointed to herself. "*I* did? *You're* the king of walking away. Who left after high school?"

He blew out the stubby candles on her farm table in the kitchen nook. She noticed the flower arrangement of baby's breath, pink roses, and yellow daisies. He'd even arranged the napkins in some S-like shape. His romantic gesture moved her to tears, but it didn't change the facts.

"You're never going to forgive me, are you? These last few weeks were a blip on the screen, weren't they? One big blip, and we fall like a house of cards. What a friendship. What a relationship. I made a mistake and you just drop me." His voice was angry, but she could hear the hurt in it too.

He strode out of the kitchen, the force brushing her skin like a departing train on a platform. She turned and followed him.

"I'm sorry," she said, turning him around to face her.

"So am I."

They both stood breathing hard.

He rubbed his brows. "Will you at least promise to tell me if you're late? It kills me that I have to ask."

Late? It took her a minute to realize what he meant. Suddenly, it was too much. She covered her face and turned away.

His arms wrapped around her from behind. "I don't want it to be this way, Jillie." He pressed his cheek against her and rocked them back and forth.

"I don't either, Bri," she cried. It was like losing him all over again.

"Tell me what I can do to make things right," he whispered in a hoarse voice. "I don't want to lose you. Forget the restaurant, forget the job offer. Tell me how to make things right *with you.*"

Since she knew how important his career was to him, his entreaty moved her deeply. She gripped his arms and then untangled them, turning around. His eyes shone with unshed tears—a rare sight. "Are you sorry?"

"More than you could ever know." His gaze never left hers. She rested on the ancient shaggy green loveseat's arm.

"I...liked her a lot. Might have loved her. I don't know. It was intense. I know you don't want to hear that, but I'm not going to hold back anymore. She was different from any woman I'd ever met." He gestured with his hands as if to include Dare in his comment. "She'd trained at the Cordon Bleu. Traveled through Europe for the best ingredients. Gone truffle hunting in southwest France for fun. Knew some of the world's best chefs."

"And she was beautiful," Jill supplied, her insides shrinking like cellophane near a gas flame.

"Yes." He lifted his head. "I won't lie and say the physical attraction wasn't strong." He tugged on his fleece's zipper, his hands jumping. "It's tough to talk like this to you."

Suddenly, she split down the middle. The Jill who loved him retreated to somewhere deep inside. The other Jill, his friend, continued to listen.

"I wanted her. She was so confident in her sexuality, and despite how much guys like to brag, I wanted that confidence. I'd been with girls, but she was...a woman. I don't know how else to say it. Do you understand?"

In some remote part of her, she realized she was nodding. Inside, she wanted to scream *I can't listen to this. I can't take anymore.*

"Somehow lust and professional enjoyment cluttered my mind. She told me they were separated, and when I found out that wasn't strictly true, I let her convince me that it didn't matter. I should have broken it off. But she was miserable with him, and we were happy. We worked well together. It all got tangled up."

When he sank back into the couch, he looked about as tired as he'd been when he'd come over to her house in the first few days after his parents announced their divorce.

Best to hear it all. "Who finally told him?"

He ran his hand through his hair. "I don't know. He found out when he came back from setting up their new restaurant in Paris. That's why we weren't caught earlier. He was gone for six months."

Jill reached for the green afghan, the emotional whirlwind making her body temperature plummet.

"He fired me in front of the whole kitchen staff and told me he'd make sure I never got a job at a decent restaurant. He said his recipe box disappeared that night. There were questions by the police, but nothing stuck."

The friend in her couldn't imagine how horrible that must have been for the boy she'd grown up with. She touched his arm for a moment, but then let her hand fall away.

His right leg was restless, dancing in place. "I didn't believe Andre's reach was as broad as he'd implied, but after my tenth job query, I gave up. His accusation had made me a pariah. My whole life was a fucking mess. I decided to regroup. I could have gotten a job in some two-bit place. But when it came down to it, I needed to come home." His eyes shone brightly when he met her gaze. "I was lost, Jill."

And devastated, her heart told her. Hadn't she read that from the beginning, but had been too angry to acknowledge it?

"I wanted to put things right between you and me. You..."

He looked away, fingers clawing at his jeans. The silence made her body tighten. When he turned back, the force of him pushed her back in her seat. "You haunted me, Jill."

Her throat closed like she was being choked.

"There's always been something more between us. I was too scared before. Still am, but I'm trying." He sat up straight. "Jill, when you offered yourself to me after graduation, I wanted to take you and never stop. But the other part . . ." He let out his breath in one long *whoosh.* "After what happened with my parents, I didn't believe anything could last. Not even us. So I pushed you away and hooked up with Kelly. I thought we'd go back to being friends."

"I knew I was leaving." He stood up, tapping his thigh. "Jill, I had to make something of myself. Prove to my dad and everyone who'd ever made fun of me that I could become a successful chef. Training locally wasn't good enough. I wanted the best, and I got it. When I left, I was sure you'd forgive me, but you never talked to me again."

She'd died a little inside each time she ignored one of his calls, but it had seemed like the right thing to do at the time—the *only* thing to do.

He sat on the coffee table in front of her. "When I got to New York, I finally realized the enormity of what I'd done. I'd lost you. I'd lost the only family who'd ever really cared for me. You can't know how much I regretted that. I put everything that was left of me into becoming a successful chef, but it never made up for what I'd lost."

Her lip started to tremble as she picked up on the anguish in his voice.

"Don't you understand what I'm saying? Jill, I *never* forgot about you."

He opened his palm and extended his hand to her. As she gazed at it, something inside her opened—a shaft of hope or longing. She couldn't be sure which. She only knew she needed to grab his hand in this moment or everything between them would be lost.

So she did.

"Jill, I was trying to swim in the shallow end and build my courage up for deep water—where I knew you wanted us to be. Then, Simca came back. I didn't tell you about her because I knew you'd be disappointed. I know how upset you were when Meredith's ex cheated on her. I thought everything in New York was over. I wanted it to be."

She thought of her conversation with Simone. "But she *can* help restore your professional reputation." It took all of her strength, but she met his eyes.

"Yes, she can. And I won't lie and say it's not everything I'd hoped for professionally." The grooves around his mouth deepened. "But this isn't only about my career. It's about us, Jillie. I love you. I need you to believe that."

His earnestness finally penetrated her psyche, but all the secrets and lies were like cement shoes, anchoring her in place.

"Everything's tangled up right now, Bri. I don't know what to think."

"We'll work out the tangles together." He kissed her palm. "Just don't throw everything away, not now."

How could she explain that the girl she'd been, who'd always saw the best in him, wanted to hold his hand and never let go, but the woman in her was wary of being hurt even more? "There's a lot to consider."

He rocked in place. "Okay, tell me about the job offer."

Dread trickled up her spine. "I can't. I signed a confidentiality agreement."

His eyes narrowed. "Can't or won't?"

"I can't. Please believe me."

His body coiled like it was ready to strike. He stood. "Okay. As a show of good faith, I won't argue with you. Promise me you won't rush into this other offer, though. Give us some time to...work things out personally and see if we can revisit the idea of working together."

She bobbed her head, afraid she was held together by nothing more than a plastic spring. "Okay. I'll...call you."

His mouth tipped up. "That's supposed to be my line. You know we still need to talk about what happened the other night."

Panic clawed its way to the surface, making her want to hide. "I'm not ready yet."

He held his hands up slowly. "I understand. I wasn't exactly ready for how it would be between us either. Jill, it scared the hell out of me." He turned toward the door, so she followed him. He tugged his gloves on. "But I'm more scared of being without you, so I'll deal. Making love with you was more intense than I could ever have imagined, Jillie. I want to be with you like that again."

Every ounce of moisture drained from her mouth. God, she wanted that too. She'd barely slept in Denver, playing it over and over in her mind. "Perhaps we should get you a life preserver," she tried to joke.

He cocked his head.

"For the deep end," she filled in, fiddling with the hem of her fleece.

"Ah," he responded, so quiet it was almost an afterthought. "So...well, this is awkward. I usually know what to say to you."

She understood. A new chasm gaped between them. Years of friendship and easy camaraderie evaporated like water on sauna rocks.

"'Bye' works," she managed to say.

He stared at her for so long she wasn't sure he was going to leave. His gaze wandered over her body. Lingered on her mouth. If a man could make love to a woman with his eyes, she'd just been ravished. Her heart beat in desperate taps.

"Bye, Jillie," he uttered, his voice deep and thick.

He shut the door, leaving her with silence.

CHAPTER 20

The *Western Independent's* morning local headline—*Gambling and Restoration Planned for Pincari's Folly*—couldn't have come as a bigger surprise to Jill. Arthur Hale didn't write articles as often as he once did. These days he spent most of his time managing the paper and writing the Sunday editorial. Wasn't it her luck he'd worked his journalism magic again by uncovering a story that involved her?

She absently waved to Margie and mumbled hello to the early birds. Despite the busy-ness of the seven o'clock hour, she closed her office door for some alone time. The smoky smell of her espresso prompted an all-over shiver.

It didn't take long to read the story, which included all the details Mac had told her just the day before. Grandpa's legendary journalistic sources at work again. Did nothing get by the man? She slapped a hand to her forehead. Oh, hell. Mac might think she'd told her grandfather everything. She eyed the clock and dug into her purse for her cell. Better leave a message for Mac now and tell him she had nothing to do with this.

"Good morning, Jill," his enticing voice said after the third ring. "I imagine you've seen your grandfather's article."

"I didn't say anything, I promise." Her emotions were a roller coaster. She could feel the climb. "I only said I was in Denver for a meeting."

"I believe you, Jill. Calm down."

Her fingers uncurled from the paper, leaving them black with newsprint. "Trying."

"Your grandfather got tipped off by someone in the Gaming Commission. I suspect I know who. He and Arthur know each other. I hoped he wouldn't leak this, but now that he has, I'll have his head on a platter."

The determination in his voice made her bite her lip. "What do you want me to do?"

"I'm driving up to Dare this morning. Your grandfather moved everything up a bit, but I'll adjust."

"What do you mean?"

"I need to submit my development plans to Dare's local government today. They can review them while the Gaming Commission decides on the validity of my gambling license. The law is on my side. The decision should come in tonight, tomorrow at the latest."

Another phone rang in the background. "I was hoping to have the decision concluded before submitting my plans to Dare's Planning and Zoning office, but I can't afford to wait. I won't have this drawn out. Jill, have you made a decision yet? A yes would be music to my ears right now."

She bounced in her seat. Brian had asked her not to rush into anything. "Well, I'm feeling the pinch here. I wanted to have a little more time to think about it. Can't I tell you once we know whether the hotel's a go? After all, the position you offered me is for the hotel."

"Well, I wanted to include your role in the proposal. It cements my local approach and will make people feel more comfortable." There was an audible pause. "All right. I won't renege on the timeline we agreed upon, but I have another proposition. My PR person can't add the value you can in Dare, and I could use your help with the locals. Would you be willing to work with me on a short-term contract until the city council vote? Introduce me to the key people. Be seen in public with me? You won't believe how much that will help, and it'll give you the time you need to see if you like working with me. You could wait until the vote to give me your decision about working together on a more permanent basis."

She had no guilt saying yes to that. This hotel would be good for the town, and she would have helped make it happen even without a contract. "You're confident. I like that. Okay. Sounds perfect."

"I'll give you a higher daily rate than I proposed in the long-term contract since it won't include benefits. You can bill me for the hours you work. I know you have other demands on your time."

His understanding made her heart leap; his excitement was infectious. "Great!"

"You've made my day," he said with such enthusiasm, she could almost hear the grin in his voice. "I want your help with the city council members. There will be a public hearing. I'd also like your help with local groups like any women's societies, the Rotary Club, that sort of thing. And it would be great to get your thoughts on our PR message and whether we're making charitable donations to the right places. There's a whole bunch of checks ready to send out. We've been ready for this launch for weeks."

Her mind raced like a bicycle tire going downhill, faster and faster. He was like a tornado in action, his mental gymnastics winding her up. A hearty dose of trepidation came with her excitement. This was a whole new ballpark. Did she have what it took? She looked around her office. Let her eyes scan the Small Business of the Year Award on the wall. Two years ago, she'd been the youngest person in Dare ever to win it. Hell, yes, she could do this.

"Count me in," she responded coolly.

"I'd like you to come with me to drop the plans off at city hall. Show your support from the start. Can you do that?"

She ran her finger down her yellow and green polka dot calendar.

"Yes, I can make time."

"Fine, I'll pick you up. It'll be after three o'clock. Where will you be?"

She glanced down at her jeans and sweater. "At my house. I'll need to change."

"How about I call you when I hit Sardine Canyon?"

"Okay," she replied, mentally reshuffling her day.

"Can you get me an interview with your grandfather? I'd like to pitch my side of the story to the paper as soon as possible."

She stilled in her chair. "I need to keep the paper separate from our involvement. The Hale family is strict about neutrality."

His silence had her fiddling with her pen.

"I see. We'll work around it."

"I don't even place ads for my shop in the paper. Someone else handles it."

"Understood. I need to run. See you soon, Jill." He hung up before she could muster a goodbye.

Grabbing her purse, she decided to visit the paper. Grandpa and Mere had some explaining to do first about their *meeting* with Brian. After they'd eaten crow, she'd tell them her news about Mac. Then, she'd find Brian and clue him in.

It was going to be one hell of a morning.

CHAPTER 21

Coming to the family paper could be as social as the Welcome Wagon. Thankfully the earliness of the hour kept the chitchat to a minimum.

She cleared a path to Meredith's office in record time. Her sister's hair hung in wet locks from her morning swim with Tanner.

"You," she pointed at her sister. "With me. We're going to find Grandpa and get a few things straight."

She nearly bumped into Tanner, who appeared behind her. "Good morning, Jill." His damp hair had a slicked back look only a strong-jawed man could make attractive.

"Were you part of the Hale smackdown on Brian yesterday?"

He flicked a glance at Meredith. "I thought I'd infuse a little reason into the proceedings. The wolves were hungry."

Meredith huffed, crossing her arms over her navy jacket.

Jill's hand swept out. "Okay, then follow me. We need to get some things straight. Plus, I have news."

She headed to the paper's nucleus. Arthur Hale didn't believe in corner offices. His kingdom lay right in the thick of things. "We need to talk," she announced without preamble.

He lifted his thinning white-haired head from the stack of newspapers on his desk. He read in order of geography, from east to west. He started with *The New York Times, The Boston Globe*, and *The Washington Post* and then headed across the country, reading the *The Chicago Tribune* and *The San Francisco Chronicle*. He added in dozens of smaller markets too, topping out at fifteen to twenty papers daily.

He lowered his rimless glasses. "What crawled up your backside?"

She stepped aside to let Tanner and Meredith into the office and closed the door behind them. "You did. You all did."

"That's no way to greet your grandfather."

She crossed her arms. "Tough. Imagine my surprise when Brian told me you and Mere confronted him like some mob family. Why didn't you talk to me first?"

Her hand pressed against her pounding heart. Damn, she hated confrontations. Facing down family was more painful than getting your tongue stuck to a flag-pole in the winter.

Meredith came over. "I'm sorry. We—"

"We knew exactly what we were doing," Arthur interrupted, standing up, his ancient chair squeaking. "We love you. It's our job to watch out for you. When that French tart made a scene at your shop, you'd better believe I checked up on her. Imagine our surprise when we read that her husband accused Brian—someone you've been talking about starting a business with—of theft." He tapped his cane on the floor like a circus master introducing the main event. "Then you went to Denver out of the blue. We were worried."

They'd get to that in a minute. "Why did you interfere? Brian and I need to work this out ourselves."

Meredith rubbed her arm. "We just—"

"Meddled with a capital M," she finished, her mouth twisting.

Tanner stood against the wall, completely still in that eerie way he had from working in warzones overseas.

"What about you? Did you think this was the best course of action?"

He scratched his jaw. "I'm taking the fifth."

Her grandpa patted her arm with his age-spotted hand. "We're only trying to protect you."

"I don't want that," she said, exasperated, but a little moved by the thought. "It's my life."

"Fiddlesticks," her grandpa said. "There are times in your life when you hear tough information and telling the person directly isn't the best approach." He fluffed himself up like a Thanksgiving turkey. "Listen to the voice of wisdom."

She rolled her eyes.

Tanner cocked his head to the side. "Jill, Mere and Arthur looked Simone Moreau up because it's what they do. When they discovered Brian's...challenges, they faced the classic dilemma. Do you tell or ignore it? They chose a third way. They told Brian they were going to leave it up to him to tell you, or they would."

"You hurt me," she finally uttered.

Mere and her grandpa crowded close, making a circle. "I'm sorry," they both said in unison, hugging her like a barrel of monkeys.

"Jill, you said you had news," Tanner reminded her, moving the conversation along with his usual finesse.

She cocked a hip. "Don't I get a hug?"

His mouth tipped up, but he didn't move. "You trying to meet a quota?"

Her grandpa gave a sputtering laugh when she stuck her tongue out.

She stepped back to get some space. "You know the article you printed this morning about Mac Maven?"

Her grandpa's face drew in—eyes narrowing, mouth pinching. "What about it?"

She took a breath. "He was the reason I drove to Denver. He offered me a job with the hotel if it passes the city council."

Meredith's mouth gaped.

Her grandpa brought his cane down. "What in the hell did he offer you? A job cutting cards wearing a slutty tutu outfit?"

"No. He wants me to be the Creative Director. Part of my job would be to draw in locals and give the place a Dare Valley feel."

"Bull pucky," her grandpa exclaimed. "He wants your name to grease the wheels with the city council." He yanked at his gray cardigan sweater. "Jill, you know we don't involve ourselves with controversial issues. We have to maintain a neutral position in the community."

She blew a raspberry. "You choose sides all the time with your editorials. Besides, I don't work here. I'm a local businesswoman and a Dare citizen."

Meredith pushed her red hair behind her ears. "But you're still a Hale. Jill, what about the restaurant talks with Brian?"

"I...don't know. He's pursuing options. So am I." Jill paced to the other side of the room.

"Probably for the best. What do you know about Maven?" Meredith asked, fiddling with her gold necklace. "He's a poker player."

And a businessman, she thought, but they hadn't met him. "You make it sound like he's some degenerate, Mermaid." She turned to her grandpa and pointed. "*You* do your homework. What's your impression of Mac, his profession aside?"

Her grandpa worried his lip. His cane tapped as he made his way back to his desk. He picked up a file, studied it, and then handed it to her. "He's driven, smart, controlled. Likes to build businesses as much as he likes to play cards. He's found a way to be successful at both. And he's a family man, which surprised me."

"Yes, he told me all that. I like him." She gazed at the file. "You're giving me your research?"

He shrugged. "Won't hurt. You need information before making your decision. Besides, I'm not saying I agree with his plans."

Meredith reached for the file. "Well, I want to read it too. I don't want him using you, Jill."

"Then take it. Why does everyone think I'm stupid all of the sudden?"

"No one's saying that, Jill," Tanner soothed. "Maven is a high roller who takes tremendous risks. He has a grand plan. We're only suggesting that you be careful. He's had time to craft every step. You haven't."

"I'm not five," she tartly responded.

"No, you're not." Arthur sat in his hallmark squeaky chair. "But you're still a woman who's been around mostly straightforward men for most of her life. Maven has layers."

And Brian had grown so many she wasn't sure she could peel them all back to see his core.

"Tanner has layers," Jill pointed out.

Her grandpa chuckled. "Yes, and he wasn't straightforward when he first came here. We had to watch him—until we knew him better."

Tanner huffed out a laugh. "Thanks a lot."

"I like your layers," Meredith admitted, taking his hand.

"Well, I'm going to work on contract with Mac until I make my decision. Help him with the city council. PR with the locals. I think his hotel is good business for Dare."

"That's your prerogative, my dear," Arthur said. "All I'm asking is that you don't take everything he says at face value."

"What does Brian think about this?" Tanner asked.

"He doesn't know yet. Now that you've outted Mac's plan, I can tell him."

Her grandpa twirled his glasses around a finger. "What does that have to do with anything?"

"Our discussions were confidential."

"Ah," he muttered softly.

That one word made her stiffen. She could almost hear the warning. Jill stomped over to the door. "Now that we've cleared this up, I have other things to do."

Tanner reached for her hand. "World peace? The end of racism?"

"Smarty."

"Since you didn't kiss me when you entered my office, the least you could do is give me one before you exit," her grandpa said, tapping his cane. "I'm an old man. My heart."

She blew out a breath. "Old, my...foot. You run circles around all of us." Still, she walked over and kissed his leathery cheek. "No one ever gets one up on you, do they?"

He grinned. "Never. That's why I'm going to be buried in a crypt above ground."

She looked into his faded blue-jean eyes, which were sparkling with mischief. "I love you, even though you're an interfering, tenacious old man."

He tapped her nose like he used to when she was a kid. "I love you too, even though you're an emotional roller coaster on wheels in desperate need of a brake valve."

Tanner and Meredith were laughing as she walked away.

Smith's Hardware store was on the way to her car. Maybe she could buy a brake valve.

***

Brian sat in his apartment with the shades drawn despite the noon hour. Mutt drooled on his bare feet, but he didn't care. He'd take a shower before he headed to the restaurant for his shift at two.

Someone pounded on the door. Brian gave Mutt a nudge and then used the Classified section of the newspaper to wipe his feet. When he opened the door, he tugged on the T-shirt he'd slept in. Swiped at his unshaved face.

Jill. He couldn't be happier to see her this soon. He hadn't expected it after last night. "Hey," he managed. "I thought—"

"Late morning?" Jill asked.

Her high-heeled boots clicked on his hardwood floor. As she leaned down to give Mutt a brisk rubdown, he eyed her getup. Instead of jeans, she was wearing a knee-length gray skirt with a dark pink wrap. She looked hot. His awareness of her increased.

"You look beautiful, but why are you dressed up and at my apartment when you're usually at the coffee shop by now?"

Her hand stopped rubbing Mutt, who immediately head butted her. She straightened. "We need to talk." She clicked over to stand in front of him.

"Great. Let's talk about the other night." He wished he'd showered and dressed. Usually he didn't care, but he wanted to look good for her.

"Not that." Jill gestured with her hands. "Did you read the paper this morning?"

Well, this was out of left field. "Yeah."

"Remember how I told you about that job?"

Right. How could he forget? Then it clicked. Brian saw the punch coming toward him in slow motion. Any hope he still had of them working together was slowly dying, of being able to stay with her in Dare and work somewhere other than The Chop House. "The new hotel, right? I thought we were going to talk first. Dammit, Jill!"

She shook her head, red curls bobbing. "Stop! I still haven't decided on the permanent offer. We don't know if the hotel will even be approved, but I think the city council would be nuts to reject it. I only agreed to help Mac until the vote. You and I can still try to work things out on the business front. I told him I wouldn't give him an answer until we know for sure whether the hotel will be approved."

Even so, he felt like she was leaving him behind. He didn't know where that left them...or him. "You move fast." Brian couldn't stand still anymore. He stalked into the kitchen and started to make more coffee.

"Grandpa's article sped things up. Mac wanted an immediate answer on his full-time offer, but I said I needed more time because I had agreed to talk with you beforehand. That's why he came up with a temporary contract. I would have helped anyway. This is good for Dare."

What she was saying made sense, but he knew her. What businessperson wouldn't want to be a part of an exciting new boutique hotel? He turned slowly and leaned back against the counter, scratching the stubble on his cheek. "Thanks for clarifying."

Her heels pounded into the tile behind him. "You're being unreasonable."

Probably, but he felt like his whole future was poised twenty feet above the earth like a high-wire act. The woman he loved didn't trust him and wasn't sure she wanted to be with him, personally or professionally. And the woman he didn't want anymore had presented him with the second chance of his dreams—but not in Dare. Then Jill had reacted to the news of his affair with Simca just as he'd expected, throwing him in a tailspin again. Now this.

His eyes tracked to the newspaper headline again. "Wait! This hotel has to have a restaurant, right? He'll need a chef. Maybe he'd hire me." Suddenly he had another option—one that would allow him to have it all. He turned and gave the beans a zoom, grinding them into exotic dust.

"Brian," she shouted over the noise, tugging on his arm.

"We could still work together," he declared when the machine stopped. No more disagreements over their different visions. And he wouldn't have to grill steaks without culinary inspiration, dying slowly inside each night.

"Brian. I already talked to Mac about that, and he knows about the stuff in New York."

His whole body stilled. It was his worst nightmare. "And?" When she lowered her head to study her boots, he knew it was bad.

"He said he won't consider you. Plus, he usually hires people with head chef experience."

The two espressos he poured looked about as dark as his future. "I see."

She waved away the cup he held out to her. "His offer gives the city council three weeks to make their vote. That should be enough time for you to consider your options. I don't think it would be fair of me to tell you not to pursue your dream job when I'm not sure I can ever trust you again."

She was slipping away, leaving him behind. He wasn't going to stand for it. He crushed his mouth to hers.

She jerked in his arms and tried to push him away, but he'd studied what made her melt. He ran his thumbs down her lower back, against her spine, and settled her firmly against him. There was no way she could miss how badly he wanted her. He changed the kiss' angle and tugged on her bottom lip. A throaty moan erupted from her, something dark and tortured. He understood. His own desire was like obsidian, formed in the deep recesses of the earth.

Brian traced her lip with his tongue, asking for entrance. When she opened, her surrender was like a drawbridge falling down after a long siege. He pressed her against the door, moving his hips in sensuous circles, taking her mouth in an even deeper kiss. He groaned when she fisted her hands in his hair and thrust her tongue against his, moving to his rhythm.

Everything in him wanted to mate. To thrust mindlessly into her, making her arch under him, swipe her nails over his back, cry out his name.

He wanted to make her his—regardless of her options and his options and the whole damned world.

"Wait," she cried.

His pulse thundered. His arousal thickened. The desire to plunder consumed him. He wanted to take her now, right against the door. His hands brushed the sides of her breasts. He eased back to fill his palms with her, the size and shape as perfect as she was in his arms. She moaned and jolted as his fingers circled her nipples through her pink wrap.

She dragged her mouth away. "This won't solve anything."

He tugged on her ear in one slow pull, wishing she wouldn't talk. When she resisted again, he feasted on her neck.

"But it's one of the reasons we need to solve it."

Her hands grabbed his and held them to her breasts for a moment.

Her head fell back. "We really need to be practical."

His hips circled against hers, communicating all the ways he wanted her. "Don't be practical, Jill."

She pushed back from the door and stepped away. "I won't have sex with you when so much is unsettled between us."

His fist slammed into his thigh. "How can I show you how I feel if you won't let us get close? How can you trust me again if you won't be with me?"

She smoothed her hair. "You know it's not that simple."

He held out his arms and approached her with caution. "When it comes to how we really feel, it *is* that simple. I love you."

Her eyes flickered for a moment before they cleared, shining with a new maturity. "You know better. Sex isn't enough. I need to trust you, and right now, I just don't."

He shrank like balled-up Saran Wrap, wondering if she ever would again.

She pointed to her chest. "I think I know what it takes to make a relationship last. Right now, I'm not sure we have it. Think about that as you consider your options."

His hands dropped. "What can I do to make you realize how much you matter to me? To get you to believe in me?"

"Other than giving me time?"

"We don't have that."

She reached for the door and turned the knob. "This isn't easy for me either. When, *if* I get my trust back in you, I want to believe I'm everything to you. No more doubts."

Opening the door, she sailed through it before he could respond. So, he had to prove himself. Well, wasn't that why he'd come back to Dare? To figure out who he was and what the hell mattered to him? He was finding answers that weren't always congruent.

Mutt paddled over, drool trailing behind him. Brian sank down and rubbed him. "Hey, Mutt, whadaya say we cook up a storm?"

Being creative in the kitchen always unleashed other inspirations. He'd clear his mind. Turn on some ESPN. Allow a solution to appear that would help Jill rebuild her faith in him.

He wasn't going down without a fight.

CHAPTER 22

leenex had become Peggy McBride's best friend. All those lines about the baby-soft, cottony texture were bullshit. Her nose's red, raw skin throbbed each time she blew. Man, she loved her kid, but he'd given her his junk. She couldn't remember feeling so sick.

"Mom! Can I go ride my bike? It's like summer outside," he yelled in one long strand of words without taking a breath.

Her neighbors might be wearing shorts, but they were nuts. It was fifty-eight degrees according to their Mickey Mouse deck thermometer. Why did people who lived in cold places wear shorts when it was still winter? Yeah, the sun was out, but the ground was covered in snow. Melting, sure. The icicles' constant dripping from her roof and their occasional crash was an ongoing musical accompaniment as she lay huddled under a blanket. Home from work. *Again.* She wanted to belt out a really dirty curse word.

She couldn't take anymore. If she didn't have a kid, she'd volunteer for a dangerous drug bust without Kevlar in the hopes that someone would put her out of her misery.

Her coughing prevented her from answering Keith.

"Come on, mom," he pleaded, dancing so his one untied shoelace skipped across the floor like a jump rope. "The sidewalks are all melted." Keith bobbed up and down. Her headache intensified. "Pu-lease."

"Tie your shoelace," she said to stop the litany.

She knew Dare's crime statistics. It was safe. Her neighborhood was the kind where other mothers watched out for your kids if you had to run an errand. The whole *Pleasantville* vibe it had going on still weirded her out.

"Come on, mom! I've *gotta* get on my bike."

Each time he jumped up and down on the hardwood floor it felt like a spike was being driven into her brain. She caved.

"Fine, but be careful. And stay on the block."

He raced off. Peggy sank onto the stairs, her chills, aches, and cough wearing her down. She thrust her ice-cold hands into an oversized black fleece. The house was a wreck. She needed to go make dinner. Could she live with the guilt of another pizza night? As she reached for her Kleenex, she realized she could. If he had to go on Dr. Phil because of two pizza nights in a row, he was not her son.

She laid her head on the stairwell, too exhausted to move. She should get up and watch him from the window, but she couldn't manage it. Her eyes grew heavy. She gave in and shut down.

Peggy awoke with a start. The clock signaled she'd been out fifteen minutes. Her whole body rebelled when she pulled herself upright and shuffled over to the window. She waited for Keith to zoom by. Her forehead fell onto the cold glass, her head too heavy to keep upright. She scanned the quiet street. No sign. The little stinker was pushing the limits, as usual. Probably racing around the other block. Kids. Why did they have so much energy? Why couldn't adults? Nature's design didn't seem fair.

She put one foot in front of the other and headed for the door. Time to go find him. Be a good mom. She shrugged on her winter gear and trekked outside. Even the warm sun on her face couldn't chase away the chills. Sunlight on snow made her squint. Damn she was too tired to go back for sunglasses.

She scanned down the street and then back. No sign. When she turned onto the next street, her heart splatted on the sidewalk like a mega-icicle. Keith lay on the ground, his distressed whimpers reaching her from a block away. Sickness faded. Adrenaline spiked. Her cop vision assessed the situation in seconds.

A strange man in a city suit was leaning over her son. Keith's green bike was lying on its side in the melting snow. A red Ferrari was parked by the curb, its door gaping wide. Rap music poured out of it.

No one drove a Ferrari in Dare.

She ran forward, child predator case files flashing through her mind. Fancy car, check. Professional clothing to build trust, check.

"Get away from my son!" she yelled. Her lungs burned. Her legs pumped faster beneath her.

"*Mommy*!" Keith cried. "Help me."

Fear crushed her heart.

"Shh. It's okay, son," the man responded.

Her fear skyrocketed as the man lifted her son into his arms in his crouched position. Was he going to make a run for it? She flashed forward with all her remaining strength.

"Let him go," she yelled in her razor sharp cop voice. "Dare Valley Police. Put the boy down. Immediately."

"If I put him down, I'll only hurt him," the man replied, still not turning around. "It's not what you think."

Terror flashed brighter. Peggy flew over the remaining sidewalk, weighing her options. She didn't have her gun. She couldn't risk putting the guy in a chokehold while he had Keith in his arms.

"Don't worry," the man called. "He fell off his bike. I think he broke his leg."

She couldn't risk taking him for his word. Smart criminals were masters of deception. Peggy grabbed a fallen stick, not breaking stride, and dug it into the man's black hair.

"Put him down, or I'll blow your brains out."

He stilled. She caught sight of Keith's tear-ravaged face. Terror lanced her all the way to her toes.

"Mommy. It hurts."

"That's not a gun, and I'm not going to hurt your son."

His voice couldn't have been calmer, which set off red flags in Peggy's brain. A normal person would be all panic and apologies right now.

"Put him down," Peggy ordered, trying to decide if a good chop to the back of the neck would knock him out. He was a big guy. Strong. Tall. Muscular. Her options were growing more limited.

"I'm not going to hurt your son, I promise, and I'd happily put him down, but his leg is broken. Do you want to cause him more pain?" he asked in that cool voice and finally turned his head.

Her mind surged with recognition. "You're Mac Maven."

"Yes," he answered like he was used to being recognized. "Since you know me, you know I'm no threat to your son. I was bringing him to you. He just told me your address."

Peggy dropped the stick and fell to her knees in front of them, huddling near a sobbing Keith. God, she could feel her own tears welling up, but she pushed them back. Her emotions zigzagged uncontrollably, the drop from terror to relief to mommy compassion a sharp descent.

"Oh, baby," she called, wiping away Keith's tears. "It's okay. Mommy's here." Her eyes took in his right leg, which was lying at an odd angle in Maven's big hand.

"There was a dog—and it ran out of the yard—I tried to miss it—and it..."

Keith's rushed, anguished explanation made her own symptoms seem like nothing. "Shh," she murmured. "It's okay. We'll take you to the hospital. Make it all better."

"I'm sorry," he cried, hiccupping between sobs.

"There's nothing to be sorry for." His good manners broke her heart. "It was an accident."

"We should get him to the emergency room," Maven said quietly.

Peggy reached for Keith. As he twisted toward her, he screamed, the sound rooting her straight into the ground.

Maven snuggled him closer, mumbling nonsensical words. "Maybe you should drive. I can hold him. The hospital isn't far, and there's no need for him to feel any worse." He rocked Keith in his arms like he knew what he was doing.

Which seemed impossible, given everything Peggy knew about him. But her gut said she could trust him.

"*Mommy*," came her son's agonized voice.

Keith's sobs made the decision for her. "Okay."

Maven stood carefully, and for the first time, she was aware of the full, devastating effect of that gorgeous face. The one that had made her body tingle from a mere picture. Flesh and blood were different. In person, he was stunning, a powerful presence that was impossible to ignore. He made her acutely aware of her red nose and unwashed hair.

When Peggy stood, her tired, achy legs returned to their cooked spaghetti texture. Balance deserted her. Maven stepped forward to stop her from teetering over, all without releasing his grip on Keith.

"Are you all right?" he asked in a gentle voice.

Now that the adrenaline was leaving her system, iciness surged through her veins. "Fine," she declared, pulling it together. She had to think of Keith.

"Good. Can you drive a shift?" His mega-expensive shoes sunk into the snow as he started toward the car.

She strode after him. "Is there enough room?"

"It's the FF model. Seats four. Don't worry. He'll be fine." His arms cradled Keith carefully as he used his natural grace to descend into the low-slung car. His murmurs and rocking melted her mother's heart.

He was nothing like she'd expected.

She turned the pumping music off and adjusted the seat so her feet could reach the pedals. Keith's crying continued, so she tried to distract him. "What an incredible car, right, Keith? You'll have to tell all your friends." She clenched her hands on the leather steering wheel, putting it into first as softly as possible.

She'd rather be gut shot than listen to her kid cry out in pain.

"You can have your friends sign your cast too," Maven added in that deep voice.

"Hurts," was Keith's only reply between sobs.

"Then Mommy will step on it," Peggy responded, zooming down the street well past the speed limit—something she never did on her personal time—marveling that a poker player was comforting her son like that.

Life certainly could throw a curve ball.

***

Forty minutes later, Peggy eyed the swarm of people in the ER who were coughing with greenish faces. They had what she had. It was a veritable germ fest. But no one looked worse than her kid, still nestled against Maven's chest.

The damn paperwork had taken too long to fill out. She wondered what happened if you showed up bleeding like a gusher. Did you still have to fill out all that crap?

"Let me see if I can't speed things up," Maven said from next to her.

She turned her head. "How?"

"I have my ways. You stay here. Anger and aggression are rolling off you—understandable—but let me try something different." He stood without jostling Keith. "Be right back."

She watched him. The abrupt woman she'd thrust the registration papers at was all smiles now, nodding like an idiot. Keith continued to cry with those terrible, racking sobs.

Maven returned. "They want us to go to X-ray. It's on the third floor."

Peggy followed him, soothing Keith. "How did you—?"

"I made her feel appreciated. Then I mentioned it might be a compound fracture."

She gasped, eyes zeroing in on her son's leg.

"It's not, but sometimes you have to stretch the truth to get what you need." In the fluorescent elevator light, he met her gaze. "Like you saying you were Dare Valley Police to protect your son. I admire your tenacity, especially since it's a crime to impersonate a police officer."

Her spine straightened. "I'm the deputy sheriff of Eagle County."

He waited for her to exit the elevator. "Still thinking I'm a threat?"

She followed the signs to X-ray. "You don't believe me," she said with utter befuddlement. Then she realized how she must look. She had on a red fleece cap she hadn't taken off because of the chills, a black North Face coat she'd gotten on sale, and a hand-knit red scarf and gloves from her mother. Add in fleece yoga pants and tennis shoes, and she had to be about as intimidating as a pissed-off parent at a PTA meeting.

"Using the stick as a gun was inspired, but I've had a gun to my head before, so I know what that feels like." His comment threw her off balance. Maven scanned her again. "We haven't been introduced. I know this is Keith. And you are?"

She reached for the red hat and stuffed it into her pocket, desperately wishing she had her badge to flash. "Hear me. *Deputy Sheriff* Peggy McBride."

"Oh." He made a muffled sound and then smiled. "Tanner McBride's sister."

"You know Tanner?"

"Only by his articles. He's a good journalist."

"We're here for an X-ray," Maven told the nurse when they arrived at the desk. "Keith McBride. We appreciate you for helping him so quickly, Miriam. He's in a lot of pain, poor guy."

Peggy watched Maven take over with ease. All the women working behind the desk had their eyes locked on him in minutes, including Miriam, whose nametag made it easy for him to butter her up. He was a natural charmer, weaving a spell on everyone with ovaries. But she didn't care if he was the devil incarnate if he helped her son. Women didn't respond well to her. She knew that. She let him work the room for Keith.

Miriam assured them it would be only a few minutes more, and Maven rocked Keith into silence once again. As her son quieted, Maven's nearness punctured her awareness. How warm his body was. She looked at the curve of the arms that held her son, the broad shoulders and chest that filled out his suit. The wet spots from Keith's tears.

As Keith slumped into Maven's arms, Peggy powered down too. The cold grabbed hold of her, making her want to lay her head against this stranger's arm and absorb his warmth.

But she didn't.

Miriam suggested a gurney, but Maven didn't want to put Keith down and hurt the leg, so they walked right into X-ray that way.

Keith clutched Maven's jacket. "Don't wanna..."

"It's okay. I'm here." Peggy grabbed her son's hand, his body so small and human against the machines all around him.

"You'll have to step outside for a minute," the tech announced. "Keith and I are going to be just fine."

Peggy wanted to sock her for such a blatant bunch of bullshit. God, she didn't want to leave him alone in this cold room, but she forced a smile. "It's going to be okay, baby. I promise. I'll be right outside. It'll only take a sec."

Maven put his hand under her elbow, and she somehow found the strength to walk out of the room with him. When the door hissed shut, she wanted to cry. Her little boy.

"So there's something I'm curious about, *Deputy Sheriff*." Maven said. "If you'd really had your gun, would you have blown my brains out?"

His thoughtful gaze met hers when she lifted her head. "In a heartbeat. No one threatens my son."

"But it's interesting you assumed the worst and ignored me when I told you he'd fallen off his bike and hurt his leg," he continued. "Do you always assume the worst about people?"

His question awakened something in her. Surprise? Defensiveness? Or fear of the truth? She didn't know, but she didn't like it. "What would you have thought if you'd come upon the same scene? Strange man, flashy suit and car, won't step away when you yell. Meanwhile, your kid's crying and not fighting back."

He made a sweeping gesture. "Flashy suit? I thought this was small-town conservative when I chose it." He leaned closer. "It was the rap music, right? The stereotypical preference of criminals."

"You're making fun of me," she observed in a flat tone. "Stop."

"I'm not. I would have reacted the same way because we have one thing in common." His hand streaked up and down her spine as if to chase away her chills. "I'm also programmed to assume the worst. You're sick, aren't you?"

His mental character assessment pushed her buttons. Then she realized he was reaching for a nearby Kleenex and handing it to her. She wanted to pull away from his hand, but the way it warmed her back was too intoxicating. "Just a cold. I'll be okay."

"I don't doubt it. Maybe you should threaten to pull a gun on your germs. They might flee from that ferocious scowl."

Was he flirting? She shivered from something other than her internal temperature. "Don't you have somewhere else to be?" Best to get him moving along.

His brows shot up.

"I don't mean to be rude, but we've taken up a lot of your time. You don't even know us."

He didn't stop that long sweep up and down her spine. "I would never dump a hurt kid."

There was something about the way he said that. She split her focus between him and the door. What was taking so long?

"You're good with kids. How does that happen with a poker player?"

When his lips twitched, making him look more playful than charming, she wanted to lean against him. He was solid. And nothing like she'd imagined.

"I have a nephew who delighted in scaring me and my sister to death with his antics." Maven looked at the door too. "Still does, come to think of it. They'll be out soon. Don't worry."

Seconds stopped ticking. Time ran like honey down the side of a bowl, unhurried and uncaring.

"Thank you," Peggy finally said. "For helping." Then her cop brain surged. "Why were you driving down our street? It's off the beaten track."

He rubbed her shoulders. "What a suspicious mind you have. I was going to see my new colleague."

Peggy pulled her gaze away from the door. "Jill Hale, right? She's a friend of mine."

His eyes flashed for a millisecond. He had a good poker face. No surprise. But she'd learned how to read people across the interrogation table. He didn't like her knowing his business.

"Yes, she's going to be helping me for a few weeks. I need to call her about this delay."

"I know you want to create a poker hotel here. I don't think it's a good idea."

His hand dropped away. "I'm sorry you feel that way. Why are you so against it?"

She stepped away, not wanting to be swayed by his nearness. "Hotels like yours bring crime. College girls hooking to pay for school. Drunken brawls. Racketeering. I'm raising my kid here. I don't want Dare to change."

When he pulled on his suit jacket and swiped at the wet spot from Keith's tears with a silk handkerchief, she felt dismissed—and a little guilty—which only pissed her off. Why should she feel bad? He was the one trying to bring gambling to town.

"I'll have my office send you the crime assessments done at my other hotels by a former police officer. I run a clean operation, *Deputy* McBride."

Gone was the man who'd held her son with gentleness and care. This man meant business.

"That's what they all say," she replied sarcastically.

He folded the handkerchief with deft hands and placed it back in his pocket, the white silk the perfect complement to his navy suit. "Ah, that suspicious nature. I don't know why I feel so compelled to convince you. But, Peggy? I mean what I say. I won't be adding any extra crime to Dare."

Her body was too tired to fight.

"Your son's finished," the tech announced when the door opened.

"Mommy," Keith called from the table. She rushed to his side.

Maven strode into the room and put a gentle hand on Keith's shoulder, leaning over him. "I need to go see a friend of your mom's. Jill Hale."

Keith's face was ashen. His little body shook with cold despite the gray hospital blanket. "Jillie? She's my friend, too."

"I'll tell her to come and see you as soon as we finish our business. How's that?"

"She could sign my cast."

Maven ruffled his hair. "I'm sure she'd love to. I'll drop by and see how you're doing. Maybe I can sign your cast too."

"Sure."

Maven bowed his head ever so slightly to her. "I'll see you later, Keith." He walked to the door. Without her son in his arms, his movements were all grace and litheness. He turned, a mocking smile on his face. "I'll see you again too, Peggy. It's been...enlightening."

The door closed behind him. The surge of aloneness caught her by surprise. She was used to handling Keith as a single mom.

It was the cold, she told herself. Her resistance was down. It couldn't be anything else.

She wouldn't let it be.

CHAPTER 23

Jill spotted Mac's sleek red Ferrari through her window. He was late, but it couldn't have been for a better cause. The way he'd helped Peggy and Keith made Jill certain she was making the right decision by working for him. He was not only a good businessman, but a good man.

When she sank into the supple leather seat of the car, her butt would have sighed if it could. Totally stoked about being in her first Ferrari, she took a deep breath to savor the moment.

His gloves curled around the leather-studded steering wheel. "Ready?"

She ran her hands down her skirt, smoothing away the wrinkles. "Ah...can I be totally honest?"

His hand poised on the gear shift. "Yes, I thought we'd covered that."

Her hands gestured in space. "The Ferrari was a mistake. The locals will think you're another transplant trying to horn in on their small town." She picked a string off her green jacket. "There's nothing we can do since people have seen you, but you might want to drive something a little...less conspicuous next time."

"That would explain the oohs and ahs I got as I left the hospital parking lot. You're right. I didn't think about it. It was such a nice day, I couldn't help myself. The roads are as clear as I could hope for in winter."

Jill eyed the shiny dashboard frame and flashy metal gadgets. "Yeah, this baby would be toast in snow."

"She fishtails like crazy but fulfills my love for speed. I won't make the mistake again."

The grim lines around his mouth made her realize he was a kindred spirit. He was mad at himself for the miscalculation. She tried to distract him with some levity.

"I thought a poker player would be more patient. I don't know. Take things slower."

"The table is different. I'm tempted to show you how fast this car can go, but that would fall under your 'flashy' category. And I've heard that word often enough today."

The bold green odometer drew her attention. "Another time perhaps. We should go. We'll be closing down city hall."

He put the car into gear. She didn't know if she was imagining it, but she'd swear the purring engine was giving her a butt massage.

"Any pointers before we head inside? I have files on the local staff, so I know the players."

"The city council won't be there, but the rank and file will be. You'll want to make friends."

The car eased around the corner. "It's what I do best."

"I believe it."

Hours later, Jill was thinking the same thing as she walked into The Chop House with Mac, waving to a few of the staff and regulars. When he'd asked her to join him for a combo celebration and strategy dinner after their successful trip to City Hall, she'd suggested the best place in town. Being seen in public together would help kick off their partnership. Dare's gossip mill twirled as brightly as a Fourth of July sparkler. She had the uncomfortable feeling of being watched as she ate her steak salad, wondering if Brian had grilled the meat. Her gaze continued to track to the back for a glimpse of him.

After their dinner, she introduced Mac to a few key customers at the restaurant and set up follow-up appointments for him. Everyone was calling him a Good Samaritan for helping Keith. He'd become a town hero. By the time they rose to leave, they'd been at the restaurant for three hours. Mac had sampled the menu with grace, complimenting the staff and asking to talk to the chef personally. Tom came out. Brian didn't.

She stopped short when Brian uncurled from the bench by the coat-check station on their way out. "Why aren't you doing your chef thing?" she asked. He was decked out in normal clothes—jeans and a black fleece—and he seemed to be suffering from a bad case of nerves.

"I didn't see your car outside, so I asked to leave early. I thought I could take you home. You must be Mac Maven. I'm Brian McConnell." He extended a hand to Mac, his mouth tight.

Mac didn't miss a beat even though there was a definite edge to Brian's voice. "Good to meet you. I enjoyed the meal. My compliments."

"Glad it worked for you." Brian crossed his arms over his chest, staring at Mac.

Jill could feel the *is mine bigger than yours* energy pass between them. Oh, for heaven's sake.

"Well, we submitted the plans," she said, hoping to keep things civil.

"Yes, I heard. Congrats. So, can I take you home?"

Clearly he wanted some time to talk to her. "Mac, why don't you go on? I'll see you tomorrow."

His hand touched her elbow. "Are you sure?"

Brian's eyes looked like they were ready to burst into flame. "I'm sure."

Mac nodded to Brian. "I'm sure I'll see you around."

Jill waited until Mac left before drilling a finger in Brian's chest. "What was that about? You weren't waiting to take me home so you could size up the guy who wouldn't consider you as a chef?"

"Nope." He held up his hands. "I have something to discuss with you.

This is too important to wait." He stepped forward, bringing their heads closer together.

Her body sizzled from the heat pouring off him. He took her hand and led her outside. She inhaled his musky scent—pine shampoo and spicy aftershave, a special hint of smoked meat knocking it out of the ballpark. "And what if I don't want to go with you?" she asked to be contrary.

He nudged a mound of ice with his hiking boots. "Then walk." Whistling, he headed to his SUV. "But I think you'll want to hear this."

He sure knew how to get her attention. She trudged after him, her interest piqued. "I might get pneumonia from walking, so I guess I'll go with you."

Opening the door for her, he caged her against the frame. "We wouldn't want you to get sick."

All their problems faded to the background, leaving only the fire between them, much like two campers caught out in a snowstorm only wanting to stay warm.

"God, I want to kiss you. Right now," he murmured, studying her mouth.

She wanted that too. So much for her *don't have sex with him again with so much unresolved* rule. Maybe a chastity belt would keep her in check.

"Let's go to your place," he said, breaking the spell. "We'll both need our wits about us for this conversation." He shut her door and came around.

When he started the car, she turned her head. "You're intentionally intriguing me."

He chuckled. "Yes, I am. Let's go home."

His use of that word made a different kind of warmth pool in her belly. The kind of warmth people sang songs about during war. *Home.*

She couldn't wait to hear what he had to say.

***

Jill pounced the minute they stepped inside her place. He should have expected it.

"Okay, what gives? You decided something, didn't you?"

He took his time, pulling off his outerwear. When he spun her around to help her out of her own, she huffed, but didn't protest. *Thank God.* He concentrated on making his mouth twist into a smile even though his heart was racing like he'd taken too much Sudafed.

"Let's go into the family room."

She sat on her insane orange couch decorated with even more brightly colored pillows. He realized there was no way he could sit still, so he remained standing.

"Okay. So, here's how I see it. You know how much I love the Broncos, right?" Watching ESPN while cooking had given him the brainstorm he'd been hoping for.

She blinked like a spotted owl. "Yeah."

He paced the room, knocking his fist into his palm like he imagined a coach would do when talking to his team. "To make the team gel, everyone goes away before the season starts, and they live together for a few weeks. I think we need to do something like that."

Her fingers tugged on an ear. "I don't think I heard you right. I work. You work. We—"

"Have some major decisions coming up. Let's start with you. You need to trust me again to see if you want to continue a relationship with me. If you can, then we're together—a couple. If this works, you might also want to re-examine the idea of opening a place together if a) the hotel doesn't pass or b) you end up not liking Mac or the work. We have three weeks until the city council vote."

She held up her hand, but he shook his head. "In a sec. Now, there's me. I need to know whether or not we're going to be together. Jill, I have to be honest here. I love you, but if you can't trust me and don't want to be with me, I can't stay here. If that ends up being the case, I would take Simca up on her offer."

Jill clutched a green pillow, her knuckles white, but said nothing.

His mouth felt as dry as day-old toast at the thought of leaving. God, he didn't even want to consider it. His idea had to work. "But if we decide we *can* be together at the end of this timeline I'm suggesting, and the hotel doesn't work, I want us to explore the idea of the restaurant again. If we're together and you decide to take Mac's offer, I'll figure out something else here in Dare. I'm willing to do that to be with you."

Her elbow dropped onto her knee as her hand cupped her temple. "Can I—"

"Not yet." He had to get out the most important part. His hands fisted at his side. "I haven't forgotten you telling me that I have to make the decision to stay for you and not a potential baby. Forgive me for being direct, but as much as I've been trying to tell myself it was only one time, I can't stop thinking about what you said and what might happen if you're pregnant." A headache spread to the base of his skull. "And you need to believe I love you and would stay for you *before* we find out."

Her long red curls caressed her arm as she curled forward.

"Do you see what I'm saying? We have to give this our full attention. Spend more time together. See if we can make things work. Make everything gel."

Her head lifted. Her green eyes were glassy. "Like the Broncos," she said dryly. "Why does it always go back to football? Never mind. Okay, I see your point. How long?"

Well, she hadn't said no yet. His shoulder lifted. "We move in together now. I can come here since you're more of a nester than I am. I'll have to bring Mutt, of course. We'll see how it goes. By the time of the city council vote, we'll both know what we need." He shoved his hands in his pockets and rocked on his heels, gazing at her with a hopeful heart. "So what do you think?"

A high-pitch laugh bubbled out. "I'm...speechless."

He sat on the coffee table in front of her and held her hands, panic bubbling up inside. "I need you to believe I love you with all these *things* coming up. This was...the best I could come up with." He didn't care what she thought. Football held the answers to most of life's questions.

Red spots rose up on her neck. "The best?" she repeated.

A frustrated sigh escaped him. "Well, I could hire some pilot to fly a banner with *Brian Loves Jill* on it, but I'm not sure that would get through your thick skull." So much for holding his frustration at bay.

She rolled her beautiful eyes at him. "You're a regular romantic."

He squeezed her hands, yanking her gaze back to his. "I will be if you'll let me move in with you. We'll call a truce. No talk about the future or the restaurant stuff. Let's just be together."

When she glanced away, he had to force his hands not to squeeze hers to death.

The scarlet dots spread to her face. "And this living together would include *everything?*"

Her embarrassment reminded him—they'd only made love once, and it hadn't ended well. Being in a sexual relationship was new to her. He needed to remember that. "I want to show you how good it can be between us, Jill."

She swallowed, making the red splotches bounce. "Well, when you finally go for it, there's no holding you back. Should I call you John Elway?"

A smile tickled the corner of his mouth. "You're the same way. We're both passionate people, Jill. That's why we're so good together."

She leaned forward. So did he. His forehead brushed hers as they both looked down.

"We'll probably argue about how to load the dishwasher."

Since he could feel her weakening, he pressed his advantage. "Consider it foreplay."

Jill pulled back and narrowed her eyes. "You'll have to do better than that if you're going to get me to agree to this crazy-ass plan. What will my family think? Heck, what will the town think? You might feel untouchable after living in NYC, but this is still Dare."

"I'm not untouchable. I know people will talk. As for your family, you have to decide how you feel about that. I'm giving you my best idea here. Do you have a better one?"

"No, I don't, but Brian—"

He put his finger to her lips. "No buts. Truce only. We deal with the present. We don't talk about anything else."

"Okay, but we can't keep the world out forever." Her green eyes flamed like basil in sunlight.

He leaned in to kiss the side of her mouth. "Jill, this is huge. Living together. Day in, day out."

"Doesn't that scare you?"

Nuzzling her cheek with his own, he pressed his lips to her ear. "Like nothing I've ever done. Not even rock climbing up that waterfall in Pine Canyon in winter."

"That was by far the stupidest thing you have *ever* done. If you'd died, you would have made the Darwin Awards."

His shoulder hitched up. "It's not the stupidest thing I've done, but I try to learn." The mistakes he'd made with her flashed through his mind.

When she met his eyes, he knew she was thinking about it too. "Yes, it's important to learn."

She didn't move away when he kissed her. He sank into her mouth, so hot and inviting. His tongue traced hers, but he pulled back before it could become too intense. He wanted their second time to be special. Romance. Anticipation. Ambience. She deserved it.

"So, can I move some things in tomorrow?" he asked.

"Okay, but this had better work." Her smile flashed and then faded, like her nerves had gotten the better of her.

He kissed her forehead. "It will, Jill." The words *trust me* didn't cross his lips although he was thinking them. "Will you let me make dinner for you tomorrow night? Something special?"

A thousand hopes fired in her green eyes. "I'd love that."

They walked to the door together. He put his coat on while she fiddled with her gold bracelets.

"I'm going crazy. First it's one thing. Then it's another. I'm struggling to keep up."

Good. It was nice to know he wasn't the only one off balance, although he felt more centered now than he had in weeks. "That's the pot calling the kettle black. Speaking of kettles," he murmured in a husky tone. "Be ready to be stirred within an inch of your life tomorrow."

"I don't usually think of kettles being stirred," she whispered.

"They are in my kitchen."

Her sharp intake of breath told him everything he needed to know. He walked down the sidewalk. Her comment about them fighting over the dishwasher came to mind, making him grin.

They were going to burn the house down if they didn't argue over how to set the fire first.

CHAPTER 24

Peggy crawled off the couch when she heard the knock. Please, God, let it be Tanner. Her cold had taken up residence in her lungs, which had meant another day at home. Keith was there with her; the poor kid's leg was hurting too badly for him to go to school.

What a pair they were. Last night, she'd held Keith while he cried, struggling not to cough all over him. Dickens couldn't have scripted a sadder scene.

Even pulling the door open took effort. When she saw Mac Maven on her front step, she thought she had finally gone crazy. Was her fever causing hallucinations?

"You look as though you've had a tough night. I brought the patient something to cheer him up." He jiggled the bag. "I also brought you lunch. Chicken noodle soup."

Surprise made her back up.

He wiped his shoes before coming inside. "Where are you holed up?"

"Living room."

He took her arm like some candy striper, minus the pink and peppiness. Her whole head was a mass of pain, congestion, and fuzziness. His presence made it wobble. Why was he here?

Keith rolled over on the floor, taking his eyes off the endless parade of Disney movies she'd stuck in the DVD player to keep his mind off his leg.

"Hi, Keith," Maven said as he led her to the couch. "I brought you something. There's this great rule. When you go to the hospital, people bring you presents. I didn't think you'd like flowers."

The fire engine wrapping paper made Keith's eyes widen. "Nah, they're for girls."

Maven sat down beside her son on the floor. The contrast between his navy blazer and slacks and Keith's Spiderman pajamas couldn't have been more striking.

"I like the color of the cast. Blue's my favorite color. How does it feel?"

"Hurts. I couldn't sleep."

Maven ruffled his hair. "I bet, but it will get better. Before you know it, you'll be riding your bike again. Why don't you open your gift? I thought it would be a good accessory for when you get back on your bike."

He tore off the paper. His breath rushed out. "Man, this is so cool!

Mom, look!"

It was the most excited she'd seen him in a week. God, she must be an exhausted, germ-infested wreck because tears welled up. She used her last strength to get a grip.

"I see."

"A Woody bike helmet. I love *Toy Story!* This is the best-est present ever."

Keith couldn't open the box, so Maven drew out a Swiss army knife and cut the tape.

"How did you know I like him?" Keith stroked the shiny helmet.

Woody's face grinned, his wide eyes reminding her of insane asylum residents. Man, animators produced some weird stuff.

"Lucky guess," Maven commented as he rose. "Besides, I thought you might like to pretend you have a law enforcement job like your mom."

Peggy couldn't take her eyes away from Maven as he came closer and sat on the couch.

"You look stunned," he murmured so Keith couldn't hear. "Did you think I'd bring him poker chips?"

Since she'd been less than nice to him yesterday, she understood the sarcasm. "No, and I'm not assuming you bought him a bike helmet because you think I'm a bad mother. He has one," she added, wanting to defend herself. "He doesn't like to wear it. Constant battle."

Maven folded his arms. "With safety being one of your principal concerns, I expected no less. He's a kid. Helmets aren't cool. I tried to get him one that was."

"It was very nice of you," she said, her heart wringing as she watched her little boy put the helmet on before turning back to the movie.

"Of course, you may have trouble getting him to take it off so you can wash his hair."

Peggy didn't move away when his warm thigh pressed against her. She simply noticed the firm muscle beneath the immaculate crease of his pants.

"I don't care as long as he's happy."

Maven reached for her arm and helped her up. "Spoken like an overtired, concerned mother. Let's get some soup in you."

Peggy sank into the kitchen chair, watching him open cabinets until he found what he needed. The domestic movements didn't diminish his manliness. With its strong cheekbones and square jaw, his face could have been the model for one of those fancy busts in a museum. When he placed the soup bowl in front of her, she simply curled forward. The steam was magic, warming the cheekbones she wasn't sure would ever stop throbbing.

"That bad, huh?" Maven commented from behind her. There was a sandpaper-like sound, and then his palms settled on her back. The warmth spread out like a shock wave.

"What are you, Mr. Miagi?" she asked, barely able to hold herself up.

He chuckled. "I played poker in a three-day tourney in Hong Kong a few years ago. By the second day, my cold had me playing on fumes. One of the locals was impressed with my playing. When he offered to help ease my cold symptoms so I could finish the game, I let him. Desperation makes you open to new experiences. Seemed a bit odd when he put his hands on my chest, but it worked. I won the entire pot ten hours later. I didn't think you'd appreciate me putting my hands on your chest, so this will have to do." His hands were still on her back.

"You thought right." Although she could imagine it—barely.

"Of course, I can't guarantee this will work, but there's something about energy medicine and the body. Like reiki. It's all the rage."

She blew on the soup to increase the steam. "Where'd you hear that?"

"I like to read. Plus, I was curious after that guy made me feel better. When I get curious, I find out stuff."

She became aware of Keith singing along with the movie he was watching. Was that *Kill the Beast* again? Whatever Maven was, he'd worked a miracle by taking her son's mind off the pain, something she'd been too sick to accomplish.

Her hands reached for the spoon blindly. When she took the first taste, she almost purred. Her throat might be the size of a straw, but the hot soup was as soothing as butter on a burn.

"Better?"

"Yes," she answered, a noodle pirouetting off her spoon and back into the bowl.

"Good." His hands rubbed her back, once, twice, before falling away.

The chair scraped as he sat down opposite her.

"Why are you here?" she asked between spoonfuls.

"I wanted to check on Keith. Plus, I'm more than a little interested by you. It's been a while since I've met someone who intrigues and challenges me like you do."

Right, he was a curious sort of guy. She'd have to remember that.

"Plus, when I get involved in something, I like to see it through."

"Me too," she agreed, realizing she'd eaten all the soup.

"You should put a pot on the stove. Steam your face."

How did he know these things? It made him seem like a normal person and not some jet-setting poker player. Then she remembered what he'd said about a sister and a nephew.

"I will. My brother's coming over to be with Keith again."

He took the bowl to the sink. "It's hard for you to ask for help."

Jeez, how did he know these things? The hot tea he put in front of her warmed her hands. But it did nothing to thaw her feelings about his plans for Dare. "I won't change my mind about the hotel."

"I'd be disappointed if you did so suddenly, but I am hoping you change your mind about it—and me."

The interest in his gaze couldn't be missed when she looked back. "You must be crazy. I look like shit."

He gave her a smile as warm as the tea. "I'm good at seeing the possibilities in a hand." When he rose, he smoothed a hand down her hair.

"And I'm looking forward to seeing you when you've brushed your hair. I'll leave you now."

"I'm sick," she explained, wishing she had a hoodie sweatshirt on so she could flip it over her wild hair.

"You won't always be." He leaned down until their heads were close together.

"Everyone's calling you a hero for helping Keith yesterday," she said, testing him.

"I did what anyone else would. Get better. I'll see you soon."

As he said his goodbyes, Keith made him sign his cast. The signature was as bold as the man. Maven winked as he passed her on his way out the door. She could only marvel at the change in the room. Keith was happier. And she didn't feel like she'd swallowed a block of ice.

Things were getting weirder and weirder. Part of her couldn't wait to get better. She'd show him.

Brush her hair, indeed.

CHAPTER 25

*M*aking Jill a fancy meal would be the perfect way to start their *we're living together* agreement. He'd arranged for someone at work to swap shifts with him. He wanted to romance her, and then he wanted to make her moan.

He studied the perfect beige color of the mushroom veloute soup, hoping she'd like it. The mushrooms' earthy smell blended perfectly with the fresh dill saturating his kitchen. Good soup needed to simmer so that all the ingredients came together. He'd take it to Jill's later and finish it off with heavy cream. The Spanish chorizo and French bread he'd made would be the perfect accompaniment.

Someone knocked on the door, and he set the bamboo spoon aside to answer it. Mutt trailed after him, dragging his slobbery blanket. Time to face the music and trust his decision. He squared his shoulders and turned the knob.

Simca gave him a warm smile, her blouse buttoned this time—so far. "I got your message." She breezed inside, her crimson pashmina shawl trailing like a matador's cape.

"I've done some thinking, Sim." He took a deep breath. "I need a little longer to make a decision about the restaurant."

She made a moue with her red-painted mouth. "Ah. The new hotel has changed things, no? I wondered."

The unfairness of his situation smarted all over again. He hadn't expected to be denied possible employment in Dare. It was just another reminder he was damaged goods professionally.

"No, he won't hire me," he said. "He heard about what happened in New York." He went into the kitchen and made them espressos. "That's beside the point, though. Jill and I are together now. Moving to New York would mean leaving her. I'm sorry to ask for more time, but it's a big decision."

Her diamond necklace flashed when she caressed her throat. "I am sorry he won't consider hiring you." She took the espresso he handed her, sipped, and sighed. "Even so, the hotel adds all sorts of possibilities. What if I were willing to open a place here with you? This new hotel's guests can't eat on-site the whole time they're there. I want to work with you, Brian. Help you restart your career. We don't have to go to New York. It won't have the same cache, but Aspen and Breckenridge have made it work. We will make people come to us."

He placed his coffee on the countertop carefully so it wouldn't spill. "Are you serious?"

She shrugged. "I could stay here for maybe two, three years. Ensure it's established. Then I would turn it over to you."

A place here. Of his own. Near Jill. "Tell me you're joking."

She shook her head, making her honey-blond hair sway like willow branches. "I told you how badly I want to make amends. Plus, this little town has its charm. I'm finding it rather nice to be away from New York's high-pressured culinary scene."

He had gotten so used to fighting for everything lately, it felt incredible to have this offer fall into his lap. "I don't know what to say." His heart pounded. "You do realize that even if you stay, I still plan to be with Jill."

"But of course. Now say yes." She laughed, caressing her fur-clad purse. "Or at least that you'll think about it."

His jaw locked. God, how he wanted to say yes on the spot. Then he thought of Jill. How would she feel about him going into business with his ex-lover in Dare?

Not good, he expected.

And they'd agreed to see if they could 'gel.' His idea.

"I can almost see it," she continued. "We'll create an innovative menu that bridges the East Coast with the West, combining elegance with rugged individualism."

His mouth watered. "It's an incredible vision."

She lifted her chin in that playful way of hers and cocked her head. He had a flashback to a time when he would have kissed her on the spot. "And I've only just started."

He picked up his cup and took a sip, realizing that working with her would be a minefield of complications. But the magic? The way they saw and created food? Well, the temptation to give it a go and deal with the complications called to his soul.

"Like I said before, I'll need some time to think about it. Would you be willing to wait until the city council vote on the new hotel? My...life is tied to it." That was all he was going to say.

"I understand. I've heard Jill is temporarily working with the owner." She set her cup aside. "I don't have to get back to New York right away. You'll have your own thoughts about the menu, of course. I can already see the food review on the restaurant. We'll show Andre. No one puts us down."

He led her out and didn't stop her when she kissed him on both cheeks. "This is our chance, *chérie*."

When she left, he sank onto the couch. Could he really have it all? If he could win back Jill's trust, would she be okay with him going into business with Simca?

Mutt head-butted his leg. A bitter laugh sputtered out. It was easier to imagine Jill smacking him than accepting that option with open arms.

***

No amount of working with Mac could keep Brian's imminent move out of Jill's head. Thoughts of them being *together* tantalized her. But she persevered, planning with Mac like a woman possessed.

Since his office wasn't ready yet due to the accelerated timetable, they used her coffee shop as their headquarters. From time to time Margie would rap on her office door to announce a local VIP's presence, and Jill would introduce him or her to Mac. He shook hands and smiled, selling his vision like a true politician but without the creepy fakeness. The guy was a natural marketer and knew how to make people feel like they were the only thing in the world that mattered. She'd only changed a few items in his spiel.

She made calls, inviting various people to lunch or dinner. The city council meeting was in less than three weeks. The vote took front and center.

Tanner strolled through the door, interrupting her thoughts. "Hi there," he said, pulling off his gloves. "I was hoping to meet the man that came to my nephew's rescue and survived my sister pulling a fake gun on him. I'm Tanner McBride."

Mac rose in one smooth line like he'd been doing for the past hour, meeting everyone from locals to graduate school professors with apparent ease.

"Mac Maven. Good to meet you. I've read your articles. Please, join us. I was happy I could help your sister and nephew."

"You have my deepest thanks."

The men shook hands. Firm grip. Brief clasp. Jill liked watching the testosterone clench. Handshakes told a lot about people. Here were two self-assured males.

Tanner leaned down and kissed her cheek. "Hi, Jill."

"Finally getting around to me, are you? We're only related."

He squeezed her shoulder and then took a seat beside them. "We've had more people than usual visiting *The Independent* today. Lots of chatter about the hotel development you're proposing, Mac."

"Good chatter or bad chatter?" Jill asked, tucking her leg under her.

As Tanner shrugged out of his jacket, he lifted a shoulder. "Some of both, as you'd expect. People have been impressed with what they've been hearing, and Jill's support has been commented on so much her grandfather is thinking about disowning her for the next few weeks to protect the paper's appearance of neutrality."

"Great," Jill muttered. "I'm being disowned."

"I'll have to pay you more," Mac mused.

Tanner chuckled and reached for Jill's paper coffee cup. "Arthur's old fashioned when it comes to objective journalism."

"Jill, would you mind giving me some time with Tanner?" Mac asked. "I'm a real admirer of your articles."

Tanner turned away from Jill, but not before giving her a wink.

"That's always nice to hear."

"You have an incredible ability to help people who've never been in war visualize it."

Mac had her brother-in-law's full attention, so Jill slipped out of her chair. God, she didn't want to tell him about Brian moving in with her. Heck, she didn't want to tell anyone in her family after the way they'd acted.

"I'm sure it's nothing like the real thing, but..."

Mac's voice faded as she headed for the counter. Time for dueling espresso machines, she decided. Nothing shut her mind down like the competition.

"Okay, let's see who gets the prize today," she announced as her customers crowded around to watch.

She beat Margie by five seconds. "Someone's been practicing."

"It's my life's dream to beat the boss."

"Hah!" Yanking the dish towel from around her waist, she sailed over to Mac and Tanner and took a bow.

"Pretty impressive," Mac commented. "I would never have thought of it."

"Not everyone can do pianos. The locals love it." She handed Tanner his favorite coffee, and plopped down into a chair. "Since you haven't ordered yet."

"Thank you."

He saluted her with the mug. "To dueling espressos."

The dueling reference made her think of Peggy. She would have been a kick-ass sheriff back in the Old West. She turned to Mac. "Hey, whaddaya say we go see Peggy and Keith? I've been wanting to drop in since I heard about his accident. Poor kid."

"Wonderful. I can give Peggy the statistics on crime at my hotels."

"You have crime?" Jill blurted out, making people's heads turn.

He cleared his throat. "No, compared to the major gambling hotels, we have a very low incidence of crime and zero tolerance. I'm just hoping to reassure her."

Tanner rubbed his jaw. "Peggy's impressions...won't be easily swayed."

Mac must have heard the same warning in Tanner's voice as Jill did. They both turned to stare at him.

"Anything you want to share?" Jill asked.

He rose quickly. "No, brother's privilege. Peg's opinions are her own, and I respect them."

Mac also stood and put out his hand. "I don't expect her to change her beliefs. All I want to do is make her feel better."

Tanner took it and nodded. "Good to meet you, Mac. Jill, I'll be seeing you." His hand gave her shoulder a gentle squeeze.

"Can't wait," she replied breezily. "Tell Mere and Gramps hello."

When he left, Mac sat back down and finished off his coffee. "Are you serious about going to see Peggy?"

"Yes." He might be a famous poker player, but even she could see the speculation in his eyes.

"Great. I can't think of anything I'd like to do more."

She waved at a group of newcomers. "I'll go get my purse."

Eyeing the clock in her office, she picked up the purse. In the silence, the hands ticked like an old-fashioned bomb in a Rocky and Bullwinkle cartoon.

She and Brian were going to have sex in a few hours.

He was moving in with her for almost three weeks.

She was trying to convince the town to reinstate gambling.

Could her life be any more complicated? All she wanted to do was get in her car and head out of town. She took a couple of deep breaths.

What she needed was serious mental discipline—the kind Depak Chopra talked about—to drive out any bad thoughts when they were together. Like anything related to the French Barbie doll and her perfect body and honey skin. Why did some older chick in her forties have the beauty edge? No, they had made a rule. No outside talk.

Nothing was more important than finding out if they could be together.

CHAPTER 26

Peggy McBride wished she really could cart her germs off to jail. But while bad guys bowed to her wishes, germs were immune to her threats. They knew about torture, though—oh yes, they had that down to an art. As far as she was concerned, having an electric prod shoved into her chest couldn't be as painful as this cold.

Thank God, Keith had wanted to go to school today. He was planning on showing off his bright blue cast—and his new bike helmet. She owed Mac Maven a sliver of gratitude for her son's transformation. Not that she'd tell him.

When someone knocked on the door, she wished for one of those door intercom thingies. Then she could tell whomever it was to go away because she was dying. When the person resorted to pounding, she dragged herself out of bed and staggered down the stairs, holding onto the rail in a vise-like grip.

Jill and Mac's presence at her door made her think the germ torturers had called in some back up. She was so not up for visitors.

"Are you *that* sick?" Jill asked, rushing forward and putting her hand against Peggy's forehead.

"Ouch," she replied, pushing Jill away.

"You don't seem to have gotten any better," Maven said silkily, shutting the door.

"I'm not. You should leave me to die in peace. These germs are diabolical."

Maven took her elbow. "Where's your gun? We'll threaten them."

She didn't care if he was leading her. "Done and failed. I've lost the war."

Jill circled to her other side and wrapped her arm around her waist. "You haven't lost. You just need rest. Lots of it. I told you you've been pushing yourself too hard."

Peggy all but fell on the couch in the family room. "Stop gloating."

Her friend eased against her side and patted her arm. "I'm not. I'm worried about you. You should go to the doctor."

The chills were starting again, so Peggy reached for the discarded blanket on the unvacuumed floor. Maven nudged her hands away and tucked it around her.

"I did. This morning. Sat there coughing and blowing my nose for two and a half hours, shaking from chills like everyone else. When I finally saw the doctor—for five minutes, mind you—he said it was a virus like Keith's. Nothing he could do. It's like I'm terminal or something. Pull the plug."

"Let's hope it's not that dire," Maven murmured, sitting on the couch's arm.

Being flanked by these two struck her as strange. Then she remembered Jill was working for him. The hotel. Poker. She wished she felt better. Not a single snarky comment came to mind. Damn congestion.

"How's Keith?" Jill asked.

"Better. Your helmet worked like magic," she said to Maven. "He couldn't wait to show it off at school. He's been shooting bad guys all over this house. Makes me proud."

Maven gave a throaty chuckle, somehow warming. "I'm delighted to hear it."

"What helmet?"

"Maven gave him a Woody helmet from *Toy Story*."

Jill gave an "ah," and then shifted in her seat. "The person who named that character was all about sexual innuendo. I mean, 'woody?' Tell me there's not some adult joke hidden in there. And he's packing a pistol."

"Just don't mention that to Keith," Peggy mumbled, laying her head against the back of the couch. "I know why Jill is here. Why are you?"

"I'm here to usher in more miracles," he said with a wink. "A glimmer of the direct, tough Peggy is already coming back."

He produced an envelope from his tailored navy coat jacket. She tugged at her own wrinkled shirt. Did he always have to look so presentable?

"Here's a copy of our laudable crime statistics and the security policy for our hotels. I hope they'll reassure you I won't turn Dare into some seedy town run by mobsters."

Jill had the audacity to laugh out loud. "If you do, can I have one of those fun names like Red Curls Jillie?"

Maven joined her, his throaty laughter making her head pound. "Sure, and we can name this one No Bristles Peg."

Covering her face didn't make them go away. "Stop talking about my hair."

The two of them muffled their laughing. "I'm only going to be more wowed than I already am when you finally feel well enough to brush it."

There was a moment of silence. Peggy peeked through her fingers. Jill was watching Maven like he was a puzzle. He gave her the hairy eyeball.

"*Oooh-kay,*" Jill finally said like she'd uncovered a new clue in a crime. "So, what can we do to help?"

"Maven, make yourself scarce for a minute. I want to hear how Jill's doing."

He set the envelope on the one clear space on the coffee table. There was junk everywhere, but who cared? It's not like she had a maid. He probably did. He owned a hotel, so he had a whole fleet of maids.

"Mind if I tour your house?"

"There's not much to see, but...sure."

As he moved out of the room with that easy, confident stride, Jill made a humming sound. "He likes you."

Peggy put a hand to her forehead. Her brow still felt feverish. "No, I pulled a gun on him—or a stick. He's intrigued."

"I don't think so. Why won't you call him Mac?" she asked, all innocent-like. "Maven is *very* formal, Peg."

So not going there. "Nuh-uh. Tell me about you and Brian." Even to her ears, her voice sounded terrible. Like she'd stuffed a sock puppet down her throat.

"Ah..." Her friend leaned closer to whisper. "We're...moving in together."

"That's..." She bit off her comment. The germs hadn't deleted all her good sense.

Jill's gaze darted to the door, but Maven was still out of earshot. "I know. I told Brian he has to convince me he's super into me before I make some important life decisions. And he needs to know I can trust him and be with him before he does the same."

Her head hurt when she tried to nod. "Moving in together would be convincing."

"And there's a slight chance I might be pregnant." Her screech made Peggy wince. "Oh God, why do those words make me want to scream and hide my head in the sand like I'm an ostrich?"

Oh crap. Now the haste made sense. Peggy wove a little where she was sitting, attributing it to shock and the stupid weakness. "I don't think ostriches scream."

"Who cares? I saw that French chick leaving Brian's house, and I got mad at him. Things got intense and...we...went nuts with each other. A tornado couldn't have stopped us. I know it sounds stupid now, but I was so hot for him, I told myself one time without a condom wouldn't matter. The whole thing was intense and wonderful, but things are complicated." Jill brought her up to date on Brian's affair with the French chick. Her words continued to rush out faster than water from a hose. "So, when Brian popped the craziest idea on the planet, I agreed."

When she smacked herself on the forehead, Peggy's face contorted. That had to hurt.

Jill told her the rest in greater detail. Her rampant energy drained the life out of Peggy like some vampire with a victim's life force. She slumped onto the couch, trying to assimilate the news.

The hand Jill was clenching uncurled, revealing Keith's mini race car. She dropped it to the ground. "What a mess, huh?"

"You're doing the best you can. That's all anyone can do."

"You're right. Everything will be...whatever the hell it is."

Peggy patted her hand, her vision wavering in and out.

"You really are wiped," Jill muttered. "Let's get you back in bed."

"I can't make it," she whispered. Colors swirled behind her lids. She rubbed her nose when it tickled, wishing she had a blanket.

A warm hand settled on her back. Her body immediately recognized the heat and size of it. Maven. Let him do that magic thingee. When he rolled her into his solid frame, she moaned.

"Leave me," she protested.

"No way."

He lifted her into his arms like she was weightless. She cracked her eyes open a fraction to see his face. He was staring down at her, his handsome face softened with gentleness. His stoplight green eyes pierced her soul. She let them close again. She didn't want anyone to see into her soul.

Still he was warm, hot actually, his body like the heat vent she'd stood over in the kitchen when the microwave was nuking her soup. Part of her wanted to crawl inside him to ward off the chills.

"It's okay, Peggy. We'll get you to bed."

Jill's voice sounded close by. Good, she wasn't alone with Maven.

"When does Keith need to be picked up?" Jill asked.

Her head lolled down onto a pillow when Maven put her down. "Tanner is getting him," she whispered.

"Have him stay a while so you can rest," Maven said, tucking the covers around her shoulders and sides. "Go to sleep, Peggy."

That warm hand brushed hair back from her brow. Then she was falling into a place where deep rest called her name along with another.

Mac.

The sweetness of his name rolled through her.

Her mind interrupted the warmth cushioning her heart. She had to find a way to stop him. He threatened everything she'd become.

CHAPTER 27

When Jill got home, Brian's car was parked on the street outside her house. She had to force herself to stop gripping the steering wheel. It was now or never.

She checked her face in the mirror. Smoothed her hair back. Her stomach had knotted up after seeing the French chick waltz across Main Street earlier that day, her perfect skin and body making Jill's old insecurities rise up. She wasn't as pretty as that woman, never would be. And she certainly wasn't as experienced.

When she opened the door, the smells of a new culinary parade made her wonder if she'd be able to eat tonight.

"Hi," Brian said a little too brightly.

Okay, so he was nervous too. Thank God. Then her brain signals crossed. His indolent pose in a simple gray pullover with jeans made her mouth water. He'd shaved recently, his cheeks and jaw smooth. Great, no beard burn tonight when he buried his face in her...

"Hi," she responded brightly, like a demented weather girl. She eyed the entryway. "Where's Mutt?"

"With...a friend."

His hesitation tipped her off. He didn't want to use Pete's name. Probably better.

"You hungry?"

Her stomach continued jumping up and down—and not because it wanted to eat. "Sure." And the pep-pep-pep in her voice made her want to gag. God, she'd spew cotton candy from her own mouth soon.

"Great." Then he lurched forward to kiss her. Since she was in the process of turning to hang her coat, he banged her nose instead. She fell back a few steps, pain shooting up her sinuses like someone had stuck a spike in there.

"Ow!" she howled.

"God, I'm sorry. Here, let me see."

"It's fine," she assured him, even though it wasn't.

When he reached for her face, she drew back. "Seriously, it's fine."

His eyes had a crazed expression as he let out a huge breath. "Let's try this again." He kept his gaze glued on her as he lowered his mouth to her cheek. "Hi. How was your day?"

God help her. She was on *Leave it to Beaver*.

"Great," she continued in the same over-bright voice. "How was yours?" Did people actually do this every day? No wonder they ate dinner with the TV on. Who could talk like this?

He reached for her coat and hung it up. "There's something I need to tell you before we start this."

His tapping foot drew her attention. Dread, dread, and double dread rolled over her like a tropical typhoon. She held up her hands. "Is it about the future?"

His head nodded like some bobble head on a car dashboard. "Ah, sorta."

"Is it something I won't like?"

"Maybe... no...probably," he replied, crossing his arms, his whole body tense.

"That's clear." She blew past him into her family room. Her heart started pounding like bongo drums as she cleaned up the crap on her purple coffee table. "I don't want to hear it."

He grabbed her hands to stop her from picking up her zebra coaster. She straightened. The sheer dread in his expression intensified.

"You *promised* this would be the Jill and Brian Bubble," she said.

When he released her hands, he took the coasters and stacked them. Sitting down, he patted the place on the couch beside him. "Maybe we should make an exception to that rule this one time. A new option opened up for me. One in Dare."

"Good for you. But seriously." Instead of sitting, she paced the narrow space by her coffee table. "We either have the rule, or we don't."

Brian put his head in his hands. "You're putting me in a position here."

All she could think about was *the position* they were supposed to get into tonight. How in the hell was she supposed to give herself to him if there were any more known obstacles? Like Siren Simca wasn't enough. "Right now I think we should just get it on. I can't stand drawing this out." She pulled off her wrap, revealing the silky tee underneath.

Brian lurched off the couch. His hands stopped her from tearing off more clothes.

"Wait," he cried. "Just wait one damn minute. This is exactly what happened the first time."

She struggled. "Worked for me, aside from the missing protection. I think we'll manage to work that in this go-round."

"Jill, can't you even look at me?" He angled his head in toward hers and caressed her cheek with his nose. "How are we supposed to make love if you can't even do that?"

"I don't know," she answered, inhaling a whiff of his cologne. "It's harder this time." *I keep comparing myself to your ex, dammit.*

"It certainly is," he drawled, shifting his hips against her.

Her gaze flew to his. His mouth quirked up. "That got your attention."

So, he was turned on. Funny, how she wasn't even close. She punched him in the arm. "That's not what I meant."

"I know. You want to be swept away. Have all that hot, sweaty desire make the decision for you. We already did that. Last night you said you thought we needed to make an intentional decision. What happened?"

"Reality! Now I understand why people have sex in the back seat of a car." They weren't thinking about ex-whatevers when they did that, she'd bet.

He snorted out a laugh. "We'll have to try that later. I made you dinner. We'll eat. Relax. Take our time. I want to treat you right, okay?" Then he pulled her into the kitchen with him before she could argue.

A large pot coughed out steam, giving off notes of mushroom and garlic. Crusty French bread lay on a cutting board. She caught a hint of roasted meat. None of it tempted her taste buds.

He pushed her into a chair and headed to the stove. The table looked as romantic as it had for their aborted dinner days ago. Bright pink daisies made her think of Jemma. Brian probably wouldn't know it had been her favorite flower, but Jill did. So did Pete. Thinking about their old friendship was more than she could bear.

"What were you planning before, when you decided you were ready to make love with me?"

Not having images of your ex in my head, for starters. She took her gaze from the table. Brian was leaning against the counter, a yellow hand towel tucked in his jeans, looking very much at home.

"That seems eons ago."

His mouth flattened. "Doesn't make my question any less relevant."

She played with an artfully arranged blue napkin and its silver ring. "New lingerie, aromatherapy candles. Music." Her cheeks flushed with heat.

Walking toward her with a spoon, he gave her a smile that punched through to her heart. "You weren't going to put on something like *Let's Get It On* by Marvin Gay, were you?" He tipped her chin up. "No smile yet? Okay, how about *Just Shut Up, Shut Up* by the Black-eyed Peas?"

She narrowed her eyes. He was laughing at her!

"No? What about Lady Gaga, *Show Me Your Teeth?*"

Even a dentist couldn't get turned on with that image. She shook her head.

"Billy Ocean?"

Crossing into 80s land was the limit. She threw her napkin at him. "Oh, for cripes sake. Would you let it go?"

"No." His arms tightened. "Tell me what's wrong with taking it slow tonight."

Her emotions popped like a champagne cork. "This!" she cried, arm sweeping across the room. "It's all a bunch of props to make me feel more secure when the truth is I'm scared shitless." She could admit that at least.

He pulled the chair out, but angled it close to her. His hands gripped hers. "Do you think you're the only one who's scared here, Jill?"

"I wish we were in some Victorian movie where the wife gets under the covers and her husband joins her, lifts their nightshirts, and just does it."

"While she's thinking about merry ol' England?" He dropped her hands, cupped her cheek. "Jill, you don't want that. You forget. I remember how you were when we made love the first time."

"That was insanity. I wasn't thinking. I—"

"Exactly, which is why this whole thing is spinning out of control. We need to relax and savor each other."

Okay, now she was getting hot. Those blue eyes of his always knocked her back. There was no way he was even remotely thinking of Simca, looking at her like that. It was time to tell him the truth. The only way they could move forward was if they were honest with each other.

"I'm afraid I'm going to disappoint you." She looked down, pulling at the wool fibers of his V-neck sweater. "I can't stop thinking about your ex."

"Stop it," Brian ordered, pulling her into his arms, rocking them back and forth. "I don't want you to think about her." He angled her back so that they were looking in each other's eyes. "Do you have any idea what I see when I look at you? I see fiery red hair that reminds me of the aspens in autumn, white skin like whipped cream, legs that go on for miles, and those eyes. They see right through me, Jill. Every time." His soft gaze melted her heart. "You're beautiful."

Her throat thickened like the soup on the stove. "Thanks."

He drew back, raised her hand to his mouth and kissed it. "We're going to be fine, Jillie. Better than fine." Then he smiled with total urbane smoothness. "Didn't I promise to stir you within an inch of your life?"

The warmth rose to a bubbling boil. Her insides clenched, and she settled her body closer to his. "Yes, you did."

He pulled a wooden spoon out of his back pocket. "It's bamboo, so it won't give you a splinter. I plan on running this all over your body tonight. Jill, I'm going to make you cry out my name until you're too hoarse to speak."

Her breath rushed out. Shock, excitement, and lust all converged into a fiery ball in her stomach.

The spoon ran down her neck in a slow, teasing gesture. "I've been dreaming about you for over a decade. I have a lot of ideas stored up."

When had she ever thought bamboo was boring? She was going to plant acres of it—somewhere. And make more spoons. All sizes. She clasped her hands around his neck. "That many years? Weren't you a child prodigy?"

"I also brought something I think you'll like."

When he stepped away, a sliver of panic resurfaced. He wasn't into anything kinky, was he? She didn't think she could pull that off tonight, if ever.

Since he was opening the fridge, it couldn't be that bad, could it? He held out a fancy bottle. "It's a Belgian beer, corked like champagne. Very unique. Like you."

As he reached into her cupboards and pulled out some beer mugs, he gave her a smile—the one she'd missed all those years he was away. "Light the candles, Jill. Let's make this a night to remember."

CHAPTER 28

The minute Jill walked out of the kitchen, Brian opened the freezer. He stuck his whole head inside, letting the arctic blast settle around him like fog. Damn, he needed a walk-in cooler right now. His head wasn't the part of him that needed the frigid blast.

He had to get a grip. She was skittish. That was understandable, but Christ, how was he supposed to make her scream his name when he could barely walk around the kitchen without wincing? It was *harder* than last time, she'd said.

She had no idea.

He waited until his eyelids stopped twitching before stepping back. Take it slow. Make her relax. Hell, make him relax. At this point, he was starting to worry whether she'd get hot enough to come. Her nerves and fears were making her mouth pinch.

Tonight had to lay the foundation for the whole *can they make it* thing? He couldn't remember ever feeling this much pressure over sex. Well, maybe a little. To please. To perform. But never before had his whole future been on the line.

He ladled the soup into the bowls and carried them to the table. The sausages looked good when he opened the oven, juices bubbling out the meat when he speared them with a fork.

When she came back in, he didn't have the heart to tell her she had red splotches on her neck. He turned back to the sausages and decided they were like a bad joke. Why hadn't he picked something that didn't resemble a dick? Like pork tenderloin. Hell, even that had "loin" in it. Why hadn't he realized how sexual meat was? Legs. Breasts. Loin. Throw in shank, and you had *Lady Chatterley's Lover*.

She came up next to him. "Can I help?" Her gaze fastened on the sausages. The red spots intensified. "Do you want me to take...these...over to the table?"

Yeah, she was thinking the same thing. Hot juicy sausages. Freud said there were no accidents. His subconscious must have had a field day—he'd made enough for leftovers.

"Sure," he managed, fighting the urge to clear his throat as he slid them onto a platter. "I served up the soup."

Her hands gave a lurch, and the sausages slid a little. He reached for the platter to avert disaster. She gave a semi-hysterical laugh. "That would have been awful. Bunch of sausages rolling around on the floor."

She set the platter down with unusual precision. He grabbed the bread board and knife and sat down across from her. As he poured the beer, Jill couldn't seem to take her gaze off the sausages.

"Jill. Your beer," he said when she didn't take it.

"Right," she murmured, eyes darting away like she'd gotten caught looking at something dirty. The red spots now resembled sunbursts.

"To us," he toasted, lifting his glass.

She almost spilled her beer when she clinked his glass too hard. "The beer's good," she commented and then focused on the soup with an intensity that made him sure she was trying to avoid the hot, steaming sausages between them. The candles flickered in the awkward silence. He nudged the platter toward her, but refused to say, *you want one?* He had clearly won *Most Idiotic Entrée Choice of the Year*. It could be a new James Beard category.

She still avoided the sausages, grabbing a slice of bread like a Titanic passenger pouncing on a life preserver. Spent way more time than needed buttering it before taking a nibble. "Everything is so good."

Everything was shit. He might as well put it out there. "So, the sausages were a bad choice."

Her leaf green eyes flew to his. "Were you trying to give me some secret message?"

"Jesus," he said, taking the platter off the table. "Not consciously."

Her breath heaved out. "Good. I thought it was some sort of strange foodie foreplay."

The idiocy of the whole situation had his laughter bubbling up and over. "Foodie foreplay? Oh God, that's a good one."

Jill gave a sputter. "Yeah, I mean, I've heard about dessert, oysters, all that, but then I saw those sausages. Couldn't be any clearer. Although they did start to shrivel in their casing as they cooled. Did you notice?"

Brian kept laughing. "Jesus Christ. This is ridiculous. I couldn't even ask if you wanted one. I was too embarrassed."

When she joined him in the hysterics, he made his way back to the table.

"I felt like I was in seventh grade. Remember how we used to giggle every time Mrs. Kelly used to say 'penis' in biology?"

His shoulders shook. "It wasn't the word so much as her lisp. Pee-nith. We almost wet ourselves. Pete used to ask the dumbest questions just to make her say it. Oh, God."

"My stomach hurts from laughing this much," Jill said, wiping her eyes. "At least the bread and soup don't have any hidden messages."

Brian put his finger to his mouth. "No, I've got nothing."

"Me either. I could barely eat as it was." A violent hiccup made her eyes bulge. "Oh, no. I've got the hiccum-ups."

"The what?" Brian asked, heading for the sink.

"You better not be getting me a paper bag like...hic...Mrs. Barret used to make me use in fourth grade," she warned. "Hic-cup."

"You looked cute that way, Red." Brian came back with a glass of water. "I don't know why this is funny, but it is. First sausages. Now, hiccups. What's next?"

Jill gave another explosive hiccup and grabbed the water. "Bed bugs?"

"Jesus, we're a pair. So much for romance."

After downing the rest of the water, she clutched her stomach. "Great, now I'm going to slosh around. Please let them be...hiccup."

He pulled her onto his lap. "Let's see if we can find a new cure."

When he pressed his mouth to hers, she sank into him. Twined her arms around his neck. Tugged on his hair. Murmured something throaty against his lips.

"I like this cure," she commented when his lips cruised her neck. "Hic-cup. Shit."

"Clearly, I need to work harder."

He took her ear lobe between his teeth and tugged gently. A shuddered breath warmed his neck. "You know I always thought people were...hiccup...crazy when they said that was hot. The ear thing."

The elegant line of her neck fascinated him, so he traced it with his tongue. "You did?"

Her fingers curled into his hair. "Yep. Do that again. Hiccup. God, I'm so embarrassed. Here you are trying to seduce me, and I'm squeaking out hiccups." She gave another explosion.

Laughter rumbled through his chest. "Beats belching."

"True," she agreed, squirming in his lap.

His gaze took in the evidence of her arousal. The spots on her neck were fading. Her green eyes made the world seem brighter. "Maybe we were focusing on the wrong thing." His mouth took hers in a quick kiss. "This is us, Jill. Laughing over stupid sausage innuendos, and you sitting on my lap with the hiccups."

"But that's so...buddy-buddy."

The white skin of her jaw was too tempting. He ran kisses from one side to the next. "Is that bad?"

"No, it's just not...the hot sizzle I think we need."

Proving her wrong would be his pleasure. "Then let's get the spoon. I'll show you what's between us."

Vulnerability came through, stark and humbling, when she clutched his forearms. "Forget the props for now, Brian. Just show me."

He lifted her into his arms and headed for the bedroom. "Fine, but the candles stay lit. I want to see your skin by candlelight."

His mouth took hers again as they bumped along the hall corridor. When he reached her room, a pungent musk tickled his nose.

His whole body was ready. This woman. This scent. This lighting.

He wanted to devour her.

Nothing mattered to him more than Jill.

***

When he laid her on the bed, she fisted her hands around his neck to make sure he didn't leave.

"So, where's that lingerie?" he purred against her throat.

"In the bathroom," she replied, hoping he wouldn't ask her to go model it for him.

"I can hear your mind working," Brian said, kissing her on the mouth. "Be right back."

He darted off the bed, looking lithe and male in the soft light. Who said only women looked better by candlelight? Jill rolled to her side, waiting for him. Being flat on her back was way too weird when he wasn't on top. He strolled back in with the green silk in his hands.

"I like this," he commented, sliding back onto the bed. "So, how about I undress you, dress you with this, and then undress you again?"

"Way too complicated." She reached for his pullover. "I can wear it later."

He helped her take it off. "It won't stay on long, Jill."

His firm skin took all her attention. His muscles curved in well-defined ropes on his shoulders and arms. The pecs could have been carved in stone. She reached out a tentative hand to touch his chiseled abs.

"You're acting like you've never seen my chest before."

What did it matter if he sounded amused? "Perhaps it's because I can actually focus on it without..." She stopped short. How much to tell?

He nudged her hands out of the way and drew her shirt off. "Keep talking."

As his hands fingered her lacy pink bra, she shifted closer. "Well, when we were just friends, it was hard not to ogle you. And lately, I've been the one without the shirt on since you were trying to keep yourself under control. I haven't really seen your chest like this." She gestured to it.

"Do you like what you see?" he murmured, his thumb running along the lacy edges. "I know I do."

She laid a palm on his pec, feeling the rapid beat of his heart under her fingers. Suddenly everything became real. Something new—and old—shifted inside her. She was here with Brian, the love of her life. A new serenity emerged. Memories of how it had been with him before added to the passion she felt now.

"I love you," she murmured, needing to tell him now.

The fingers unhooking her bra stilled. His eyes flicked up to hers, allowing her to see inside him. The boy. The man. The human. The triumphs. The mistakes. The search.

Whatever else there was in the world, he was hers. And she would always be his.

He cupped her neck with one warm palm, held her eyes. "I love you too."

Emotion rolled through her. This, she thought, this was how it was meant to be.

They moved with a new ease. Nerves faded and warmth grew into heat as their mouths met and urged them toward passion.

He tugged off her bra, and when his mouth took her breasts one at a time, she arched, seeking more, giving more.

How could she have doubted herself? An inner knowing emerged inside her. Her hands knew how to caress his skin. There was no hesitation when she reached for his jeans. No embarrassment when he pressed her hand to him, jerking his hips once. His groan was symphonic to her ear. The zipper hissed its way down in the quiet room. Helping him out of the denim until he was naked made her grateful to be alive.

It seemed the most natural thing to touch him, stroke him, while his eyes watched her.

"I want to see all of you," he finally murmured, reaching for her skirt.

When they were both naked, he trailed his hands down her chest to her center, then angled down her thighs to her knees. "God," he uttered. "Look at those legs. I've been wondering about this forever. I didn't have the time to really look last time. Didn't I say you were beautiful?"

Her stomach seemed designed for his kisses. But he didn't stop there. The tops of her thighs seemed to summon him. Then the line where leg met hip. The kisses moved back up her torso to her breasts, and he continued his path until he found her mouth. She opened to him, letting their tongues tangle as he smoothed his hand over her leg, lifting it to him. Pressing belly to belly was a new sensation. She contracted, ready to spring ahead for whatever was next.

Something silky slid over her breasts. When he broke contact, she saw the green negligee in his hands.

"See how beautiful it looks against your skin. Put it on for me, Jill."

The fabric's silky slide down her body made her shiver in delight. Brian played with the fabric's edge at the tops of her thighs and then parted her legs.

"Open for me. I need to touch you."

His harsh, nearly hoarse voice made her remember how his touch had felt last time. Heat suffused her, and the gentle passes he made at her core had her back arching. Then he increased the pressure, rubbing in quick strokes before easing back to lighter caresses. Her nipples tightened, and she stretched back against the pillows, wanting more. Gave a throaty moan before opening wider to him.

"That's my girl," he whispered and parted her with his fingers.

A finger eased inside, rubbing, circling, making the heat peak. Her hips moved once, then twice as he deepened the touch. Inside. Outside. All forcing her toward something stronger and more powerful. Something she couldn't resist.

The satin hiked higher up her thighs. She opened her eyes to see his hand easing it up over her stomach. His feverish eyes met hers. He deepened his caress inside her and pressed his warm, open mouth to her belly.

Sensation took over as her eyes lids shut, her hips lifting. Need rose from her throat in one long, low moan.

"That's it," he whispered, raising the green silk above her breasts, taking one in his mouth. The pull on her breast. The beat of her blood. The caress between her legs. It was all too much. Everything seemed to contract and then spring forth. The climax hit her in one strong burst. She pulsed against his hand as he heightened her pleasure, murmuring against her skin.

She licked her lips, panting. Felt his hands leave her. Shift the green silk over her head with gentle care.

"God, you take my breath away."

The guttural note in his voice made her crack her eyes open. He shifted. A synthetic package ripped, which she realized was a condom.

"I need you, Jill."

She opened her arms. He settled against her body, took her mouth in a deep, dark kiss. Passion spiked again. His hands settled under her butt, lifting her. He penetrated her slowly.

Her head writhed back and forth on the pillow as her lids fell. His size, his heat, the movement. So slow. So deliberate. Everything fired her up again. When he sank to the hilt, she opened her eyes. Knew he was looking at her. At them. Joined.

"Move with me," he murmured and sank out and then in, letting her adjust to the motion, the penetration.

Soon she was mindless. Passion flooded her, making her lock her legs around his waist. He took over, sinking deep inside her, his thrusts powerful and consuming. Her hands slid off his sweaty back to grab his hair.

He groaned when she tugged, his body pounding into hers, opening her up even more. With a thrust she was sure pierced her wide, she peaked again, shaking against him as he lunged deep. Teeth bared, he groaned as he came, hips jerking.

When he folded onto her, his face pressed into her neck, she sank into the pleasure, awash on a wave of pink light. She drifted out to the shore she'd discovered with him before.

In her haze, she listened to his heart, his breath. Savored their connection. The beauty made her eyes tear. Hope—as fragile and precious as a soap bubble—rose within her.

He didn't move for some moments. Simply held her.

Then he rolled to his side and slid out of her. When he left the bed, she curled a hand under her cheek and reached for the sheet without opening her eyes. The pink light receded. Surely he was coming back.

His body eased against her before she knew it. His hands pulled her close and adjusted her to him. She caressed his chest. God, *finally*, was all she could think.

They'd gotten through it.

Hell, more than through it.

Up it, under it, over it...

Over the river and through the woods started playing in her head. She stopped when she got to grandmother's house. She was so not thinking about that now.

She gave a breathy sigh with a hint of sound—from now on she'd think of it as the love-me sigh.

"Happy?" he murmured, kissing the top of her head.

"Uh-huh." Real words couldn't be uttered yet. It felt incredible to float on pleasure's waves. Better than espresso in the morning after an all-nighter. Better than the first ski on the first snow of winter...

"Me too."

They stayed that way for a long time, quiet, bodies cooling. Jill continued to stroke him when the mood struck her, and he did the same for her.

She realized it was the longest they'd gone without talking in ages. It was perfect.

When she was sure her eyes could finally open without a forklift, she let them flicker on the new scene. Naked. Brian's fingers dancing across her stomach. The sheet tucked around his waist. All that golden skin calling out for her touch. Candles sputtering. She took a deep breath, inhaling musk and sweat and aromatherapy.

She wanted to raise her hands to the ceiling and belt out a *Hallelujah*, but it seemed sacrilegious. She decided she didn't care, so she settled for something else.

"Finally!"

His throaty chuckle rumbled near her ear. "Exactly." He tipped her chin up. "Do I even need to ask?"

The smile simply burst from her, seeing his mussed hair, puffy lips. "What?"

"Whether you enjoyed it?"

They looked at each other, grinning like loons. She couldn't do anything else. He couldn't seem to either. It was like they'd sniffed glue or something.

"We *so* need to do it again—just to make sure it wasn't a one-time deal."

He snorted. "What about last time?"

Shadows danced on the walls of her mind. Pleasure, yes, but more. Irresponsibility. Fear. Heartache. She shoved it all in a box, trying to stay in this perfect moment.

"That was insanity. Hot insanity," she corrected when his eyes narrowed. "This was..."

"The perfect epilogue to sausage and hiccups?"

"Don't remind me," she pouted, giving him a light punch.

"Maybe we can manage a meal now that the pressure's out of the way. I'm starving." He kissed her on the mouth and rolled out of bed.

She watched him move to her closet. God, he had a fantastic butt. Hell, the whole back of him was pretty incredible.

"Turn around," she called, starting to enjoy herself. Jillian Marie Hale had herself a lover. Hah! "I want to see if the front's as good as the back."

His laugh snorted out. "You just want to see my sausage."

She threw a pillow at him. "Well, your sausages are going to be cold. Do you want me to heat them back up for you?"

He turned around and stole her breath, completely calling her out on her own request. When he raised a brow, she smirked.

"Yep, it's as good as the back."

"I'm glad you think so." When he pulled out a navy terrycloth robe from her closet, she had a moment of disorientation. She looked closer, seeing more of his clothes next to her own. As she scanned the room, she realized there were other signs of him. A pair of boots. His wallet on her dresser. He really had moved in. It was kinda weird.

"You're not thinking about my sausage anymore," he commented, drawing her attention.

His eyes held hers as he shrugged on his robe. She could all but hear him telling her to take a minute. Get used to him being in her space. Calm down.

Clearly sex had only heightened their ability to read each other.

"So, when you reheat the sausages, do you recommend a nice hotdog bun or cutting them into itty, bitty pieces?" She made the motions with her hands.

He belted the robe. "Well, then... I'd suggest the bun."

Were they even talking about eating anymore? "Fine, then go warm them up for us." She waited for him to move. When he leaned against the wall, she narrowed her eyes.

"If you think I'm walking out of here without seeing *you* walk over here buck naked, you're crazy. I've been fantasizing about this for years."

Her belly jumped. "You truly are a sick man."

"Yep." He held out her robe. "You can have it if you come to papa."

"I'll kick you to the moon if you say that again." She fingered the sheet. "I'm not ready for this."

"I just kissed about every inch of you... Well, I might have missed a few spots I'll have to take care of later."

Her thighs contracted.

"This is part of it. Jump in the deep end, Red. Strut your stuff."

Shoulders back, she drew herself out of bed, her posture as elegant as a swan's. His gaze flicked down her body in one sweep. Plucking her robe from his hands was easy. He was almost drooling.

"Are you going to go heat those sausages or what?" she asked, belting it.

"It's already heated," he announced, pulling her back to the bed. "I'm hungry for something else, after all."

When he crushed his mouth to hers, she flung her arms out.

This was what it felt like to be ravished, to not care if you ate anything other than lust and sex for days. She was happy to be on the Sex Starvation Diet.

At last!

Jillian Marie Hale had arrived.

CHAPTER 29

Jill jerked in bed when the alarm blared *All Night Long*. God, she was tired. She reached blindly to stop the assault. Encountered flesh. Shrieked.

"Jesus," Brian muttered, shoving his pillow over his face. "You really know how to wake up in the morning."

Memories flashed through her blurry mind. Sweat, skin, tangled sheets, *the spoon*—and a relaxation even yoga couldn't equal.

They hadn't been able to keep their hands off each other. It had been like some crazed sex orgy for two minus that goat-satyr guy with the flute. Years of wanting had turned into hours of unimpeded passion and release.

Dammit, she wanted to call in sick today. If it weren't for Mac, she'd cuddle up to Brian right now, waking him up in a way she'd only dreamed about. Mouth, hands, tongue. God, she was hot already.

The sheet twisted around his waist, so she took a minute to admire him. Man, oh man, yards of tantalizing skin and muscles. And he was finally hers. She reached out a hand and ran it down his chest and then snuggled up to him, fitting herself against his body.

"Good morning," she drawled, knowing happiness was helping her wake up faster than usual.

"You chuckle snore." He slung an arm around her waist without cracking his eyes open. "Kinda cute."

"I was exhausted." God, she'd snored? Wasn't that the guy's prerogative?

His stubble scratched her when she leaned in for a long kiss. She refused to think about morning breath. They both had it. Deal with it.

"Don't go. You've barely had three hours of shut eye."

Nuzzling his neck, she firmed her shoulders so she wouldn't give into the desire to fit her skin to his. "Lots to do."

"I want to have morning sex with you," he murmured.

"You're still half asleep." Inner delight made her want to do a cartwheel. Morning sex. Yeah! Another check.

He pulled their hips together and undulated. "Not all of me."

Her insides melted, and she was pretty sure her toes curled. Her damn work ethic made her look at the clock. It would have to be a quickie. Did she really want to settle for that?

Hell, yeah. She launched herself at him.

She was sore. He was slow, all sleep-eyed and languid, his body warm and relaxed as he guided her to the peak and found his own.

She wanted to wallow in the afterglow, but she forced herself out of bed instead. She had a reputation to uphold. Mac didn't strike her as someone who liked waiting. Plus, what would she tell him? Saying she'd gotten banged until she was too sore to move didn't exactly count as an excuse.

She sang in the shower. Got ready in record time. When she cracked the door, steam billowing out, Brian wasn't in bed.

Bacon's enchanting scent drew her to the kitchen. He'd pulled on a pair of boxers and was flipping thick-slab bacon onto a paper towel. Talk about a dangerous outfit.

She wrapped her arms around his middle. "You *never* get up this early. And you're cooking for me?"

"Never say I don't treat you right," he replied, scooping the bacon inside toasted French bread from last night. He flipped a sizzling egg on top and dotted it with cheddar cheese. "Thought you might need to eat on the run."

She kissed his back again and simply savored the moment. Great sex all night. Morning sex. And now breakfast. Who said the morning after sucked? "I could get used to this."

"Yeah, I don't think either one of us is worried about this being a hardship."

"I could have picked something up at my shop."

"I know," he simply replied. "I wanted to feed you." He gave her a quick kiss. "I like feeding you. Now, you'd better get going before I decide to delay you further."

Her mouth dropped open, her gaze flying to his crotch. "Again? What are you? A machine?"

He chuckled and pointed to the door. "So it seems. Go."

"You got inspired by the left-over sausages, didn't you?" She gave him one fast kiss. Ruffled his hair for measure. "See ya later."

Wishing she could share her new sex glory, she talked to Jemma in the car on the way to work. Told her all the details like she would have shared if her friend were still alive. By the time she arrived at the coffee shop, she needed to wipe the tears from her eyes.

Her morning with Mac went like clock-work. They planned and plotted. He made calls. She made calls. They huddled. When they were a few minutes shy of heading to a meeting, Meredith walked into Don't Soy with Me.

She exchanged greetings with a few locals, but moved with purpose toward Jill. "Hey there," she called, leaning down for a hug. "You're a hard woman to track down these days."

The dig turned up guilt's clingy roots. Why did family always know how to give you the thumbscrews treatment?

"I've been busy with my new boss," she replied. "Meredith, meet Mac

Maven. Mac, this is my sister, Meredith Hale."

"It's good to meet you," Meredith said, shaking his hand. "Tanner said he enjoyed talking to you. Of course, we're all grateful for the help you gave Peggy and Keith."

"I'm just glad I was there."

"I heard both of you were over at Peggy's yesterday." Meredith's gaze simply screamed questions about that visit. "She's feeling a bit better today, and we're hoping she's on the mend. Keith is coming to our place after school. This virus has her wiped."

Jill glanced at her watch again, hoping Meredith would take the hint. "Yeah, made me want to wear one of those masks you always see in Tokyo. We have a meeting with Kim Ploy. Since it's our first lunch with a city council member, we don't want to be late."

Meredith smiled, her mouth a flat line. "I understand. This won't take long. Excuse us." She grabbed Jill's arm and all but dragged her to the back.

"Hey," Jill protested, but she knew what this was about. *The move.*

"You can go nicely or be herded."

The entire coffee shop was watching, so Jill gave a breezy wave. "Big sisters," she called out as an explanation. People laughed. Some rolled their eyes like they knew exactly why Meredith was dragging her off.

Her sister pushed her into her office and shut the door with a silky rap.

"You have some explaining to do," she said without preamble.

"Okay." Guilt made her stare at a point over Meredith's shoulder.

Her sister's hands went to her hips. "I heard from our new copy editor that she saw Brian moving things into your house. Like *boxes*. That's not a few pairs of underwear and a change of clothes, Jill. What's going on?"

At times like these, living in a small town sucked. Jill fiddled with a paperclip. "We're giving it a trial run. I'm sorry I didn't tell you. I didn't know how." Plus she knew her family wouldn't like it. Coming on the heels of the French chick's arrival, right after she and Brian had started dating, no less, and the Hales would be worried about her getting hurt. Hadn't they already called Brian out?

Meredith planted her hands on Jill's desk, leaning over. "I don't like this. Mom's already gotten some calls, and she's wondering about this sudden move. And don't even ask me what Gramps said this morning over coffee."

The paperclip twisted into modern art with the flick of Jill's fingers. "I'm sorry I didn't keep you updated."

Meredith slapped her hand down, startling Jill into dropping the metal swizzle. "I'm your sister. I'm not someone you update."

A combination of fatigue and guilt made Jill dart around the desk and pull Meredith into a hug. "You're important to me, Mermaid. You all are. I just need to handle some stuff on my own." She squeezed her hard enough to crack her ribs. "Things are complicated."

Meredith gave her own version of a bear hug. "I know you don't want us to think any less of him, Jill, but he's distancing you from our family." She pulled back. "It's a dangerous thing to start. I know. I did it with Rick-the-Dick when we got married. Is that really how you want to play it?"

Jill thought back to how Meredith hadn't come home or called as often when she'd been married to her loser ex. "It's not like that with Brian. He's not Rick-the-Dick."

"Isn't having Brian move in on the tails of his ex's arrival a little over the top? Seriously, Jill, this looks like you're going off half-cocked to try and keep him."

Jill inhaled sharply. "Are you implying I'm desperate?"

"I don't know. Your behavior kinda smacks of it. I don't trust him right now, Jill, and I'm surprised you're embracing him with open arms given everything that's come to light. That just doesn't seem smart."

Having an older sister had many benefits, but not when it involved this kind of talk. "I don't expect you to understand."

"Jill!" Meredith cried. "You've always been an open book."

She decided she could go for part of the truth. "That was before I started having sex with him."

Meredith's hands dropped from her arms. That shut her up. For a second.

"This is about more than sex." Her eyes narrowed. "I don't mean to piss you off, but don't you think that's odd? You suddenly have sex with Brian at a time like this when you were so concerned about waiting for the right moment. Now, he's already moved in with you? Gramps thinks you've lost your mind."

She didn't need a lecture. "Gramps can think what he wants. So can you. It's my life, Mere."

"Why are you fighting so hard to keep us out, Jillie?"

She was afraid of their judgment, she realized. If she and Brian didn't work out, she didn't want them to act like she'd been stupid for not taking their advice.

"Sometimes you need a little space from your family to find your way. I have things to sort out. With Brian. And the long-term job offer from Mac. A lot of things."

Meredith's face fell. "That says it all then."

"I'm sorry!"

"Me too," she said and left.

After kicking her desk until her toe hurt, Jill walked back to Mac and signaled that she was ready to leave. She watched Meredith emerge from the bathroom as they headed to the door, wiping her eyes. She'd hurt her sister. Just when their relationship had grown back into something special.

But she didn't need a lecture. She had enough on her hands.

CHAPTER 30

Jill and Brian fell into a pattern over the next few days. She took a nap when she got home so she could stay up late with him, and as soon as he got home from his shift, they tore each other's clothes off. Their hours were totally lop-sided, but their schedules didn't seem to matter.

She was sore and sated, sleep deprived and serene. Who could ask for more?

Yet the friction with Meredith still grated. And her call with her mother had gone about as well as expected. Even though she loved Brian like a son, all the rumors and revelations had made her question Jill's judgment. Plus, didn't she care about her reputation? The whole town was talking about them shacking up right after the French woman's arrival. She'd tried to defend herself and Brian, but her mother had been on a tear.

Her grandpa didn't swing by, but he called to ask if she needed anything. When she asked if he was going to give her the what-for, he said he expected Meredith and her mom had pretty much outlined his concerns. Yeah. They had.

She knew they'd done it out of love, but it still grated. And hurt.

Things with Mac clicked like clock-work. Lunches, dinners, even coffees. They were making progress, gaining more votes. The man was a genius at reading people, knowing what to say. Jill liked him more and more and thought she could easily work for him full-time.

Her mind spun out future scenarios, but none of them stuck.

Fragrant aromas of onion, garlic, and spiced meat surprised her when she swung into the door after another long day. Mutt greeted her with a drooling smile. She was glad he was back from Pete's house. Being obligated to Pete was less welcome than shower mildew when she was too lazy to clean.

"Hey, why aren't you at work?" she called out.

Hands on her hips, she waited for her favorite moment of the day—Greeting Time, as she called it. Brian appeared with a dish towel tucked in his snug, worn denims. The navy blue fleece only made his eyes brighter when they met hers. He leaned against the wall, all male nonchalance.

"I switched shifts with someone," he responded, gazing from her chocolate brown boots up to her caramel-colored wool skirt to her burgundy sweater wrap, lingering on her breasts. "I told you, we're like the

Broncos."

"Who agreed? They can have free coffee for a year."

Was he going to pounce on her or draw things out? She never quite knew what he had in mind, but since they always ended up making love, she couldn't complain.

"I'll be sure to tell him."

She toyed with her smoky quartz necklace, which had seemed an appropriate choice. She *felt* smoky lately—and pretty damn happy over how easily they shared the house together. They'd become a unit faster than she would have imagined. Flicking that to the back of her mind, she sauntered forward, but Mutt ruined it when she had to step over his fat brown and white folds. The right corner of Brian's mouth tipped up, but he didn't move.

"I was wondering when you were going to get over here," he murmured as she twined her arms around his neck.

She smoothed her fingers through the maple-colored hair at his nape and simply stared at him. "How was your day?" she asked as he pulled her against his hips. She gave a throaty moan. God, she was easy.

"Shut up." He fitted his mouth to hers, taking her on a steamy, erotic ride.

Clothes flew. Being taken in the hallway against the wall was another notch in her Position Belt. When they sank to the floor, she listened to his pounding heart. Panting, she cracked her eyes open. Mutt was breathing heavily too, his saggy eyes staring right at her.

"I'm never going to get used to having your dog watch us." She reached for her wrap, squirming.

"He's just jealous," Brian commented, tracing her back. "Besides, since you can't keep your hands off me, it's not like I can lock him away all the time. He hasn't done anything to deserve a stint in bulldog prison."

She snorted. "Did we burn the meal?"

He crossed his arms behind his head, naked and at ease on her floor. "After the other night, I always turn the burners down."

"Yeah, having the fire alarm turn on as we were getting off is not something I'd care to repeat."

He chuckled. "Thank God you don't have a security system."

The image made her grin, something she'd been doing a lot of lately. "Yeah, I can see it now. The firemen will come in brandishing their hoses, and I'll say, 'Fellas, this girl's already got all the hose she needs.'"

His shoulders shook as he sat up. "Let's eat. I'm starving."

"Me too," she said, pulling on the rest of her clothes alongside him and following him into the kitchen.

When he served the food, she jumped up and gave him a smacker. "You made Indian food!"

"Well, I know you love it, so I figured I'd give it a try." He pushed her back into her chair.

His thoughtfulness made her heart squeeze in a good way. "You're the best."

She dove into the butter chicken and squealed at the steaming naan bread. The sticky rice released a coconut fragrance, calling to mind exotic beaches.

"If you moan any more, I won't be able to keep these pants on," he finally remarked when she served herself a second helping.

"Take them off then," she ordered, waving the spoon with rice stuck to it. "This meal deserves a few good moans."

He edged the naan closer. "You've given off more than a few. It's like a chorus."

She smirked. "Don't worry. You'll get a few good moans later."

He ripped a sliver of bread. "Can't wait. So, tell me about your day."

Talking about her day wasn't the mundane recanting she'd feared. The stories could be as dull as dirt, and he would still smile. Ask questions. Laugh when she mentioned something funny. Then she would do the same for him. It was like comedy hour.

He produced a chocolate mousse for dessert—something non-Indian since they both agreed sweets with rice didn't work. She moaned some more as the hazelnuts and bittersweet chocolate hit her mouth.

After they finished eating and cleaned up the dishes, she took his hand and led him into the family room.

"Now I'm going to do something nice for you," she said, unable to contain her smile. This was going to be so much fun.

His lashes lowered, and he ran his nose along the length of her neck. "I can't wait."

She shoved him back playfully. "Not that—yet." Walking over to her stereo, she hit the play button.

Abba's classic song, "Dancing Queen," rolled out. Her hips wiggled to the beat.

He sunk back onto the couch, groaning. "Please tell me you're at least going to give me a strip tease or a lap dance."

Snorting, she grabbed his hands and tried to pull him up. Thankfully, he didn't resist, but he groaned again.

"Seriously, Jill. Abba?"

"You know how much I love them. Plus, this is how I'm going to help you."

He stared at her patiently. "By ruining my taste for music?"

Her hand punched him in the chest. "Hey, you don't like me making fun of Julia Child, so don't make fun of Abba." She looped her arms around his neck. "I got to thinking about the past."

His gorgeous eyes narrowed. "Okay..."

"Every time we went to a school dance together, you put on a horrible exhibition of White Man's No-Rhythm Syndrome. I'm here to help you overcome it."

His breath sucked in. "Are you saying I can't dance?"

She tilted her head to one side. "Yes."

"Hey, I've got moves." He pulled her to his hips and moved against her slowly.

"Yes, in the bedroom," she replied, taking a deep breath and putting more space between them. "Now we're going to translate them to the dance floor."

"No way," he said and reached for the TV remote.

Was that a red flush spreading up his neck? "Come on. Show me what you can do."

He paused. "Like now? Come on, Jill. *Please*."

Oh heavens. He was begging? "Bri, I love to dance, and you need serious help. I didn't feel it was right about intervening back then, but don't you remember Jemma trying to show you a few things?" Her smile dimmed for a moment at the thought. God, she missed her friend.

His mouth twisted. "I *thought* she was being sweet. She was trying to stop me from embarrassing myself?"

"It wasn't that bad," she said half-heartedly. Not if you called jerky hand motions and hip gyrations smooth.

"Great," he said, falling back on the couch. "If I agree you were always the better dancer, and I felt like a moron next to you, can we stop this?"

"No." She pulled him back up. "Come on, this will be fun. Plus, you get to put your hands all over me like you always wanted to at those school dances we attended. Why did you always ask me anyway? You could have gone with other girls." Hadn't she always wondered?

He lifted a shoulder. "We were a foursome, you, Jemma, Pete, and me, remember? The Four Musketeers. I wasn't going to mess with that on one of the biggest nights of the year. Plus, I liked buying you a corsage and picking you up. Seeing you all dressed up. You were always beautiful—even in that purple satin dress that I kept tripping over junior year. I guess it was my way of going out with you without changing how things were between us."

A soft glow encased her heart. "I loved that dress. Those are great memories."

His mouth tipped up. "The best."

"Okay, let's get started," she said, re-playing "Dancing Queen."

"You're going to make me listen to it again?" he asked.

"Stop whining. It's my favorite song, so you'll be hearing lots of it. Now, I want you to watch me." She closed her eyes and let her body sway to the music. Her hips wove a perfect figure eight. Her arms floated as if suspended on clouds.

"I could watch you all night," he murmured.

Her eyes flickered open. Sure enough, he was watching her with a heavily lidded expression. She knew what that look meant. Her heart rate increased. She held out her hands. "Dance with me."

He rose as smoothly as a tiger. His palms slid slowly over hers before she took his hands and settled them around her waist. She rested her own hands on the defined muscles of his shoulders. Heat poured off him. She took another step closer, so that there was barely a hairsbreadth between them.

"Move with me," she said.

"Oh, I plan to," he responded, his tone wicked.

And yet, even as she tried to fall under the spell of the music, she could feel the uncertainty in him.

"Stop fighting it," she counseled.

"Stop leading," he fired back, jerking his hips against hers.

She angled her head back and cupped his face. His stubble shot fire through her fingertips and up her arms. "Close your eyes."

He rolled his.

"Hey!" she said, wanting this for them, another connection, another thing for them to enjoy together. "I said close your eyes."

This time he did, but his mouth tipped up like he was fighting off a laugh. She pulled away. "Keep them closed."

Dimming the lights, she lit some sandalwood incense and the candles on the coffee table.

Her second favorite Abba song started to play, "Knowing Me, Knowing You." He'd stopped moving, but his eyes were still shut.

"Are you planning on inviting some hippies over later?" he quipped.

"Shut up," she whispered as she returned to him, pulling him close. "Now, keep your eyes closed and feel me."

Her body brushed his in perfect time to the beat. His hands remained firmly on her hips where she'd planted them. She slid across his torso, breaking his hold, and then flowed to the spot directly behind him. His breathing changed.

"You're playing with fire," he said, his voice husky.

Instead of responding, she kept dancing around him, sliding her hand across his body—his chest, his back, even cruising down to his spectacularly tight ass.

His hands finally brushed tentatively against her. The incense rose in her nostrils, its scent exotic and tantalizing. When she went to make another pass around his body, his strong arms pulled her close. His body seemed to know her, moving against her with the perfection they found when they were making love. Her eyes closed. "Mama Mia" started to play, and the heat rose between them as her head lolled from side to side with the music.

Brian's fingers trailed up her back. His erection pressed into her hip, but he continued to brush gently against her, finding the beat. She surrendered to the rhythm, to him. Her hands twined around his neck, his hot skin enticing her.

When his hands settled on her butt, she sputtered out a laugh. "You certainly learn fast."

"I couldn't dance with you like this when we were in high school, but you can be sure I thought about it. Why do you think guys always let girls walk ahead of them?"

Their bodies continued to sway, but she knew his eyes were open. His eyes were like hot coals when she looked into them.

"Not out of being a gentleman?" she asked, her own voice breathy from arousal.

"No, it's to watch a girl's ass," he said in a hushed tone. "I'm glad you thought of this, Jill."

Her smile was easy. "Me too. Dance with me, Bri."

They continued to move against each other, their bodies brushing together.

When she could resist no more, she pulled his head down for a hot, wet kiss. They continued to move to the music. But soon, her body could take no more. She had to have him. Right now.

Pushing him lightly on the chest, he danced backwards with her to the couch until he fell back. She undressed slowly in front of him, letting her body sway to the music as he watched. It was unbearably arousing.

He seemed to know she wanted to be in charge, and testing her new confidence, she undressed him as slowly as she'd undressed herself. Sinking to her knees in front of him, she met his heated gaze.

"Now it's my turn to try something new," she whispered, and even though a moment of nerves entered, she took his arousal in her hand.

His mouth broke out into a smile. "Don't fight it," he joked, using her words.

Right. Good idea. She closed her eyes, took a breath, and then lowered her mouth onto him. As she'd done for him, he guided her through the movements until she got the hang of it. An inner knowing took over—as it had when they'd made love the first time—and with his hands guiding her head, she brought him to a heated release.

Abba continued to play as she snuggled into his arms, and when he came back to himself, he made love to her with a sweetness that stole her breath away.

An hour later they were reclined on the couch well sated, watching TV, her head in his lap.

"So," he commented conversationally, but with an edge, like he was testing the water he'd set to boil for spaghetti.

Even though her whole body was a ribbon of relaxation, her muscles tensed.

"PolarFest is next week," he continued.

The mention of Jemma's annual party ruined her easy mood, and she wondered if he'd purposefully waited until after sex to bring it up.

She and Jemma had created PolarFest together after drinking too many margaritas one night during a blizzard, wishing they were in the tropics. They'd decided to celebrate winter with an annual party so they wouldn't have to bitch anymore about February being the most *boring* month of the year. Hence PolarFest.

"I've heard," she responded, wishing Brian would stop talking so they could just lie here in peace. Pete hadn't even run his plan to host it by her. Granted, she didn't want to speak to him, but still. She'd thought about doing it herself, but in the end, she hadn't been able to face it.

"Pete wanted to keep the tradition alive since everyone loves it so much. He asked me to help, so I'll be...doing that."

"Great," she answered, staring straight ahead. Their easy mood seemed to have evaporated. She was back in the thick of anger and grief and confusion.

His mouth flattened. "Look, I know it will be tough without Jem, but I want you to come with me." He cleared his throat and looked back at the TV. The lights flickered across his tense face.

God, she so didn't want to see Pete, but it would be a good place to bring Mac. He'd be able to hobnob with the professor set from Emmits Merriam.

"Is this going to be a problem?" he asked.

They'd had such a great night, and she wasn't about to spoil it. "Nope. I'll be there. Yay!"

He snorted, obviously picking up on the sarcasm in her voice. "Great. Let's get some sleep."

She had trouble settling down once they were in bed. Thoughts of the past kept swirling in her mind. Perhaps it was the earlier talk about high school dances, but she found herself missing Jemma more than ever. The grief welled up. Tears spilled over.

He slid on his side and pulled her against him. "Hey, what's this?"

She clutched his hands. "Jemma," she said simply as the hurt spread.

"Shh," he whispered. "It's okay, baby. I miss her too. Cry it out."

And she did, soaking his chest. He tightened his arms around her and didn't try to stop her like some men might have. When she finally finished crying, totally hollowed out, her gratitude toward him for comforting her overwhelmed her.

"I love you."

He laid his cheek on hers. "I love you too. Come here." He turned her gently. When he took her mouth, she gave him everything. He did too. Grief shifted into comforting caresses, long kisses, throaty murmurs, soft sighs. The rawness changed into something else—love and a sense of belonging so sweet and encompassing she didn't want it to end. They loved each other slowly, deeply until they came apart in each other's arms, shaking. When he rolled away and came back to the bed moments later, he fitted her against him again.

With his arms around her, she realized it was time for her to start wearing the necklace he'd given her after graduation.

She fell asleep to the now familiar rise and fall of his body next to hers, realizing that everything in life was easier when they shared it.

Being with him was exactly as she'd imagined.

CHAPTER 31

Brian slid the strip steak marinated with adobo sauce into the fridge and kicked the door shut. He was meeting Pete at Hairy's for a beer, and he was already running a little late, so he hustled out the door.

Hairy's happy hour crowd talked raucously. With St. Patrick's Day just a couple of weeks away, the bar was proudly displaying two blinking signs in orange, white, and green. A leering leprechaun had a female draped over his body, her boobs spilling out with the subtitle, *Sit On A Leprechaun's Lap. Ask About His Pot of Gold.*

Brian smiled as a blond chick asked Mike, the bartender, what the other sign meant: *Tell the Man Póg Mo Thón.* She giggled when he translated, "Kiss my ass."

Mike pulled him a Guinness. He took a sip. Scanning the crowd, he spotted Pete chatting up some dewy-eyed grad student in the corner. Brian headed in their direction. If Pete waved him off, he'd play darts. He wished Jill was here to play a game with him. She loved playing and beat him more often than not. Still, he liked watching her green eyes narrow and her mouth purse right before she launched her shot. It was yet another sign he was toast.

Pete signaled him, so he moved through the crowd, greeting the people he knew. There was new speculation in their eyes when they looked at him. The scrutiny made him uncomfortable.

"No luck?" he asked Pete as the girl moved on.

"She had to get back to her friends. I got her number though."

"She's cute." He leaned against the wall, careful not to knock the drunken green-haired fairy picture off the wall. The dark foam tickled his lips when he drank. The meaty brew called to mind hops and chocolate. After drinking half the glass, he settled it against his chest. "So, when are you going to shop for the party stuff?"

"Thursday. It's cold enough to leave everything outside."

"My meat needs to be defrosted, Pete. It'll be hard as bricks in this weather, and I don't want it to burn on the grill."

Pete slapped him on the shoulder. "Oh, lighten up. Hey, your future in-laws just walked in."

The beer almost slipped from his hand. In-laws. Jesus, he thought, as he spotted Tanner and Meredith.

Pete raised his brow. "So, all's not well with Jill's family? That's gotta be tough. I know how much they meant to you while we were growing up"

He thought of them calling him out. "Yeah, it is."

"Whoa!" Pete's mouth dropped. "You've got a new problem. Hot French chick at five-o-clock headed this way. Man, anyone who ever thought you were gay for cooking French food is eating their words now."

Brian elbowed him as Simca approached them, decked out as usual in a black pencil skirt, ice-pick boots, and a red cashmere pashmina shawl over a white silk shirt.

"Hello, Brian," Simca said in her husky accent, but stopped short of giving him the French greeting of a kiss on either cheek. He smiled so she'd understand his appreciation.

Her mouth curved.

He shifted on his feet. Everyone was staring. A thread of discomfort slithered down his spine. He sipped his beer. How was he supposed to consider going into business with her in Dare if he couldn't handle an innocent run-in at Hairy's?

"I decided to explore more of this town since I might be staying here," Simca said.

Pete coughed as he took a sip of his drink. "Excuse me?"

Well, great. Now he'd have to trust Pete to keep his mouth shut. Brian drilled him with a stare. "We might be opening a place here in Dare, but nothing's been decided, so don't say anything."

"I won't. Do you want to pinky swear?"

Brian snorted.

Simca put her hands on her hips. "You look pretty trustworthy. You're Brian's best friend, Pete, right?"

Pete's eye twitched. "Yes, how did you know?"

"Brian talked a lot about you in New York."

His friend looked about ready to slump to the floor from the attention. "Can I get you a drink?"

She wrinkled her nose. "Is the wine terrible?"

"Abominable," Pete confirmed, shuddering.

"How about an Irish coffee? Thank you, *mon cher*."

Pete stumbled away.

Another man under Simca's spell, and she knew it. Brian looked over his shoulder. Tanner's dark gaze didn't even blink when their eyes met. Meredith shook her head in disgust.

Brian turned back to Simca, angling her into the corner. "Well, this is awkward."

People around him had grown quiet and were leaning closer.

"I'm happy I ran into you." She opened a designer black purse and handed him a manila envelope. "I drew up a draft menu to further our conversation. This one's for Dare. I'm still working on the one for New York, depending on what you decide."

He scanned both copies, his heart thumping in tune to the angry Irish band playing. "This is...genius. I love how you included game meats with the organic produce. Farm-to-table is a great selling point here."

"I'm glad you like it." She edged closer, taking him through the menu. The stares and whispers disappeared, eclipsed by visions of venison on a bed of Kale with white beans—a daring Western take on the French dish cassoulet.

He set his beer aside. "This is exactly what I envisioned."

Their gazes locked. He saw the pulse beat in her neck.

She still had a thing for him—he could see it in her eyes, her body language. He took a step back.

"I'm not sure this is going to work, Sim."

Her hand brushed his arm. "Let's not decide that tonight. I'll go find Pete and have my coffee. People are *terribly* aware of us, no? New York is so different. I'm not sure the locals will ever stop staring at us—even if we only run a restaurant together. And while I don't mind attention, this isn't the type I want."

Bingo. "I know."

"We'll talk soon." The crowd parted as she walked away.

He headed to the men's room to get some air. No one could stare at him there without coming off as a perv. He tapped his head against the Kelly green tile wall. The concept and the menu were everything he could have hoped for, but she still had feelings for him, even though he no longer shared them. Jill wasn't blind. If she saw Simca looking at him that way while they made a duck confit, she'd be jealous. And he wanted her trust above all things. Could Jill possibly support his partnership with Simca if he convinced her to trust him?

He firmed his shoulders to face down the stares. For a moment, he wanted to be in New York again, any big city where he could be anonymous. When he left the bathroom, Tanner was standing by Dare's only remaining pay phone.

"I had to talk my wife out of coming into the men's bathroom to ask you why you're talking to that woman. That doesn't make me happy."

He put his hands on his hips, letting righteous anger cover the hurt he was feeling that the Hale's didn't trust him anymore. "I've done nothing wrong."

"You're crossing the line with Jill's happiness, and it's starting to piss me off."

Brian stepped into his face. "You have no fucking idea what you're talking about. Everything I'm doing right now is for Jill's happiness." Hadn't he moved in with her? Wasn't he trying to prove how much he loved her?

"Then you'd better be careful how you look at Simca."

"You misunderstood the situation." Brian fisted his hands to keep from shoving him. "Maybe Mere should mind her own business since she wasn't privy to our discussion."

Mouth curling like a wolf ready to defend his mate, Tanner said, "Mere is only looking out for her sister, which is also what I'm trying to do."

The Guinness in his stomach burned like he'd drunk a half bottle of Irish whiskey. "You don't need to. We're fine. Leave us alone."

He walked away. Meredith was waiting for him when he left the hallway to the restrooms.

"Brian—"

"No," he nearly barked. "I've already had it from Tanner. I'm outta here." He would text Pete when he was outside. Pete would understand why he had to leave.

He weaved through patrons to the front door. When the cold smacked against his face, he welcomed it. Bracing his shoulders, he headed to Jill's, well aware of the stares that followed him as he crossed Main Street and turned the corner.

How was he ever going to stay in this town with everyone waiting for him to fuck up?

CHAPTER 32

Peggy threw *The Western Independent* in the trash can. Was it immature to want to ball up the page with Maven's hotel plans and stomp on it?

She booted up her computer. There had to be some way to stop him. His assistance to Keith had made him the town's hero. The conflict between gratitude and gall warred in her tight chest. She tapped the computer keys, logging into her police background software.

As she worked, she thought about her father, coming home drunk and broke from a spontaneous trip to Atlantic City. She refused to allow other families to be destroyed because of gambling. Her fingers keyed in her search. When the doorbell rang, she tucked the laptop away and headed downstairs.

Her conscience felt like a snake slithering down her spine when she saw Jill. She was trying to undermine her friend's plans.

She flung the door open. "Hi, there."

"Hey, you feeling better?" Jill asked, wiping her feet on the rug.

"Getting there. Come on in."

When Jill walked into the family room the hitch in her gait gave her away.

"Someone's had a whole bunch of sex," Peggy commented.

Her friend's head whipped to the side. "Wait. How did you know?"

Peggy snorted. "I know a prostitute walk when I see one. Close your mouth. I'm used to watching suspects. Prostitutes who've been well used have a walk."

Jill immediately stopped walking. "Well, thank you *very* much."

"No need to get your panties in a twist. Although you probably haven't been wearing them much. Having fun?"

Her grin called to mind giant sunflowers. "Yep."

"Then enjoy the prostitute walk. It's not like you got arrested or anything."

Jill tucked her arm through Peggy's. "Right, nothing illegal. Just hot sizzling nights of sex after—"

"Please, don't make a single mom cry. I'm sick. And I haven't had sex in...I am *so* not sharing." She tapped her temple. "Must be the cough medicine. I'm babbling worse than a first-time offender."

She almost rushed to clean up. Kleenex puffed out of the waste basket like popcorn. The heating pad's orange light shone on the couch. Her place could be called The Sick Zone. After a moment she gave up, and settled onto the couch, patting the cushion next to her.

"I'm heading back to work tomorrow," Peggy said. "Thank God. This Kleenex could be made of silk, and it would still hurt. I'm hoping there's a scuffle or something at Hairy's bar. I want to cuff someone."

"That's pretty sick."

"You make lattés. I arrest people. It's what we do." She put the heating pad on her chest. "And you're sleeping with a hot guy, while I'm left with this for warmth. How sad is that."

Sitting cross-legged, Jill put her hands on her knees. "I want to talk to you about something."

Uh-oh. "What?"

Jill rearranged Keith's books on the coffee table. "Would you go to PolarFest with me? I need moral support."

Phew. Nothing serious, and nothing to do with the hotel. "I don't like parties."

"Please. It's the biggest party in Dare since Halloween."

"Are you going to tell me the real reason?" Peggy said gently, reaching for a Kleenex. She wished she could do without a nose. At this point, she'd have it removed if it would stop running.

Jill sat on her knees. "Okay, Brian asked me to go. He's helping out, but you know how angry I am with Pete, who's going to be hosting. I *need* to take Mac to mingle with the professor set. And I need to go with Brian, because he's still Pete's friend." She held up a hand when Peggy opened her mouth. "I'd like to have all my friends around me."

"Jill." She let her voice break down her friend's walls.

Jill rocked in place. "And okay, this will be the first real party I've been to since Halloween. I don't want to be thinking about that night."

Finally. Peggy sighed. "Okay, but you'd better not be asking me so you can set me up with Maven."

A goofy grin broke across her face. "Do I look like Cupid?"

"I can see you wearing a diaper and wings."

Throaty laughter bubbled out of her mouth. "Why, thank you. It's a lifelong dream, shooting people with arrows.'"

Peggy threw the tissue aside and missed the waste can. "I'm the one who likes to shoot things."

"I'll only say this once. Mac's more than easy on the eyes. And his voice. Margie almost has an orgasm every time she hears him talk. She's spilled more coffee this week than—"

"I've got the drift. But you need to leave it alone. I don't think he belongs in this town."

Jill's mouth twisted. "Fine. Keep telling yourself that."

"I hope our different views..." Peggy pushed the heating pad aside. "Don't screw up our friendship."

"My family has always managed it. I don't see why we can't."

She reached out her hand. Peggy grasped it. "So we agree to disagree?"

"Yep." Jill stood up. "I'm going to go wash my hands now."

"Now I know how a leper feels."

"Haha. I'd hug you, but...Eww. Germs."

"Germs are like radiation. You've already been exposed by being in this room with me." She started hacking to mess with her.

Her friend's full-body cringe made Peggy fight a grin. "Yuck, thanks for the image. I'll be sure to wear a Haz-Mat suit next time I visit. Thanks for agreeing to come, Peg. It means a lot."

Peggy coughed into another Kleenex. "You're welcome. Just don't meddle with Maven and me. If you do, I'll have to arrest you for your prostitute walk, and then you won't be able to keep having hot sex."

"The horror," Jill replied, dancing out of reach. She headed out, strutting her prostitute walk the whole way, making Peggy laugh.

She headed up to her office to resume her investigation of Maven. The water she'd poured coated her dry throat as she pulled open her laptop and scanned his background. When she only saw one criminal charge years ago, she almost snarled. Why couldn't he have a rap sheet as long as her arm? That would have helped. She clicked on it. Well, well. So, he'd been charged for assault and battery, but he'd found a way to weasel out of it. Why was she surprised? Time to find out why.

She called Atlantic City's police department. The arresting officer didn't remember anything, but he dug out the short case file and read it to her over the phone. Maven had apparently beaten up some rich kid so bad he'd been hospitalized, but he'd refused to explain his reasons. The family had pressed charges after their son was hospitalized, but they had dropped them a few days later without saying why. When she hung up, she set the phone down and tapped the arm of the couch. Was it enough? She'd be skating an ethical line.

But he couldn't bring poker to Dare. No one here understood what that meant, how it changed families, increased alcoholism, domestic and random violence, but she did.

She'd used this because the ends justified the means. Everyone in town needed to be reminded of gambling's darker side, and this incident would throw Maven's reputation into the muck. It might be enough to shift public perception toward him. She needed some seriously concerned speculation from the town, especially the councilmen and women. Did she spill everything now or wait for the vote? No, he was as slick as a lobbyist. If she put this out now, he'd find a way to spin it.

Better to inform the paper she had something on him and then announce it at the town council meeting. If law enforcement had taught her one thing, it was that the mere speculation of guilt could tarnish a reputation.

She picked up the phone to call *The Western Independent*.

CHAPTER 33

Perhaps it was the slight guilt Brian felt about the scene at Hairy's, but he decided it was time to unveil the surprise he'd been planning for Jill since their Valentine's Day picnic.

"Hey," he said, calling her at the shop. "Can you sneak home to have lunch with me? I'm going to be working late tonight."

She made a humming noise. "Miss me, huh?"

If she only knew... She was on his mind all the time—just like in the old days. "Yeah. You?"

"Yeah," she responded.

"So, can you?" he asked again.

"Uh-huh. We're close to securing enough votes for the hotel. I think I can take a break. Let me just check with Mac."

So the hotel was looking like a go. His breath huffed out. Given how darn happy Jill was with the work, it didn't take a genius to figure out what she wanted to do.

She would keep working for Mac and the new hotel.

Which meant his best option for staying in Dare to be with her was starting the restaurant with Simca, which he wasn't sure she would support. Shit.

"I can get away," she said brightly when she returned to the phone. "When?"

"How about noon? And Jill." He paused for effect. "It's going to be a long lunch."

"Excellent," she replied, the smile in her voice obvious. "See you soon."

At the appointed time, she pranced through the door looking beautiful in a brown wool skirt and one of those sweater wraps she favored in a bold lime-green. "A nooner!" she cried, reaching down to give Mutt a good rubdown. "I've been wanting one all my life."

His laughter floated out. "Well, then, Red, you're in luck."

Sailing into his arms, she took his mouth in a passionate kiss, but he broke away. "Later. I have a surprise for you. This time you have to close your eyes."

Her lids closed immediately, making him aware for the first time how long her lashes were. "Are you planning on showing me some new moves?

Have you started taking dancing lessons with Mrs. Ellison?"

He shuddered. "Jesus, Jill, she's got to be seventy. Now quit chattering and give me your hands."

He took them in his own and led her into the kitchen.

"Ummm, it smells awesome in here. Are you brewing some new coffee?"

She couldn't see it, but his smile could have beaten the Cheshire cat's. "Kind of. Here, sit down and keep your eyes shut."

As he helped her into one of chairs at the kitchen table, he surveyed the four bags of coffee he'd artfully arranged on a platter.

"My God, whatever you're drinking," she said, "I want some. Is that a floral scent?"

Damn, he should have known her nose would be able to pick up on what was going on.

"You're too good, Red. Okay, you can open your eyes now."

Those green eyes darted from him to the platter. Her mouth dropped open. And then she shrieked and shot up from the chair. Started jumping up and down, crying out, "Oh my God, oh my God!"

He grinned and pulled her into a hug. "I'm glad you like your surprise. I thought you might appreciate a specialty coffee tasting."

She levered back, her hands still gripping his waist. "Are you kidding?" Her head swiveled to the platter again. "These are some of the priciest coffees in the world. Like fifty to two hundred bucks a bag—and super rare. How did you manage it?"

His shoulder lifted. "Someone I went to school with has incredible connections with the specialty markets, and he managed to arrange it for me."

"This is too much," Jill said as they both sat down. "I can't take it all in...So, we have Panama's famous Hacienda la Esmeralda Geisha." She brought the bag to her nose and inhaled deeply. "Ah, this is the source of the floral notes I was smelling. And it has a strong fruit aroma too. Yummm."

"You're too good, Red. I've worked with some incredible sommeliers, and you have the same knack for coffee they have for wine."

She waggled her brows. "Well, I should, babe. I own a coffee shop, after all. Oh, Bri, this is like the best-est surprise ever. How can I ever thank you?"

His throat thickened. It seemed like just being with her every day was the way she constantly thanked him. "Just by enjoying it."

She picked up the St. Helena coffee and took a deep inhale. "Oh my God."

"Yeah, pretty cool, huh?" He'd inspected them earlier. "It's made on the island where Napoleon was exiled in 1815." His friend had sent descriptions of each of the coffees.

"He was the French Revolution dude, right?"

He almost rolled his eyes. "Yep. And the little guy."

She snuck a hand under the table and caressed him through his jeans, making him instantly hard. "Yeah, I don't know any guys like that."

His snort carried across the room. "Lucky you. Now, how about we try these coffees?"

"Okay, no offense, but *I'm* in charge here."

He settled back as her hand stopped stroking him. Plenty of time for that later. "I wouldn't have it any other way."

He'd sat through thousands of wine tastings, so he knew how long the process could take. And it was so much more complicated with coffee. They would have to grind the beans first and then analyze their aromas before putting a couple of tablespoons in individual cups with six ounces of hot water to "break the crust," Jill explained, inhaling deeply as they pushed the grounds to the bottom. Of course he'd researched how coffee tastings were done, but he could tell how much joy she took in sharing with him.

After the grounds settled, they slurped each brew from a spoon to take in the flavor, the sounds rudely filling the kitchen. The table was littered with mugs—one of them was an official Abba cup, which made him smile.

She moaned with each taste. Hell, he did too.

"You're spoiling me for other coffee," she said, sipping from a cup of the enticing Jamaican Blue Mountain Coffee, the spoon now discarded.

As he watched the light from the kitchen window play upon her hair, he thought about how she was doing the same for him when it came to other women. He couldn't imagine ever wanting anyone but Jill. Hadn't he always known she could do that to him? Isn't that why he'd been so afraid in high school?

"Come here," Jill called, standing up and pulling him out of his chair. She turned back and grabbed a few El Injerto coffee beans in her hand. She ran them along his neck and then leaned in and inhaled, moaning. "God, you smell good. We might have to look into a coffee-scented cologne."

"I like your coffee-scented lotion," he told her. Funny, everything about coffee reminded him of her now.

She raised his shirt and ran a few beans down his chest and then kissed the path she'd made. His breath sucked in. His arousal, ever-present when Jill was around, spiked.

"I want you here," he told her. "With the coffee all around us."

Their clothes flew in their haste. He pulled her into his lap and entered her forcefully, causing her to cry out.

As he thrust into her, his gaze pinned on the necklace bouncing against her collarbone. It was different from the amethyst one she always wore, the one that had been Jemma's. There was something familiar about the heart-shaped pendant, and when the memory clicked into place, his heart burst in his chest.

It was the necklace he'd given her after high school graduation. *J&B, BFFs.*

He pressed his forehead to hers, gripping her hips, wanting to be absorbed into her. She came with a loud cry.

She'd never mentioned the necklace. To his knowledge, she'd never worn it until today.

His release poured out of him with a harsh shout.

He stroked her hair, then raised her chin so he could meet her gaze. It was a sign. The feeling of redemption blew through him.

"I love you," he whispered. "More than anything."

Her green eyes looked like melted glass. "And I love you more than anything."

His fingers trailed to the necklace.

Her gaze stayed locked with his as he traced the heart.

He swallowed thickly. Couldn't speak.

So he pulled her close and held her until their bodies cooled, wishing he could go back in time and thank the scared kid who'd entered Dare's finest jewelry store on a windy May morning eight years ago to buy her this gift.

He'd known the truth back then.

And now their connection had grown into so much more.

CHAPTER 34

"Mac, I think you've addressed all my questions," the head of the planning commission said. "I can't officially tell you which way I'm voting, but I can tell you not to lose any sleep over it."

The two men shook hands. Jill had to hold herself in check. Doing a celebration dance in public would look immature, but they now *unofficially* had enough votes for Mac's plans to pass.

"Jill, we're delighted you're involved. We know it will make the whole project reflect our community."

She took Lane Brikens' hands in a warm clasp. "I'll do my best for the town."

"We know you will. I'll see you at the meeting."

Jill sank back into her chair, watching his humpty-dumpty figure cross the restaurant.

Mac crossed his arms and leaned back in his seat, a Cheshire grin on his face. "Okay, now you can let loose."

"You won't think any less of me?"

He huffed out a laugh, unbuttoning his navy suit jacket like it was his one concession to relaxation. "No. In fact, if you didn't, I would think it out of character."

"We have enough votes," she chanted, clinking her fork against her plate like it was a drum stick.

"Yes, we do," he murmured, tugging a yellow poker chip from his pocket and rolling it across his fingers. "You do good work. Not that I'm surprised."

"Back at ya." She threw her hands out. "It's why you hired me."

"It is," he agreed. "Have you decided to join me full-time yet? I'll add another third to the salary I quoted you. You're worth it."

Her mouth dropped open. This acknowledgement from someone like Mac was everything she'd ever wanted. "Are you serious?"

He pocketed the chip. "Damn straight. You're a kindred spirit. A natural rainmaker. If I don't tie you up, you'll be running this town before long."

The daydream went wild. More brightly-painted shops lining Main Street with cute names. Her hot self flitting in and out of her businesses. People waving to her. Calling her a business prodigy. Hell, she could run for mayor.

She fingered her heart-shaped pendant, so proud to be wearing it. Brian's reaction had melted her heart.

"I told you! I'll let you know *after* the vote." She didn't want to share her whole saga, though, so she said the first thing she could think of. "I don't want to jinx anything."

He snapped his posh burgundy leather briefcase shut. "You're not a woman to be rushed. I'm trying to respect that. Let me take you back to your other job—for now."

When he dropped her off at the coffee shop, she darted for the door to escape the cold. Damn, she was tired of winter, which only made her think about why she and Jemma had started PolarFest. Depressing.

The early evening crowd hummed with activity. Students took breaks from studying, their discarded textbooks unopened. Friends huddled close, laughing and smiling, letting go of the challenges of the day. The milk frother roared under the low jazzy voice of Miles Davis. Cold nights, the darkness descending down the snowy mountains, and the heat from the gas fireplace all made Don't Soy with Me the perfect place to unwind. New artwork from the public school's second grade class hung in funky frames on the walls, adding to the ambiance.

Margie waved her over. "When is the coffee order going in?"

Shit. She'd forgotten about it. "Right now."

"That's what I thought."

Jill made a face and hustled back to her office. She sank into the chair and shuffled through her files for their ongoing order, adding notes in the margins about new products they'd agree to try on her patrons. What would people think of the java from Indonesia? A knock on the door gave her a start.

"Knock, knock," said a familiar, age-roughened voice. "I thought it was time for me to see how you're doing in person." Her grandfather made his way forward, tapping his cane. He held a coffee cup. "Peace offering."

She'd wanted to be like him ever since she was a little girl, so it had frustrated her when her journalism classes had bored her to tears. Who wanted to go through life being objective? Telling the news. She wanted to live it all in technicolor. He'd never been disappointed in her, but she felt he was now. He was from another time, and moving in with a man who wasn't your husband simply didn't work for him.

"I'm glad you came," she said, her words their own olive branch. The cup warmed her hand when she took it from him.

The brow he raised should have been waxed when Kennedy was president. "Meredith's on a rampage after seeing Brian and that French woman at Hairy's last night, discussing some sort of menu. And your mother...well, you know how she feels."

The spasms in her gut intensified. It made sense for Brian to talk with *that woman*, but she still felt a pinch of jealousy.

"This whole moving in with Brian thing was so fast, which got me thinking." He peered down his nose at her. "You aren't pregnant, are you, girlie?"

"What?" The cup spilled when she flailed her arm. "Shit." She plucked her coffee order out of the way with the speed of a pedestrian fleeing an approaching bus. Hefting a wad of Kleenex onto the spill, she mopped it up and tossed the soggy mess in her garbage can. "No, of course not," she said, secretly praying it was true.

He clapped. "Thank God you didn't go into acting," her grandfather harrumphed, folding his hands across his lap.

Brezhnev hadn't fooled her grandfather during the Cold War, and she didn't have a prayer.

Eyes as sharp as a red-tailed hawk's pinned her in place. "You are, aren't you?" He clucked his tongue. "So, one mystery solved. I can't believe your mother and Mere didn't think of that."

Her whole body flushed red as she realized she couldn't lie to him. "Look, I don't know yet." Her damn period hadn't shown up yet, but she kept telling herself it would any day. She lowered her head into her hands. "How did you guess?"

The chair scraped on the floor as he moved around. His hand stroked her back. "Reporter's deductive reasoning. Come here, kiddo."

"Oh, Grandpa," she cried, resting her head against his chest and finally giving into all the emotions she'd been trying to bottle. When he bent down, she smelled the familiar scent of red hots.

"Here now, it's not the end of the world. Not the best situation, I'll grant you, with this French tart in town, but you're a tough girl and a Hale. You'll pull through."

His support surprised her. "You're not disappointed?"

His hand gently whacked the back of her head. "I'm not delighted that you're shacking up with Brian without a ring on your finger, I won't lie, but it doesn't make me love you any less. You're tougher on yourself than I could ever be. I've reached an age where I've seen enough of life to know one thing."

Tears popped into her eyes. She sniffed and reached for a Kleenex, relieved that he wasn't as upset as she'd thought. "What's that?"

"I only want you to be happy, and if I can help with that, then I'm on the case. Of course, part of me wants to kick McConnell in the balls, but that won't solve diddly."

"It's not just his fault. It—"

"Takes two, I know, but he's an easy target. Were you keeping us in the dark because you knew we'd be angry with him now that his ex-girlfriend is thinking about staying and buying Morty's place? Please tell me you're not allowing Brian to go into business with that woman. There's no way that woman doesn't have an agenda."

The tissue slid from her hand. Suddenly, it was like gravity had sucked everything down. Her mouth. Her hands. Even her legs.

"She's thinking about *staying?*"

He rubbed his hip and leaned on her desk. "You didn't know?"

Her mind flashed back to the first day she and Brian had moved in together. Was that what he'd wanted to tell her? That they were going to open a restaurant in Dare *together*? It would be the best of both worlds for him. And it would mean he wouldn't really have to choose her—not like she wanted.

"Oh, my God," she whispered. How was she supposed to handle him working with that woman day in and day out when she knew she was planning to win him back? "How did you find out?"

"Morty Wilson gave her an advance tour before the property officially hits the market. Said she was charming."

"Charming!" Everyone seemed to fall under her spell. She sank back into her chair.

"I can see the misery on your face." He tapped her crown. "Seems like this is news to you."

"Yeah, Morty left a message for me to call him, but I haven't had time yet," she replied in a listless voice.

"That's not what I meant."

Right. "Brian tried to tell me, I think." She didn't want anyone to heap more blame on Brian. She stood up, needing to move. "We moved in together to see if we could work things out between us before deciding on our career options. We agreed to table all the difficult stuff."

Her grandpa's whistle pierced her ear. "What kind of stupid idea is not talking about the tough stuff? That's what relationships are all about."

She stomped her foot. "I know that, but we didn't think we could make it without some...stupid moratorium."

When he pulled her into a hug, she wrapped her arms around his waist, his wool cardigan tickling her nose.

"Well, at least he'll be here if you're pregnant."

"I don't want to be pregnant," she whispered. "Does that make me a bad person?"

His sigh couldn't have been more heart-felt. "No, sweetheart. Only human."

"Oh, grandpa. It looks like we have enough votes to get the hotel passed. I want to work for Mac." Her voice was so soft she could have been in a confessional admitting to a mortal sin. "He's great, and it's an incredible opportunity for me."

He leaned back, his faded blue-jean eyes rimmed with the laugh and worry lines of a long, full life. "You're like me, Jill. You want to build empires. I knew it when we started playing Monopoly when you were eight. You always had to have your hand in everything."

A headache spread across the base of her skull. "I don't want Brian to open a place with that woman here in Dare even if it keeps him here. She does want him back." Could she support his decision and trust him to stay true to her? God, that was like trust with all capitals.

"Of course she does."

"But he wants to be a serious chef, and I don't see that happening here, especially since I'd rather work for Mac than open a restaurant with Brian." She didn't need the vote, after all, to know what she'd decided. "But

I love him. I don't know what to do."

"You'll figure it out."

"I've missed you, Grandpa."

He tightened his grip. "I've missed you too, missy. If something like this happens again, God forbid, I hope you'll remember I'm not some judgmental ogre. I love you, kid."

She burrowed her face into his sweater, smelling Old Spice. "I love you too."

"You let me know if you need anything, okay?"

There was a hidden meaning in his words. She didn't want to go there. "Okay."

He released her and used the desk as a prop to get back to his cane. "The rest of the family might want to kick Brian's butt, but they love you too. Now, go talk with your sister. She's upset. Her copy is suffering."

Jill doubted that since Meredith had written kick-ass articles even through her divorce. "You've got it."

"Well, better get back to my own empire. And so should you," he added, tapping her nose. "Still can't believe people pay that much for a cup of coffee. In my time..." His voice trailed off as he shut the door behind him.

Jill put her head in her hands. Her mind was spewing up all sorts of scenarios. Stop, she ordered her thoughts and reached for the coffee order. After placing it, she left the office, steering her emotions back inside. Time to make things right with Meredith.

***

Tracking down her sister wasn't tough. Jill knew she'd be at work. When she walked into the headquarters of *The Western Independent*, phones were ringing everywhere and people were arguing passionately over sentences. Ink and paper had never smelled as good to her as coffee, but the combo warmed her heart nonetheless. Memories of coming here after school, her dad and grandpa letting her design her own ad for the lemonade stand she ran with Brian or write an announcement for her Oscar-winning role in the Christmas play, rushed over her. Nostalgia sang through her veins.

Jill knocked on the open door. The proverbial Hale red pen halted on the page. Meredith looked up and frowned.

Shutting the door behind her, Jill slid her hands into her coat pockets. "I know you're pissed at me—and hurt. I am too, but I don't want it to be this way anymore. I'm sorry we fought, but I felt like you weren't trusting me to make my own decisions...and you were being super hard on Brian when I need to work out my feelings for him—my own way." She took a deep breath to ease the tightness in her chest. "Plus, there's something else I need to tell you. I...there's a chance I might be pregnant and didn't want to tell anyone in case I wasn't."

Meredith blinked a few times. Put down her pen slowly. When she didn't respond, Jill continued. "I didn't want you to be disappointed or worried if there was no reason for it. Plus, I was scared you'd tell mom."

Standing, her sister crossed the space between them and gripped her shoulders. "You might be pregnant?" Her green eyes bugged so wide, her irises looked like Jupiter's ring. "Holy shit."

"Yeah, holy shit."

Her hands slid down her arms. "Mom's going to have a cow."

"See, I knew you'd tell her." She jumped up and down. "Listen to me. I don't even know if I'm pregnant yet."

A ping sounded, signaling an email. "Wow, it's a shock. So him moving in was about—"

"Needing to see if we can make our personal life work when we have a lot of other decisions looming, like Mac's offer for me and that French chick's offer for Brian. And I wanted to see how we'd work as a fully functional couple before finding out for sure about the whole ...pregnancy thing."

"Wow," Meredith commented dryly. "That *is* a lot. And I don't know how to tell you this, but Tanner took Brian aside at the bar yesterday..."

And then proceeded to describe the whole incident.

Jill stepped away from her and started pacing.

"I'm not saying he wants to go back to her or is doing anything questionable right now," she said.

"God, Mere, I don't know what to do. I think we have enough votes for the hotel, and I really want to work for Mac. If I do, that woman seems to be Brian's only chance of regaining the career he wants in Dare. I want him here. We've been doing so great, Mere. Should I set aside working with Mac and open a place with Brian? It's the only way to keep Brian here and happy without that tart being involved."

Her sister put her arm around her shoulder. "But you said you and Brian didn't want the same things in a restaurant. Jill, I don't know what to tell you. You won't be happy if you settle for something you don't want."

Her head throbbed in time with her heart. "God, this is terrible. I don't see how this can work out. But I told him I'd respect his decision, and he mine."

"What if you're pregnant? What then?"

Jill looked down. "We agreed to make our decisions before we find out for sure. I have to know he's staying with me for the right reasons. Now, I'm afraid I won't know if he decides to open a place with that bitch."

"I know you love him, but deep down, can you really see yourself trusting him with that woman?"

"I don't know. We've had a few bumps, but it's working between us. I guess I'd give it a try." Her fingers touched the smoky quartz necklace at her throat. "Being a chef is his goal in life. He loves me, Mere. I know that. I just don't know if he can choose me over everything. Am I asking too much?"

"No, we all deserve to be someone's priority. Trust me, one thing I learned from my last marriage is that marriage won't work any other way. And I trust that's where you want this to go with Brian?"

"Yes."

Meredith circled the desk and hugged her close, holding her for a long moment. The phone rang four times, filling the silence.

"If he decides to go into business with her here, I guess I'll have to trust him. It wouldn't be fair of me to say no if I don't want to pursue a business with Brian."

Letting go, Meredith cupped her shoulder. "But you need to share your concerns about the French chick. There has to be an open dialogue, especially if he's blind to her plans."

Boy, wouldn't that be a fun conversation? "Can I ask another favor?" she asked.

"Sure."

"I need moral support for PolarFest tomorrow, more than just Mac and Peg. It's going to be the first one without Jemma."

Another email pinged. "Sure, but I'm bringing Tanner along. I've heard Pete's professor crowd from the university can get a little frisky."

Understatement of the century once the hot tub antics started. "Yeah, they can. Thanks, Mere."

Another hug warmed her heart. "Jill, I'm here for you. I always will be. Whatever happens, okay?"

Jill tunneled her hands into her hair, massaging the tightness in her neck. "That means a lot. I need to get back to work and let you do the same."

Meredith bumped her with a hip. "I'm glad we're okay again, sis."

"Me too."

Even though the reconciliation was a relief, it didn't erase the worry in her solar plexus. What in the world was she going to do about Brian and the French chick?

CHAPTER 35

"We have a problem," Mac announced when Jill took a chair next to him in the coffee shop on Friday morning.

"What's wrong?" she asked as Margie put her Americano in front of her.

His hand slapped the paper onto the table. "Read it. Peggy is suggesting she found something in my background that might give council members pause. She's not saying what, which is damned smart of her and irritating as hell. There's also a group that's mobilized at the last minute to stop us."

Her mouth gaped. "But everything was fine yesterday."

"Welcome to the fast lane."

The Western Independent's story was about a concerned citizens' group called FOLD—Friends of Limited Development. The article outlined FOLD's concerns, citing statistics about the interrelationship between crime and gambling.

Peggy's quote rocked her back in her seat. *Hotels with gambling like Mr. Maven's statistically attract criminal elements such as prostitution, loan sharking, and drunk and disorderly conduct. There's no question Dare Valley could use the financial boost his hotel would generate. It's what comes along with it that makes me think it's wrong for our community. Additionally, I've come across some information about Mr. Maven's background involving the law that has me seriously questioning his character. I plan to share that information in person at the city council meeting.*

"Take a deep breath," Mac suggested when she looked up from the article. "I can almost see the steam coming out of your ears."

How could Peggy take it this far? "Do you know what she's talking about?"

"Stuff involving the law? It's so vague I could run a truck through it." He smoothed his tie with calm hands, but his eyes burned with repressed rage. "That's the genius of it. She's a regular Machiavelli."

Funny, how Jill had always liked that about Peggy until now. "Can we make her tell us?"

His brow shot up. "Are you serious?"

Snorting would have been unprofessional. "Right. She's like steel."

"I'll have to handle it at the city council meeting. Now tell me about FOLD's spokesperson."

She blew on it and then took a sip. "It's that damn Florence Henkelmyer. She's tight as a screw when it comes to money and hates seeing people with it. And who came up with the name like FOLD? Definitely not Florence. She's not that creative."

"If they're willing to meet with us, I'd like to try and convince them the hotel's not evil incarnate."

Breathe, she told herself. "I'll get on it. What about Peggy?"

"Leave her to me," he replied. "She's entitled to her opinion, but I won't let her ruin this for us."

His voice was a little too smooth, so she studied him. His cleanly shaven jaw looked tense, the dent in his chin more accentuated than normal.

"She's coming to the party tonight. You can talk to her there."

He slid files into his briefcase. "Fine. I have some calls to make, so I'll head back to the hotel for a while. Call me when you have a meeting set up with these folks. I'll clear my schedule."

"Good I'll see what I can do."

When they stood, he patted her shoulder. "It'll be okay, Jill. The vote is Monday. They don't have much time to put up a fuss."

She gave him a brave smile, but worry ran rampant through her mind. Last minute campaigns had altered elections in this town. "What if they won't listen?"

"Then I dust off my feet and leave. If I can't convince them, I'll stop caring what they think. It's a waste of energy."

God, she wished she could do that, simply stop worrying about what other people thought. Maybe there was a secret substance in Dare's water that caused that malady, which is why Mac seemed immune.

She reached for her coffee cup. "Right. I don't like any of the people who are quoted in this article anyway. Well, other than Peggy." But not at the moment.

He tugged on his gray wool overcoat. "See. If they don't see reason, we'll just have to hope the others will."

After he left, she thought about her options if the vote didn't pass. She and Brian could figure out a way to bridge their creative differences and open a restaurant together.

And boot that French chick back to New York.

She headed behind the counter, needing the ebb and flow of customer orders and chitchat to distract her from the sadness she was feeling about the new threat to her dream job. She wanted to strangle her friend for muddying the waters.

Everything seemed to be up in the air once again. Maybe if she renamed her coffee shop Don't Toy with Me like Brian had suggested, the Universe would get the message.

***

Brian lugged the bazzillionth cardboard box of brats and chorizo down the deck steps. Chili pepper lights lined the rails, reminding him he needed some red pepper flakes. "Dammit, Pete, you'd better shovel this snow. Someone's going to take a dive and break their neck."

Pete popped his head out the back door. "I'll send someone out to take care of it."

Thankfully, he did. Mike, the bartender at Hairy's, scraped the snow off as Brian arranged his meat station a short distance away. One hundred pounds of meat. Four grills. And an open fire pit twenty yards off the deck where he would stake the chickens. Pete had bitched about the birds, but Brian couldn't resist. Something about men and fire. If he'd thought about it in advance, he would have ordered a whole pig. Spit the thing with a brown sugar glaze. Now *that* would have been a party.

Feeling heartened, he rubbed his gloved hands together. Despite the gray day and the breeze, there was something uniquely enjoyable about cooking outside. Add in the hauling he'd done, and his body was plenty warm. He was glad he'd worn his ski shirt under his jacket so it could wick away his sweat.

The easy camaraderie of the volunteers who were helping set up for the party only added to his good mood. People had been a little standoffish at first, but after they'd all hefted a bunch of shit around together, that attitude had faded. He'd become one of them again.

He was dumping beer into the industrial container for the marinade when Pete shouted his name. Turning, he caught a shape like a red straw before seeing blond curls cascading out of a cap. Simca gave him a wave like she was royalty skiing at Chamonix-Mont-Blanc. He tossed the empty bottle into the garbage with a loud clack.

"Hey," Pete said, "look who volunteered to help the other night. Having two professional chefs make the food. How lucky can I get? This is going to be the best party ever." He headed back inside.

"Hi, Brian," Simca said, her voice a soft purr.

So, this wasn't her best idea, but since Brian didn't want to be a dick and tell her to take a hike, he inclined his chin. Well, Jill had to start trusting him sometime. And this was as good a place to start as any. At least they were in public.

"Hi," he replied, sensing a few people edging closer as they carried lights and Chinese lanterns by him. It was like Hairy's all over again. Shit. He'd been way too optimistic.

She fingered a package of ribs. "That the marinade?" When he nodded, she squatted down and inhaled long and deep. "I've never used beer in a marinade, but I like it. It's earthy."

"Yes," he replied, trying to tune out the attention they were attracting.

She stood and held out her hands, like she was ready to receive her marching orders. "Then let's start. You can show me how Americans do cook outs."

The role reversal was refreshing, and it erased his feeling of unease. "You'll be a natural."

They fell into an old, familiar rhythm, discussing the stages and steps—planning, tasting, and sharing.

He ripped off another bottle cap and poured more beer into his marinade. Assuming everything went through on Monday and Jill took the job with Mac, he would ask her how she'd feel about him working with Simca.

As the foam rose in the bucket, he realized it had to work.

He jerked guiltily when Simca's hand brushed his.

"Let me stir," she commanded gently.

"Sure," he replied, stepping back, once again aware of the stares. He wasn't in love with her anymore, but she clearly had feelings for him.

Why did the past always have to confuse the present?

Deep down, he knew Jill wouldn't understand.

And maybe in that she'd be right.

CHAPTER 36

Keith pushed around his macaroni and cheese, kicking the legs under the table like he was in soccer striker tryouts.

"Stop the kicking, please," Peggy asked in her nicest voice.

Heading back to work had delighted her for all of five minutes until she saw the stack of new files on her desk and the hundreds of emails in her Inbox. She hated being behind. It would take days to dig herself out of the hole. Even worse, her red nose could still pass for Rudolf's.

The doorbell rang. She jumped and frowned. God, she hoped it wasn't Maven. She'd been waiting for him to track her down all day.

Keith swiveled in his chair.

"Stop right there. You can get up when you finish your dinner."

"But mom," he whined, inducing a shudder. The whining had started up full throttle as soon as he got the cast. She prayed it would go away when it came off.

"No buts. You know the rules."

She winced when the mirror in the hallway produced the expected results. The only thing with color was her stupid nose. Well, it would serve him right.

Peggy opened the door. Jill stood there with her arms crossed.

She forced herself to meet her eyes. The tightness in Jill's mouth made Peg's conscience squirm. Hadn't she been dreading this? "You're early. Your grandfather's not showing up to watch Keith until eight."

"Yes, I thought we should *chat* beforehand."

Jill's outfit seemed utterly befitting for a party called PolarFest. Her boots had fake fur on the tops, reminding Peggy of sheep, a fleecy green cap made of squiggly yarn covered her head, and a cream scarf cinched her neck, tight as a garrote. A knee-length burgundy bubble coat completed the look.

"Look, you're mad about my statement in the paper. Fine. I get that." She crossed her arms too. "You know I don't support the hotel."

Jill tugged on her scarf. "Yes, but did you have to give them such a humdinger quote?"

"Jillie," Keith called. "Come see me, pul-leeez."

"Be right there," she yelled, making Peggy wince. "What the hell do you think you have on him?"

"I'm only saying at the council meeting. Sorry, Jill, but we agreed to disagree."

"Yeah, but you threw out a character assassination without any facts. Does that seem like fair play to you?"

She steeled herself. "I'm doing what I have to do."

"He's been nothing but nice to you. I didn't know you could be so mean."

Even though suspects had called her all sorts of bad names, this one stung. "I have to do what I think is right."

Jill's mouth pursed like she'd sucked sour lemons. "Fine, but since we're still friends...the French chick is thinking of buying Morty's shop. She wants to open a place with Brian in Dare."

"Uh-oh. She must really want him back. This isn't her scene. She's like some exotic animal in a petting zoo."

"Wow, that's an image. And based on the six calls I've received from friends who are helping set up for the party, Pete apparently invited her to help with PolarFest. The asshole. She and Bryan have been cooking together. They've said it looks 'intense.' Whatever that means."

Probably what you think it means, Peggy thought. She let out an undetectable breath of relief. By switching to a personal topic, Jill was showing her they were still friends—for now. She led her to the formal living room she never used so they could talk away from Keith.

"Start from the beginning." She realized it was the same phrase she used with crime victims when they babbled.

Jill nodded and started in on the story. When she finished, she put her head in her hands. "I'm going crazy."

"Hold on," Peggy ordered when she saw Keith peek around the corner. "Back to the kitchen, young man." So much for keeping little ears away.

"But I'm done with my dinner," he protested, sticking out his cast—a new ploy for sympathy. "Jillie, why are you so sad?"

Peggy's heart melted. She treasured the moments when her son showed he would grow up to be a good man, canceling out her ex's asshole genes.

Jill held out her arms. Keith hobbled over and gave her a hug. "Oh, why can't you grow up so I can marry you?" Jill asked.

"Because it takes like years to grow up," Keith informed her. "Didn't you learn that in science class, Jillie?" He rustled free. "Besides, you're going to marry Brian."

How did a seven-year-old know something like that? "What makes you think so?"

His right shoulder inched up. "'Cause he makes you happy and act like a girl."

"Who told you that?" Peggy asked.

"Uncle Tanner."

Peggy wanted to roll her eyes, but it was impossible to diss Tanner in front of Keith. Blood would be spilled.

"Can I watch TV, mom?"

"Sure. Grandpa Hale will be here soon though."

"Cool." He left with a cheeky wave.

Jill sighed. "He's right. Brian does make me happy—when he isn't busy making me nuts with this whole French chick thing." And she gestured to her clothes. "And he does make me act like a girl. Do you know how long it took me to choose something warm *and* cute?"

Peggy had a moment of panic when she thought about her own wardrobe. Her warmest jacket was police issue. Not exactly party gear. She shook herself. When in the hell did she ever obsess over what to wear? Must be catching—like a virus.

"And you know what," Jill said. "I'm dying of heat."

"Then take some of it off."

With the bizarre cap, she could have auditioned for the Muppets. "It would take too long to put it back on. Why don't you go upstairs and get ready?"

They walked to the foyer, and Peggy headed for the stairs. "Where's Maven?" she asked before she thought to stop herself.

"He's meeting us there." Jill's head swiveled. Her eyes narrowed. "See, you *do* have the hots for him, but you're trying to deny it by using his last name—and throwing out humdingers in the paper."

"I am not, and I do not like—"

"Peg and Mac sitting in a tree—"

"Oh, shut up," Peggy interrupted. "He likes a challenge. He sees me as an obstacle, so he's trying to sweet talk me into supporting his project, that's all."

"I don't think so."

"You can think whatever you want. He's a poker player. I'm a cop. Oil and water would be more compatible."

"Brian tells me they make a good vinaigrette."

"That's oil and vinegar, you idiot."

Jill crossed her arms. "How would you feel if you weren't a cop, and he wasn't a poker player?"

"That you're a moron. I'm going to get ready."

"You can run, but..." Jill's voice faded when she disappeared from view.

Oh, she could hide all right. She'd been doing it for years. Still, Maven's ruggedly handsome face kept popping into her mind, making her kick the staircase. She could all but hear her heart sigh. Pathetic, simply pathetic, especially given what she knew of him.

Still, her pulse sped up. She was going to see him. Her thoughts turned to her closet. What in the hell could she wear to this popsicle party that would make her look good?

When she realized she was thinking like a girl, she gave a little shriek and mouthed a really bad word.

***

"I hate parties," Tanner muttered when they arrived at Pete's house.

Surveying the scene, Jill rubbed her gloves together. "Welcome to PolarFest."

About fifty people stood in the front yard, milling around the open garage, huddled together, drinking beer. More chili pepper light strings decorated the front door and the bushes. Someone had stolen a blinking leprechaun sign from Hairy's and shoved it by the bay window. It looked better than she'd expected. Pete hadn't half-assed it after all. Reluctantly, she gave him points.

Despite her beef with Pete, a shiver of anticipation ran through her. She had always loved PolarFest. The speakers were already blasting classic Bon Jovi, and it seemed like the whole town had shown up—the place was packed, inside and out. Jemma would have been proud.

"It's three degrees out," Meredith complained, leaning closer to Tanner.

Jill pulled out packets of hand warmers and shoved them at the trio. "Here, these will keep you warm. They work great in your bra. Adds a little stuffing too."

"Please," Tanner muttered, cursing under his breath.

"I'll have to adjust my clothing. Tanner, block the view," Meredith ordered. "Peg?"

"I don't stuff—anything."

Jill snickered. "Your loss."

Spotting a keg station in the front yard. Jill trudged forward for a couple of beer maps. She traced the paper, remembering when Jemma came up with the idea a few years ago. Shaking off her sadness, she headed back over to the others.

"Here's the setup," she announced, passing one to Meredith. "Winter ale in the kitchen. Chocolate stout in the garage. White wheat on the deck. You can read the rest."

"Okay, that's cool," Tanner commented, taking the paper from Meredith.

They all jumped when something cracked. Rainbow lights in the sky drew their attention.

"Oh, and sometimes the guys hoard fireworks from the Fourth and set them off."

"That's against city ordinance," Peggy informed them, scanning the yard like she was looking for other signs of criminal activity.

"We've never gotten into trouble for it. Hell, it's safer than in the summer. No danger of wild fires now. God, I hope Mac calls me when he gets here. I don't know how I'm going to find him in this throng."

"How are you even going to feel your phone vibrate dressed up like a puffer fish?" Meredith asked. "How many layers do you have on anyway? You're going to roast inside."

"Trust me, you're going to wish you looked like this. You're talking to a veteran of six PolarFests." She puffed her cheeks out, mimicking the fish she resembled. "The wind chill is going to start dipping, making it feel like it's ten below zero."

"I'm sticking to the house then," Meredith said with a shudder.

Jill waved her hand. "Trust me, you're going to be driven outside. It gets way too crowded and hot in there. You'll barely be able to move. Guys try to cop cheap feels, especially the old profs."

"Wonderful." Meredith grabbed the beer map from Tanner's hand. "Well, if I'm going to get groped all night long, I'm going to need a drink."

"No one's groping you," Tanner declared.

Hearing the tinkle of bells, Jill spun around. Down the lane, a horse tossed his head, his breath frosty white from the cold. "Oh, my God," Jill cried. "It's a sleigh."

"Holy shit," Tanner muttered.

"Hey, Jill," Clark Terrence called from the buggy seat, reigns snug in his gloved hands. "I borrowed Old Man Jenkins's sleigh in memory of Jemma so that I can give rides in the vacant pasture adjoining Pete's property. Remember how much she wanted this last year? Damn, I miss that girl."

Her tears nearly froze. "I remember, Clark," she called out, her voice breaking. "She would have loved it."

"You'll have to come for a ride."

"I will, Clark. Thanks."

So Jemma had her legacy after all. It was all around them.

"Oh, shit, I'm going to bawl." Jill sniffed and dug out a Kleenex.

"Unbelievable," Meredith declared, pulling her in for a one-arm hug.

"I told you. It's PolarFest."

Memories overwhelmed her. The first year they'd held PolarFest was when they were both twenty-one. The scope and size of the party had continued to grow each year as they planned increasingly more unique events. One year they'd made an ice rink in the vacant pasture and played ice skating bingo. And now PolarFest had a sleigh.

"We missed you at setup, Jill," someone called out. "Brian's cooking a shitload of meat. Spit a whole flock of chickens. Jemma would have loved that."

She waved in the general direction since she couldn't see who was speaking. She hadn't been prepared for how many people would talk about Jemma.

"You gonna be all right?" Meredith asked, rubbing her back.

She wiped her nose. "Yeah. Jemma would be happy about this. I need to find Brian." And see for herself how things were between him and the French chick.

Peggy took Jill's elbow. "No reason for delay, right?"

"Right," Jill responded, leading them around the house.

White Chinese lanterns hung along the side of the house and dotted the trees, lending everything a magical glow.

The powerful smell of roasted meat reached her when the wind blew. She caught sight of a huge bonfire, emitting tons of smoke. She wouldn't have been surprised if someone had been dancing in the middle. Jill spotted Brian basting a whole row of chickens with a kitchen mop. He was standing in the middle of a ring of fire with only a narrow path leading into the circle of four grills and an open pit. All he had on was a long-sleeved T-shirt, and he was sweating at the temples. When Brian cooked, he went all out.

She waved at a few people as they walked deeper into the back, but she kept her eyes peeled for the French chick. "Tell me that's not the mop Pete and his boys use to clean their kitchen floor," Jill commented as they reached Brian.

"Like those guys ever clean anything," he replied with a shudder, dunking the mop back into the gallon bucket of basting sauce before dabbing the glistening birds again. "I'm getting slammed. Can you turn some brats for me?"

Clearly, he was in drill sergeant mode. When she didn't answer right away, he turned toward her, the roaring fire illuminating the side of his face.

His eyes narrowed, and he pulled her to him, kissing her on the mouth. "I'm glad you're here. You've been crying. You saw the sleigh, didn't you?"

His comfort helped soothe the ache a little. "Yes."

His finger stroked her cheek. "Jemma always did have great ideas."

"Yeah," she mused, picking up a meat fork the size of her grandpa's cane.

"Hey guys," Brian called out to her group of supporters, but even she could detect the tension in his voice. "Glad you came."

"We're trying to get into the spirit," her sister responded.

Jill almost let out a sigh. Good. Everyone needed to put their recent interactions aside. Her family and Brian both meant the world to her, and they'd have to deal with each other.

Meredith linked her arm with Tanner's. "I need a drink. Peg?"

"I'll wander around. See if they're breaking any other ordinances."

"We're already breaking the fire code given the number of people inside." Brian darted over to what looked like fifty hamburgers frying in neat, precise rows. "Tell Pete to announce that the meat's coming off the grill in five. Hey, we laid the sausages from right to left," Brian informed her.

"So?" Her eyes watered from the smoke.

"So, turn them from right to left. It's the cooking order."

"Order-smoder," she replied, but fell into a rhythm with the heat on her face, inhaling the scent of the roasted meat, listening to Brian mutter as he darted back and forth between the cooking stations.

"Sorry that took so long, Brian. I see you found yourself another helper."

Jill turned, grill fork in hand. She wished Simca's all-red outfit looked like a fire hydrant, so the dogs could all do their business on her. Instead, it accentuated her svelte figure. Simca picked up another fork and opened the grill, turning hot dogs and hamburgers like she was a gold medal winner in the Grilling Olympics. Even her stocking cap made her look like some sleek ski kitten in a Bond film. Suddenly Jill felt like a slob.

Jill walked over to her, her anger flaring like the fire. "I can handle this. Why don't you go get a drink?"

They shared a look of pure understanding that went all the way back to women in the caveman era. *He's my man,* Jill conveyed, while Simca shrugged, *try and stop me.*

"As you wish," she replied, turning the last of the meat.

Brian stepped between them. "Sim, why don't you grab me a Guinness?"

When she left, Jill was aware of the stares, the conversations that halted mid-sentence.

Brian dropped the mop into the bucket, causing marinade to slop out onto the shoveled snow. "I can tell you're upset about her being here, but we're only cooking."

She realized she couldn't wait to ask him. "Grandpa said she looked at Mr. Wilson's property for a restaurant? Is she really thinking about staying here?"

His eyes swept between her and the roasting chickens. "I...tried to tell you—"

"The night you moved in," she finished. "Yes, I remember."

He turned a chicken and then rushed over to her, gripping her arms. "If the hotel is approved, it'll open up a market for high-end cuisine in Dare. The guests won't always eat at the hotel. It's a good option, Jill. I can stay here with you and do the kind of work I really want, but it's only an option. We'll talk about it after the city council vote comes in."

His reasonable tone made her grind her teeth. "Do you really think you can work with her without getting all tangled up?"

"Yes! I love you, and you need to start trusting me. Look, smoke's pouring out of your grill. Can we talk about this later?" he asked, picking the mop back up.

Ignoring the smoke, she stood her ground and changed tactics. "I saw you, how you two worked together, how you look together. You're a team."

"Jeff's tapping a keg," Pete said, coming into the circle and slapping Brian on the back. "Where's the ever-helpful Simca?"

"Don't ask," he responded, nudging him with an elbow.

Pete's eyes widened when he caught sight of Jill. "Right. What can I do?"

"Turn the burgers," Brian ordered. "Jill, we'll talk about this later."

Both of them turned away from her. Jill finished flipping her meat, even as the rage grew inside her. Pete liked Simca. He had invited her here. It was the last straw. She put her fork down and walked over to him. He didn't look at her as he arranged the burgers.

"I came here tonight even though it was one of the hardest things I've ever done. Jemma's not here, and tonight makes that even more obvious."

"Jill," Brian warned.

"No, I'm not done." She drilled her finger into Pete's chest. "I came anyway, and what do you do? You invite Brian's ex-whatever over to help him and then act like she belongs more than I do. Who in the hell do you think you are?" She stepped back, arms wide.

"She volunteered to help, Jill," he responded, his eyes narrowing. "You need to calm down."

A crowd started to gather—either everyone had developed an appetite at once, or they were all listening to her. Suddenly she didn't care. The words were bursting from her chest. "I'm glad Jemma can't see what you've become."

Someone pulled on her arm. She realized it was Brian, looking at her with slitted eyes.

"Enough. Go inside." When she didn't move, he gave her a nudge. "You're not thinking straight."

The only sound in the backyard was the rock music blasting over the speakers, she realized. People passed in a blur as she hurried into the house. Coming here had to be the stupidest idea she'd ever had. If it weren't for Mac, she would have taken off.

As she dodged through the throng of people in the kitchen, a few pitying glances were thrown her way. When she caught sight of the French chick popping champagne in clear celebration mode, she wanted to break the bottle.

The party swirled around her, but the coldness of grief grew inside her.

Everything had changed.

***

"Fuck," Brian muttered as Jill ran inside. He checked the meat, his heart pounding in his chest. His hopes of everything falling into place had gone up in flames.

The wind blew briskly, and the plastic plates he'd weighed down took flight like Frisbees.

"Goddammit," Pete growled. "When is Jill going to stop this shit? I mean, I hate to say it, but Simca's growing on me. I think she's got your best interests at heart. Buying Morty's place to open a restaurant with you. Now that's loyalty."

The fire burned Brian's face. "Look. Keep your mouth shut."

The last thing he wanted was for that particular gem to start circulating in the town's gossip mill. Pete had said he'd keep it to himself. Right.

"Seriously, Bri."

"Look, I haven't decided on anything yet, so shut it." And after seeing Jill's reaction, he knew she would never support it. An angry depression overtook him.

Pete flung out his arms. "Are you crazy? What's your other option? Stay at The Chop House? You know you hate it. You'll die of boredom, man."

The words dug into his skull. He wanted to lash out at the unfairness of it all. Most of all he wanted Pete to stop. It was more than unprofessional to air his feelings about The Chop House in public.

"Jill's leaving you behind with the potential big new job at the hotel. You know she wants it."

"I said, 'shut up, Pete.'"

"Why won't you take what you want?"

Brian slugged him before he knew what he was doing. Pete fell back, making the crowd gasp.

Brian took a deep breath, reaching for his control. "Shit, man. I'm sorry."

Pete slipped on the snow, trying to get back up. Brian reached out a hand to help him. His friend flung it aside and stood.

"You just crossed the line," he announced, brushing at his lip.

"Pete—"

He walked away.

The fire over the birds whooshed. Brian concentrated on pulling the chickens off the spit so he wouldn't have to meet anyone's eyes.

God, he'd totally lost it. But why hadn't Pete just shut the hell up?

When smoke rolled over him, he stabbed the meat with blurred eyes. Flung it on the plate in an odd assortment without a care for presentation.

Lifelong friendship flickered like the flames.

***

Peggy surveyed the guests at the party. College towns really were weird. Gray-haired profs flirted with dewy co-eds like it was completely normal. She'd heard something about a hot tub from an old guy in an ugly green cardigan sweater who looked like he must be part of the English department. A few bleached blonds had shrieked—actually shrieked—and run after him. God, she hoped they weren't breaking another city ordinance.

She hated busting naked people.

Especially if they were wet and sloshed.

A warm palm squeezed her behind, making her head swivel. A feverish, middle-aged man had his eyes glued to her butt.

"Get your hand off my ass before I break your arm."

His glassy eyes didn't so much as blink. She slapped his hand away.

His gaze swung up like he was being pulled on a lever. "You're *intense*, like one of the black holes I study. I appreciate that in a woman. Wanna go somewhere and make out?"

Astonishment flashed through her. Who in the hell were these people? "What are you? Some demented prof from the astronomy department? Get lost."

He made some humming sound like a bee that'd just been diverted from a blooming flower and didn't intend to be put off. "Make me."

She took a wide stance. "Look, I'm a cop, so take off."

His grin made him look even more dopey-eyed drunk. Seriously, what was with this guy?

"I love role play. You're a cop, and I'm a dangerous criminal. Wanna cuff me?"

"Seriously, I am *the deputy sheriff* of Eagle County, and you need to back off."

He reached for her face. A man seized his hand mid-reach.

"Trust me. She really is the deputy sheriff." Mac Maven leveled the guy a dangerous look. For Peggy, it only confirmed what she knew of him— Mr. Poker wasn't all charm. "And she told you to back off."

"She's only saying that," the professor mumbled. "She really wants me. I have a PhD. Women like that."

"I don't think so," Maven said, stepping closer.

"I've got this," she interrupted, putting her hands on her hips.

"I said," Maven uttered in a silky voice. "*Leave.*"

The guy back peddled. "She doesn't want you either, man," he said over his shoulder as he stumbled away.

"I'm well aware of that," Maven said, turning to face Peggy.

"I was taking care of it," she ground out.

He lifted his brow. "I didn't mean to impugn your abilities. I'm sure you could have put him in a deadly Colga hold. My way seemed faster."

"That headlock is no longer used by police officers. And your way wasn't faster. You just didn't give me the chance to deal with it," she commented, knocking into him when someone pushed her from behind.

He caught her shoulders with his hands. They felt big and warm on her body, and the woman inside her was awakened by the touch. His brown leather jacket called to mind old war pilots. Add in a V-neck gray sweater with the hint of a white T-shirt underneath, and he looked relaxed and casual—more so than she'd ever seen him. The jeans hugged his thighs, making her wonder how it showcased his nice butt.

He didn't let go. "Your hair looks lovely tonight, and is that color in your cheeks?"

His face took up her whole field of vision, like a microscope zoomed in on a prized specimen. God, he was gorgeous. Why did she have to feel this jolt with him? And why wasn't he giving her the cold shoulder after that quote was published in the paper?

"Have you found Jill?" she asked in an effort to divert his attention from her *brushed* hair. He'd noticed. Part of her sighed.

"Not yet. Let's get some air. We have something to discuss." He took her elbow, leading her through the crowd and down a hallway. They stepped onto the wrap-around porch, his efficacy and speed indicating he'd been at the party for a while. He must have taken the time to scope the place out. A few people stood smoking, chatting in low voices near the tiki torches.

Maven swung his jacket off and had it on her shoulders before she could protest. She wished she hadn't shed her coat. His actions made her edgy. If he thought he could convince her to back off, he had another thing coming.

Her chin went up. "I don't need your jacket."

When she reached to take it off, he laid his hand over hers. "If I asked you what you think you have on me, would you tell me?"

"No."

"I didn't think so." He raked a hand through his hair. "So, it's going to be a shoot out then. You and me at the city council meeting."

Her mind conjured up a dusty street in the old west at high noon. He would make a good adversary. "If you like."

"Peg, whatever you think you have, let me warn you it's not going to play out like you expect."

She stiffened. "Don't warn me off. Your charm won't work on me."

"I know you're tough. You don't have to prove that to me."

His eyes could have been spotlights into her soul. His intense stare made her want sunglasses, which was stupid since it was pitch black out. "Glad you picked that up."

A devilish grin slashed across his face. "After our encounter on the street with Keith, it would be impossible for me to forget. But that's not all you are. It's good to see your hair brushed and that ghastly green off your face. It's a nice face."

A door slammed somewhere, startling her, or was it her imagination? His deep voice was as mesmerizing as the cadence of her gun shooting at the range. It held her in place like she was his personal target.

"Mother and cop vie for first place, but mother always wins. You can be tough, yes, but you're also incredibly loving, gentle. Even playful, I'll bet. Being a good friend is important to you as well. I would bet you're intensely loyal. But it's the side of you that's hidden best that has me thinking about you more than I'd like."

Her throat might have turned to sand because she couldn't breathe or swallow. She gave herself an internal shake like she did sometimes when she heard dark, nasty details about a crime. No intimidation. No fear. No reaction.

"Oh, yeah?" she replied in her most flippant voice. "What's that?"

He cocked his head, those jade eyes wandered over her face. "Don't you know? It's the woman." His hand smoothed a tendril behind her ear. "She's buried deep, but she's still there."

His touch burned her skin. Made her lips tremble slightly. For the first time in many years, Peggy had to reach deep for imperviousness. "I don't know what you're talking about. Of course I'm a woman." She gestured towards her chest as if to say *duh*.

Those bow-shaped lips curved, accentuating his dimple. "Yes, there's no denying nature's finest trappings." His gaze dipped lower and then rose to her face. "But you don't let yourself act like a woman anymore. It's like you consider it a weakness. I wonder about that."

The pressure in her chest came out of nowhere. Suddenly she couldn't fill her lungs. "Well, don't overtax your pea-sized brain. Keep it focused on how you can swindle more people out of their money at cards."

"I already know how to do that. I won't take exception to your use of 'swindle' since I know what I am."

Well, she didn't have a clue. He was a threat to her system. Intoxicating and interesting, but unnerving all the same.

"Why aren't you more upset with me?"

He leaned back, all nonchalance. "I was at first, but then I did what I did when I'm playing poker. I took stock of who I was playing against, thought about her motives. I realized you wouldn't be fighting this hard if I didn't threaten you. Why don't you stop trying to approve or disapprove of what I do for a living and simply let yourself go?"

Was his jacket growing heavier? It could have doubled for concrete. "Go where?" she quipped.

He didn't touch her, but she felt the punch of his gaze all the way to her toes. "If you have to ask, the woman's buried even deeper than I suspected."

Old vulnerability sprung up as if from a jack-in-the-box. Memories and emotions flooded her system. A whisper surfaced. *If you let yourself be a woman, you'll be destroyed again.*

"You need to stop looking for layers. I'm Peggy McBride. Mom. Deputy. End of story."

The hollow at the base of his throat drew her attention. What would his skin taste like and how warm would it be? The thought shocked her.

"Some people's stories are as short and simple as children's books. Yours isn't one of them. You're as long and complex as *Great Expectations*, but you're trying to give the world a *Cliff Notes* version. Most are content with that. I'm not."

She jerked his jacket off, ignoring how it released more of his spicy scent. "I don't care what you are. And stop trying to read me like I'm sitting across from you at some poker tournament."

When he didn't take the jacket, she thrust it at his chest. He grabbed her hand and held it against his heart. The rapid beats matched the tempo of her breathing.

His chest seemed lovingly carved by a sculptor's hands, the angles defined, utterly masculine, begging for her touch. She yanked her hand back and fisted it at her side.

"I know you're not ready, Peg, but you're in luck. I have a reputation for being patient." He gestured to the door. "Shall we?"

Since she had no idea how to respond, she strode forward. Part of her didn't want to dissuade him. There was a new thrill inside her, like when she had burst into a drug dealer's house without her Kevlar vest. Stupid, but exhilarating.

His finger brushed her nape, making her spine arch, but she didn't turn around.

"Peg," he whispered in the cold night. "I'm not your enemy. Remember that when we face each other down at the council meeting."

He was wrong. He was as much an enemy to her body as he was to her town. She simply had to defeat him.

CHAPTER 37

Jill wanted to find a corner where she could quietly grieve.

The half-hearted conversations she'd been having were draining her soul. Finding Mac was her main goal. Then she could escape. When she finally found him, he was already chatting away with the dean of environmental science, who was also head of the Environmental Club. Why hadn't she guessed he'd figure out who to target in this crowd? He turned when she approached and ended the conversation with élan. The dean headed off with a wave.

"You don't have to babysit me, Jill," Mac said. "I can tell tonight's been difficult for you. Why don't you head home?"

"No, this is my job," she responded, aware of the strained glances. It was like she had a *Party Wrecker* sign around her neck.

He leaned close. "Take it from someone who knows. Fold your cards when the odds are against you."

The urge to fight rose, but he was right. She nodded.

"I'll call you in the morning." Mac disappeared through the crowd.

She supposed she should be glad for his understanding, but humiliation made her red spots pop. She was a liability tonight.

A tap on her arm made her swivel around. Terry Ployke had the look of a man who'd been given an unwelcome job, his face pinched like he'd eaten bad sushi.

"Hey, Brian's looking for you. Said he'd be at the sleigh. It got stuck out back."

"Thank you," came out like she'd downed a teaspoon of gravel. She wondered if he'd chosen the sleigh because of Jemma. She rubbed her throbbing head and wove through the tense crowd. And caught sight of Kelly Kimple. Of course, she'd be here. It was the biggest party of the year. She was engaged to a young biology professor now, but she still radiated that perky, sleek cheerleader look. Old memories and feelings rolled back in, making Jill feel small.

Thankfully no one could see her flushed skin in the dark room.

The wind blew snow on her face when she opened the back door. A number of people who were clearly impervious to pain were singing a song she didn't recognize about mountains and moonlight. At least one of them didn't have much of an ear for music, but they were all shouting at the tops of their lungs.

Her eyes watered from the cold when she stepped out to find Brian.

***

Brian turned when he heard the crunch of snow. He froze when he saw Simca coming down the path, a beaming smile on her face.

"What is it?" he asked.

She gestured to her phone. "Glorious news, *mon cher*."

He squinted into the distance, looking for Jill. This was all he needed. If she saw him with Simca... "Okay, tell me quickly. I'm waiting for Jill."

Her smile faded. "You really do love her, don't you?"

So, she really hadn't believed him. Part of him knew she hadn't stayed around for the restaurant, but he'd wanted this chance so badly. He sighed, his breath cascading to the sky like smoke. "Yes. I told you I was with her now."

Those sherry eyes sought his. "And us?"

He shook his head. "We have some wonderful memories, a true respect for each other professionally, and a shared passion and understanding of food. But that's all."

"Then that makes what I am about to show you harder. I told you I would make things right, but I had hoped... Well, just read it."

He took her phone. His eyes widened at the title of the article, "New York Chef's Confession." The interview covered Simca's rise to fame with her celebrity chef husband and their difficult marriage. It ended with an account of her affair with Brian, the injustice her husband had done to him, and her emphatic statement of his innocence. She pleaded with the culinary community to stop making him the scapegoat for her failed marriage.

His whole body flushed with an emotion so strong, he couldn't speak. She'd made everything right again.

She retrieved the phone from his lax hand. "I could tell last night at the bar you didn't share my affections anymore. I had hoped I was wrong, but after being here tonight, I think it's better for us to part ways. I've just texted a few chefs in Manhattan and received positive feedback. They'll interview you for a sous chef position, Brian. You don't have to go into business with me." She wiped her nose. "And I...I can't be around you and not care."

His entire career was coming back into focus. He wasn't a pariah anymore. "Oh, Sim," he whispered, moved beyond belief. Eager to comfort and thank her, he took her into his arms. "I'm so grateful, but the last thing I want is for you to be hurt."

She rested her head against his chest. "I will mend. Perhaps I was trying to hold onto something that was no longer there."

When she lifted her face, he brushed aside a lone tear. His muscles tensed. He'd never seen her cry. "How can I ever thank you for restoring my reputation?"

Her mouth tipped up in a small smile. "Did I not tell you I would make amends?"

The warmth in his chest spread. He cupped her cheek. "Yes, you did. Thank you!" And the gratitude burst from his heart. She'd forsaken her own privacy for him.

Her eyes softened. "You are most welcome, *cherie*. I wish you success—whatever it is you decide to do. Of course, should you change your mind..."

His heart hurt. It felt like he was saying goodbye to a part of himself, a piece of his past. "So this is goodbye, then?"

"I'm afraid so. I'll...miss you," she whispered.

Lover. Teacher. Friend. And now savior. "Yeah," he whispered back, thinking of all the meals they'd made and shared in the sweltering heat of the kitchen—or at home when it was just them. "Me too."

Kissing her goodbye seemed like the most natural thing in the world. When she settled against his chest, he pulled her close. "We had some great times."

"The best," she agreed.

The mountains rose before them, seemingly closer than usual. Brian's mind filled with scenarios. He had his reputation back. Everything seemed possible again. He couldn't wait to tell Jill. Freedom beat a heady rhythm in his body.

***

The light from the porch and Chinese lanterns faded the farther Jill stepped away from the house. Moonlight gave the shoveled path an eerie glow. Footprints stamped the snow, an echo of a path already taken.

The red sleigh was hard to miss, an unnatural intrusion in a scene perfect enough for a Conservation International calendar. The horse stood tethered to a large maple, bobbing its head in place, snorting white puffs resembling cotton balls. The bells around his neck jingled, making her think of Christmas.

Two figures stood talking against the backdrop of the mountains. As she came closer, the sleek red suit froze her in her tracks. And she'd know Brian's body anywhere.

Her boots gripped the snow as she leaned forward, peering in the muted light. Brian was holding what looked to be a cell phone, its light illuminating his face. Even from the distance, she could see his face soften with shock and then love. When he cupped Simca's cheek, her heart tore. She watched them murmur, but she wasn't close enough to hear.

Paralyzing fear emerged. It couldn't be true! After everything they'd shared, he couldn't still love Simca.

When he leaned in to kiss her, his arms holding her like they'd done it a thousand times, she stumbled as she tried to turn. It *was* true, and the old Jill told her she'd been stupid to believe otherwise.

He had chosen the pretty girl over her again.

She jumped when a hand brushed her arm. She turned to see Peggy, her mouth grim.

"Let's get you out of here," she said in a flat voice, pulling her away from the scene.

Jill slipped down the path. Without Peggy, she would have fallen to her knees and simply broken down. Her heart lay shredded inside her, a raw wound burning and throbbing.

Everything was lost.

CHAPTER 38

When Jill didn't come outside, Brian headed into the house to look for her. No one had seen her recently. They thought she might have left with Mac, but couldn't be sure. Peg, Tanner, and Meredith were all gone too. He took out his phone to text Jill.

Where are you? I have news.

He hung out with some old high school friends, still scanning for Jill. After thirty minutes without a response, he called her again and was bounced to her voicemail. The party was in full swing, but he didn't want to be there anymore, so he gathered his cooking utensils and left. He couldn't wait to tell her what had happened.

When he arrived at Jill's, all her lights were on. The first thing he saw when he walked inside was a tower of boxes in the hall. His already acid stomach burned when he caught sight of his own handwriting. They were his. Something was so not right.

His legs turned rubbery as he walked the short distance to the family room. Jill sat on her orange couch fully dressed, a pillow clutched in her lap. Her face bore the traces of tears.

"Hey!" he said gently. "What's wrong?"

"I need you to get out," she ordered. "Mere, Tanner, and Peggy helped me pack everything up. If we missed anything, I'll leave it for you at my shop."

Her cold tone was a slap in the face. "What are you talking about?"

"I saw you with her," she whispered. "We're—"

Oh Jesus. "I don't know what you think you saw," he said, knowing exactly who she meant. He flew across the room and sat beside her, meeting her tear-drenched gaze. "But you're jumping to the wrong conclusion."

"I saw you kiss her. Embrace her." Her words lashed out like a whip.

Jill edged away when he tried to touch her arm. Shit, he thought, thinking back to his final moments with Simca. Yeah, it probably had looked bad. "Listen. I was saying goodbye to her."

"Bullshit!" she cried.

He held out his hands, desperate to make her see. "It's true. We both ended up deciding we couldn't work together. I'm with you, Jill. I love you. Simca still has feelings for me, and I told her it wouldn't work."

She punched him in the arm. "And you still have feelings for her too, or you wouldn't have touched her. I *saw* you!"

"No!" The feeling of sinking in quicksand came over him. He wasn't sure how to dig himself out of this hole. He yanked out his phone and pulled up Simca's interview. "Read this. Seriously, Jill. She talked to a major culinary magazine about our affair, and how Andre set me up. She texted some major chefs in New York, and some of them are willing to interview me. Don't you see? I was grateful. I was saying goodbye to a friend."

She threw the pillow aside and stood, not reaching for the phone. "We tried your experiment. It failed. I can't trust you."

Oh God, it was his worst nightmare. He rose in a flash and gripped her shoulders. "Don't say that. I love you. I swear to you nothing happened. Please, Jill."

"You just said people want to interview you in New York. I think you should go for it. It's what you've always wanted."

His anger suddenly exploded. "What the fuck! I can't believe we're here again after everything we've shared."

A tear slid down her cheek.

"You *think* you see something, so you come home, pack me up, and kick me out? What the fuck kind of relationship is that?"

She scrubbed her face. "One that's not working."

He punched the air. "That's bullshit. It *has* been working. I can't wait to come home to you each night, and I've never been happier than these past couple of weeks. What more can I do to convince you I love you?"

Her lip trembled, and seeing it, had him fisting his hands at his side so he wouldn't reach for her.

"Clearly you can't." She inhaled a jagged breath. "You broke my heart again. Do you have any idea what that feels like?"

He grabbed her hand and slapped it against his chest. "Fucking yes. You're breaking my heart right now."

The muscles in her face tensed. A fresh onslaught of tears crested over. "We don't have what it takes, Bri. I just can't trust you after what I saw."

He strode across the room and kicked one of the boxes, had the sudden urge to hurl it across the room. "You're throwing everything away between us because of your insecurities. This is that stupid Kelly Kimple shit all over again."

She fisted her hand to her ribs. "It's not *stupid* to me. How do you think you'd feel if I'd done the same thing?"

"I don't fucking know. You're the saint. I'm the sinner. Am I ever going to be redeemable in your eyes?"

"Please." She couldn't meet his gaze. "Don't make this any harder than it is."

A laugh snorted out. "Harder? What the fuck does that look like, Jill? From where I'm standing, I'd pretty much say you've gutted me as clean as a fish."

"I thought you were going back to her when I saw you touch her. That you wanted her again. That you didn't want me anymore. I don't want to ever feel that way again."

"So you cut me out. No discussion. No nothing. Well, maybe you're fucking right. I guess we don't have what it takes. I'm tired of having to prove myself to you. I thought we were past all this."

"You shouldn't have put yourself in that situation!" she cried, sweeping her arms out.

He shoved his hands to his waist. "I didn't mean to. I was waiting for you to meet me by the sleigh. Simca found me because she had exciting news. I thanked her. Maybe not as 'purely' as you would have, but goddammit, I have history with her. I was saying goodbye. I waited outside for you for half an hour! I couldn't wait to tell you I'd been vindicated, that my career looked promising again. And you left without a fucking word."

She strode across the room and shoved his chest. "I cried the whole way home, damn you! What was I supposed to do? Intrude on your tender scene?" Her hand dug under her shirt and before he had time to process what she was doing, she yanked her necklace off and flung it at him.

She might as well have thrown his heart on the floor as well. He grabbed her fists. "Okay, that's it! You want to toss everything away, fine. I'm done trying to convince you how much I love you. When I head to New York this time, you can be goddamn sure it's your fault."

Her sharp intake punctuated the silence as he grabbed a couple of boxes and started to load his car. When he finished, his heart was thundering in his chest. Kneeling down, he picked up the broken necklace. He stood and strode down the hallway to her bedroom after not finding her anywhere else. For a moment, his hand almost couldn't turn the doorknob. He pressed his forehead against the wood, the necklace heavy in his hand, and reached deep for courage. Then he let himself inside.

A single lamp shone on her bedside, illuminating her in the fetal position, crying into a pillow. A searing pain shot through his heart. Nothing had ever hurt this bad.

"Jill," he called.

She jerked back and turned her flushed face toward him.

He held up her key in his other hand. "I'll leave this on the kitchen table. If you find any more of my stuff, throw it out."

A sob rushed out of her mouth. "I'm sorry," she whispered.

His throat thickened. "Me too," he said and left, unable to hurl the necklace across her yard in the snow and let it go.

CHAPTER 39

City cuncil meetings were new to Jill. Since it was open to the publico, they'd scheduled it for nighttime so more citizens could attend.

Through the large windows of the court-room-style council chamber, gas street lamps gave the snowy town square a Norman Rockwell feel. Inside, the chamber's high ceilings, burnished wood, and brass chandeliers created a cozy atmosphere.

"Stop fidgeting," Mac ordered under his breath.

Her fidgeting had more to do with her lack of sleep and cry-fest over Brian than it did nerves. No amount of concealer had worked on her puffy eyes. "There's a lot of people. Everyone's waiting to hear what Peggy's found out."

He smiled and nodded as more people settled into chairs. "Yes, but there are more on our side, so stop worrying. I'll handle her."

Her pencil skirt was going to have wrinkles if she didn't stop clutching it. "I can't help it. It's the biggest thing I've ever been involved in. Plus, you don't know what she's going to say."

Mr. Cool stood. God she wished she could be more like him. She was a freaking mess right now.

"Everything's going to be fine." He started making the rounds.

A hand tapped her shoulder, making her look back. "Grandpa!"

He bussed his grizzled cheek against hers. "Big night, sweetheart."

His endearment had her blinking back tears. "The biggest."

"Maven's not a man to underestimate. He's charmed his way into the most starched unmentionables in this town. Of course, everyone's wondering what Peggy has to say. Even a seasoned journalist like me couldn't get her to reveal her information. I was crushed." He tapped his cane. "So, I heard the Frenchie left town."

"What?" She made her mouth curve as the mayor cruised past them with a nod. Had Brian really been telling the truth? She'd tossed and turned all weekend thinking about it. Had her old fears ruined everything?

"Meredith told me about you and Brian. I'm sorry, honey. Come 'round the house tomorrow for dinner. Cry on this old man's shoulder."

She rubbed her nose when it started to tingle. "Okay."

Someone rapped a gavel. Her grandfather pressed her back into her chair when she jumped a few feet.

"Here." He reached into his pocket. "Have a red hot. They always calm me down. Remember who you are, and you'll do just fine."

"Sorry, I'm late," Mere announced in a rush. She kissed Jill's cheek with a loud smack. "Someone made a few too many red marks on my article for tomorrow's edition."

"Wonder who would do a thing like that?" Grandpa commented, pulling out a red pen and twirling it with his fingers.

Meredith gave him the fish eye and then turned to Jill. "You all set?"

Her sister had come over with movies and ice cream the last couple of nights, offering her unconditional support. She was so grateful for her right now. "As I'll ever be."

"You'll do fine. My sources tell me there are four people on the fence after Peggy's bombshell."

Grandpa gave a huff. "My sources say five people are on the fence. Given what Maven did for Keith, people are thinking it must be pretty bad for her to turn on him."

Just like Peggy had hoped. "Great."

"This might be one of the most exciting meetings Dare has seen." He tapped his cane for emphasis.

"Would everyone please take their seats?" Jim Kartens called loudly, banging the gavel.

Tanner approached them. "I found us three seats on the 'for' side. Good luck, Jill."

After kissing her on the cheek for luck, they wove through the crowd to their chairs behind the table where Mac and Jill were sitting at the front of the room. When Peggy strode forward with Keith, Jill's stomach gave a little jump.

Keith waved at their family. "Mommy, why can't we go sit with Uncle Tanner, Aunt Meredith, and Mr. Hale?"

"Because we need to sit on this side," she answered, guiding him toward a couple of seats across the aisle. She was careful not to meet Jill's gaze.

"But Mom," he protested, kicking his feet under the chair until reprimanded.

Mac waved to Peggy and Keith as he walked back to the front of the room, making Keith grin and Peg scowl. Jill scooted over to give him space. He unbuttoned his gray wool jacket and smoothed his burgundy tie.

"How can you be so calm?"

"I play poker for a living." He winked. "You ready?"

"I was born ready," she announced with false bravado. It was time to ignore everything but this moment.

The city council's chairman, Oscar Smithens, called roll and then went through some stupid-ass process to get the minutes from the last meeting approved. Didn't these people have email? When Jill didn't think she could stand it anymore, the chairman finally read their order of business. The hotel vote was the only item for this special meeting. Sitting up straighter, Jill clenched her hands in her lap.

"We've elected to read the correspondence we have on this issue and then take comments from visitors in the audience," Oscar announced. He began to read, shuffling the papers near the microphone. Most were in support because of the economic boost the hotel would give the town. A few mentioned their excitement at seeing Pincari's Folly renovated to its original glory. The dissenters talked about preserving the town's family-centered culture and protecting Dare from crime. A few environmental concerns were raised, but Jill knew they were bogus. Mac had high standards for environmental protection and preservation.

When Oscar opened the floor to visitors, Mac immediately raised his hand. The chairman looked between him and Peggy and then finally called on Mac with a friendly smile.

"Good evening, everyone. As you know, my company has proposed plans to renovate a condemned historic hotel in the mountains. We're concerned with providing the best services to our clientele, but more importantly, becoming another seam in the fabric of town life. This is why we hired someone you all know so well to help us for this vote—and hopefully the future. Jill Hale."

When he reached for her elbow, she stood up, trying not to obsess about whether or not she had a wedgie.

"Jill is one of you, from a family that's deeply invested in Dare. With her guidance, we have crafted a socially responsible and environmentally-friendly plan to make Pincari's Folly a premier boutique hotel. Since this town prides itself on unique brands, our niche fits in perfectly. A hotel that exclusively offers poker, no other type of gambling. It's totally legal and will be carefully controlled. Like you, I don't have any tolerance for shady gambling establishments that feed on crime to fuel other-than-legitimate-business concerns."

Some people nodded. Their encouragement made it easier for Jill to smile in the spotlight.

"Let me begin by saying we estimate our hotel will generate $5 million per year in taxes for the city of Dare, and $2 million each for Eagle County and the public school system. Additionally, we have made a commitment to work with the local business community, and we'll fill up to ninety-five percent of jobs with Dare-area residents."

As Jill took her seat again, Mac ran them through the poster-board sized plans for the hotel. His presentation took about twenty minutes. He finished by placing a blown-up black-and-white photo of the original hotel next to their model for the new one. No one could miss how close Mac's restoration plans were to the historic landmark. It kicked ass.

Mac stood between the images, resplendent in his suit, an easy smile on his face. "As I've outlined, our plan is respectful of Dare's values. It will recreate a beautiful sanctuary in the mountains while bringing a great deal of money into this town. We look forward to your support and thank you for giving us the opportunity to propose this plan."

When he turned to her, smooth as butter, her heart jumped. "Jill? As the first Dare resident hired for this project, do you have anything you'd like to add?"

They'd rehearsed this, so she wasn't surprised. Still, her nerves skyrocketed as she stood up. "Some of you might wonder why I decided to back this plan. I mean, an exclusive poker hotel in the mountains? Who would have thunk it?"

As she'd hoped, her folksy language made people laugh.

"I grew up here. Went to school here. Own my own business here. And after having my grandfather lecture me time and again about the importance of being a good judge of character, I can tell you I not only chose to work on this hotel because of the economic boost it would give our town, I also decided to put myself into it one hundred percent because of Mac Maven."

She gestured to him with a warm smile. "He's the real deal, folks. A self-made man who has continued to better his life through his unique set of skills. Honestly, I can't give him a higher compliment than to say that if I didn't know better I might have thought he'd been born here. He's the kind of man Dare produces—a true maverick, just like his poker nickname. Plus, he's honest, loyal, and wicked smart."

She looked pointedly at Peggy, who only stared back.

"When he says there will be none of the usual 'shenanigans' you find at other casinos, he means it. And we have the statistics to back that up. Dare's businesses will boom with this new hotel in town. We look forward to your support."

When she sat back down, Mac patted her hand. Her hot face could have melted all the snow outside. She wanted to fan herself, but didn't want to attract the attention.

Other people stood, making innocuous comments about the hotel. Nothing they hadn't expected. Florence Henkelmyer didn't persuade anyone with her rant about the evils of alcohol and gambling. The woman should have lived during Prohibition. When the chairman asked if there were any more comments before the vote, Peggy raised her hand and stood.

The whole crowd seemed to lean forward on the edge of their chairs, causing a massive medley of squeaking wood.

"Like my brother, Tanner McBride, I'm new to this town. As a police officer, I've seen a lot of bad things. Jill and Maven may say there will be no crime at his hotel, but I can only tell you the facts are against them."

She cited stats she'd given the newspaper, drawing out the suspense. "Our town is particularly vulnerable because we have a university here. High rollers tend to be power-hungry types who like young women, which is why gambling and prostitution have been constant bedfellows since the first cavemen carved their own dice. Young college students looking for a fast ride and easy money are especially susceptible. Policing this type of thing is tough, I can tell you that right now."

Peggy continued to talk about violence and domestic abuse. She hooked her hands in her belt loops. Jill realized she was playing the who-blinks-first game with Mac.

"I'm not questioning whether Jill's a good judge of character. Or saying Maven's not a nice guy."

"I like Mr. Maven, mommy," Keith said loudly. "He helped me when I broke my leg, and he gave me a Woody helmet."

Her friend's mouth thinned, but she just stroked her son's head. "As I mentioned in the paper, I came across something in Mr. Maven's background that calls his character into serious question. I feel I'd be remiss in my duties if I didn't mention Mr. Maven has been arrested for assault."

The bombshell silenced the room. Jill gripped Mac's sleeve and looked at his face. His easy smile faded. He turned in his chair like a jungle cat. So whatever he'd expected, it hadn't been this.

"You're well informed, Deputy McBride, but those charges were dropped."

She planted her hands on her hips. "Doesn't mean you didn't beat someone up enough to send him to the hospital. What do you say to that?"

The accusation drew some gasps from the crowd.

He rose in one fluid line. "Did your source provide you with the reason for the so-called 'assault'?"

Her brown eyes flickered under the hall's fluorescent lighting. "Neither the report or the arresting officer spelled out all the details."

"I see, so you were simply planning to tarnish my reputation? Mr. Chairman, I wonder if we might have a short recess? I will respond to this statement afterwards."

Jill locked her hands at her side. He needed a break? Oh, this wasn't good.

Oscar's mouth flapped, but he nodded and whacked the gavel down. "Ten minutes."

The crowd's din immediately rose.

"I'll be right back." Mac strode out.

Jill's heart rapped against her chest so hard she clutched it.

"Any idea what's going on, Jill?" Oscar asked her.

"I'm sure everything is all right," she reassured him as best she could.

Her family hovered close, and all around her people peppered her with questions. She kept repeating that Mac would answer everything. The crowd began to turn.

Florence's voice rose in volume. "See, he's nothing but a two-bit gambler. We don't want his kind in Dare."

Meredith patted Jill's back, and Tanner squeezed her shoulder before pushing through the crowd toward Peggy. Keith's lip wobbled. He threw his arms around Tanner's leg. Her brother-in-law hoisted him up and bent his head down to Peggy, whose expression was grim.

A door smacked against a wall, arresting conversation. The crowd took their seats and fell silent as Mac strode back into the room, his mouth tight. "Thank you for your patience. The answer to Deputy Sheriff McBride's accusation involved someone close to me. I needed permission to speak of it."

Well, that explained the break. Jill hovered on the edge of her seat as Mac scanned the audience, the sheer force of his will evident.

"So, it seems we need to clear up something from my past, doesn't it? I don't want anyone to think I'm a 'bad' guy. I can assure you this was a singular incident." He unbuttoned his suit jacket. "I'm a private person, and this was a private family matter."

Peggy stilled as Mac strolled over. "You're to be commended for your diligence, but you really should have researched the details of the so-called assault more thoroughly."

"I made my best effort," she asserted without breaking eye contact.

Keith wrapped his hand around Peggy's leg.

"Folks, I was twenty when this happened. I found out another college student had been highly inappropriate with my younger sister, who was a senior in high school."

A few gasps came from the crowd. Jill clutched her chair, thinking oh, Peggy. This couldn't have been what she'd had in mind.

Although his mouth had grim lines around it, he shrugged. "What can I say? I was acting like a protective older brother. Who isn't a bit impetuous in their youth? If that makes me a 'bad' guy in Deputy McBride's eyes, I fear we disagree on the definition. I was protecting my family. If you choose not to approve the plans for the hotel because of this information, that's your decision. And I'll respect it."

He walked back to his seat and sat down. Jill rubbed his arm in support, the muscles rigid with tension—the only sign he was upset.

"I'm so sorry," she whispered.

He just patted her hand.

Peggy stood and faced the crowd, but it was obvious she'd lost them. Mac looked like a hero again.

"All I'm saying is we're getting a Pollyanna version of this poker hotel. I hope you vote against it."

"Thank you, Deputy McBride, for that *enlightening* information," Oscar said, his voice heavy with censure. "Any more comments?"

When no one raised a hand, Jill expelled her breath. She struggled with her anger at Peg. She knew her friend was only trying to do what she believed was in the town's best interests. But it was hard not to feel she had gone too far.

"We're going to put this to a vote now. Would all those in favor raise their hands?"

The showing of hands made Jill's toes dig into her soles in anticipation. The motion passed with only three against. Oscar pronounced the plan approved, and the meeting closed.

At least one thing in her life had turned out okay. Jill surged to her feet. "We won!"

"Yes." Mac put his files in his briefcase.

"Are you okay?"

He snapped the clasps in place. "I will be. Peggy's accusation pissed me off, so I'm not as happy as I'd like to be right now."

Join the club. She couldn't find her inner Dancing Queen either.

He leaned in as people swarmed in around them.

She felt like the MVP of the Superbowl with all the people thumping her on the back and pumping her hand, telling her what a great job she'd done. She spied Keith hobbling over to her family, his blue cast etched with signatures. She threaded her way over, reaching them just as Tanner launched his nephew into the air, making him squeal.

"Be careful. He might give up his mac and cheese," Peggy warned from the sidelines.

Jill crossed her arms as she met Peggy's eyes.

"Congratulations." Her grandpa pulled her against his mothball-scented cardigan. "Remember who you got your business sense from."

She kissed his cheek, welcoming the interruption. She wasn't sure what to say to Peggy right now. "How could I forget?"

"Can I have a red hot, Mr. Hale?" Keith asked.

"Sure thing, young man."

"I know you're pissed at me," Peggy said, walking over to her. "We just don't see eye to eye."

Funny how that was happening in all of her relationships lately. Jill pressed her lips together, trying not to say the first thing that popped into her head. No need to hurt their friendship. "Well, you made it personal, but I hope you'll do your duty and support us now that the vote's in."

Peggy shifted on her feet. "My duty is to protect and serve this town."

"Exactly so, officer," Mac said as he joined the group. "Actually, I'm glad Dare has someone so *dedicated*. Since I'll be moving here for the next few years, I don't want to have any trouble sleeping at night."

"Do you see the boogey man in your room too, Mr. Maven?" Keith asked from Tanner's shoulders.

The innocent question broke the tension in the group. Everyone chuckled—everyone but Peggy and Mac.

"We all see the boogey man, Keith," Mac said. "Not all of us are as lucky as you are to have a mom who can make it go away. I'll bet there's nothing she wouldn't do to keep you safe—even if it meant breaking the law."

The veiled glance he gave Peggy made her look elsewhere. Keith put his arms out to Jill. She drew him against her chest, realizing Mac and Peggy would continue to clash. Now that the hotel was coming to town, this would only be the beginning.

"Where's Brian, Jillie?" Keith asked.

She forced a smile to quell the pang in her heart. "He's working."

"Cool. I bet he'll be so happy for you." He kissed her cheek and threw his arms around her neck.

She doubted that very much. What happened to her no longer mattered to him now that they'd split up. Her chest suddenly hurt from repressed tears.

"Can we get ice cream?" Keith asked.

"I'm buying," her grandpa announced, tapping his cane.

"I promised I'd call my sister back after the vote," Mac replied, stepping out of the circle. "I'll celebrate with you another time."

Jill put Keith down. "No, please come."

He stood apart in his gray wool suit and designer watch. His body language was fluid, but his face had grown distant. All charm had faded. "Not tonight. You did a great job, Jill. I hope your family knows how lucky they are to have you represent them in this town. And I look forward to hearing from you about your long-term decision."

Yes, the time had arrived.

Mac's eyes locked with Peggy. Jill didn't think they'd notice if lightening struck between them. The corner of his mouth tipped up. "Deputy." Then he ruffled Keith's hair. He waved to their group and headed off, surrounded by well-wishers.

Jill tried to shake off her anger. "Well, without Mac, I don't feel much like celebrating." Not just that. Her bubble had burst. "I have something else I need to do." It was time to face the music all 'round.

She kissed everyone goodbye—except Peggy.

When she let herself into her house, she firmed her shoulders and immediately walked to the bathroom. It was time to find out if her worst fears had been realized. Her period still hadn't come. Better to stop hiding her head into the sand.

Jill went through the whole testing process numb. As she waited for the results, she brushed the tears falling from her eyes. When she saw the plus sign, she put her head in her hands. The unimaginable had happened. She was pregnant.

The thought of having Brian's baby without him overwhelmed her. She gave into the emotional storm that left her spent and hollow.

What in the world was she going to do now? Keep moving forward, she could almost hear her grandpa say. She'd have to tell Brian tomorrow. God, give her strength. Now that they were splitting up, she expected he'd be leaving Dare soon. For a moment she thought about not telling him until after he'd left. This would slice him in two. He'd have to choose between seeing their child frequently and living in New York pursuing his dream job.

Her hand cupped her stomach. After all these years of dreaming about them having a child together, it was happening. Only they wouldn't be together.

God, their baby. It didn't feel real.

Heading back to the family room, she reached for her phone and texted Mac, *I want to accept your offer. Let's talk. I have other things to discuss.*

Moving forward was the only thing she could do now. Thank God the hotel had passed. She'd have a new focus now, one that would she hoped would fill the hole inside her.

She'd tell Mac she was pregnant when they spoke. Legally, he couldn't make an issue of it, but ethically, she wanted to make sure he was okay with her situation.

Tomorrow, she'd share the news with Brian.

A part of her tore in two. She'd have to find a way to become Jill-the-friend again.

She'd call Meredith in the morning and let her sister hold her and tell her it would all work out. The Hales always banded together in a crisis.

Her phone immediately buzzed. Mac's name appeared on the screen. She picked it up.

It was time to take control of her life.

CHAPTER 40

Brian heard the news about the hotel from his boss when three city council members showed up for drinks and dessert. He had trouble arranging the orange slices on the New York cheesecake, so he had to take a deep breath to calm himself. What happened to Jill didn't matter anymore, he told himself. Still, he knew she'd take the job with Mac.

He needed to focus on his own career. His reputation had finally been restored. He needed to start making plans to head to New York. He had no doubt he'd find a job in a Michelin restaurant now.

Orange juice squirted onto his chef coat when his hand clenched around the oranges. He couldn't bear the thought of never seeing Jill again.

God, he wouldn't have imagined it, but this hurt more than when he'd lost his reputation as a chef.

More news trickled back to him. Pete was leaving town tomorrow for a new job. Well, hadn't he said he'd put some feelers out? His stomach clenched with dread, remembering what had happened at PolarFest. He'd tried reaching out to apologize, but Pete hadn't called or texted him back. He'd have to do some thinking about how he wanted to leave things between them. They weren't the friends they'd been, but it felt like he was losing another vital part of himself.

***

After another sleepless night in his empty bed, he cruised over to Pete's house. His friend came down the porch, holding two boxes stacked on top of each other. He inclined his chin in greeting, but didn't walk over as Brian pulled in front of the house. The tires on Pete's SUV bulged from the weight of the boxes blocking the back window.

"You didn't respond to any of my messages, so I'm here to say I'm sorry."

"Fine," he snapped.

"I heard you were taking off." The words spread the hurt in his chest.

"Yeah." Pete stuffed the boxes in the passenger side. "I decided to take a job at Yellowstone and get the hell out of here. Simple enough to finish my doctorate there while getting paid."

While the words were easy, the tone wasn't. The strain between them was as obvious as dried herbs in a fresh salad.

"I'll say it again," Brian said. "I was out of line the other night."

"I was too," Pete replied, jerking his shoulder. "We were all a bit wired from being at our first PolarFest without Jem."

"Yeah," Brian agreed. "Why are you really leaving?"

Pete leaned against the car. "I told you. There are too many memories here."

God, didn't he know it? "I don't like you leaving like this."

Pete shrugged. "It's for the best."

Brian rested on the frame, not knowing what else to say. They both looked out over the snow-covered yard.

"I heard you've been staying over at your place the last few nights. Something wrong between you and Jill?" Pete asked.

He cleared his throat. "We broke up." It was the first time he'd said the words out loud.

"What happened?" he asked.

Staring across the yard, Brian told him everything.

For a long moment Pete didn't say anything, but he finally said, "I'll be right back," and then took off for the house.

Brian rubbed his chest where it hurt while he waited. When Pete returned, he handed him a photo.

"I found this when I was packing my things."

In the photo he and Jill were sitting close together on a blanket, laughing. It made his breath stop. He remembered that day when they were sixteen. They'd gone hiking in Eagle Pass when all the wildflowers were blooming. He'd wanted so badly to kiss Jill that day.

"Look, I've had some time to think about stuff. Things with Jill...have bothered the shit out of me. I understand why she wants to hate me. Hell, part of me hates me. What I'm trying to say is that despite all the crap between Jill and me right now, I know you've always wanted her. I saw how much you fought it when we were young, not wanting to lose her or her family when your own was shit."

Brian looked away. "What are you saying?"

"Fuck, I'm saying that I didn't feel the way you're feeling when I broke up with Jemma. I don't care if it makes me a dick, but I felt *free* when the two of us split. I missed her, yeah, but we had outgrown each other. You're torn up over this. It fucking bothered you when you and Jill...fell apart after high school. And this time you've really been with her, man. Are you sure you want to go through that again?"

"No." It would be much worse this time.

"Look, I know your parents' divorce messed you up, but you know what? They didn't really lose much when they split."

He turned his head. "What?"

"They didn't love each other anymore. Why else could your mom hook up with some other guy so quickly? There was nothing to fight for, man. But you and Jill, well you two fight because you care so much. There's always been this crazy energy between you."

Brian's sigh came from a place deep inside him. "No one knows how to push my buttons like she does."

"Do you remember your parents ever being as happy or passionate as you and Jill are?"

He thought back to his early years. Nothing popped. "They got married young. I don't know. Maybe not everyone acts like we do."

"Exactly!"

The photo seemed to mock him. "What the fuck am I supposed to do? Turn my back on the one thing I have back, the one thing I can count on—my career. She doesn't trust me, Pete."

His friend laughed out loud. "Can you really blame Jill? Simca is super hot."

Just what he wanted to hear. "Fuck."

"Maybe all Jill needs is time. If you leave suddenly like last time, you won't know. I'm just saying, man."

Pete was right. He would always wonder if he had given in too easily if he hit the road without talking to Jill again.

"You don't have to leave town, Pete." He bumped him like they used to when they were horsing around.

Pete turned all stiff next to him. "It's...too much here. It's not the same. I realized that the other night."

Brian kicked some snow with his boot. "Are *we* gonna be okay?"

"Yeah." He slammed the car door and slapped him on the shoulder. Gave him a one-armed man hug. "I gotta finish packing. I want to get going." He jogged away. "I left something for you at Don't Soy With Me since I wasn't sure if I'd see you."

Brian started to follow. "Pete—"

He turned around. "One last thing. If you decide to stay and get Jill back, will you guys host PolarFest next year? I think we should keep it going." He tugged on his ball cap. "Jemma...would want that."

His friend darted inside, the swinging door cracking in the frame. Brian stared at the house. Kicked around some more snow. "Jesus," he muttered.

He studied the photo of him and Jill again, tracing her face.

Pete was right. Jill had always been it for him. Now, what the hell was he going to do about that?

CHAPTER 41

"Hey, Jill. Thought you'd be taking the morning off after your big win last night. Congrats!" Margie said, pulling the red lever for hot water.

An early morning talk with her sister had been the highlight of her morning. Meredith had been shocked by the news of her pregnancy, but supportive. She'd held Jill as she'd cried and told her she'd be with her when she told her parents and grandpa.

Her hands clutched her purse, trying to keep herself grounded. "Thanks. I haven't been around as much lately. I appreciate the way you and the crew have picked up the slack."

And she'd need even more help now that she'd accepted Mac's job. He had assured her that he still wanted her to work for him. He'd even congratulated her on the baby and outlined his generous maternity benefits. She'd struggled not to blubber on the phone. Her insides twirled like a roller coaster when she thought about all the changes ahead of her. Finding a new manager for Don't Soy With Me was her next priority.

Her work with him would grow over the next few months while the construction occurred. Mac had an ambitious timetable for the build. The clearing crew had already started, impressing everyone in town. Mac planned to have a grand opening on Independence Day. Having seen the construction company's references, she believed it would happen.

Margie sidled closer to her. "Pete dropped something off for Brian. Asked you to give it to him." She patted her on the back.

The pain of not seeing Brian again tore through her. "That's weird."

"Pete said he was leaving town, and after the other night..." Margie finished the latte she was making. "It's on your desk."

He was leaving? Jill headed for her office with a cup of coffee. She caught sight of Pete's parting gift as soon as she opened the door. She approached it with a sense of wonder and pain.

The worn football showed over a decade of love. The white seams had turned ivory, the pigskin a dull and worn brown like an old suit. Someone might have thought it was worthless if not for the signature. She picked it up and traced the name—John Elway—the Denver Bronco's most hallowed quarterback.

It was Pete's prized possession. And he'd given it to Brian.

He wasn't coming back for a long time.

She sat there in the silence. The damn Broncos reference made her think back to Brian's suggestion they move in together. Memories of that time flooded her mind. Just when they'd become closer than she'd ever imagined, she'd run like a rabbit and fallen behind the old walls of hurt. She'd shut him out like he was meaningless to her.

Reaching into her desk drawer, she bypassed their Valentine's Day photo and pulled out one taken a few weeks ago, after their first dinner. He'd set up his phone to take the shot and tugged her onto his lap. They were gazing into each other's eyes, her hands fingering the brown hair curling at his nape. No one could mistake the love in their eyes.

He did love her.

She was an idiot.

Her hand caressed her belly. It was time to tell him about the baby. And to ask him for a second chance. She couldn't bear for him to leave again. Whether he would forgive her or not remained to be seen.

And if he wanted to pursue his dream job now that she had hers, she'd find a way to understand. They could share the baby if nothing else.

Grabbing her phone before she lost her nerve, she texted him. *I'm sorry about the other night. Can we talk?*

She waited. A few minutes turned into ten. An hour later, she still had no answer.

He wasn't going to respond. She eyed the clock. He'd be heading to the restaurant soon. Not the place to tell him about the baby, since it was clear he didn't want to talk to her. She couldn't blame him. She'd go by his apartment tomorrow.

Her head lowered onto the desk as the tears started.

She'd made a mess of everything, and she'd have to live with that.

CHAPTER 42

Brian received Jill's text as he was getting ready to head to work. Just seeing her face pop up on his home screen made him double over in pain. Her message only made him feel worse.

Since he didn't want to talk to her without something concrete to say, he went to work like a robot. Burned himself on a sauté pan. Overcooked three orders of steak—a first. His boss finally sent him home since it was a slow night. News of his break-up with Jill had spread. Everyone knew why he was fucking everything up.

His apartment was a tomb. He didn't want to be there. He missed Jill as badly as he'd missed Jemma in the first days after her death, the grief so fresh he hadn't functioned for days.

And then he realized something so simple he felt stupid.

Jill was still alive. Jemma wasn't.

What the fuck was he doing?

He didn't want to be without Jill. He'd rather fight with her than live a passionless existence with anyone else, particularly when making up was so fun. And hadn't they been happy living together until the shit hit the fan?

He and Jill's relationship was nothing like his parent's. What a fucking epiphany!

The situation with Simca would have been tough for even a time-tested couple to handle.

Jill needed more time to trust him and understand just how much he loved her.

As he stroked Mutt's folds on the couch, he came to the decision to stay in Dare. It was the only decision.

But keeping the job at The Chop House wasn't an option. He'd suffocate there. So, he needed another plan. Something long-term because that's what he wanted with Jill.

He fell into cooking, opening himself up to inspiration. The perfect idea came at 4:11 A.M. as he was baking Jill her favorite raspberry scones.

He would open his own place here and find another partner. And there was only one man he respected enough to approach.

After a couple hours of sleep, he headed up to Arthur Hale's house. Knocking on the door, he stuffed his hands in his pockets, trying to control his nerves. The door opened.

Arthur tapped his cane on the hardwood floor. "You've got a hell of a nerve coming here after what you did to my granddaughter," he growled.

His reaction wasn't unexpected. "If I really *had* done anything, do you think I would have shown up on your doorstep? Will you let me explain? I could use your help—and advice."

Those bushy brows drew together. "Jill blasted me for getting in the middle last time."

He snorted. "You're always in the middle when it comes to your family."

The cane tapped in rapid beats. "Fine! Come in, but don't expect me to make you coffee like it's some social call."

"Understood," Brian answered and followed him inside.

The house still bore the vestiges of time. Generations of possessions—from black-and-white photos on antique furniture to a cherry wood record player—gave it a homey feel. He hoped to have a place like this with Jill someday.

"So, why are you risking being caned by an old man?" Arthur fired off.

"Let me explain." Brian sat on a flowery upholstered chair and ran him through what had happened the other night, even showing him the article in which Simca had cleared his name.

Arthur squinted at the screen. "Damn small type. Hard to read, but I get the drift. Isn't this something you need to tell Jill?"

"I tried, sir."

"So what are you going to do about that?" Arthur rolled a red hot between his fingers.

Brian took a moment to clear his throat. "I'm going to stay here and try to work things out."

Arthur stared Brian down over his glasses like a quizzical professor. "That's a good start. Jill's in overdrive with you—always has been. It's the crappy thing about love. You're humming Handel's "Messiah" one day and crying in the gutter the next. Highs and lows. But with trust and time, you might find a middle ground where you can experience more highs and hold tight in the lows. That's the key to marriage, son. I assume that's where you're headed if you're staying here and not dashing off to some big-time career in New York."

Brian nodded emphatically, even though ice still swirled in his stomach. Would she even be receptive to the idea?

Arthur reached for a photo of him and his wife, showed it to Brian, and then studied it himself. "You know, when I think back on my years with my wife, I don't remember the bad stuff. I only think about her smile. How she felt in my arms. How she hummed when she baked cookies all day during a snowstorm. I have to really think to remember the lows." He put the photo back. "We had them. Everyone does. But you don't stop loving."

Brian swallowed and gazed at the photo for a long moment. Arthur and his wife looked so young, no lines on their faces, no gray in their hair.

Brian rubbed his hands on his knees. "So, I have a proposition for you."

"You're not my type," Arthur quipped, taking a seat on the adjacent couch.

If he'd been less nervous, he would have made a smart-ass comment. "As you know, Morty's property—the one Jill and I were originally planning to buy—goes up for sale pretty soon."

"Yes."

He bounced his foot. "Well, Jill's here. I love her. I want to be with her." He put his ankle on his knee to stop jittering. "But I can't work at the Chop House forever. I'll go nuts. I'd like to buy Morty's place, but I can't do it alone." He took a deep breath. "I don't want to approach a Californian who doesn't understand Dare."

Arthur harrumphed. "They'll have us all eating tofu and sprouts."

He didn't want to get into an argument about all the good things they were bringing into town, like organic produce. "I want this place to be a Dare staple."

"And you can't get a loan by yourself," Arthur summed up.

He should have known Hale would understand. "Right."

"You're not worried about competing with Mac's restaurant?" he asked, steepling his hands.

"No. My place is going to kick that place's butt."

"You and Jill are like two peas in a pod when it comes to your careers." Arthur rested his cane on his lap and caressed the wood. "All this career talk is giving me heartburn. What about how you feel about each other? When are you two going to stop talking shop and realize what's important?"

Uncomfortable, Brian lowered his foot to the floor. "We'll work it out." Since Hale was being candid, Brian decided to be equally so. "Shit got in the way."

He pushed his glasses up his nose. "And what do you do when shit gets in your way? You shovel. As hard and long as it takes."

"That's what I'm trying to do," he declared.

"Good. It worries me. My heart." He patted his chest for dramatic impact.

Brian had to bite his lip.

Arthur dug into his pocket, pulled out two red hots, and threw one at Brian. It bounced against his chest. They tore the wrappers off and popped them into their mouths, candy crackling against their teeth.

"I'll co-sign the loan. You'll run the show." Arthur put out his hand. "Unless you start serving crap. No tofu. That's not negotiable."

Brian gripped his hand. "No problem. I hate that shit."

"Me too," Arthur agreed and made a motion to the door. "Now, go get a haircut and wash that crud off your face. Women like that kind of stuff."

He wasn't sure it would make a difference. "Yes, sir."

"My final piece of advice. Forgiveness is as important as love. We all screw up."

"Thank you." He wished for more adequate words.

"You're welcome." He stood, cane tapping as they headed to the front door. "I'm only helping you because I'm a bachelor now. Can't stand to eat mac and cheese every night."

Brian gripped his shoulder, knowing he was all bluster. "Think up your favorite meal. We'll put it on the menu as the Hale special."

Arthur laughed. Brian left feeling like one enormous weight had evaporated. He had a plan.

Now he needed to share it with Jill and pray they could bridge the gap between them.

CHAPTER 43

Jill received Brian's response nearly twenty-four hours after she'd sent hers. *I'm sorry too. Can you meet me at Jemma's?*

The sweetness of the spot had her blinking back tears. Yes, they could both use their friend's support for this talk. She texted him back and suggested a time. He immediately agreed.

When the appointed time rolled around, she drove to the cemetery. The quiet immediately wrapped around her like a blanket. The birds chirped as she walked to Jemma's grave, wearing her friend's amethyst necklace for support. The bench by the graveside cushioned her. Sitting there, watching the clouds flutter by, she imagined Jemma sitting beside her, being her angel.

A car door slammed in the distance. The sight of Brian walking toward her made her heart twist. His maple syrup hair looked freshly cut and his cheeks shone with a close shave.

His eyes locked onto hers. "Hey," he called, stopping a few yards away. "Are you ready to talk?"

"Yeah," she answered. This was going to hurt.

His finger pointed to Jemma's headstone. "I suggested we talk here because when Jemma died, everything between us changed. Do you remember?"

The wind swirled around her as she thought of that time—the shared hurt, opening her heart to him again. "Yes."

Brian's hands fell to his hips. "I don't know how to start this, so I'm just going to do the best I can. I'm sorry I hurt you again. It was the last thing I ever wanted. And I'm sorry I lost my temper, but you hurt me too, Jill."

His bloodshot eyes conveyed that. "I'm sorry I hurt you."

He sat beside her. "I realize how much this whole situation with Simca must have damaged your trust in me."

His understanding cooled her flushed face as much as the bitter wind. "Thank you for that."

"But I have to know, Jill, Simca aside, if you can ever trust me again?"

The skin on her face suddenly felt stretched across her bones. "I want to. I've been afraid from day one that you were going to choose her over me. Like you did before with Kelly."

His jaw clenched. "Dammit, Jill. I love you. You're fucking *everything* to me! Why can't you see that?"

Her eyes burned. "I was scared I wasn't enough. And then I saw you with her. I can't offer you everything Simca can. A new career. Life with a confident, sexual courtesan. I'm just Jill. Simple, plain ol' Jill."

He grabbed her face in his hands "That's bullshit. There's nothing simple or plain about you."

And staring into the certainty in his eyes, something inside her shifted. She realized it was true. She wasn't Simca, but she was herself. She had talents. And she needed to stop comparing herself to other people and start loving her body for itself. Hadn't Brian shown her how much he enjoyed it?

She could almost hear Jemma applaud.

"Jill, you stir me up, rip me up, and cut me up until I don't know if I can put it all back together."

Everything in her shook at his outpouring of emotion, like the windows in an old house when a plane went over too low.

He yanked her to him, the warmth of his body taking away the cold inside her. His hands twisted in her hair, and he kissed her. She could feel the pull of him, the draw. Her body leaned forward until they were flush against each other. Feeling the heat. The hurt. It lasted all but a minute until she wrenched back, needing to know what this meant.

"Brian—"

His head swooped down again. The hard press of his lips took her under. Opened her up. Desperation, longing, and the endless bite of love turned the kiss into a brutal act. Tongues dueled. Teeth scraped. The flash of lust turned her body to lava. She moaned—deep and long in her throat.

He tugged her back by the hair. "Do you think Simca ever did this to me? Or Kelly Kimple?"

Breathing hard, she stared at him. Looked at him. His eyes shone like the noontime sun—hot and intense. A flicker of hope took root. "So, what does this mean?"

His hands framed her face. "It means I'm not leaving you. I'm staying here. I'm going to do everything I can to help you trust me—the whole way this time. It doesn't matter how long it takes."

Her mouth parted. He was staying? "But—"

"What about you? I assume you're taking the job with Mac?"

The first stirrings of a smile broke across her lips. He was staying—for her—and before he knew she was pregnant. "Yes, I took the job with Mac. I'm sorry I didn't wait to talk to you, but I thought you were out of the picture. I hope it's—"

"I'm one hundred percent behind you. You've been so happy with this new project, Jill."

"Part of me wanted to open a place with you so you'd have to stay with me," she said in a low voice. "It was my insurance policy, so to speak." She leaned her head against his shoulder. Drew in the warmth and the heat. "But I could see it wouldn't work. I was afraid I would start agreeing with you just so you'd stay. Our ideas were totally different."

He caressed her hair. "Yes, they were, which is why I'm going to buy Morty's place. I'm done working for someone else. With the new hotel on its way, my vision has a chance to succeed here."

Her heart soared like the crows flying out of the nearby tree. "That's wonderful!"

He traced her brow. "And I'm going to partner up with someone who understands Dare almost as well as you do. Your grandfather."

Like a shot to the heart, it paralyzed her for a moment before the real impact sunk in. "My *grandpa* agreed to go into business with you?"

All the misery in those Bengal-tiger blue eyes evaporated, replaced with pure mischief. "He'll be a silent partner on one condition: I can't serve tofu."

That wonderful old codger. He always supported her—and did it on his own terms. She had to bite her lip to keep it from trembling. "Sounds like him."

"Of course, you might be wondering why I asked him and not someone else."

She cupped his face in her hands. "I know you, remember? You were asking for his approval after everything that's happened."

He pressed his forehead to hers in one rapid motion. "I should have known you'd get that."

"And he gave it to you." Arthur Hale was no fool. He knew his approval counted. God, she loved him.

"And you have clear warning. I'm going to marry you," he whispered. "One way or another. Sometime in the near future or in a few years. Whatever it takes. I'm through with letting my parents screw with my head. We're not them. We're us," he said, leaning back, "and I love you. You're my most important thing in the world to me."

Hadn't she been waiting years to hear him say that? Her face fit into his neck like the space had been waiting for her. She breathed him in. Spice and forest and something else—red hots, she realized. She took a moment to savor it, him. He was telling her everything she'd ever wanted. Now it was time to share her other news.

"I need to tell you something else," she whispered.

His eyes beamed. "What?"

She caressed his chest, feeling his heartbeat beneath her palm. "I'm pregnant."

His mouth dropped open. He didn't blink. Didn't say a word.

"Brian? I know it's a shock. I took the test after the city council vote since my period still hadn't come. Isn't it our luck that we struck gold, so to speak, on the first—"

"When were you planning on telling me?"

"When I texted you."

"Wait. Is that what you wanted to talk about?"

Was he freaking out? Changing his mind? She knew how scared she was thinking about taking on a new job with a baby on the way. "Please—"

"Stop. Give me a minute.'" He paced a short distance away. But he didn't head to his car. With his back turned, she couldn't see his face.

She gripped Jemma's gravestone, scared their future hung in the balance again.

***

Her news had him struggling for breath. She was pregnant?

Jesus, what in the hell would have happened if he hadn't stayed? Being separated from his kid would have ripped his guts out. His knees almost gave out at the thought. The shock rolled over him as he tried to make sense of it—and what it meant for them.

He rose and started toward her. Her hair shone like hot coals, a reddish orange so rich it kindled warmth. The breeze twirled the ends of her curls, tracing her tear-streaked face and neck like his fingers itched to do. Her green eyes reminded him of the spring coming in a few months. Soon, these grounds would be a rich emerald carpet, the showcase for granite gravestones and flourishing flowers.

He pulled her to him. When he kissed her, everything inside him settled. Her mouth opened under his, giving him her tears and love and the promise she'd always be there, wanting the best for him. He soothed her as she cried into their kiss, her breath coming in harsh intakes until she finally laid her head on her shoulder and went to pieces.

"I thought you were running away." she said.

"No, I was just trying to take it all in. Jill, you—the baby—it all overwhelms me. I don't want to screw it up." He rocked them back and forth.

When she lifted her head, he brushed the wetness from her cheeks. "Then don't," she whispered, eyes shining, nearly destroying him.

Simpler words couldn't hold more truth. "Right. Or like your grandpa told me, you work harder." Arthur's other words about forgiveness popped into his mind. "Jill, I need to know one more thing. Do you truly forgive me for leaving Dare the way I did when we were kids?"

Her smile dimmed for a second, making him wonder if she was ready. "Oh, what the heck? I'm in a good mood." She launched herself at him again, locking her lips to his. "Speaking of the past, I heard Pete left town," she whispered, reaching for a Kleenex in her navy jacket.

"Yes." The reality hadn't quite set in.

"He left his John Elway football for you at the coffee shop."

For a moment, he couldn't breathe. He remembered the moment Pete had called him to tell him about his *best Christmas present ever*. They were eight at the time.

"He was here too," she informed him. "He left Jemma's favorite flowers."

The Gerbera daisies looked like giant multi-colored lollipops all wrapped up from the candy store.

"I'll teach our kid how to catch with it." Brian traced the headstone, the angel in the center.

"That would be nice."

She went into his arms as liquid as water. Fitted against him with a perfection that could only have been designed.

He tucked her collar up around her ears when the wind gusted. "So, about the baby..."

And he realized releasing the past meant creating space for the future.

***

Their hands found each other on her flat stomach. "We're having a baby," she announced like it still hadn't sunk in.

"Yes. It's rather a lot to take in. Have you gotten used to it?"

Her leg hopped in place with equal parts nerves and excitement. "Uh...I'm not as afraid, knowing you're going to be with me, but I'm still scared shitless."

"Me too," he confessed, "but I'm getting happier. It'll be a new adventure."

"That's an understatement. It complicates everything."

A slow smile touched his mouth. "When haven't we had complications?"

"You're right. We're the master of complications. It'll be great!"

She rocked him. Then he picked her up and spun them around, making wet snow fly across the ground.

"We have to get back to the basics," Jill declared. "Remember why we love each other."

"I know why," he uttered in a shaking voice, sparking a whole new crop of emotions inside her. "Because you're home for me. That's why I came back. It wasn't Dare. It was you, Red."

"I'm so happy about your restaurant." She threw out their arms in a Victory formation. "You're going to kick culinary ass, Bri. Make everyone who ever called you a mean name eat their words—literally."

"Yep." His grin made her own pop up like toast in a toaster. "And you're an empire builder in the making, just like your grandfather."

"It's nice to be able to support each other's dreams, isn't it?"

"Yeah," he agreed, tracing her cheek. "But know this. I'm planning on courting you a little longer, and then I'm gonna propose, Jillie. You have fair warning of my intention."

"You're not going to propose in a cemetery? Brian, you're so unromantic," she teased. The banter felt good, right.

He narrowed his eyes. Scanned the place. "Hmm...Jemma might like to see it. Maybe it's not such a bad a place after all. That whole 'death do us part' would really ring true."

She drilled a finger in his chest, hearing Jemma's light-hearted laughter in her mind. "Don't even think about it."

"I do have something though. It's not a ring—yet—so don't freak out." He pulled out the jewelry box and held it out.

The expectant look on his face told her what was inside.

"I had your necklace fixed. I hope you'll wear it again. I don't wear necklaces obviously, but I had the back of my watch engraved." He took it off and showed it to her. *"J&B, BFFs. And so much more."*

"Oh, Bri," she whispered, fighting tears as she opened the box and tried to put it on.

When her gloves got in the way, he took his off and spun her around, fitting the clasp together. Their hands brushed the pendant.

"You'll always have my heart." His hand curled around her neck, fingering the chain, and pulled her by inches until their mouths all but brushed. "I love you, Jill. God, how much," he breathed against her lips.

"I love you too," she whispered and leaned up to fit their mouths together. Inside her, the rain receded. The sun came out. A new day dawned.

After a tangle of arms, a string of kisses, and drumming heartbeats, he pulled away. Grabbed a flower and handed it to her. "I don't think Jemma would mind."

She took the red daisy. Traced the gravestone with a finger tip.

"She's not here, you know," he reminded. "She's here." He pointed to her heart.

"I know," she answered and pressed the flower to her chest. "Maybe we can go play some catch with the John Elway football."

"Any other time, I would baulk. That's an official autographed football. But in this case, I think Pete might like that."

"Moving on sucks sometimes," she whispered, thinking about their losses.

He drew her to his chest, letting them sway in the wind like the tree branches. "And sometimes, it doesn't."

Since she knew what he meant, she smiled. They'd both come a long way. Isn't that what love was supposed to do? Make you better.

She took his hand and led him out of the cemetery, realizing that after every burial, there's always a new beginning. They had theirs. And if they had a bad day and forgot about what was most important, they could always come here. Jemma would remind them.

Life really was precious. They would soak up every minute.

Dear Reader,

I hope you enjoyed reading about Jill and Brian coming together after so many years. It's great seeing friends become lovers. I know I couldn't be happier for them. Jill's finally found her NORA ROBERTS LAND.

As always, reviews really help other readers find my books. Your opinion matters. I would deeply appreciate you giving a review if you feel so called.

Additionally, we'll be giving away Don't Soy with Me swag and other fun prizes from Dare Valley. Should you like to participate, you can sign up for my newsletter at www.avamiles.com and connect with me on Facebook at www.facebook.com/authoravamiles.

Peggy and Mac's love story is up next in THE GRAND OPENING. Those two are quite a pair, and with their individual family dynamics, it keeps everyone on their toes. Keep reading for more information about their book.

In the meantime, since many of my beta readers said FRENCH ROAST made them hungry or want to cook something fun, I've included the recipes for the meal Brian makes Jill on their first date. Who doesn't love a man who cooks for her?

Thanks again for spending some time with my characters in Dare Valley. We hope to see you all real soon.

Much light,

Ava

BRIAN'S FIRST DATE SPECIAL

CHICKEN FRICASSEE
1 Fryer Chicken (around 3 pounds) cut into pieces
4 tablespoons of butter

In a Dutch oven, fry the chicken pieces in the butter, careful not to burn the butter. After 10-15 minutes of cooking the meat on both sides, remove the chicken and place to the side.

Add the following chopped vegetables to the butter and chicken drippings:
1 onion
1 carrot
1 stalk of celery

Sauté for about 10 minutes. Then add 8 ounces of quartered mushrooms to the mixture and continue cooking for about 5 minutes. Add 3 tablespoons of flour, mixing thoroughly but slowly, and cook until the sauce is thickened, about 1 minute. Then add 3/4 cup of white wine and 4 cups of chicken broth. Stir gently to ensure the vegetables do not break. Add the chicken pieces back into the pot on top of the vegetables. Add a bouquet garni to the pot. After the mixture has boiled, reduce the heat to simmer and cook covered for about 30 minutes. Remove the chicken.

Whisk 2 egg yolks and 1/4 cup cream together and then temper the mixture with the warm sauce. Then add this into the pot, stirring gently, and cook until thickened, about 2-3 minutes. Add 2 tablespoons of butter and incorporate. Finish by adding the chicken back into the pan with 3 tablespoons of tarragon, fresh preferred, and 2 tablespoons of fresh lemon juice. Stir gently for 2 minutes and then serve. Bon appétit.

POTATOES WITH BEURRE BLANC SAUCE
Sauté about 3-4 medium-size potatoes in olive oil until crispy on all sides. In a separate pan, prepare the beurre blanc sauce.

Boil 1/4 cup white wine, 1/4 cup vinegar with one finely chopped shallot until the mixture is thickened and reduced, about 5 minutes. Add 1/3 cup of cream and a dash of white pepper. Boil about 1 minute. Quickly cut two sticks of butter (1 cup) into small pieces and then add a few at a time to the sauce, whisking constantly until the sauce is thickened. For a smooth sauce, strain out the shallot (or leave the shallot pieces large enough to remove with a fork). Add in about 2 tablespoons of fresh parsley, stir, and then pour over the potatoes, tossing gently. Serve.

WATERCRESS SALAD a L'ORANGE

Wash the fresh watercress and lightly snap the stems into smaller pieces. Peel either a regular orange or a blood orange (preferred) and remove the fruit from the inside of the skin by placing a delicate cut across the top of the orange segment. Then arrange artfully on top of the delicate leaves. Make the pecans.

Honey Bourbon Pecans
1 cup pecans
1/8 cup honey
1 tablespoon butter
1 tablespoon bourbon

Add ingredients to a shallow pan and cook over medium heat until the mixture foams and coats the nuts, about 3-4 minutes, careful not to burn the mixture. Spread the nuts onto a buttered piece of parchment paper on a cookie sheet and cook in the over at 375 degrees for 5-6 minutes, watching the color of the nuts. You want them toasty brown. Once finished, set onto a wire rack and let cool for 30 minutes. Add to the top of the salad and enjoy.

The Dare Valley Series continues...
Book 3: THE GRAND OPENING
Peggy and Mac's story

When Peggy McBride moves to Dare Valley, Colorado, the last thing she wants is to meet a man. If she's learned one thing from her divorce, it's that love is a messy business, and as a single mom and the new deputy sheriff, she has her hands full. But when hotel magnate and poker player Mac Maven moves to town, she becomes enthralled by the very last man she would ever consider dating...

Mac Maven has come to Dare with ambitious plans for his new project, the restoration of The Grand Mountain Hotel as a boutique poker venue. Only one person offers him a less than warm welcome: Deputy Sheriff Peggy McBride, who is dead set against gambling. But although Peggy's a fierce opponent, Mac senses a tenderness and passion within her that he longs to free. Having helped his sister raise her teenage son, he understands Peggy, and can see past her tough-as-nails exterior.

When a threat to Mac's hotel surfaces, he and Peggy must join forces to find out who's responsible. Working together ignites the white-hot connection between them, and their cooperation takes a decidedly personal turn. But can Mac convince Peggy to set their differences aside and take a gamble on love?

ABOUT THE AUTHOR

USA Today Bestselling Author Ava Miles burst onto the contemporary romance scene after receiving Nora Roberts' blessing for her use of Ms. Roberts' name in her debut novel, the #1 National Bestseller NORA ROBERTS LAND, which kicked off her small town series, Dare Valley, and brought praise from reviewers and readers alike. Ava has also released a connected series called Dare River, set outside the country music capital of Nashville.

Far from the first in her family to embrace writing, Ava comes from a long line of journalists. Ever since her great-great-grandfather won ownership of a newspaper in a poker game in 1892, her family has had something to do with telling stories, whether to share news or, in her case, fiction. Her clan is still reporting on local events more than one hundred years later at their family newspaper, much like the Hale family in her Dare Valley series.

Ava is fast becoming a favorite author in light contemporary romance (Tome Tender) and is known for funny, emotional stories about family and empowerment. Ava's background is as diverse as her characters. She's a former chef, worked as a long-time conflict expert rebuilding warzones, and now writes full-time from her own small-town community.

If you enjoyed reading this book, please share that with your friends and others by posting a review. Thank you!

Made in the USA
Monee, IL
18 April 2021